NO REGRETS

The wagons were ablaze. They watched the flames crackle for a moment.

And then, in an enormous explosion, the rear wagon blew itself to splinters. The remaining daks collapsed in a twisted mass of dakflesh.

Some were killed outright. Some blew notes of agony through their horns. All were yoked together and could not flee into the Redlands to die.

They would die right here.

I wish I'd set them loose. I should have, maybe.

But the thought hadn't occurred to him when he'd been back at the wagons. There hadn't been time. Besides, he told himself, domesticated daks wouldn't last long in the Redland wilds. Probably.

For a moment, he remembered the woman's pleading face just before the ball struck her.

She'd have done the same to you, lad, Raj said.

Then the other two wagons exploded one after the other in great black plumes of smoke, and, looking upon the scene in excitement and amazement, Abel felt every bit of regret fade away.

He'd done that. Him. Abel Dashian.

No regrets.

All he was left with was the firm resolution that next time he would hold on to his rifle no matter what.

THE HERETIC

TONY DANIEL & DAVID DRAKE

THE HERETIC

This is a work of fiction. All the characters and events portrayed in this book are fictional, and any resemblance to real people or incidents is purely coincidental.

Copyright © 2013 by Tony Daniel and David Drake

A Baen Books Original

Baen Publishing Enterprises
P.O. Box 1403
Riverdale, NY 10471
www.baen.com

ISBN: 978-1-4767-3637-2

Cover art by Kurt Miller

First paperback printing, April 2014

Library of Congress Catalog Number: 2012051344

Distributed by Simon & Schuster
1230 Avenue of the Americas
New York, NY 10020

Pages by Joy Freeman (www.pagesbyjoy.com)
Printed in the United States of America

For Cokie and Hans

—T.D.

THE
HERETIC

Braun
Sea

Schnee
Mountains

Nedlands

Fourth
Cataract

Orash

Progar
District

The

Third
Cataract

Montag Island

Second
Cataract

Cascade
District

First
Cataract

Brunebers

Nedlands

Nedlands

The River

Hestinga

Lilleheim

Alwu-Alawaha

Garangipore

L. Treville

Box Canyon

Upper Cliffs
Scout Base

Ingres
District

Treville
District

Bigsticks

The
Tables

Land

Lindron

Lindron
District

Nedlands

Mims

The

Delta

Fyrpahatet

Braun
Sea

Duisberg

950 Miles

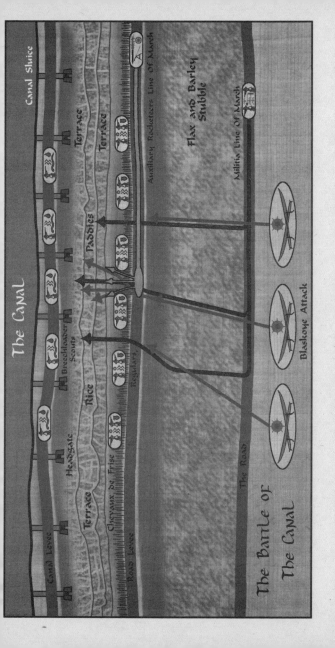

The Battle of
The Canal

"Yesterday won't be over until tomorrow and tomorrow began ten thousand years ago."

—William Faulkner, *Intruder in the Dust*

PART ONE

The Scout

1

"Bows and muskets, blood and dust—" six-year-old Abel Dashian sing-songed as he played in the yard of the temple storehouse. The afternoon was hot and humid, and the air was still.

He jumped from capstone to capstone upon the carved blocks of reddish-yellow stelae that surrounded the storehouse, teetering perilously, gloriously, on the brink of a fall to the hard-packed dirt below.

Teetering, yes—but never quite falling. Abel knew he would make his next jump, and the next. He liked that he was good at stuff like this, better than most boys his age.

"Flint and powder, broken bones—"

Nearby was the pile of baggage he was supposed to be watching while his father checked in with the district's ruling cleric, Prelate Zilkovsky. Abel and his father had been in Hestinga for several days, having hooked up with a fast caravan to arrive earlier than

3

expected. His father had used the extra days of leave to acquire a dwelling near the military compound, to find a nanny for Abel, and generally to set up house-keeping. Abel had gotten to know some of his new neighborhood, but spent most of his time unpacking his cache of personal belongings, including the treasured locks of his dead mother's hair.

Today was the first official visit Abel's father had made to the district priest, and custom required that he present his family—which was, in his case, only Abel—when he reported in. His father, whose name was Joab, had brought along the official deliveries he'd been charged with transporting from the capital to Hestinga.

The day before, Abel had finally given in to his curiosity, pulled back the large reed mat that covered the stack of items in a corner of the common room at his home, and taken a peek at this material. He had no idea what most of it was, but he had noticed a basket full of blank papyrus scrolls. Abel loved to draw, and spent a few moments lusting after them. Then he'd turned his attention to a carefully wrapped case with something hard bound within in it—carefully wrapped, but not so hard to open, even for smaller fingers. The case revealed a shiny new set of obsidian sacrificing knives. His father had walked in from watering the donts and caught him just before Abel made the major mistake of touching one of the knives.

"These were sent to the district prelate by the Abbot of Lindron himself," his father said. "How do you think it would look if Zilkovsky found a bunch of fingerprints all over them?"

Seeing Abel's downcast eyes, his father had taken pity upon him and given Abel one of his old throwing knives as a consolation prize. Abel had spent a happy afternoon practicing with it against a wooden post.

Today, Abel had been put in charge of watching over this baggage while his father went in to make his initial presentation, and he was determined to keep himself away from the sacrificing knives, which he still longed to play with.

I want to see one of those knives split papyrus, Abel thought. A friend back in Lindron had seen a prelate do that once with an obsidian blade. *No. Absolutely cannot touch. Father will whip me ragged.*

So he'd looked around for something to distract himself, and soon noticed an interesting picture that was carved on the sides of the standing stones that ringed a nearby large building. He'd wandered over to see what it was.

A carnadon. A dangerous river beast. And a really good likeness, too. Carnadons were Abel's favorite animals.

The carnadon carved on these stelae was a symbol the priesthood liked to use—he'd seen it near all the holy sites in Lindron—but he wasn't exactly sure what it meant.

Each stela had a carnadon relief carving on it, and who could resist climbing up on top and jumping from stone to stone to get away from them?

Not Abel Dashian, that was for sure.

Each of the roughhewn stone uprights was rect-angular, flat on top, and wide enough for a boy to stand squarely upon with a couple of steps to spare. They were squat, planted deep into the sandy ground, rising to about the height of a tall man's chest. The gap between the stelae was perhaps a stride and a half, which was a length that Abel could span with a jump—barely.

"I'm the one you'll never catch," he chanted and leaped through the air. He landed on the next stone, took a stutter step, and leaped again, continuing the ancient jingle, a song his mother had sung to him on the cradleboard and then, because he often requested it, through the years up until her death. "I'm the one who catches *you*."

Land on a stone top, leap, land, and leap again.

"You don't scare me, carnadon. Beer and barley, lead and copper, I'm the Carnadon Man!"

Abel pretended he was crossing the River at one of its rare fording points and must leap from rock to rock to avoid being snatched and eaten. The carnadons lived in hunting packs thick along the riverbanks near the wide spots in the water's flow. River carnadons were creatures horned with scale. They walked about on land with small legs, but in the water they possessed a powerful swimming tail. Their main feature, however, at least by Abel's lights, was a large mouth equipped with a jaw on a flexible hinge that could open wide and swallow a young boy whole.

Abel was both terrified and spellbound by River carnadons. When he'd lived in Garangipore as a very young child, one of his first memories was of watching from the terrace porch of the officer's residence where his family dwelled as carnadons wallowed on the riverbank below. Then in Lindron, his father had taken him to see the Great Tabernacle moats, which were full of well-fed carnadons kept as pets by the high priests.

He'd watched an afternoon feeding and seen the creatures swallow chunks of meat as big as barrels without once chewing. In the River, the creatures made their grisly living on fish and weak land creatures. In Garangipore, he'd seen one bring down a young herbidak that visited the riverbanks to graze. Carnadons also didn't mind feasting on the occasional villager when they got the chance—a fact which his mother had never let him forget.

I won't forget, Mamma.

"Teeth all snapping, tails all whapping, try to bite me if you can!"

Even though Abel was only six, he knew that the stone from which the stelae were made was not local. It was rock from the desert wastes beyond the River: the Redlands. Here in the valley, the natural stone was always black or dark brown like river mud unless you dug a hole *very* deep. You never saw buildings made of stone like this in Lindron, the city where Abel had lived for the past year, and the city where his mother had died. But here in Hestinga, near the Valley Escarpment, there were official buildings and even a few houses made from the red stone.

"You can't catch me, I'm the Carnadon Man!"

Abel completed his second circuit of the storehouse yard and sprang down. He took the landing with bended knees and rolled as his father had taught him Scouts did when jumping from a rooftop or a cliff. He came up facing the door to the building the stones circled. It had the look of some kind of storehouse, maybe an old granary. The structure was made of the same Redlands stone as the stelae, but the door was of thick-plaited river cane and looked solid, many layers thick. A pile of windblown sand had built up at its base. There were no hinges on the door that Abel could see.

Maybe it swings inside to out, Abel thought. *Or maybe it slides to the side into an opening. That would be interesting to see.*

Abel had always been good at picturing sizes and arrangements of things in the world, and figuring out how things moved or might look on the other side just by thinking about them. He'd been surprised to find that not everybody could do this, not even some adults.

On the right side of the matted door was a metal plate with a long piece of flat, dark metal emerging from it. Abel moved closer and saw that the flat piece was the shaft of a key. It was sticking out of a keyhole.

Abel had seen metal locks like this before in Lindron on the *very* old buildings, but this was the first he'd come across in the week they'd lived here in Hestinga. He'd been interested enough to ask his father how locks worked, and his father had demonstrated a wooden version on a small reed chest in his office that held his military credentials and the jade insectoid scarab he used to set a wax seal on official documents.

This key is larger. It's huge.

Abel approached warily. It was at about eye-height to him. He reached up, touched it.

Cold metal. Old metal.

It was made of steel, not iron, and was perfectly smooth. He ran a finger along its edge. It had the fine-cut profile of *nishterlaub*, a holy metal item from the Chaos Times, the nightmare days before the Law had been revealed to the priests by Zentrum, and the priests brought peace to the Land. Abel knew what to do if he found nishterlaub. *Don't touch. Tell a priest.*

But the storehouse was in the midst of the Treville District temple compound. Everyone obviously knew about it. This nishterlaub had been collected by the priests themselves. So what could it hurt to—

Before Abel quite realized what he was doing, he turned the key.

Click.

The lock was well-oiled and offered no resistance. Turning the key caused a plate on the door to pop out from its recess by a finger span to reveal a small pulling ring.

Never saw anything like that *before.*

In fact, the lock seemed as complicated as the most complex thing Abel knew: the firing mechanism on his father's musket. Abel had seen plenty of those. He was the son of a soldier, after all. But complicated or not, with a musket what it finally came down to was pulling the trigger.

So just pull it. See what happens.

Abel grasped the ring and leaned backward. The door didn't budge.

The sand. The buildup at the base of the door was keeping it in place. Abel swept it away with the sole of his sandal.

He tried again, this time throwing all his might into the effort. The door moved, swung outward an arm's length. Abel stumbled back a step as a whoosh of musty air escaped. It set him to coughing.

After he recovered, Abel glanced inside. Dark, but some light got in through window slits set in rows around all four walls. Still, pretty scary in there. Abel stepped away, glanced around the storehouse yard.

There wasn't much by way of a weapon to carry along with him, not even a stick. There was a stone, a black rock from here in the Valley, sitting not far away that, upon further examination, Abel figured must have been intended as a doorstop.

It was all he could do to pick it up with both hands and carry it next to his belly, but any weapon was better than nothing. So armed, he returned to the door and slipped inside the storehouse.

The air inside was cool and stale. He looked up and saw that the window slits near the ceiling were covered with actual glass. Glass was not considered nishterlaub, but it was something you could only find and were not allowed to make, so windows were rare in the Land. Windows were for priests and high officials. Windows were for keeping out rain and wind from important places.

And I guess for some storehouses, Abel thought.

Anyway, you normally didn't need windows in the Land. Strong gusts sometimes blew up the Valley before the spring floods, but usually the winds of the Land were light. Abel had never seen any rain, but his mother had sung him jingles about it. The songs were about water falling from the sky, as strange as that sounded. It wasn't that he didn't *believe* in rain, it was more that he had a hard time picturing it. Abel imagined rain as thick and syrupy, falling brown and silty like the River's water, and leaving everything with a fine coating of mud.

After his eyes adjusted, Abel stepped farther inside the storehouse. It was a large room, large enough to contain an average-sized house. The ceiling stretched a good twenty spans above him. The official residence he and his father shared could fit in here easily, with space to spare for an outhouse and stable.

This is sure no granary.

All about him were shapes. Twisted, strange shapes like midnight shadows. Large, square shapes. The glint of iron and copper and steel. Glass. Wood. In front of him, a white-colored pipe stretching out perpendicular from some sort of box with what looked like dead briars curling out. Odd. The pipe glinted almost a bit like metal, a bit like glass.

He reached out and touched it—

And recoiled in shock. *Plastic.*

The pipe was nishterlaub. Abel looked around again and realization dawned. The pipe, the strange shapes, everything in the storehouse. It was *all* nishterlaub.

His immediate thought was to turn tail and run, find a priest or his father, tell them what he'd found.

But that's stupid, he thought. *The priests* know *the nishterlaub is here. They must have put it here. But I'll bet I will still get in trouble.*

Was it wrong for him to be here?

Most of his friends from Lindron would sure think so. Of course, most of them wouldn't have opened the door in the first place. He'd barely been able to convince those guys to leave the alley behind the married officer's quarters. He'd dared them to go out and explore, and when nobody accompanied him, he'd gone himself.

Abel felt the familiar pain of remembering Lindron. Lindron was the before life. All gone.

Gone with Mamma.

She'd called him her brave boy, her little Carnadon Man. Was he still brave without her?

He would try to be. And the priests could give him a hiding if they wanted, he didn't care. Besides, he knew he'd start wondering about the nishterlaub and have to come back to have a look at it sooner or later. He'd be back.

So might as well look around now.

Interesting, said a voice. It was a dry voice, high pitched. Abel was unable to tell if it had come from a man or woman. He spun around. Nothing. No one there.

He moved deeper into the storage house.

A *likely lad, maybe*, another voice said, this one deeper and definitely male. ***Then again, maybe not.***

Abel lifted the rock he carried in his hands to his shoulder, ready to strike.

"Who's there?" he said, trying not to let his voice quiver with the fright he felt.

No one answered.

After a moment, Abel decided he must have heard soldiers speaking outside. The storage house was next to the temple guard exercise yard, after all. Maybe a platoon had shown up for morning duty.

But the voices had sounded close. Very close.

Okay, it's time to get out of here.

Abel turned to go.

But all this nishterlaub, he thought. *I have to see it.*

He looked to his right, to the strange box-shaped thing growing briars with the white plastic pipe emerging from it.

Not briars. Not anything that grew from the earth. Abel stooped down, looked closer. They were like vines, yet unlike. A sheath of colorful skin covered a core that glinted reddish-brown, like copper. No, it *was* copper, somehow.

Electrical wires, the high-pitched voice said. **To carry a fluid that is more powerful than**

gunpowder, than water gathered into a ram. You could think of it as liquid sunlight. The liquid sun brought the machine alive, and it—

Show him, said the low, gruff voice.

Very well. Observe:

Suddenly, the nishterlaub was alive. It beeped like some kind of strange, wounded flitter or an insectoid in the trees at night. Flames like evening glowflies flickered across its surface.

Abel gasped, stumbled back.

This is a simulation. It's a picture painted inside your mind, child. Observe:

And Abel did observe. He was in the room, but not in the room, and the machine, the nishterlaub, was different.

It was fixed. It *worked*.

The machine chimed, a door slid open in its side, and from it emerged...

Made things. Wonderful things. Like an oven that baked bread in all sorts of shapes, only this oven baked useful items. Tools. A procession of items emerged: hammers, rakes, shoes, scissors, pens...and then other things whose names began to flood Abel's mind: simple navigation computer, powerpack for kitchen appliances, medical diagnostic meter, pellet gun, wristwatch.

This thing was the Oven of Zentrum. It baked... *nishterlaub*!

And then it stopped. The vision disappeared, and the ancient machine stood before him, as destroyed as it had been moments before.

One of many such three-dimensional printers, said the dry, high-pitched voice. Nothing special to those who came before the Collapse. Resolution

moderate to low. Production value self-limiting. Cheap goods, made to become obsolete quickly. Unfortunately, no independent power source remains, and key metallic elements have been removed and destroyed or repurposed. Quite useless.

Abel started back. The voice again. He picked up his rock, which had fallen to his feet when he'd touched the . . . now he knew its name . . . the three-dimensional printer.

No one was here.

Who was speaking?

It has to be the nishterlaub talking, doesn't it?

Was·this why the priests kept it to themselves? But if the nishterlaub spoke, why did they abandon it here in the storage house? Obviously no one had been inside this building for a long, long time.

Three point five Duisberg years, said the high-pitched voice. **It was opened for the delivery of a piano.**

The meaning of what a piano was suddenly flooded Abel's mind—along with quick images of its use. Abel tried to grasp what he was being shown, but shook his head stubbornly after a moment.

"Cut that out," he said aloud. "Stop making me think things I don't ask to think. Anyway, I get it. It's a kind of musical instrument, right?"

Correct. The strings and other metal elements were stripped and recast. You can see the remains and the keys in a pile by the door over there.

Abel turned and looked. There was indeed a mass of broken wood and a neat stack of rectangular white stones. They looked like giant teeth.

*Boggles the mind. Three years ago the piano—
and nobody has been back since,* said the low voice.

*If I were a priest, I would spend all my time
talking to nishterlaub,* Abel thought. How could you
not, once you knew it could answer, that it could tell
you what it was, and, more importantly, what it *did*?

Abel looked away from the piano remains and
turned to the holy item behind him. Its surface was
a kaleidoscope of colors.

More plastic, Abel thought. Pretty.

It was larger than he was and looked like an enormous flitterdont. Well, it had what looked like wings,
anyway. Flitterdonts hunted in flocks and could be
dangerous. Abel had been warned by one crusty old
Scout in the caravan that the flitters sometimes made
a meal of human blood. Maybe the Scout had been
having him on. Maybe not. The flitters allegedly lived
in the Escarpment overhangs, and there were plenty
of those around here.

But this thing, whatever it was, was not alive, and
didn't look likely to suck his blood. He gulped, then,
after a moment of indecision, reached out and touched
its smooth surface of swirling colors.

Abel tried to forget about flitters and to clear
his mind and concentrate. Maybe the next flood of
information wouldn't make him feel so dizzy if he
was prepared.

"Okay, tell me," he said.

**An impulse flyer, used for personal transport.
This is a foot-mounted model peculiar to this sector, pre-Collapse, and this one obviously belonged
to someone with extravagant design tastes, perhaps an adolescent. This flyer here is perched**

**on its side, of course. Obviously the priests had
no clue as to how to arrange it after depositing
it. Imagine the item rotated horizontally. That
is its correct position.**

Abel ran his hand along the surface of the flyer, trying to do just that. His hand passed over a depression
in the surface. Nearby was another, similar depression.
Both were about two elbs across and a half-elb deep.

**Footholds. They activated the stabilization field
and allowed the passenger to ride standing up
without fear of overbalancing.**

I don't get it, Abel thought. *They stood on this
and* flew?

Show the boy, said the gruff voice.

**I am not sure that such a young subject will be
able to properly integrate a full virtual immer-
sion. There is considerable risk to his neural
networks.**

***He'll either adapt or break. Either way, we'll
have our answer***, the gruff voice replied. ***Show him.***

"Yeah," said Abel. "Show me!"

Very well. Observe:

And then Abel was flying.

He was standing on the flyer *in the air*. The ground
was far, far beneath him. For a moment, he almost did
break. This was impossible. He was outside. He was
flying like a flitterdont through the air. The world spun
like crazy as dizziness overcame Abel. He started to fall.

But couldn't. Something held him in place.

**Stabilization fields. Of course, this is merely a
simulation, but it is an extremely precise approximation of what a flyer ride was like.**

Abel shook his head, regained his balance. He looked down again. Far below were the roofs of Hestinga. It was perched on the edge of the oxbow lake that formed the great Treville oasis, one of the few places within the Land that was more than a day's walk from the River. From this height, the waters of Lake Treville sparkled as a small breeze caused the surface to ripple.

"I'm flying! Am I really flying?"

Unfortunately, no, answered the high-pitched voice. **This is a form of make-believe. A projection based on extrapolation. You are still physically within the storehouse. But given the historical records in my databanks and an accurate survey of the local geography prior to landfall, this simulation should be accurate to within one tenth of one percent of a hundred.**

In other words, lad, this is what it feels like to fly, said the gruff voice. *How do you like it?*

Abel looked around. Far to the west, the River was a shining strip barely visible on the horizon. Between were the rolling hills of the Treville salient with its massive irrigation system, its ditches and canals, derived from the River and culminating in Lake Treville. Abel's father had explained to him how it all worked, how the alluvial paddocks and washes along the way were watered by a system of ditches and aqueducts, and coaxed to yield wheat and barley, flax and rice.

Duisberg barley, said the high-pitched voice. **The planet was renowned for beer and whiskey. Liquor was the principal export, pre-Collapse. Since settlement, Duisberg has remained mostly agricultural, which is probably why the Sector**

Command Control Unit AZ12-i11-e Mark XV remained set in his ways. Cultural accretion often creates waves of repetitive behavior to which even artificial intelligence units find themselves subject.

"Huh?"

Zentrum is stuck, lad.

We have come to unstick the unit. More importantly, we have come to reintegrate Duisberg into the reconstituted Galactic Republic.

"Zentrum?" replied Abel, confused. "But Zentrum's just a special name for God."

Zentrum is not a god, and he is not God. He is a computer.

It is the being your priests serve, boy, said the gruff voice.

Zentrum was the word for God that the priests used when they were talking about the Laws. The Edicts. The Stasis. All the stuff you learned in Thursday school.

Whatever. It was the most boring stuff in the world. He wanted to fly, to keep flying, forever. This was so much fun!

The wind was whipping past him and, in the process, making a terrible din, like a storm. He leaned to his left. The flyer tilted sharply with him, and Abel quickly straightened back up. Too much. "How do I steer this thing, anyway?" he shouted.

Quiet lad, said the gruff voice with a laugh. *You'll accidentally summon the guards. Remember, you are actually still in the storehouse. You needn't speak. We can hear words if you think about saying them.*

Can you hear this? Abel thought.

Yes, boy.

Abel didn't know if he liked the fact that the nishter-laub voices could eavesdrop on his inner thoughts. But for the moment, all he really cared about was keeping this trip going, to fly like a flitterdont across the landscape.

I dreamed of this. The day before Mamma died.

The sickness had grown worse, and she was wrapped up and shivering on her pallet even though it was a hot day outside. And that night, he'd dreamed of flying with his mother beside him, her flowing robes trailing behind her as they both laughed and zoomed over Lindron, over the River, and into the beyond.

But that dream was nothing compared to this!

He shifted his balance slowly and carefully to the left again. The flyer reacted by swooping into a graceful arc.

I can do this! I can steer this thing like a reed boat.

He leaned to the right, almost overbalanced, but caught himself, pulled the flyer into a sweeping curve.

I want more, he thought/said to the voices. *I want to go farther. Let's go. Show me! Show me everything!*

Done, said the high-pitched voice.

Abel leaned back and, yes, the flyer tilted up as he'd hoped it would, climbed higher. The River was now in view below him, as were both sides of the Valley. It wasn't at all straight, but twisted like a legless dont whipping through the dust.

How high am I?

In local terms? Approximately half a league. Seven thousand feet. You are at the maximum recommended altitude for an uncovered flyer such as this. But this should be sufficient for the purpose.

What do you see below you, boy? the gruff voice asked.

The River. There's Garangipore to the north, where the main canal and the River meet. I see the Valley. The Land. But not all of it.

You couldn't see all of the Land, not unless you flew nearly to orbit, out of the air itself.

Air ends *somewhere in the sky? That's a lie. Has to be.*

What I say to you will never be a lie, Abel.

Whatever.

He looked back down.

Like a map. Like one of my father's maps. I love maps. I can almost read, you know. Mamma taught me a lot. And Father has taught me all about maps, too.

We are aware of your strong literacy skill set, replied the high-pitched voice. **This is one among several latent abilities, some of which you do not yet realize you possess. As you see, the Valley here at the branch-point of the Treville salient is at its widest. To the southwest, it becomes narrower until it finally reaches the capital of Lindron and then Mims, the city just above the River Delta. At Mims, the River widens, drops its alluvium to form the Delta islands and the tidal estuaries, and then flows into the Braun Sea. The average width of the Valley is two days' travel on foot.**

The Valley is hardly twenty leagues across at its widest, said the gruff voice. *But its length from the top of the cataracts to Fyrpahatet on the coast—now, that's another story. In fact, that's the whole story of the Land and why things are the way they are.*

I don't get it.

Wouldn't expect you to, boy. You've never known anything else. The River drains the whole of the western continent on this planet, northeast to southwest.

Don't know what he's talking about and don't care, Abel thought and tried to keep the thought to himself. He had a feeling the gruff voice could be just as impatient with what he viewed as foolishness as his father. *Just let me keep flying!*

He must have at least partially formed the words in his mind, however, because the gruff voice stopped short, let out a growl.

You either care or you'll be made to care, lad, the voice grumbled. **Center, impress upon our young charge what it means that we are inside his thoughts.**

Are you certain that's wise?

We have to push now. If the lad's what we're looking for, he'll survive it.

Agreed, said the high-pitched voice, which must be "Center," the possessor of the high-pitched voice that the gruff voice was speaking to. **This may prove disorienting. I will physically alter certain neuronal firing sequences within your brain and impart to you sufficient strata of term denotations to enable you to understand otherwise undefined referents.**

Didn't sound good. Not good at all. Whoever or whatever this Center was, it or he or she was about to alter his thoughts. Could it alter his memories? Everything?

Cause him to forget.

Mamma.

No!

I'm afraid this will be necessary.

I'll jump. I'll fall and die.

You are, in actuality, already standing on the floor.

Don't poke inside me, I mean it!

I will perform only necessary poking.

Please! No!

I'm ... sorry, Abel.

"Wait!" Abel screamed, this time sure to do so aloud. Maybe he could summon the priests or a guard. The gruff voice had cautioned him against shouting. Maybe he could use this against them. "I'll yell!"

No, said Center, **you won't.**

Abel's opened his mouth to prove Center wrong. Not a sound came out. He struggled to shout. Nothing, not even a voiceless puff of air.

Okay, Abel said. *Okay, you win. It's going to hurt. It's going to hurt, isn't it?*

Yes, said Center.

And suddenly his head exploded in pain.

And understanding. Continent. Orbit. Energy. Northern hemisphere. He began to comprehend.

The world is round!

Yes.

And the Land is not all of the world. Not by a long shot.

The Land and its surrounding desert reaches, which stretch to the Schnee Mountains in the east and the Braun Sea to the west, are the only portion of Duisberg inhabited by humans.

You keep saying Duisberg. That's the name of this ... planet? asked Abel.

Correct.

And there are lots of other planets?

Lots, said Center. **And other suns.**

And he was made to understand.

That's what the stars are.

Correct.

"Why should I believe you?" said Abel, speaking aloud. The thought was too hard to form completely without hearing it first. "You're probably lying to get me to do something, like those beggar boys in Lindron who said they'd show me a hardback riverdak out of its shell. What they really wanted was to steal the slingshot Father made me. I had to fight six at once when they chased me to the barracks row."

And did you win, lad? asked the gruff voice.

"Nope," Abel replied. "They got the slingshot. But it took all six of them to lick me."

Abel leaned hard to the left, then hard to the right. The flyer yawed, and he could feel a buzz as the invisible stabilization fields, whatever they were, gripped him tight. He leaned to the left again, attempting to rock the flyer into capsizing.

If I'm not really flying, then I can turn this over . . . and fall! I won't die, because I'm really in the storehouse. But maybe that'll get them out of my head.

Another gruff laugh. **Good try, lad.**

General Whitehall, we have much to accomplish today, said Center. **Foundations must be laid.** It, he—Abel decided Center sounded more male than female—seemed irritated.

Almost. The flyer was almost tipped over on the right side. One more hard rocking motion and—

Enough!

The flyer froze in place. If he'd been on the edge

of a cliff, Abel's momentum would have made him fall. Instead, the stabilization fields seemed to absorb his motion like a down pillow.

We must decide if this child is the one, the gruff voice said. *If so, then agreed, we will proceed. If not...* The voice trailed off.

That doesn't sound good. That's the kind of voice father uses just before he takes out his sharpening strop.

Abel stopped rocking and ceased trying to end the flying simulation. Besides, he really didn't want to, not yet. It was time, however, to change the subject. "So you, the squeaky one who sounds like a cross between a three-year-old and a priest, you're Center?"

Correct.

"And the other, you with the mean voice, you're General White-something?"

Call me Raj, lad, the gruff voice replied. *It's my first name. I have a feeling we're going to get along fine. May even be friends.*

You wish! But Abel did his best to keep his misgivings to himself and tried not to let them form into a full thought. He found it helped if he considered other things at the same time. Feeling like a flitterdont flapping around. The wind in his face. Clouds.

It did seem that the two voices couldn't know *exactly* what he was thinking unless a thought was so complete he was on the verge of speaking it out loud.

At least so he hoped.

Well, Raj, *you can call me Abel,* he said, a*nd I* don't *think we're going to be friends.* He hoped the tone of defiance was clear in his thought-speech.

From Raj's quiet chuckle afterward, he figured it had been.

Abel turned his attention back to flying. He'd now reached the River. He'd approached from the east, and he leaned to his right to tilt the flyer into a north-northwest direction, parallel to the general trend upriver, although the water's course itself wound back and forth in a completely crazy fashion.

The wind whipped by his ears and caused his hair, plaited by the nanny into a single pigtail, to stick out like a riding dont's neck plumage. He leaned forward, and, to his delight, this increased the flyer's speed.

You'll notice that there are very few clouds to obscure your view of the Valley below, Center intoned.

Yeah, so?

Precisely, said Center. **There are *never* many clouds. Due to the extreme height of the Schnee formation—we are still not level with the smallest peaks, even at this altitude—almost all westerly wind current is blocked on the eastern side of the massif. The prevailing winds on this side of the continent are strong northeasterlies, channeling up from the Braun Sea to the wastes above the River's springs and, ultimately, flowing through the high passes and into Duisberg's Arctic, where what moisture there is becomes locked up in snowfall and ultimately ice. The northern glaciers calve into the Braun, and the cycle continues, for this geological moment, at least.**

Massif.

Continent.

Arctic.

Abel winced as each of the unfamiliar words seemed to twist and squirm inside him before they locked on to a set of meanings. Every moment of new knowledge acquisition was also a moment of pain. Center had not lied. It hurt. But in the end, he made sense, or believed he made sense, of what the voice was saying. He understood.

The River itself originates near Chambers Pass in the Schnees and is the sole drainage for the western continent. It flows south-southwest to the Braun Sea. Duisberg is extraordinarily dry as settlement planets go, and there is no comparable hydrological system anywhere else, not in either hemisphere. The terrain created by the River provides the only planetary region capable of feudal-style agriculture such as is practiced in the Land.

Your deserts and scrublands are herder territory, said Raj. *Fit only for nomads. And the Redlands will only support scraggly grazing animals at that, given the present condition of development. That's one of the reasons that raiding has become such a way of life for those... what do you call the tribes outside the Land?*

"Redlanders," said Abel. "Even talking to them can get you crucified."

And yet talking goes on all the time, I'll wager, answered Raj.

Correct, said Center.

"But if you touch a Redlander, you'll get sick and die!" Abel exclaimed.

You never really believed that, did you, boy?

Raj was right. When Abel mentioned the Redlander curse to his father, his father had nodded, but he'd smiled in the same way he did when Abel asked him if it was true swimming in a temple pool made a baby grow in a mommy's tummy.

"I guess not."

In fact, the current aristocracy is made up of Redlander stock, said Center. **Observe. The Land is merely two to three leagues across roughly east to west, but is over two hundred leagues long north to south. It would take the better part of a Duisberg year to walk its length from the Delta to the upper cataracts.**

A strategic weakness, said Raj. *Would be fatal if the scrub lands weren't so poor. So it is in the interest of Zentrum to keep them poor or at least to keep them sedated. And he doesn't care how he does it, either. When the Redlanders have built up to any extent, he doesn't just allow them to invade. He practically invites them in.*

Your people have myths of these nomadic invasions. They are called the Blood Winds.

"I know about that," said Abel, again returning to the spoken word to expresses a more complicated thought. "Elder Newfeld taught us about it in Thursday school."

The people of the Land had grown wicked and disobeyed the commandments of God, the elder had said. So Zentrum, God's voice, allowed their enemies to attack and destroy every other man, woman, and child. Even the donts. That was the part Abel particularly hated.

Zentrum made an accommodation with the invading Redlander tribes. They were given lands, titles, wealth. They stayed, interbred—and were absorbed into the surviving populace. This has happened time and again.

It's going to happen again, Abel, Raj said. ***Soon****.
What's going to happen?*
Blood Winds. They're coming.

Abel leaned back, slowed the flyer. He suddenly
felt sick to his stomach. In the stories, the Redlanders hadn't just killed the people of the Land. They'd
spitted babies on the ends of their spears. They'd
taken kids away to be slaves forever.

And worst of all, they tortured *the riding donts
before they slaughtered them. Cut off their hoofpads.
Tied their mouths closed and plugged their blowholes
so they couldn't breathe.*

Abel loved riding donts, loved everything about
them. It hurt him inside to hear a dont scream in
pain. It really bothered him if that pain came from
a whip lashing or the kick of a glassrock spur. If he
hated one thing more than all else, it was people who
were mean to donts.

"They're going to kill the donts? All of them? They
can't do that!"

Maybe they can and maybe they can't, Raj
said, his tone softer. ***That's part of why we're here,
Center and me.***

You can stop it? But you said God wants them to
win, to—

Raj cut him off. ***Zentrum. Again, lad, Zentrum
is not God. God doesn't care who wins or loses
a fight. Well, let's just say God's thinking on
such matters is a bit hard to figure. Zentrum,
on the other hand, has a very simple plan. Keep
things the way they've always been. Forever.
Maintain stasis.***

He has achieved this aim on Duisberg for

**nearly three thousand years by restricting the
population to this peculiar blend of Neolithic
and early industrial-age technology.**

Abel pictured the Land, the rolling fields of barley
and flax he'd passed on the way from Lindron to Hestinga. The flitterdonts and the hardbacks and especially
Mot, the little riding dont that was his special mount.

"What's wrong with Stasis? That's what all the Laws
and Edicts are supposed to be for."

Can't last, Raj said. *And there's no fallback.*

**Zentrum has made a fundamental miscalcu-
lation that will destine this planet to ruin,** said
Center. **It was based on insufficient information.
After all, when the Collapse came, the slide
was rapid due to nannite viral infection of elec-
tronica via the Tanaki Net. A secured military
or planetary defense computer of some sort, a
being such as myself in original configuration,
is often the only electronic suite that survived
intact. My kind can be an extremely protective,
even paranoid, lot.**

*Creativity, innovation, people having a say in
their own governance,* said Raj. *Zentrum hates
all that.*

The words and their meanings again exploded in
Abel's mind. He closed his eyes against the strain,
but it didn't seem to help. This was not a headache.
It was more like a *mind* ache.

And within all the words, one shining, horrible,
wondrous, amazing fact stood out.

What the voice said was true.

Zentrum was not God. Not even the voice of God.

Zentrum was a mean Thursday school teacher who

wanted you to sit up straight and recite the Law for watch after watch. Who never let you do anything that wasn't Edict. Who whacked you with the correction stick when you got out of Stasis for even one second.

In the Land, it's Thursday forever, lad, said Raj.

When Abel opened his eyes again, he was hovering over the Fourth Cataract near the River's headwaters as it cascaded out of the Schnee.

A village stretched below him. Its rooftops not flat, as were all roofs Abel had ever seen so far. These were oddly tilted and joined at the center in ridges.

They're for shedding the autumn rains, lad, Raj said with a chuckle. *Never seen the like, have you? Not only that, sometimes in midwinter they're topped with snow.*

White, like in the stories?

Yes, lad. At least for a day. Then the dust settles in and browns it down.

Behold Orash, Progar District, said Center. **Behold the gateway of the Blood Wind.**

2

Observe:

The Redlanders flooded down the Escarpment toward the forts at the choke point of the River. The donts they rode upon were Valley stock sold to them by the very villagers they were now attacking. It didn't matter. The Redlanders cut through the villagers like a scythe.

Time to go down, said Raj, and abruptly Abel found himself off the flyer and standing in a village street.

The principal street of Orash in a not-distant future. Observe:

Screaming people were running past him. Babies were crying. Children were yelling for their parents, for their brothers and sisters.

Nobody knew where to go or what to do.

Because there wasn't anywhere to go.

The rumble of massed riding donts in the distance. Men on dontback. Abel recognized the sound well enough without Center's data planting.

Screams that were screams of pain.

A single villager charging down the street straight at Abel, a wild look on his face and insanity in his eyes.

It was the eyes that frightened Abel the most.

He's seen something, Abel thought to himself. *Something horrible.*

Their eyes locked, and the man headed directly toward Abel at a quick pace, as if tugged by a lanyard.

Abel flinched. The man with the crazy eyes was going to run right over him. There was no time to dodge, no time to jump away.

But then the man stumbled. Slowed.

Still his eyes remained locked with Abel's.

And then he keeled over and fell on his face at Abel's feet.

The man's back was pierced with arrows as if he were a human pincushion. And there was a gunshot to the left shoulder blade. Meat and muscle hung loose, and the ball had wreaked terrible damage to the bone.

It looks like a ragged, bloody cave, Abel thought. Bone glinted within torn skin.

Enough, said Raj.

Abel was back in the storehouse in Hestinga. He stumbled back from the upended flyer he'd been touching. He gasped for air.

"That man—" Abel managed to wheeze.

—one of many, said Raj. **Many thousands who will die.**

The Redlanders will sweep down Valley. The Second Cataract forts were designed as bases for forays into the surrounding desert, not north-south defense bastions. Their rear works are practically nonexistent. Most of them are unwalled

and back up to the River. The Central Granary on Montag Island will burn. Rotten Bruneberg will crumble. Lindron will fall. The priesthood will flee to Mims. Mims will burn along with the priests. Thousands more will die from famine.

How do you know? Abel asked.

I am a fifth-generation artificial intelligence running on a one hundred gigacubit quantum superimposition engine. I complete more calculations per one of your eyeblinks than all the computers of the first millennium of the Information Age could produce together if all of them ran at full power for each of those one thousand years.

Huh?

Trust me, Abel. I know.

Zentrum will reach an accommodation with the Redlanders, said Raj. *As always, Zentrum believes he is taking the long view.*

There is a tactical purity to the scheme, said Center. If one's time horizon does not extend beyond a century or two.

Bloody hell, you sound like you agree with him! Raj practically shouted in Abel's still spinning mind. *Have we not seen this before? Have we not seen where it leads?*

Merely tactical, *not* strategic, Center replied without missing a beat. There is an enormous error at the heart of Zentrum's calculations. Stasis is error.

Abel pulled himself upright. He started to back away, to back out of the room, but something stopped him. He had another question. More to learn. Even after all this, after seeing the crazy-eyed man and his ripped apart back, Abel still felt—

Curious.

"H-how?" he said aloud.

How what? said Raj brusquely.

Abel experimented with keeping his thoughts to himself.

Ask. Ask the question. Just because you want to know. Maybe they *had* heard. Were these his own thoughts, or Center's, somehow beaten into his mind?

No. No, they weren't.

Mamma liked it when I was curious. Mamma liked it that I wanted to know everything.

"How is Stasis wrong?" Abel asked.

For many reasons. On a mere physical level, consider: Duisberg has three moons. The gravitational tides created by their interactions have created an enormous debris field in a nearby orbit. The very rotation of the planet, opposite that of the rotational momentum of the system as a whole, speaks to this fact, as well. There have been cataclysmic strikes in the past, and a future meteor strike is a virtual certainty, geologically speaking.

Each unfamiliar word lit up with a definition as Center spoke it. Didn't help. This was the way all adults were, explaining things that had no earthly use right now.

So what?

I don't understand your response.

I said, so what?

Rephrase, please.

Am I going to get hit by a giant rock from space?

Unlikely that you yourself will be hit.

Is my father?

Again, unlikely.

You're stupid, then. And I don't care.

Human cognitive integration error. Due to your limited experience, you will require time to process.

Raj laughed heartily. It was not a pleasant laugh, either.

There's no error. He may be six, but he gets it well enough, don't you, lad? Your mother—there's the key. Was she not going to always be there for you? Where is she, Abel?

Mamma.

Not fair.

It was one thing to fight, even to get beaten up. He was tough, and, even if he cried, he knew he didn't really care. But to have a presence in your head that knew the places that *really* hurt—that wasn't shy about touching those places if it served a purpose . . .

Mamma. Sunken eyes. Gurgling breath that smelled like pus. Face twisted in pain at something inside that was eating her, killing her.

That did *kill her.*

It had only been a toothache.

Only a stupid toothache the week before. And then she left me.

Lad, I'm sorry.

"Not fair," he whispered. "It was just a bad tooth. She had it out. That was supposed to cure her."

Bacterial sepsis, no doubt.

I know it's not fair, lad. It's not. But there's your answer. Nothing stays the same.

Zentrum has fallen into a logical trap of his own creation.

"Not. Fair."

Something heavy in his hands. Abel glanced down. It was the rock, the door stop. He was still clutching it. He'd been clutching it all along.

See there in the corner? See the cone-shaped thing?

Abel looked around. He had to step past the upturned flyer to see what Raj was talking about. It was indeed a cone shape, white with black markings upon it, as if it had survived a terrible fire.

"I see it," Abel said. "What is it?"

Another laugh, this one not so unsettling.

Why, it's the spaceship we came in, lad, Center and me.

And Abel understood—because he was made to understand. The capsule speeding through hyperspace in a tunnel of stars, their light extended into lines about the spaceship. This capsule. Hundreds of others on their way to different worlds, other fallen human worlds.

Like puffer-rod seeds, when you blew them, flying every which direction.

"I don't get it," Abel said. "I mean, I know what a spaceship is, you just showed me. But why? Why'd you come here?"

Change, replied Center. **Change *will* occur, and if all upward change is blocked, what eventually occurs will be downward. Another Collapse. And this one longer and more complete than any other. Maybe final. This world must be readied to rejoin the awakened Republic. Those ships will**

come. And when they do, if they find nothing
but primitives crawling among the ruins, they
will pass by. There is much else to do.

"So what?"

Things can get worse, Raj said. *Like they got
worse for your mother.*

"Leave my mother alone!"

**If this society had the most basic antibiotics,
your mother would still be alive,** said Center. **We
could have helped her.**

"You're gods from the heavens! If you want to help
me, bring her back!"

We can't do that, Abel. We're not gods.

"But you *are.* I know what you say, but you have
to be to show me all this. I'll do whatever you say.
Whatever it is you want." Tears were streaming down
Abel's face. "Just bring Mamma back."

You don't understand, Abel Dashian, Center
calmly replied. **It is *we* who need you.**

He gripped the rock tighter. "Then what good are
you?" With all his might, Abel raised the rock over
his head. He stepped toward the capsule. "Get out."

You can't harm the capsule, said Center. **Not
with a simple stone, Abel.**

"Get out of *me.*"

A moment of silence. Then Raj's deep voice, now
tight with concern. *His plan isn't to hurt the
capsule,* Raj said. *Abel, lad—*

"You don't scare me," said Abel. Despite himself, he
found himself laughing through his tears. "You don't
scare me, I'm the Carnadon Man."

Then Abel brought the stone down hard upon his
own head and fell into darkness.

3

When Abel awoke, he was looking at his reflection in still water. His head ached.

Not still water. Probably blood, he thought. *My blood. I'm seeing my reflection in my own blood. Must be a lot of it.*

He reached for the blood to see if it was still warm. Maybe this was what it was like to be dead.

His hand stopped against the shiny surface. He pushed harder. The water was solid, and it wasn't water at all. More like stone. Smooth stone.

Abel sat up. He was surrounded by himself. He moved. Many other Abels moved with him.

Reflections. But there were dozens. It was as if he were inside a gem.

Where am I?

Abel stood up. He walked forward. One step, two. He ran into himself, nose to nose. Reached for his face. More smoothness.

Not blood, not reflecting water. This was a room made of looking glass. Mirrors. He'd only seen one once before. His mother's friend Dagmar in Garangipore had a small glass she used to apply the kohl liner to her eyes. That she could do this without poking her eyes with the liner pencil had fascinated and scared Abel, and he'd liked to watch.

Yet this glass was different. Brighter. Completely reflective. Where did the light come from, anyway?

Suddenly Abel lashed out, swung at a wall as hard as he could with his fist.

Pain shot through his hand.

Ow!

Nothing, not the slightest effect on the wall. A smarting hand. Abel nursed it to his side while considering his next move.

It might help your plans for escape if you had some idea where you are, wouldn't it, lad? And just who and what you are dealing with. The gruff voice had returned again. He hadn't managed to smash it out of his skull after all.

Then, as a man might step through a waterfall at the Second Cataract (Abel had seen it happen once; there were caves behind the falls), a tall man with pale skin, dark hair, and a curly black beard stepped *out* of one of the mirrored walls and came to stand beside Abel. The man wore strange garb. Abel had never seen fabric so uniformly smooth. His own trousers and tunic were made from beaten flax fiber and always felt scratchy.

In addition to a shirt that covered his arms down to just below the elbow, the man wore not a well-bred man's muslin trousers but the kind of baggy-legged

pants that only beggars and wastelanders wore in the
Land. These pants were stuffed into black boots of
what looked like the finest herbidak leather Abel had
ever seen. He wanted to touch those boots just to see
if they were as supple as they looked.

"Hello, lad, I'm Raj Whitehall," the man said. He
gestured at the surrounding mirrored walls. "And this,
all around us? This is Center."

Greetings, Abel. The voice came from everywhere
and nowhere in the mirrored room. **We were concerned, but the danger has now passed. I am
effecting repairs on the trauma your actions have
caused to your brain. My efforts will allow you
to avoid a convalescent period and, in fact, keep
you from experiencing any ill effects at all, to
a ninety-three percent probability.**

"This is like the flying, isn't it?" Abel said to Raj—
mostly because he knew where to look when speaking to him. "It's not really a...a simulation. This is
a"—he searched for the new terminology, found it
implanted—"mind-space."

"You're in the district prelate's house, lying on his
wife's sleeping pallet," Raj replied. "Your father and
she are watching over you until you wake up. You
managed to give yourself a fine concussion."

Raj smiled. His big white teeth shone brightly in his
black beard, making him look less like a wastelander
and more like a Redland barbarian.

"Father found me?" Abel asked.

"That he did," Raj replied. "The high priest was with
him, too. It caused quite a stir. You got picked up and
taken to Prelate Zilkovsky's home on a private litter."

"Father must be worried."

"He was. And by the sound of his voice, a bit terrified that he would lose you as he did his woman. I would not expect him to be in a happy mood when you wake up."

Observe:

Abel was in the priest's house. He lay propped up on pillows upon a sleeping pallet. The walls of the room were painted white with a wash that Abel knew had to be very expensive. He smelled the familiar odor of surkrat cooking somewhere, a dish his mother had made. His father paced back and forth, his sandals slapping in rhythm against the ceramic tile floor.

Then Abel was back in the mirrored room.

"I want to wake up. I want to tell Father I'm all right."

"In good time," Raj answered. He hunched down to face Abel eye to eye. "Let Center do his work upon you first, lad." Raj settled into a crisscross position on the floor. He did not fidget, and seemed like a man accustomed to occasionally sitting on floors—or wherever the situation called for.

"You're Raj."

"Yes, lad."

"You dress funny, but you look kind of like a man."

Raj smiled. His teeth flashed within his dark beard. "That's right, lad, I'm a simulation," he said. "But a good one. I even manage to fool myself."

"You're not real."

"I used to be." Raj nodded as if remembering, though how could a simulation *really* remember anything? "A fighter. Then a soldier. Helped bring a world or two out of darkness."

"And Center?"

"Center is no simulation. He's here on Duisberg, contained in that capsule in the storehouse. And, in a way, so am I."

"Then how come I see you when I'm supposed to be asleep in the prelate's house?"

Raj nodded, thinking. Then he smiled and spoke. "You know how the Signal Corps has those towers along the road?"

"Those are for wigwag. You can send a message, or get one."

"Well, think of it like this: there's a little wigwag tower in your head now, lad. We talk to you that way."

"And you can change things?"

"What do you mean?"

"In my head. Like make me forget about my mother. Wipe her out. You could do that, couldn't you? And when you find out I'm not the one you're looking for, you're going to wipe her out. Like a rake on sand."

He felt a sob coming on. How could you sob in simulation? You shouldn't be able to. It wasn't fair.

"Lad, we won't take your mother away."

Abel felt his teeth clenching, his whole body clenching. He didn't want to say it, didn't want to admit it even to himself.

"You won't?"

"No."

"Doesn't matter anyway."

"What?" said Raj. "I don't understand, lad."

"Because *I'm* forgetting what she looked like," he said.

Raj's hard face softened. "So that's it."

Interesting. The room filled with Center's voice. **Your precipitous action was a distant outlier in**

**my own calculations. It's not often that I am
outthought, especially by a six-year-old.**

But now that he had his point, Abel was not going
to let go of it. He was being stubborn. He didn't care.
"You *can* wipe my mother away, can't you?"

Raj nodded. "We could, lad."

"Leave her alone," Abel said. "Just leave her alone."

Raj reached out, touched Abel's shoulder, but Abel
jerked away. "I'll kill you both if you touch her," he
murmured.

"You have my word, lad," Raj said. "Wouldn't serve
any purpose."

"You're a simulation. You're just . . . you're just a
nothing. I don't like you. I don't trust you."

Raj shook his head. Abel risked a glance at him.
He seemed sad.

"It's the way of all things," he said. "Maybe we'll
earn your friendship, Abel. But we're going to have
to stick together anyway."

"How come you are doing this to me?"

"We have to reach you when you are little, before
the Law of Zentrum gets all the way beaten into your
brain, that's why."

Suddenly, as loud as he could, Abel formed a
thought. He wasn't going to say it. He was going
to shout it. *I can get both of you out of my head!
Any time, I can!*

**That is correct, Abel. But at the cost of your
own life,** said Center.

I'd rather be dead than a slave.

Raj rose to his knees from the crisscross sitting
position. For a moment, he looked Abel straight in
the eyes. Abel returned the gaze with a glare.

Raj took Abel by the shoulders. Abel looked down at the backs of Raj's big hands.

He could shake me to death with those. Well, let him try.

Abel pushed Raj's hands away, crossed his own arms, and continued to glare.

Then Raj threw his shaggy head back and began to laugh. "Oh, we've found the one, all right!"

4

The classroom was stuffy and smelled of dont piss. It had once been a stable; there were no windows, and the floor sand was not packed, much less paved over. Bits of straw from its previous life could still be kicked up, and Abel suspected this was where the urine odor still resided. Abel knew he ought to feel lucky. Most of the people of the Land, even those from First Families, never learned to read, and resorted to an abacus when numbers began to move much past twenty. With his father's permission, the officers with children had pooled their resources to hire a teacher and had rented the space from the military garrison.

Reading had come easily to Abel. Math had not.

With class a half day on Mondays and Fridays, and, of course instruction in the Law and Stasis taking up all of Thursday, Abel had begun to spend a great deal of time inside his thoughts, talking to the voices he still was not quite sure were real, but that he *knew* had proved to be quite helpful at times.

But the voices, Raj and Center, would not *give him the damn answers*. At least they hadn't yet. He was determined to keep asking for help, because wheedling was easier than attempting another meaningless word problem of the sort the instructor, Lieutenant Milovich, seemed to take such pleasure in assigning.

I hope you know us better than that now, lad, Raj said. *We're here to give you more options, not turn you into a suckling babe again.*

Yeah, right, thought Abel. *Prove you want to help by doing this math problem for me. What's the angle of the triangle Lieutenant Milovich wants us to calculate? I've got two angles and a side. It's not a right angle, so how do I do it?*

If we told you, how would that help you learn trigonometry?

You could just put it in my head.

That is correct, Center put in. **I could instantly provide you with the answer to this question. But I could not condition you sufficiently so that you will know how to work out the problem for yourself, or how to approach future problems.**

Give me the answer.

No.

I don't care about ballistics or land surveying. I care about being a Scout.

And do you not think knowing how to estimate land areas might come in useful out there in the wastes of the Redlands?

No. Abel considered. *Well, maybe. Give me the answer anyway.*

No.

I know about the Redlands, but if you tell me the answer, it will get me out of this stuffy garrison taking lessons from a junior officer with too much time on his puffy little rich-boy hands.

The lieutenant's hand swelling is from hypothyroidism. He'll be dead before he's thirty from autoimmune system collapse, Center said. **A Fibonacci projection using Seldon values for social normatives does indicate an upper-class upbringing, however. Reconstruction of formative moments should be possible—**

Center took longer than usual before he spoke again. Abel had learned that this usually indicated he was performing some sort of *extremely* complex calculation.

Yes, I have it now. Observe:

Milovich as a boy Abel's age, standing next to a window in the upper stories of a residence in Lindron. He was sipping a steaming liquid (smell was present in the vision), and Abel detected the odor of cured yerba mate. Milovich—or the boy, as Abel had to think of him now—was wearing a linen wrap twisted about one shoulder and clasped at the hip by a belt of well-tanned carnadon leather.

Just what I figured, Abel thought. *Sipping mate and clothed in carnadon.*

Observe:

The boy suddenly broke into a smile and turned from the window. He spoke to a young girl who sat in a corner working at a loom.

Servant or concubine?

Try sister.

"Father's home," said the boy.

His sister nodded placidly, but remained at her work. The boy rattled down the stairs and emerged in a finely furnished receiving room below. He waited nervously as the door swung open.

"Father!"

A man in the door in the blue robes of the high priesthood's service. A dark scowl on his face. "What's this?" he said. "What the hell have you done?"

The boy glanced down at his father's hands. They held a creation of balsa and glue that had taken the boy a full day of labor to create.

His father lifted this creation in front of the boy's face.

"It's . . . it's a glider," said the boy. "One of the boys at school showed me some scroll drawings. I just looked at them and figured out how to make one, and I wanted you to—"

"You wanted me to what?"

"I worked really hard on it," the boy said, desperation slipping into his voice. "Because . . . I know you think I can't do anything right. I wanted to show you I can, I mean sometimes—"

"You left it on the stoop."

"So you'd see it," replied the boy. "When you got home, I mean."

"And the neighbors? Did you consider that they might see it?"

"I didn't think about that."

"Of course you didn't, you stupid fuck," said the father. "Of course you didn't."

Shaking with anger, he crushed the balsa flyer in front of the boy's eyes. "You could've gotten me fired.

You could've gotten you and your sister dragged away.
Do you see what you've done?"

"But I—"

The boy didn't have the opportunity to finish his
sentence. His father lashed out with a backhand and
sent him spinning across the room. And when he
fell, his father stepped up and kicked him hard in
the abdomen.

"Don't you ever, *ever* do anything like that again!
Do you hear?"

"Yes . . . yes, sir."

Another vicious kick. His father's sandal strap broke
with the effort, and, cursing, he kicked the boy with
his bare foot—but this time in the face, for good
measure.

"I was right about you," the boy's father said. "You'll
never make a priest. I have my doubts if you'll even
make a soldier."

He turned away, leaving his son gasping and bleeding on the dirt floor.

"Stupid little shit."

Abel shook his head. *He should've known the glider
was against the Law. He could've made it and hid
it somewhere.*

**In this instance, making a glider was only
a means to an end for Milovich. I believe you
understand that, Abel.**

*Would your own father have reacted in the
same way, lad?*

Maybe. Abel considered. *Okay, no. But he would've
been mad all right if I'd left something like that out
on the porch. And how's this supposed to help me*

*figure out the area of some pointy piece of farmland
without walking it, anyway?*

**Maybe you could show a little respect for the
young lieutenant and ask him to explain it to
you again. That would be one way, don't you
think, boy?**

*Yeah. Okay. You two know how to take the fun
out of hating a guy's guts.*

Raj laughed his not-so-pleasant laugh. **There'll be
plenty of time for that, lad. And plenty who
deserve it more than Milovich.**

Abel completed the assigned work as well as he
could, but he could not shake off the feeling that
Center was assessing his mathematical abilities the
entire time and finding them severely lacking.

As class recessed he forced himself to get over
his irritation and approach Milovich to ask for extra
help. The young lieutenant seemed shocked at first,
and then pleased. They arranged for a review session
before the next class, and Abel was finally set free
from the stinking classroom.

He rushed out into the garrison exercise yard to
see if the Scouts had returned. They hadn't. A few of
his classmates lingered about, two of them—Xander
and Klaus—sparring with musket rifles from the
broken-weapons bin.

Musket rifles were a special exception to nishterlaub
edicts. They contained metal, and lots of it, including bayonets, and shot lead minié balls. They could
not be manufactured, but they could be repaired,
and this only by the priest-smiths at special facilities within the temple compound in each district.
Zentrum allowed the production of a new batch of

rifles once per decade, as well, but only in the the Tabernacle of Lindron.

Gunpowder was a different matter altogether. Its manufacture was a fiat granted to only a very few places: Orash in Progar. Bruneberg in Cascade, Mims in the Delta, and near the Tabernacle at Lindron. Those who oversaw the magic creation of powder were called the Silent Brothers. They were selected from a young age and had their tongues removed at age eight as part of their induction ceremony. They were also castrated at that time.

I'd like to know how gunpowder is made, but not that badly, Abel thought.

The broken rifles that Xander and Klaus were using were fixed with blunted wooden bayonets for practice. Grunts of exertion and the clack of the practice weapons filled the courtyard. Klaus, who was a stickler for military detail, was wearing his full cadet's uniform even while sparring. His brown knickers and black tunic marked him as one of the Black and Tans, the army Regulars. His lower legs were wrapped in leather strips for protection.

Xander was shirtless. He was Black and Tan, too, but his cadet's tunic was thrown over a nearby dont hitching post, and his leg wraps were coming undone and trailing after him as he moved around the courtyard practice area.

Despite appearances, Xander was a military brat. His father was stationed several miles to the east at the outlying settlement of Lilleheim. Xander's father was part of the teaching subscription, and he, his mother, and his sister had remained in Hestinga for school. Klaus, on the other hand, was the son of a priest in the local administration. Yet Abel knew, because he'd heard him say it enough times, that Klaus hated the priesthood and longed for a life in the regiments almost as much as Abel longed to become a Scout.

Abel's own formality of dressing fell somewhere between the two cadets. He didn't bother to wrap his lower legs every day unless he knew duty called for him to be out of the military compound, but he never forgot his cap, which most cadets kept stowed under an epaulet and didn't wear in the compound.

Most telling of all, Abel kept his tunic on even when days were as hot and humid as this one. His father viewed the Scouts as an indulgence and expected Abel to go into black when the time came for a real commission. But Abel knew what he wanted, and it was the Scout service. His tunic was russet, a color that matched the iron-tinted rock of the Redlands perfectly, and he wore it proudly.

Abel ducked around the cadets' melee and made his way across the hard-packed exercise yard. On his left were the dont corrals where the cavalry, Scouts, and signal corps mounts were pooled when not in use. The larger of the donts had quickly established dominance and took up half the space, while the rest of the herd had carefully packed themselves against one railing, leaving plenty of space for the stags to saunter about at their ease. The stags held the entire line of their spinal plumage erect at all times, which Abel thought had to get tiring after a while. The beta donts only bothered flicking up their large neck feathers from time to time when they became agitated or aroused, and the few does present studiously ignored the males. Rutting season was many months away.

Abel liked donts and, like most military brats, had been around them all his life and figured he understood their ways far better than any civilian. Herd and territory were everything to a dont. When you could see the world in those terms, you could almost always get why donts did whatever they did. Mostly though, Abel knew that a Scout's life depended on picking out good dont-flesh from bad, and he aimed to become an expert, because he aimed to become a Scout.

Abel passed the corral and arrived at the large building of black River brick that served as District Command Headquarters. The entranceway was strung with a beadwork screen of Delta shells to keep out the flies, and it rattled as Abel passed through into the cool interior. An outer room held his father's staff and his adjutant, Lieutenant Terian Courtemanche. Courtemanche was everything the puffy-featured Milovich was not—hardfaced, impatient with nonsense, and muscled like a fighter. Abel admired him, but was also a little afraid of him.

"Cadet Dashian reporting," Abel said, pulling himself to attention.

Courtemanche looked up from a scroll he was proofreading for errors. He motioned Abel past him. "Go on in," he said. "I think the old man has a bin of filing for you to tackle." Abel groaned, which caused Courtemanche to indulge in the slightest smile. Then he returned to checking the scroll—and ignoring the presence of a lowly cadet.

Abel passed through another bead curtain and entered the office of District Commander Joab Dashian, his father.

Joab was not alone. There was a man in tan pants

and belted overshirt. On a nearby table, a pith helmet rested, the mark of a civil engineer. Abel knew him slightly, but couldn't remember his name.

Sigismund Reidel.

Okay. Thanks.

Reidel and Abel's father were examining a plan for what looked like, at a glance, an extension of the Hestinga irrigation system. Abel had seen (and filed) many such plans before. This one was drawn on a rolled-out scroll weighted down on either end by smooth River stones. Light from a skylight covered by a translucent section of herbidak hide poured down from directly above the deployed plan.

"So the water ram would go here," Joab said and pointed at a spot on the plan. "But that's a bit far downstream. Will there be enough water remaining to raise it to the second plateau on the Escarpment?"

"I'm *fairly* certain there will be," Reidel answered, but from quavering tone of his voice, even Abel could tell he was very much not so sure.

"Fairly?"

"It seems the best place."

Joab sighed. "Politically, you mean." He looked the engineer calmly in the eyes, then pointed to the plan. "This is Hornburg land, isn't it?"

"I believe so," the engineer replied, "but there are no ownership boundaries on the plan, as you can see. It's a district project, after all."

Joab shook his head. "Believe me, after five years serving here, the boundaries are etched in my mind. Move the ram upstream to the original location."

"But—"

Joab held up a hand to cut Reidel off. "I understand.

I will deal with the Hornburgs. This is no longer your problem."

After a moment of tension, the engineer nodded. He lifted the edge of his robe and used it to wipe a bit of sweat from his face. "We should double-check the flow, Commander."

Joab smiled, nodded toward the plan. "Let's go over the figures again, Sigis," he said. The two men began discussing ditch widths and flow rates, and Abel tuned them out. The pile of scrolls to be filed was on a broad table that his father used to spread out the really large maps, and Abel began to sort them by type. An upper border dipped in green pigment was command. Ochre was the color of logistics, and yellow represented communications with the local temple. Red was for messages sent and received by semaphore flag or courier. Secret documents were sealed with wax and scarab marking.

Abel sorted the scrolls, about fifty in all, into their various baskets according to content. The baskets would be delivered and filed by date in the large company library adjacent to headquarters. Abel was occasionally assigned that job when a soldier who was literate could not be located. It happened more often than Abel would have liked. He *hated* filing.

After more wrangling, Reidel received his instructions and left the office. Joab rolled up the irrigation plan.

"File that," he said to Abel, "under trouble."

"Yes, sir. Ochre, sir?"

His father nodded, and Abel began to carefully roll up the scroll.

"So, how was class?" Joab settled into the chair

behind his desk and poured himself a cup of wine from a clay pitcher.

"Okay."

"Just okay?"

"Calculating land areas."

"Useful."

"Yeah, I guess." Abel didn't look over at his father. *Was this the time to ask?* Maybe. Maybe not. "Why did you have the water ram moved, Father?"

"Oh, you were listening in, were you? Good." His father took a sip of the wine. "The Hornburgs put pressure on the builders to move the ram downstream."

"Where there's less water in the irrigation ditch," replied Abel.

"A ram needs lots of water moving fast to push a smaller amount of water uphill."

"I know that, Father."

Joab smiled. "Of course *you* do, Abel, but most don't have the faintest idea how the things work. Matlan Hornburg, for instance. I'm sure he doesn't know and doesn't care."

"Then why did he want the ram on his family lands?"

Joab looked at Abel, sighed, and took another, longer drink of wine. "Why? So the Hornburgs can control the water supply to the second Escarpment, that's why. In a couple of years, that plateau is going to be filled with barley fields. Imagine if you have the power to cut off the water to all those fields from one point. Those farmers are going to do anything you ask."

"Like what?"

"Like go through you as the middleman to broker

grain supply to the temple and military. Act happy and keep their mouths shut when you claim two-thirds of their grain and pay them back one-third of the profits."

"That's not fair."

"It happens all the time, son," Joab replied. "But not this time. Not in my district." He drained his wine, set down the cup.

"Whoever has the River has life." It was a basic Thursday school lesson.

"Exactly."

"What if Matlan Hornburg doesn't like it, Father?" The Hornburgs were one of the big three families in the district. Everybody knew it.

"I can guarantee you he *won't*. He'll be here within a week trying to browbeat me. I won't budge, so he'll take it up with Prelate Zilkovsky. Zilkovsky will sweet-talk him, but won't give in, either, because he knows he can count on me. We have a pretty good working relationship, the prelate and I."

"Count on you to do what?"

"Enforce the decision. Deal with the fallout," Joab said. "Hornburg won't let it stop there, you see. He'll do something like cut off a grain delivery or two to the garrison, try to starve us into line. I'll send a patrol to confiscate it from his warehouse. He'll set his hired men to defend it. It's going to be interesting."

"Or you could just give in, give him his ram, and avoid the hassle."

"That's what he's counting on. That's what men like that always count on."

"What if the prelate gives in?"

Joab glanced over at his son, chuckled. "Your mother used to ask me questions like that. She had a way of cutting to the heart of things, even when she knew the answer wouldn't be pretty." He looked back at his wine. "It's simple, really. I'll do what the chief priest orders."

"But Father, you just said—"

"I've been in districts where the district military commander ran things. Gets ugly, corrupt, and violent. People need to trust in the civil authorities, or it's every man for himself." Joab smiled. "Anyway, Zilkovsky's got a hide like a carnadon. He's not about to let a Hornburg tell him how to rule Treville District."

"You could also have Hornburg killed now. Save the trouble."

"And become another Hornburg myself? I don't think so, Abel." Joab nodded toward the chair on the other side of his desk. "Sit down, son." Abel sat down while Joab turned another cup over from the stack next to the pitcher and poured wine into both his own and the other. He pushed the cup toward Abel. "Drink. You look like you have something stuck in your throat. Something you want to tell me. Or ask me."

He knows, Abel thought. But how could he? It wasn't as if his father was inside his thoughts in the same way as Raj and Center.

Abel took a swallow from the glass, carefully set it down. "Father, I think I should be able to go out with the Scouts. Okay, maybe not into the *deep* Redlands," he hastily added. "But at least on Rim patrols."

"And what makes you think they'd have you?"

"Corporal Kruso said they could use an able body for water carrier."

"You've been talking to Kruso a lot?"

"Mostly listening," Abel said. "He likes to tell stories."

"And you believe his nonsense?"

Abel frowned, looked down. *I love to hear it. Because things happen in Kruso's stories. Dangerous things, sometimes. But never boring. Never always the same.* "Yeah, I guess."

"Good, because it's all true," said Joab. "Kruso's half Redlander and half lower Delta scum, but he's one of best Scouts I've ever seen." Joab considered his wine, still untouched. Abel knew the level would only slowly go down, Joab nursing his second cup throughout the afternoon with small sips. "I'll tell you what. You keep good marks in school, and I'll assign you Scout water duty starting next week."

Abel felt the weight, the need he'd felt for weeks, lighten. It was going to happen. He was going to get Scout duty! "Thank you, Father."

Joab held up a hand. "But only to the Upper Cliffs. No Rim patrol, not yet."

The weight returned. "But Father, I can—"

"You can lose even that privilege if you aren't careful." Joab finally sipped his wine. "When you turn twelve, you can go out on the Rim. But only on routine patrols, and absolutely only with Captain Sharplett's and the other Scouts' permission."

Twelve. He would be twelve in . . . three months. He could make it. He could wait. And in the meantime, he would at least get to the Scout bases in the upper cliffs. You could *see* the Redlands from there.

"And Abel, let me tell you something," Joab continued. "Scouts are a hard breed. Have to be. They won't care that you're the son of the DMC. They have a tendency to let nature and events take care of the fuckups among themselves. And sometimes they're willing to help nature along, if you understand what I mean."

"Would they take care of *you*, if you were a fuckup, Father?"

Joab smiled a hard smile. "Well, I know what *I* would do if I were a Scout and my commander was a fuckup," he said. He glanced over at the rolled-up irrigation plan, sighed. "It's my job to make sure it never comes to that." He looked back to Abel. "You make that your job, too, Abel. Because you *are* my son, after all."

5

"Blaskoye over thet hill fartleken," said Kruso. "Peers out of Cascade comenz they."

The Blaskoye are coming over the hill. It looks like they're coming from Cascade.

Abel did not have to ask for a translation from Center. He'd grown up around Scouts and heard enough of the patois to understand it well, and to speak it so that he could make himself understood. It was far easier than Redlandish, which he was working on now. Most Scouts spoke at least some of that language, and he was learning what he could from them.

Scoutish is a true patois of Landish and Redlandish, Center explained. But it is on its way to becoming a creole. Many similar patois have sprouted and died in the three thousand years since the Collapse. You must remember that Redlandish is far from a unified tongue, and that Landish itself did not start off as a single

**language, but as a mixture of tongues that were
as different from one another as Spanish and
French were from Catalan.**

What?

***I think he's referring to old Earth, lad. That
kind of speech was long gone when I was a boy.***

True to his word, Joab had permitted the twelve-year-
old Abel to go on Rim patrol with the Scouts. It had
been a year now that he'd been allowed to accompany
them. Abel had spent every moment he could with
them. Abel had been worried that the Scouts would
hold his age and his relative lack of rank against him,
but he'd quickly learned that the Scouts didn't give a
damn about any of that. If you could pull your load and
make yourself useful in some way, you were in.

He'd also found out more disquieting things. Things
he didn't know quite what to make of. Like the fact
that most of the Scouts were *very* religious, but religious in a manner that Abel was fairly certain wouldn't
be approved of by any Thursday school teacher he'd
ever had. They had a semi-secret cult that worshipped
Zentrum's mother, Irisobrian. She was a figure of
veneration to many of the Scouts, and a Scoutish
swearword to them all.

According to the cult mystery story, Irisobrian had
died in childbirth, but then, miraculously, had nursed
the young Zentrum on her breast for fifty days and
fifty nights while lying beside the River and herself
decaying to bones.

It was Irisobrian's mystical breast milk that was
said to have made Zentrum invisible, so there was a
lot of oath making among the Scouts on the bones
and mother's milk of Irisobrian.

Furthermore, there was an Irisobrian dispensation on several Scout items that would otherwise have been declared Stasis proscriptions or even nishterlaub. For instance, instead of employing flint and steel as directed by the Law, the Scouts sometimes needed to light a quick fire with the aid of a *lucifer*. These were made from powder taken from a broken percussion cap and mixed with glue from a desert cactus that grew near the Rim. The lucifers stank of sulfur, but were highly effective for getting fires going. Scouts often carried punk sticks on longer trips, but punk was notorious for burning down and leaving you with not a trace of fire to start with at the end of the day. At such times, the last thing you wanted to do was to spend a quarter-watch striking sparks and puffing into tinder to get fire going. And sometimes to do so was perilous.

Kruso had given Abel his own box of matches for emergencies, and Abel carried it in the inside pocket of his tunic, as did most Scouts. Sometimes when he heard the lucifers rattle there, he felt a faint qualm at the almost-nishterlaub feel of possessing them. But mostly he didn't think much about carrying them one way or the other.

"Well and secret guard tham. To the civvies showez them is a bad thing," Kruso had intoned. "Comenz of it a quiver of troubles."

Kruso was wrinkled and weather-beaten. He was almost as short as Abel, and built like a gnome. He seemed old, but Center had told Abel that Kruso was only thirty-five.

Every evening Kruso placed a wad of Delta tobacco into a clay pipe, pulled a smoking wand from the fire, and puffed away by the evening fire. He never used the pipe during the day, however.

"Hide sign and go to the Lady tomorrow, leave sign and she'll take you today," Kruso had once pronounced with his usual dry chuckle.

Abel figured Kruso had given him the matches not so much as an aid, but to draw Abel into the cult. Kruso was quite devout when it came to Irisobrianism. Abel had attended a couple of rites, but, on Center's advice, had declined to become a full initiate.

You would not like the communion meat they share, Center had said. **It must be at least three days old to have achieved sacred status.**

After he was permitted to accompany the Scouts, Abel concentrated on finding ways to become useful. At first, this had taken the form of being a simple water carrier. Men who moved fast and light through the Redlands needed to drink a great deal more than Abel had ever imagined. Even though the Scouts were famous for being able to go a very long time without taking a drink, he'd found that this ability was not something they cultivated or celebrated among themselves. On the contrary, it was a constant Scout obsession to have plenty of water along—because one setback, one extension of a mission, would soon mean you didn't have enough, and had no way of getting more. It was quite possible to die, and to die horribly, in the Redlands if you went too far out without the liquid to take you back.

Over the months, he'd demonstrated his usefulness and abilities to the Scouts in other ways. He'd graduated from water boy to dont keeper, and finally worked himself up to what was, for all intents and purposes, a squad regular. He'd proved his worth several times in that regard. Abel knew himself to be generally dexterous and naturally stealthy, and it didn't hurt to have Center, who could use his quantum-computing ability to predict what lay on the other side of a rock, hill, or clump of desert plants.

Abel understood in a general way how Center pulled off this feat. He also knew if he requested specifics of any one prediction, he was likely to get a lengthy lecture that left him feeling sorry he'd ever asked.

And as he had grown more a part of the group of Scouts and more adept, the deeper into the Redlands his "Rim patrols" had taken him. He wasn't technically disobeying his father at the moment. The Rim, and the Valley below it, was still in sight, several leagues to the west. Well, they would be if you climbed a very tall hill and strained your eyes to make them out. Furthermore, this was not technically a mission—where one expected and planned for battle—but a patrol, where danger had to come to you.

It looked like danger had done just that.

"How many do you make out, Kruso?" called out a nasal, brassy voice. It was a voice made to cut through a harsh desert wind, and it belonged to Sharplett, the captain of the Scout squad.

"Ten," Kruso replied. "Ten of many."

From the vantage of the overhang where he and Kruso shared lookout, Abel could clearly see that they were more than ten. Then he remembered that Kruso could not count any higher.

"I make out twenty...twenty-three on foot," called Abel. "At least...fifteen armed with muskets."

Correct, based on tactile input and spectral

analysis of your visual stimuli for metallic content, Center announced.

Isn't that the same thing as what I just did on my own?

As in mathematics, it is often useful to check one's work.

"Three wagons, three drivers, Captain," said Kruso, perhaps in an effort to redeem his counting skills. "Too, a passel of Blaskoye does. Wear they thom ugly robes what hiden thar milkers, curse tham to darkness."

"How many women?"

"Five . . . no, six," Kruso replied, looking down at his fingers, where he'd been enumerating his sightings, to be sure his tallies matched. The only problem with that method was that his left hand was missing a pinkie.

The Blaskoye clan were generally excellent at evasion both of Scouts and of one another and did not repeatedly follow the same travel routes through the Redlands. In addition, they almost never returned on a route by which they'd left. Redland pathways often frayed into dozens of possible paths, especially when there were no features in the landscape such as rocky outcrops or higher mountains to avoid. Nevertheless, this time a caravan had come back precisely down the path upon which, two weeks before, it had traveled north. A single lookout had spotted them at a great distance, and soon the flags wigwagged across Scout-held territory from signal hill to signal hill—all the way back to the High Cliffs, the Scout base on the upper Escarpment. Abel had been there and had been part of the general scramble for muskets, bows, and donts as Fleischer, the signalman among the Scouts, translated the incoming message from the next hill over. Sharplett had instantly ordered the troop to ride.

I really can't be blamed for going along with them. If I'd stayed, I would have been alone at the High Cliffs, and that could have been dangerous, too.

Except, of course, the squad cook and those two Scouts getting over their heat blisters stayed. They should be able to mount a drawn-out defense if they're attacked, said Raj. **And that base is at a hell of an excellent locus point, too. Three men could stand off a hundred for who knows how long, if the three were brave, fed and watered.**

And given the stores, the interior spring, and the possibility of slaughtering stable donts, eating them or drinking their blood if need be, that would not be a problem, Center added.

Whatever, Abel thought. *I'm here now. I can apologize to my father later.*

Kruso strode up and slapped Abel on the shoulder. He said in a low voice: "View you tom waginen. Dre, t'is peer. You so tally?"

Abel took a close look through the gap formed by two boulders next to one another. "I see two high wheeled carts . . . no, you're right, three," he replied. Abel knew that Kruso understood Landish well enough, and Abel still wasn't as comfortable speaking the Scout patois as he was understanding it when spoken to.

"Wagonen be goodsheavy, thay are hitched wid wubblebund donts ableatinz," Kruso said.

The carts must indeed be loaded down with goods, for the donts teamed to pull it were straining and groaning. Their cries could be heard even at this distance.

"They're coming from upper Treville, down the Pricklebush Route. Think they're getting back from a raid?"

"Never," said Kruso. "Our wigwag be quiet as fuckabone."

There had been no semaphore traffic from the north, no indication that a raid on the Land had taken place in upper Treville or the Cascade District. So it was possible these Redlanders had utterly wiped out a Land village, leaving not even a survivor to report, or that they'd acquired the goods by trade or raid on another Redlander clan.

There's another possibility lad, Raj growled in his low voice.

What?

It's a payoff from Cascade.

From people in the Land? But the Blaskoye are bloodthirsty killers. Why would someone do such a thing?

I'd say they're quite as bloodthirsty as their reputation makes them out to be, Raj said. *But where they decide to drink that blood is another matter, isn't it? Maybe the goods are an effort to persuade the Blaskoye to take their muskets and bows elsewhere. Somewhere like Treville District, where the protection geld doesn't flow like honey.*

As if to confirm Raj's suspicion, Kruso nodded and muttered, "Dortgeld," the Scoutish word for ill-gotten gains.

Because they were the two best pairs of eyes in the squad, Kruso and Abel had been put on lookout. The entire squad was on a rise in the desert. It was a rocky area, bare of Redlands vegetation. They'd left their dont mounts in the brush below. Near the highest point on the rise was an uptilted stone of darker basalt that Kruso and Abel had scrambled up to get the best view. It was from here they called down their report.

The trade route cut through the center of the rise north and south. The forbidding brush of the desert surrounded the rise in a thorny, dense thicket, whereas the bare hilltop with the path running along it provided a quarter league of prickle-free travel.

When they'd first arrived at the place, Captain Sharplett had remarked in Landish that it was "not the best place I've ever seen for an ambush, but it'll do." Sharplett, unlike Kruso, came from a better-off family from the lower Delta and, although he understood Scoutish well enough, spoke Landish with only a trace of downriver accent. But however educated and skillful he might be, he was still a Delta man. He was considered a lesser breed by the military Regulars, who were almost entirely upriver men—and, Abel had to admit, it was hard not to think of the squad commander as a bit of a marshland barbarian.

Abel and Kruso climbed down from the lookout. Sharplett had already sent the main body of six Scouts down the western side of the rise and into the brush. There the hardy, desert-bred donts were grazing on the thorny vegetation.

"Kruso, I want you and Himmel on the east in them bushes. Looks like there's a couple of piss trails cut into the thicket over there that go a ways back. Use them for your retreat."

The Redlanders, though they lived in a land with

no trees and only limited concealment, were fanatics about not being seen when defecating or urinating. They had been the ones who had cut those offshoot trails. Abel reflected that this was one more fact about the enemy that you picked up from being around Scouts that you would never find out in the Regulars.

"You two'll hit first, one shot, draw their fire and pull 'em east. When they hit the bushes, fire a second round—Himmel with your gun, and Kruso, use your bow. That'll be our signal. We'll ride out, hit 'em hard from the west."

Kruso nodded and Himmel answered with a smart "Yes, sir."

"And one more thing," Sharplett added. "After that second round, you get lost in that brush, hear me? They'll be madder than a carnadon mam with a raided nest, and they'll be after *you*. Himmel, you reload and cover. And Kruso..."

"Captain?"

"Make use of that bow of yours after we turn 'em around."

Kruso smiled a crooked smile. "Yes, sir. That I will."

Kruso's composite bow was a thing of beauty to Abel. He carried it over his back, left to right, with the bowstring securing it in front. The outside was carved from the thick, pliable river pufferwood that grew only in the Delta, and Kruso had told Abel he'd picked out the tree himself on an expedition. The wood was laminated by special glue made from the tuskhorn of a gigantic ocean-going creature called a grendel that Abel had never seen, but only heard about.

Kruso reached down to the quiver suspended from his belt and ran a finger along the fletching of one of his brace of arrows. Some were white fletched, some black. The feathers of the white arrows were notched once for tactile identification. The tips were clad with copper for longer range but ultimately smaller damage—unless you got lucky and placed one in an eye or a joint. Black feathered arrows were notched twice and tipped with sharpened and barbed iron for maximum destruction of flesh.

Then Sharplett was beside Abel giving instructions.

"We'll mount up, and I want you up at the edge of the west thicket, Dashian, to give the sign to charge. When yon sharpshooters fire round one, they'll fall back a bit, then turn and fire again. Then they'll hightail into the brush. On the second volley, you'll wigwag, and we'll swarm the donts."

"But sir, I—I want to fight, sir."

Sharplett gave him a wry smile. "I expect you'll get your chance, don't worry. As you said, there looks to be thirty of them and only nine of us." Sharplett spat on the sand, wiped his mouth. He chewed the desert herb *nesh* incessantly. Lots of Scouts did. This was another trait the Scouts shared with Redlanders. Abel had tried nesh, but had never liked the bitter taste.

Pay attention, lad. This is a fine disposition, and Sharplett's a good man. But one band of Blaskoye is neither here nor there. We need to know what's in the wagons. You need to find out and tell him, lad.

But he won't let me go, I'm just a kid to him.

You might be surprised. After these past few months, I have a feeling these men don't look at you quite like that anymore.

Still, I—

Make yourself heard, lad. Do it now, and be forceful.

Sharplett had already turned to walk away. It was now or never.

"Captain, I have an idea."

The Scout captain paused, turned back to Abel. "Yes, Dashian? What is it?"

"I was thinking Kruso and Himmel should go after the wagons, sir."

"How do you mean?"

"After they've drawn them to the east, they could circle around and hit the carts. They'll be mostly unguarded, with the Redlanders out front fighting you. That way, we could see what's in those wagons, sir, even if you and the others have to beat it back to cover."

Sharplett swirled a lump of nesh in his cheek and considered. "I *would* like to know what's so important it's got near thirty buck warriors assigned to bring it down from Cascade." He spat again. "And maybe they'd have time to ruin some of that cargo, too." He slapped Abel on the shoulder. "Good plan, Dashian. Now, you run over and tell Kruso and Himmel about it while I see to the others. And take care not to break the horizon or all this'll be for naught."

"Yes, sir. I won't, sir."

Abel breathed deeply as the Scout captain stalked away. He hadn't realized how tense he'd been until this moment.

He thought it was a good idea.

Raj chuckled coarsely. **Of course he did, lad. It was mine. Now go make sure the Scouts get those orders.**

Abel ran to do just that, and, after Kruso nodded his understanding, he crossed the rise one last time, careful to keep a line of boulders between himself and anyone coming up the rise from the north. He was about to take his position at the edge of the brush when Sharplett tapped him on the shoulder.

"Get me another look," the captain said, and ordered him up the basalt lookout post a final time. "But take care. They'll be able to see you even through their own dust at this distance."

"Yes, sir."

Abel scrambled back up the rock and raised just his head and eyes above its peak.

The caravan was still on its way. It was at the bottom of the rise, a hundred strides to the north. Not long now. He could make the caravaners out quite distinctly, and he confirmed his previous count of warriors in the vanguard.

So close. They seemed nearly naked, small. Certainly not the giant warriors of the stories, clothed in dont feathers and the skins of their enemies. The Scouts knew not to underestimate them, however, as did Abel.

The wagons were in the rear. They rolled upon very large, very thin wooden wheels. Each wagon was pulled by a team of four herbidaks arranged in the typical Redlander manner, three abreast behind with one in the lead dak position.

The daks were similar animals to the riding donts, but without a dont's spinal plumage. Daks also had much more rounded heads—heads with a single plated horn that terminated in a breathing hole at the very top. Both donts and daks were closely related, and each was capable of producing eye-stinging droplets

of acidic drool and phlegm from their breathing holes
when they huffed and puffed.

Abel, nevertheless, thought of daks as an inferior
species to the riding donts, not nearly so noble. But
they were useful animals, nonetheless, and they could
and would interbreed with riding donts to produce
remarkably strong mules on occasion.

Abel scrambled down and took a narrow, barely
perceptible trail into the brush to deliver the caravan's
position. He found the Scouts gathered in a clearing
not far inside the thicket.

"Hundred strides, no more."

Sharplett took in this news, then turned to the
other Scouts and gave the hand signal for them to
mount up.

The donts had been waiting patiently. But these were
experienced beasts, and the fact that their neck plumage
was erect indicated that they were aware something
was afoot. The Scout squad mounted adroitly and
trotted up to the edge of the clearing they occupied.

Dont tongues flickered out to taste the wind. One
dont pawed the ground with a fore claw. Abel knew
that, at speed, these donts would rise up on their
rear legs and run like a human. And when they did,
those forefeet became rending appendages that could
tear a man in half.

The men unlimbered muskets from saddle holsters
and unlatched the black-powder cartridge boxes hanging upon their belts. There were only so many rifles
to go around, and it wasn't only Kruso but several of
the Scouts who preferred a bow to a musket or pistol
in a close fight. Three of the Scouts had decided to
go in with bows rather than muskets. What the bows

lacked in firepower, they made up for in rate of fire. Reloading a musket rifle was a three-stage process, and stage one required tipping the muzzle up to receive powder—not an easy task to perform while riding a charging dont. Reloading a bow could be done in a single, one-handed motion.

Abel returned up the trail to the thicket's edge. Kruso and Himmel were in position across the way.

He waited nervously for the first shot.

Remember, those carts are what matters here.

Why? Why are they so important?

Because I am not sure what is inside them, even after extended extrapolation, Center said. **I have made a good guess, but I require specific confirmation for our future plans.**

So they're payoff goods or whatever, and somebody in Cascade's a traitor? What of it?

For one thing, the goods themselves may point to who is to blame, Raj replied.

On a larger scale, Center put in, **knowing which of the Redland clans is most likely to initiate the new round of Blood Winds will be essential if we are to mitigate its effect and use the results as leverage against Zentrum's strategy of prolonged technological stasis.**

I'm a Scout. I want to fight, not be a signalman and a slink!

Really? Let us assume you have your way. Observe:

What do they need a signalman for? They'll know when to strike from the muzzle blasts.

And it seems Abel is correct, for when he neglects to give the signal, but instead charges at point, his rifle at ready, his bayonet affixed, the squad soon comes thundering after. The donts race past him, and he's left sprinting in their dust, but he doesn't care.

But his appearance on the rise has been spotted. It is a matter of a few seconds. But those seconds are enough.

A shout goes up from the Redlander leader. Ambush! He calls his men to turn back from pursuing the sharpshooters, and soon they are in rough formation facing west. Not perfect. But good enough.

Scouts and donts charge.

Instead of being taken by surprise, the Blaskoye meet them with a ragged volley. The Scouts are close. It is difficult to miss, although most of the shots do. Four do not, and the Scouts are literally cut to half their numbers. And before the still-mounted Scouts can meet the line—the space of a breath, a gasp, but long enough, long enough—the reload is done and another volley of lead scythes into the Scouts.

This one leaves no survivors.

Except for the two sharpshooters, who are attempting to escape into a desert that their pursuers know too well.

And Abel, who rushes forward, nearly trips over a fallen, screaming dont, drops his rifle in trying to regain his balance, pulls up short to find—

Thirty Redlander faces staring at him.

The leader begins to laugh. He rides toward Abel.

Abel fumbles, lifts his rifle up.

The hammer is down, the charge spent.

The gun had fired when he dropped it.

He begins to reload. He tries to stay calm. He pulls out a cartridge, bites the papyrus end off. Pours powder into the muzzle. Like the Scouts have taught him. Carefully. Agonizingly carefully. Now take out the ramrod, tamp it down, tamp it—

He jerks the musket up to cock it, take aim.

He's left the old percussion cap in.

Flick it out. Get another.

Abel is fumbling in his cartridge box for a cap when the Redlander leader arrives and, with the butt of a musket, strikes Abel to the ground.

Abel awakens with a pounding headache. It is night. Two moons have risen, while Churchill, the largest of the Land's three moons, is on the horizon.

He moves to put a hand to rub his aching forehead.

He cannot move.

It is then he notices that he cannot even see his hand.

The moons are bright enough, he reasons. He ought to be able.

Beside him, he does see a human head, its blank eyes staring at him.

With a start, he realizes it is Himmel.

Just a head.

Then Himmel's eyes open. He takes one look at Abel, and the disembodied head begins to laugh. It is a dry laugh that soon turns to coughing, then choking, then gasping for air.

"Himmel," Abel says, "what happened? What are you?"

Again Himmel rolls his eyes toward Abel. "And what are you, boy, what are you?"

He spits in Abel's eyes. Why? How?

Abel attempts to wipe the saliva away, and realization dawns.

Sand around him. Sand above his chin, to his lower lip.

He's buried, with only his head above ground.

He struggles.

His arms will not move.

"They've bound and weighted us," Himmel coughs out. "No use."

And then on the other side of Abel, a plaintive wail. Abel just has the ability to turn his head to see. Facing in the opposite direction, looking toward a back that Abel can never turn toward again, it's Kruso.

"Alaha Zentrum, nish thet me over!" cries Kruso. *Oh great God, not over me!*

What was Kruso seeing? What was going to happen?

"Nish thet me over." Kruso's voice had become a whimper now.

There was no way to turn his head. There was only waiting.

On the horizon in front of Abel, Churchill rose fully above the horizon.

And then something came down from above and blocked the view. Blocked the moon. Blocked the stars.

From the smell of it, Abel knew immediately. One of the transport urns. An earthenware pot that had lately contained liquor, now emptied. Someone had, perhaps, been celebrating a victory and drained the wine.

True night descended forever.

Ninety-four percent probability, given known Redlander torture methodology, with a nine percent chance that arrows will be set through hands and feet in lieu of binding with weighted rocks, Center intoned. **More unfortunate—**

More unfortunate! How?

More unfortunate is the cascade of consequences. Your father will blame himself. There is a significant chance he will take his own life. In any case, Treville governance degrades inexorably. The Scouts will only desultorily be rebuilt, and a moment for Redlander containment will be lost. Zentrum will accommodate and incorporate the invasion, as he has before, and the chance to break Stasis will be lost for several more generations. In fact, there is a probability function trending toward one hundred percent that, should he decide against self-slaughter, your father will be killed in a manner similar to you as the victorious Redlander forces make an example of regional military leaders.

Okay, okay, I'll obey orders, damn it, Abel thought. *I guess that's what you're trying to tell me.*

Wrong lesson, lad. How about you merely avoid doing anything incredibly stupid that's liable to get you killed in horrible ways, Raj replied.

Okay.

He could hear the Blaskoye donts that were hitched to the wagons groan as they strained to pull the heavy-laden vehicles forward into the sandy defile.

What you need to do is get to those carts, said Raj.

So—you want me to obey orders or do what you say?

Yes.

A cloud of dust from the north, and the Redlander caravan came into sight and into range. Himmel fired the first shot from his long rifle. Abel saw no effect, and counted three heartbeats before the Blaskoye vanguard began to scramble. It seemed the ball had hit something, if not someone. Then Kruso fired. A man fell into the dust as if his legs had been cut out from under him.

Himmel must have quickly set aside his rifle and rearmed with his riding gun, a carbine, its shorter barrel intended for shooting from dontback and for close work. *Crack!*

With that, the Redlanders charged to the east. Evidently, whoever it was Kruso had dropped was important, and they shouted with rage.

Abel glanced over his shoulder. Sharplett had led the Scouts up from the bushes on the narrow piss trails, and they stood only a few strides deep in the underbrush behind Abel. They still did not have the view of the action that Abel did—which was the point, of course, for that also meant they could not be seen by the Redlanders.

Abel raised a hand.

The five Scouts behind him shifted in their saddles, and a dont pawed the ground.

Kruso and Himmel came into view through gaps in the Redlander grouping. They both charged toward the Redlanders. Himmel carried his bayonet-tipped rifle. He had probably not reloaded, but the Blaskoye had no way of knowing this. Kruso was armed with his bow and let fly arrow after arrow. Abel had never imagined the gnomish man could be so graceful. He simultaneously sprinted forward, fired, reached for an arrow, notched it, and fired again.

Several of the Redlanders returned fire with muskets as they ran, but no bullet hit either Himmel or Kruso.

Then, when the Blaskoye were within only a few

paces, Himmel stopped short, took aim, and calmly dropped the Redlander's point man.

I guess he did reload, Abel thought. It had been with amazing speed.

At the same moment, Kruso put an arrow into a man's chest.

Abel dropped his hand.

Across the rise, the two Scout sharpshooters turned on their heels and ran as fast as they could back in the direction from which they'd come.

As if on cue, the enraged Redlanders followed.

The remainder of the Scout squad flowed over the hill crest, thundering past Abel, and charged into the rear of the Redlander soldiers full tilt with bayonets fixed.

It was not a fair fight, which was a good thing, for the Scouts were outnumbered threefold.

At a shout from Sharplett, the dontback Scouts raised their weapons and, at the same time, urged their donts into a full bipedal sprint. Each Scout aimed over his dont's shoulder. The Scout carbines crackled to life, spewing minié slugs or buck and ball shot—in either case, death and destruction.

But there were ten more Blaskoye, plus the drovers and passengers of the wagon retinue. It was going to be a long, hard fight.

As if to underline this fact, one of the Scout's necks exploded with blood. He clutched at it as he fell from his mount and into the dust. At least one of the Redlanders had found the presence of mind to turn and shoot.

The wounded man looked to be Dornberger, a Scout who was not that much older than Abel.

Don't think of rushing out there to drag him off, lad. You'll just get yourself killed.

Besides, he is already dead, Center intoned.

Time to get into the brush and mount up.

Abel went back into the thicket to find his dont, a creature he'd named Corie. His personal riding dont, Mot, was safely in a stable back at home. Mot was far too old and too much of a Valley-bred creature to be used for Scout work. Corie was patiently waiting, chewing on a needleplant.

Check your carbine, lad, and have caps and cartridge limbered, said Raj. *The blunderbuss dragon from your father, as well. Put it in your belt.*

Joab had insisted he carry a flintlock sidearm in addition to his military-issue rifle when he went on patrol and had given Abel his own old dragon, which had been in the family for generations. The dragon had seemed an encumbrance at times. It was singular among the Scouts, and it caused him to stand out as different among them—something he strove not to do—but now Abel was glad of having it. He checked that the dragon was at half-cock and the flashpan frizzle had not come loose and spilled his powder. It had not. Then he stowed the pistol in his belt and took up his rifle, a shorter, carbine model of more modern vintage, and ran a finger down and felt the edge of the percussive cap where it covered the fire nipple leading to the barrel. *Should I cock my rifle now?* he asked.

What, and tear the head off poor Corie with a misfire? answer Raj with a chuckle. *Wait till you reach the wagons, then give it the flick.*

Abel spurred his dont and raced up and out of the brush. Then he turned the beast to the south to circle around the melee in front of him and get to the wagons if he could. He pushed his dont to her ultimate speed, and with only Abel's light weight to support, she was soon up on her back feet and racing.

The wagons loomed ahead. Abel fumbled for a moment, then managed to cock his rifle.

He felt his finger snaking toward the trigger and consciously pulled it away. He'd been lectured time and again on the need to keep one's finger out of the trigger guard until it was time to fire, but in the heat of the moment, he found it extraordinarily hard to do so.

There were three carts with half a dozen occupants or attendants nearby. Two wore the billowy blue and white pants and shirts of Redlander men. The others had the flowing white robes worn by the Blaskoye women. He'd heard tell that Blaskoye women were not only allowed to serve as muleskinners and drovers, but were actually the clan's traders and merchants as well. Abel found this hard to believe, but Kruso and Sharplett had assured him it was so. In the Land, a female merchant would have been inconceivable.

Just another way the Redlanders behave as complete heathens, Abel thought.

Don't be so sure, and don't underestimate the does, lad. Might be your last thought.

I think I can take a woman, at least.

You must concentrate on the animals first, boy, said Raj sternly. *At least one on each cart must be put out of commission to bring the wagons to a halt.*

The motley-clad driver of the first of the carts was armed, and he pointed a gun at Abel and fired. A flintlock. Even running at full tilt, Abel saw the flashpan ignite and the smoke rising. A whistling sound nearby.

Was that a bullet?

Aye, lad. Be glad about the ones you hear. It's the ones you don't hear that are the problem.

He grew closer, closer—the driver with the rifle was attempting to reload by pouring powder out of a horn down the muzzle. Abel smiled and aimed the carbine at him.

The move must have registered, for the driver suddenly gave up what he was doing and leapt behind the cart in blind panic.

Abel adjusted his aim for one of the daks in the middle of the team.

He pulled the trigger. Nothing happened.

Damn it, bad cap or—

Look down, lad.

Abel did as instructed. His Scout tunic had wafted up and gotten between the hammer and the cap. He quickly cocked again, pulled the fabric free, took aim.

Bang! The rifle's report was startlingly loud, even though he was rushing forward full tilt on the dak. And this time, the ball had its effect. The dak he'd been aiming at let out a roar. It rose into the air, pawing at the sky in agony and spurting its milky blood over the other herbidaks, terrifying them.

He grew so fascinated, watching, that he nearly forgot to turn his mount to avoid a head-on collision. As it was, he reined just in time and headed for the wagon that was next in line.

He drew his pistol and didn't waste time trying for a middle animal, but shot the lead dak of the pack team straight in the head at point-blank range.

Dak blood and brains spattered across his chest, and a bone fragment popped him smartly in the cheek. Abel rode on.

To the next wagon and—

He was riding into the muzzle of a musket pointed directly at him.

A swirl of flowing white robes, a headscarf. It was a woman, a young woman with crystal blue eyes. A fierce, beautiful face. Her mouth curled to a snarl.

But the musket had his attention now. There was no way he could turn his dont in time. The Redlander woman would shoot him in the chest. He reared back to throw his pistol at her, sure the move wouldn't work, but unable to think of anything else to do—

An arrow took the woman through the neck.

Startled, she dropped the gun, reached for the shaft protruding from either side, and let out a piercing scream. It did not sound like pain. It sounded like anger to Abel.

He charged past and swung his mount around as quickly as he could. More arrows were flying into the remaining occupants of the cart. Kruso emerged from the western thicket and was firing his bow in a steady rhythm. His rate of fire was like nothing Abel had ever seen before.

Abel pulled his mount to a stop and leapt to the desert floor. Corie stopped expertly without shying.

"Good girl," he muttered, then reached for his rifle in its saddle scabbard. The rifle was nowhere to be found. He'd dropped it after firing and hadn't realized it.

In his belt was the blunderbuss dragon, however. Would it take a minié ball? He supposed he'd find out. He reached into the cartridge box at his waist and dug out a cartridge, which consisted of a ball and powder charge wrapped in a thin layer of knife-peeled papyrus. He bit off the end to expose the powder.

Okay, okay, thumb up the frizzle, shake gunpowder into the pan. Not too much, not too much. Close it up. Half cock the hammer.

He flipped the pistol over. It had a bell-shaped muzzle. This was not to spread the charge upon firing. Instead, it had been given this shape in order to funnel the powder down the barrel more effectively. He poured the powder in and followed it with paper and ball. The lead seemed to be a close enough caliber, and maybe the paper would serve as a makeshift patch to form enough of a seal.

Or maybe not, and he'd have an exploding pipe bomb in his hand.

No time to worry about it.

Abel yanked out the small ramrod from the pistol's underside and stuffed it down the barrel once to set and once again to pack.

The wagon was blocked by the others ahead, and the packtrain had stopped moving, but the lead animal was attempting to find a way to get around the jam. Several arrows quilled its hide, but they didn't seem to faze it. Daks were smart, and their toughness must never be underestimated.

He cocked the hammer on the pistol all the way back and strode quickly past the other animals. When he got to the lead, he took careful aim and pulled the trigger. A flash in the pan, and a crack as the pistol went off.

The dak screamed and fell. The pistol had worked.

He walked back toward the wagon.

There on the ground before him lay the Redlander girl. The arrow was still through her throat. Blood covered her robes, and she was gasping for breath. She had located her dropped musket and held it up, its muzzle pointed toward the sky.

Their eyes met.

Such blue eyes she had.

He reached for the musket, and, instead of yanking it away or pointing it at Abel, the woman handed it to him.

She tried to say something, but only a moist gurgle escaped her throat. It didn't matter. Abel looked into her pleading eyes and understood what she wanted.

He pointed the musket at her head, turned his face way, and fired.

The world blurred. Abel blinked. He had not thought he would cry.

"Thas weakness wastes time," Kruso said as he stepped up beside Abel and took the musket from his hands. "Wagons to burn have weh."

"Yes," said Abel, rubbing a forearm across his face to clear his tears. "You're right."

They climbed into the bed of the last wagon, and Kruso used his bayonet knife to cut a line that held down a tarp. By this time, Himmel had arrived, and the three of them pulled back the tarp together.

Barrels. Hooped barrels with Landish markings. There was no mistaking what they were. Abel and the other Scouts had seen enough of them before from the Land's principal powder plant in Cascade.

Gunpowder. Kegs and kegs of it.

Excellent, said Center. **The variable necessary for further calculation.**

"Neh good," said Kruso, shaking his head. "At all, neh good."

"Let's check the others," Abel said.

He and Kruso ran to the other wagon and found that it too was laden with similar cargo. The lead cart had no barrels, however. In its bed were earthen urns that, when struck open with a rifle butt, were revealed to be full of barley grain. There was also a row of jugs the size of butter churns. Himmel was about to break one open when Abel motioned for him to hold up.

"Lamp oil and wine," he said. "Let's soak the tarps in the oil."

A gunshot nearby. Then another.

"I thought you took all the wagon riders out with arrows," Abel said.

"Might somebody tham missed."

They skirted around the middle wagon and found Himmel near a Redlander male. The Blaskoye was gut-shot and attempting to crawl away. He trailed a steadily increasing length of gut behind him that was winding out from his body. Himmel stood on the trailing end of the man's intestine, holding it in place. As he watched the other crawl, a horrible smile played over Himmel's face.

"Bastard took a shot at me," he muttered.

Kruso did not waste time speaking to Himmel, but jogged up to the Redlander. He quickly took the man's head in his gnomelike hands, then, with a jerk, twisted and broke the Redlander's neck. The man collapsed, kicked twice, and was dead.

Kruso strode back to Himmel, looked him straight in the eyes for a moment. The smile left Himmel's face. "Nonsense is such," Kruso said with a shake of his head, and turned away.

"Can we burn the wagons now?" Abel said.

They quickly went and did just that, dividing the wagons among them, with Abel taking the middle.

Himmel reloaded and fired a gun point-blank into the rear tarp, expecting the muzzle flash to catch fire to the lamp vapors that filled the air.

Nothing.

They tried again with Abel's dragon. No fire.

Abel reached into his tunic pocket and retrieved his wooden box of matches. He thumbed it open and pulled out a lucifer.

Himmel backed away. He, like Abel, was not an initiate of Irisobrian. Unlike Abel, he was a Stasis literalist. "Nishterlaub," Himmel said. "Neh good."

Kruso shook his head. "Not nishterlaub. This lucifers myself made of cap and splinter. Nishterlaub it neh is."

"Still," said Himmel, "against edict. I don't like it."

We haven't got time for argument. Do what you must, lad.

Abel struck the match upon the glued grain on the box lid. It sprang to life instantly, its acrid sulfurous fumes filling the air all about them. Kruso made very trustworthy matches.

"It ta thet corner set," Kruso said, and Abel followed instructions. Within seconds, the tarp was ablaze.

They did the same for the other two wagons, with Himmel muttering of doom the whole time. When they were done, Kruso bent down, grabbed something, then stood up and handed what was in his hand to Abel.

He'd found Abel's dropped rifle.

"Best quickly we go," Kruso said.

Abel ran back for his dont, careful not to trip in the mess that was the Redlander girl's splayed body, her blasted face now turned to rapidly drying slop upon the thirsty desert sand.

Abel mounted up, and the three rode away as quickly as they could. After they'd gone what Kruso estimated was a safe distance, the Scout signaled them to turn around for a final look.

The wagons were ablaze. They watched the flames crackle for a moment.

And then, in an enormous explosion, the rear wagon blew itself to splinters. The remaining daks collapsed in a twisted mass of dakflesh.

Some were killed outright. Some blew notes of agony through their horns. All were yoked together and could not flee into the Redlands to die.

They would die right here.

I wish I'd set them loose. I should have, maybe.

But the thought hadn't occurred to him when he'd been back at the wagons. There hadn't been time. Besides, he told himself, domesticated daks wouldn't last long in the Redland wilds. Probably.

For a moment, he remembered the woman's pleading face just before the ball struck her.

She'd have done the same to you, lad.

Then the other two wagons exploded one after the other in great black plumes of smoke, and, looking upon the scene in excitement and amazement, Abel felt every bit of regret fade away.

He'd done that. Him. Abel Dashian.

No regrets.

All he was left with was the firm resolution that next time he would hold on to his rifle no matter what.

6

"I won't ask what you were thinking, because I believe I know the answer to that," said Joab. "What I would like to know is what I'm going to tell the prelate to somehow keep you in the military." Joab stopped walking, and Abel came to an abrupt halt beside him. His father eyed him. "Because with that kind of judgment, I frankly don't know if you *are* officer material, son."

Abel met his father's gaze, but said nothing. He had the feeling that any reply he made would be the wrong one at this point.

"You do understand the seriousness of the situation?" Joab's voice was low and intense—which Abel feared far more than his father's shouts or curses.

"Yes, Father."

They continued walking, Abel a half step behind his father.

One thing I hadn't counted on, Raj continued,

almost, it seemed, speaking to himself, **when I had Center copy my mind and blast us both to the stars: having to go through puberty again and again and again.**

After a few paces Joab began talking again, this time to himself. "The problem is that you not only defied me by going out there, you went against Stasis by using the lucifer that way. It's not what you did, it's how it *looks*."

"I get it, Father."

They made their way through the streets of Hestinga. Hestinga was only half the size of the capital, Lindron, but it had many of the same amenities and was considered a good posting by both priest and soldier. The centers of the thoroughfares were paved with Redland stone, and the gutters were swept at least once a week to clear out the collections of sewage, garbage, and dont and dak manure that piled up there in the interim.

Abel had been to villages that *never* got swept, where people lived on layer upon layer of their own garbage. Hestinga smelled like a bloomherb flower in comparison.

Furthermore, once a year during floodtime, the lake filled to the point a bucket line was possible and the streets were actually washed down. This annual event didn't even happen in Lindron.

The Hestinga buildings were not as grand as Lindron's, however. Most were simple mud-brick structures with cut-hole windows that were closed with woven rush mats during the heat of the day. Glass was *far* less common here.

The Hestinga market square was a group of temporary stalls. In Lindron, most of the merchants had permanent shops.

And in the market square were women. Not just at

the market, either. Abel spent a great deal of his time inside walls behind which females were not allowed. Here, they were simply...everywhere. He knew enough to hold his status and not to allow his head to jerk about like a springleg every time someone of the opposite sex walked past. He liked it better when he and his father approached from behind. That way, he could spend lots of time staring at swaying hips and shoulders without being noticed, and then steal a glance at the face in profile as he and his father, who were walking at an soldier's pace, passed its possessor.

After several blocks of temptation, Abel began to forget who he was with and where he was going. He began to think instead of the problem of how he was going to get laid for the first time. Xander had told him about a whorehouse on the outskirts of town, but Abel somehow didn't want this to be his first experience.

Yet if this feeling kept building inside him, and he never got a chance to meet any girls—well, then, the whorehouse might have to do.

Any advice on that, o inner voices? What, nothing to say?

When the time comes, I am capable of providing the proper physical instructions.

One world at a time, lad. But here's one that's all right. Looks like she bathes in butter and honey does that one.

A raven-haired young girl who looked only a little older—and a little taller—than Abel wafted by in a cloud of flowing vermilion robe, silver belt and bracelets, and clean-smelling soaps and unguents. She was gone as quickly as she arrived, and Abel fought mightily the urge to stop in his tracks and gaze longingly after her.

It was only when they arrived at the temple gates that Abel was jerked from his female-induced reverie.

The district temple compound differed from the surrounding edifices in that it was mainly built of stone, and Redland stone, at that. It was at least five hundred strides wide, and housed all manufacturing facilities that were allowed under the Law. This was where nishterlaub was reworked into permitted materials. A plastic casing for an ancient nishterlaub machine might be fitted with a wicker handle and made into a bucket, for instance. A plough might be made from a piece of the incredibly light, incredibly durable pre-Collapse ceramic.

Spacecraft tile beaten to ploughshares, Center had once said of it.

And it was here and only here, in the temple compound, that bullets could be forged and cartridges packed. There was an entire team of priests who did nothing else. Abel had once spoken with one of the priest-smiths, as they were called, and had learned of the intricate prescriptions and prohibitions the priest-smiths must take account of. One slipup, and an entire run of bullets or cartridges would have to be scrapped and recast in the proper manner.

In the center of the compound, a stepped pyramid rose a thousand spans into the sky. It was visible throughout Hestinga, and from quite a few leagues outside the village, as well.

Abel and his father struggled up the oversized steps of the temple pyramid as best they could. There was an easier path with human-sized steps on the backside of the structure, but this method of climbing was reserved for priests.

At least the steps keep Father occupied, Abel thought. *I hate even watching his face. His being disappointed is ten times worse than his yelling at me.*

A wise parent, Raj said, followed by his low, not-so-nice chuckle.

Finally, they reached the apex plaza and entered the small stone building that occupied the center of the plateau.

District Prelate Zilkovsky's office was an inner chamber within an inner chamber. It was the chilliest room Abel had ever been in. A temple priest outside the entrance was on fan duty. He continually pushed and pulled a cane rod through a slot in the wall. The cane connected to a rush-woven fan inside set on a dont-leather hinge. The rod kept the fan continually moving air across the chamber.

Zilkovsky was fat. There was no way around that fact. The folds of his priestly robes could not hide the belly that lurked behind them. He was also nearly bald, with a wispy layer of hair that he combed to the side as if to hide the shiny skull beneath. It did not.

Yet for all his girth, the prelate moved gracefully. His eyes, though small and closely set, sparkled with animation.

Don't underestimate this one, Raj said. **I've known his like before. He'll never be your comrade, but he's best to keep as an ally, not have as an enemy.**

Zilkovsky had no desk, but instead worked in a sitting area with several chairs gathered round. When Joab and Abel entered, he motioned Joab to sit. Abel, not having received such permission, remained standing.

"Commander, correct me if I'm wrong, but is this

not the young man who once managed to drop a rock on his own head in the nishterlaub house?"

"You've got the right one, Mr. Prelate."

"And now he's managed to destroy a wagon transporting munitions to the Redlander scum, but, at the same time, has used proscribed methods to accomplish this?"

"That's about the size of it, sir."

"And only one casualty to the Scouts?"

"That's correct."

"Dead?"

"Yes."

Zilkovsky settled back in his chair. He took up a clay mug of beer, nodded toward a pitcher and cup on a nearby side table. Joab shook his head, indicating he didn't want any. Zilkovsky had a sip, smiled a mild smile of peaceful pleasure.

Abel had a feeling the beer had a much better taste than the vinegary wine in his father's office.

"Allow me to scan with Zentrum," the priest said. He closed his eyes, breathed out.

And for a long moment, his body jerked and shuddered. Then it relaxed.

"Yes," he said in a low voice. "Yes." Zilkovsky opened his eyes. "Alaha Zentrum."

"Alaha Zentrum," Abel and Joab murmured in the automatic response inculcated by years of Thursday school lessons.

"Scan completed," Zilkovsky continued. The priest finally turned his head and looked at Abel. It wasn't merely a look, but a stare, as if Zilkovsky was peering deep within, seeing things Abel would prefer hidden. Could he detect the presence of Raj and Center?

No, Center replied. **No known methods of quantum broadcast discovery are in use. Zentrum is unaware of our presence on Duisberg. We, however, are faced with another issue. The encryption mechanism within the implant Zilkovsky is employing to communicate with Zentrum in Lindron is secure. Breaking the code will take some effort on my part but should be possible in time.**

"It seems that your dual actions cancel one another out. So you are not to be punished for the breach in edict, but you are likewise not to receive a commendation for your admittedly brave behavior in helping to torch the wagons. What do you have to say to that, young man?"

"Alaha Zentrum," Abel said, "I accept this judgment."

Zilkovsky nodded. "Good, good." He motioned for Abel to take a seat next to his father. Abel gratefully sank into the chair and, when the prelate offered beer, took a half cup—even though this action caused his father to raise an eyebrow. When he took a sip, he found he had not been mistaken—it *was* great. He could almost chew on the sweet barley that had gone into the brew.

Zilkovsky turned back to Joab. "So we have a problem, my friend. These wagons with the gunpowder, there was no semaphore traffic concerning a raid up north?"

"None whatsoever," replied Joab.

"I, too, have received no message flitters."

Interesting. He speaks of message-carrying animals. His implant must not allow him to communicate with his fellow prelates, but only

with the central computer. No doubt he really does believe he is hearing the voice of God. An interesting choice on Zentrum's part.

Do I have one of these . . . implants, then? Is that how you do it?

No, Abel. I am an advanced model. I am able to narrowcast to you using quantum uncertainties within the small bits called molecules that make up your brain. Zentrum will not have the means to detect this.

Good. You two get me in enough trouble already.

"Based on their direction of movement," said Joab, "the Redlanders were coming from the northern borders of Treville. But, as we both know—"

"—Treville manufactures no gunpowder," put in Zilkovsky.

"Exactly. So the point of origin must have been Cascade. That is also the Captain of Scout's evaluation."

"Sharplett," said Zilkovsky. "Good man. Pity he's of Delta stock."

Joab nodded. Abel knew there was no use arguing against class distinctions in the Land. They were, if anything, more deeply carved in stone than the Stasis itself.

"The problem then becomes to figure out if this is a regular flow. Are the Redlanders planning something?" Joab said. "My Scouts report that the Blaskoye have been on a tear of consolidation in the past couple of years. They've incorporated at least five neighboring tribes by conquest or negotiation."

"What are they up to, do you think?"

"I'm not sure, Mr. Prelate," Joab answered, "but it can't be good. I was hoping you might tell me."

Zilkovsky sighed, sat back in his chair, took another swig of beer. "Unfortunately, this is a matter on which I've received no guidance from Zentrum. I do, however, have a few watchers in Cascade who send me the occasional report."

Joab smiled a toothy smile. "I'd hoped you did, Mr. Prelate."

"Cascade has problems. Rot at the top, I'm sorry to say. As you and I have long discussed, it's a happy district when District Military Commander and District Prelate get along and truly share power with one another. You and I are blessed by Zentrum to be in such a relationship."

"I agree," Joab said.

"Many times in . . . more *unhappy* places . . . it is the military commander who takes control, since he possesses the force."

"Or believes he does," said Joab. "More than one DMC has found out the hard way that what he believes he has is a relative matter in actuality. Zentrum often finds a way to swat such a man down."

"Yes," said Zilkovsky, "quite. But the problem in Cascade is worse. Both the priesthood and the military have allowed themselves to become pawns of the gentry."

"Surely this can be remedied," replied Joab. "I'd think a lesson or two would go a long way to doing just that. Burn a farmhouse, save the Land."

"It might," Zilkovsky said. "But the monopoly on gunpowder production at the Bruneberg plant would continue, for that is the Edict of Zentrum. So the enormous inflow of wealth would likely tempt another group to misbehave. This is how it has been in . . . well, *forever* . . . in Cascade. It is a corrupt place."

Joab looked perplexed. "So what's the solution, Hiram?" Abel had never heard his father use the prelate's first name in another's presence. He hadn't even known Zilkovsky *had* a first name.

Zilkovsky now turned to Abel and pointed to his father. "Behold the military mind," he said mildly. "Your father wishes to order things that are fundamentally chaotic."

"The Blaskoye are building up to something," Joab replied. "We can't resign ourselves to being unprepared for attack just because Cascade's a dirty mess."

"No, we cannot," replied the priest. "I also do not believe Zentrum will allow it."

That's where he's wrong, said Raj. *This is exactly the sort of thing Zentrum will allow, so long as it ultimately keeps the Stasis in place. Zilkovsky has come to enjoy his job so much, he's forgotten Zentrum's ultimate purpose.*

Zentrum takes the long view, Center put in, in what, for Abel, had become a mantra akin to a Thursday school lesson. But it was a lesson he knew he ought to heed.

"At the moment, however, I am open to suggestions, Commander," the prelate concluded.

Joab nodded grimly. "I'll garrison the Escarpment strongholds with Regulars. Set the Scouts free to roam. We'll need more supplies, and I have to secure a Valley water source. That means somebody's water rights on the second plateau will have to be requisitioned. And we may as well requisition their fields as a way station, because it'll be no good for grain."

"I believe I can find funds in the temple coffers to cover such a requisition."

"It's still going to scare the hell out of the landowners."

"As well it should."

"I'm also going to need more Scouts. That means recruiting Delta elements. Unsavory sorts. I'll keep them out of Hestinga proper as much as possible."

"Yes, do." Zilkovsky had a definite opinion about the social worth of Scouts, it seemed, no matter how much he might value their abilities. He nodded toward Abel. "And I would think twice about letting this young man associate with them overmuch."

"Pardon me, Mr. Prelate, but I know my place," Abel said. "And so do *they* when they're around me. We are not of the same blood, but I can handle it."

Zilkovsky smiled thinly. "That may well be. But remember: all Scouts are borderline heretics. Heretics are hated of Zentrum, the same as infidel Redlanders. They're outside the Law. And when you're outside the Law, you're outside the Stasis. And when you're outside the Stasis...well, you are outside the Land itself."

Abel started to reply, but thought better of it. He met the priest's steady gaze as best he could.

"Here's the real lesson I want you to learn from your recent adventures, Abel Dashian, son of Joab. You come from a fine line of soldiers on your father's side. I don't have to tell you the high standing of your departed mother's family in Lindron. There is a clear path ahead of you to high command. Maybe even a place among the Temple Guardians one day."

Zilkovsky leaned closer to Abel. A stray breeze from the fan caught the thin strings of hair on his scalp and lifted them up for a moment like a riding dont's feathery crest. "So, my young friend, don't fuck it up with heresy."

PART TWO

The Powder

1

Bruneberg had not begun as a settlement, much less a town. It started as a scattering of unrelated clumps of families, a congregation of tribal settlements that had congealed in the area of the first cataract of the River, the cataract nearest the broad plain into which the River spilled itself after a thousand-league journey down its self-carved valley from the glacial drip of the Schnee Mountains. The Schnee were invisible from Bruneberg. They were over the horizon of northeast or, as all the Land referred to that cardinal direction: up-River.

The Collapse here was quite literal, Center explained. **The River cuts through the alluvial remnants of an ancient mountain chain in this area, and as a result, the Valley constricts to a few leagues across. Duisberg's original settlers found it a good place to build a dam to compound water for irrigation and recreational purposes.**

It burst, and the rocks of the cataracts are the remains of its duracrete masonry.

But a dam doesn't need nishterlaub technology to stay in place, Abel thought. *We have dams all over the place today.*

A good example of why the Galactic Collapse was so complete and all-obliterating, Center replied. **If the Duisberg colonists had built their dam of rebar and concrete, it would still be here to this day. Instead, they relied on exotic molecular configurations held in place by molecule-by-molecule algorithmic maintenance.**

So they built a dam that could be infected by the Plague, did they? Raj's rough and bitter laugh echoed in Abel's mind. *The wonder isn't that the Empire of Man fell to ruin, but that it lasted as long as it did. It's as if we built a Blood Wind into the very ground beneath our feet.*

Abel reined his traveling dont, a huge stag named Spet, through the southern gate of the town. At seventeen, he was grown to what he imagined would be his full height now (and he overtopped his father by half a head) and had begun to fill out with the wiry, desert-bred muscles created by many hundreds of Scout patrols and expeditions. Even two years before, he would not have chosen, or been allowed, to ride such a beast as Spet, a herd alpha if ever there were one. The dont would have simply been too big for him and impossible to control.

Now Abel sat the saddle easily and the dont responded smoothly to the rein. Spet, he'd discovered on the fourteen-day journey up-River, was a sensible creature, if not the most intelligent dont Abel had ever encountered. It had taken a day and a night for dont and rider to become used to one another, but a special evening meal of blood-soak, barley marinated in the purple-brown blood of a local herbidak, had cemented the bond between them.

An interesting hemoglobin-hemocyanin mix in the Duisberg fauna, Center intoned. **Probably due to selective pressure brought about by geologically recent planetary volcanism. Hemocyanin is not susceptible to carbon monoxide poisoning as is hemoglobin.**

As usual, Abel had let Center rattle on, knowing that any comment of his might lead to another lengthy disquisition.

Abel was more concerned with the dont. He had rightly assumed that Spet, who had conquered all dontflesh he'd ever surveyed, was done with the challenge and dominance rituals most dont stags spent half their lives and all of their free time engaging in—or was simply beyond such pettiness—and his thoughts were those of a fledge-dont again, concerned with a good meal, comfortable bedding, and taking on his allotted burden for the expected period of toil, no less, and most definitely no more.

Upon first smelling the proffered blood-soak, the feathers of Spet's flank crest had flared in happy surprise, and the dont had snorted with delight when Abel refilled his feed basket with a second helping.

Bruneberg was sprawled down both sides of the River up and down the First Cataract. Its original reason for being had been as a portage stop and watering hole for transports coming down or being rowed, sailed, or pulled back up-River by dak towline.

It was a fortunate fact—the Hand of Zentrum, said the priests—that the prevailing wind in the Land was always off the Braun Sea and up-River.

After fighting for a century of more, the local tribes had finally joined together to form the town with a sentiment less of civic pride than pure exhaustion with feuding, and it showed in the architectural design, or lack thereof. Even Abel, who didn't much care, thought the town an ugly place.

Yet there was a bustle, an air of liveliness and even danger, present in the jumble of stone and wattle edifices that did impress him. Every alley seemed to be crowded with the stalls of merchants, vendors, auctioneers, and hawkers. Groups of men threw the bones openly in the shadow of dusty stoops, betting on the marks. Women lounged at corners, and some offered the promise of more than just a flash of breastcurve and ankle—for the right price.

Money itself was everywhere in the form of palm-sized clay promissory notes etched with quantities along with one- or two-glyph simple terms of sale. These were known as barter chits. When discharged, the chits were broken into shards and scattered for luck. For this reason, the streets of Bruneberg were littered with the remains of deals made and unmade, lucre gained and spent. You might very well gash your feet on the stuff if you weren't wearing a good pair of sandals or didn't have tough footsoles to tread upon it.

The whole town smelled of dak shit. Nobody cleaned the streets—the concept probably hadn't even occurred to most of the citizens—and to do so would have been near impossible, in any case. The droppings mixed with the clay barter shards to produce a noxious slurry that defended itself with shit-coated barbs against all that was sanitary and sweet smelling.

Riding beside Abel on a dont doe was a priest whom Abel had gotten to know fairly well over the past fourteen days. His name was Raf Golitsin, and he was the chief priest at the gunsmith works of Treville, and, according to Joab, was considered a fast-rising protégé in Prelate Zilkovsky's retinue. Golitsin was in his late twenties, and Zilkovsky trusted him enough to send him on this journey. In fact, Golitsin had confided his hope that this meant big things ahead for him at the temple, with a possible promotion to chief of staff in the near future—especially if they returned successful. The old priest who currently held the position would be retiring soon.

In general, Golitsin was garrulous, amusing, and not at all what Abel had encountered in most priests before. He found himself liking the man.

The mission was to acquire gunpowder. The allotment for Treville district was now months overdue, and Scouts were going out on half their patrols armed with bows only, so dire had the situation become. The Regulars had not been able to hold target practice for over two months lest they risk having zero supplies on hand if called upon. Some districts might have let this situation slide, left matters to luck, Redlander indifference, or for the Scouts to deal with, but Abel's father had no intention of doing so. Joab had appealed to Zilkovsky, who had organized the trip and personally requested Abel as the military representative. Abel had been pulled from Scout duty to comply, and the move had angered several of the Regulars who believed they were much more capable for such a mission than some half-wild lieutenant of the Scouts.

For that was Abel's rank. Gone were the days of being the band's water carrier or dont wrangler. He was a full-fledged officer in the group now, one of four under Captain Sharplett's command. Abel's first act upon assuming his new title was to appoint Kruso as his squad NCO.

Abel's squad was now under the temporary command of Klaus Blauscharf, his old schoolmate, who was taking advantage of Abel's absence to serve his required rotation in the Scouts. Abel had left instructions with Kruso to go lightly on the young officer and to take inevitable insults he would be throwing out as the result of ignorance and not intentional disrespect. Kruso had dealt with enough Regulars in his time to understand exactly what Abel was asking of him.

"Steer not tha young commander into tha prickle-reed thicket," Kruso said. "Kin I."

"And when he runs into one on his own, which he will, for the Lady's sake, help him out, will you?" Abel added.

"Aye, sur," replied Kruso, "to tha hardpack keepen."

Golitsin served as the guide, since he had been to Bruneberg before, and Abel followed a half-dont's length behind him as he led the way through the streets. The broken piles of clay shards along the streetsides grew smaller and eventually disappeared as they neared the main temple complex, although the smell of dak excrement did not lessen. Eventually they arrived at a large temple square housing a central adobe building surrounded by a shabby willow-wood fence constructed of wrist-thick poles and uprights not a one of which ran straight for more than the length of a man's hand.

Nearby was a yard to tie the donts. It had an arbor made of the same willow-wood that looked like a bad attempt someone had given up in the midst of building to provide shade for the animals. A clay cistern of muddy water sat nearby, however, so at least their mounts could drink.

A couple of guards lounged near the entrance, one sitting on a bench, the other leaning into a shady spot along the wall. Neither wore tunics or leg wrappings. The leaning guard watched Abel and Golitsin dismount and approach, and when they were a couple of paces away, he turned his head and spat out a brown stream of nesh-laced spittle on the dirtyard. He eyed first Abel then Golitsin, whom he addressed.

"What can I do for you, brother?"

"We've come on an official visit from Treville District to the Bruneberg Powder Works. We want to report to the prelate before we travel to the plant."

The guard smiled and shook his head. "Official visit, huh?"

"Yes," Golitsin said. "Now if you will kindly announce—"

"Prelate isn't seeing anybody today," the guard replied.

"But . . . I assure you, I work directly for Prelate Zilkovsky and am his designated representative. I'm sure Prelate Asper will want to admit us immediately when he finds out we have arrived—"

"Prelate is busy today," the guard cut in. "Come back tomorrow. For an appointment."

"Our time is limited, I'm afraid, and our business of the utmost importance."

"Come back or don't come back," said the guard, "it isn't any of my concern."

"But, but—" Golitsin stammered. As a chief under-priest, he was most definitely not used to having his requests treated so cavalierly.

The guard who had been sitting now roused himself and brought the muzzle of his gun to bear on them.

"You heard the sergeant," he said in a low voice. "Move on."

I should teach these slovenly crap-haulers a lesson, Abel thought. *This is beyond insolent. It's downright stupid.*

I'm inclined to agree, Raj answered.

Not worth the effort, in my opinion, put in Center. **And in fact, analysis shows that whatever the attitude of these sentinels, they are telling the truth. They believe that the prelate is not inside.**

Still, I wouldn't mind knocking some sense into them.

You may get your chance later, Raj said, **but Center is right. You should go directly to the plant now.**

Abel took a long breath, held it for a four count, then slowly exhaled. *All right,* he thought. *But I hope I get my chance.*

"Come on, Brother Golitsin," he said softly. "We have other ways to fulfill our task." He put a hand on the priest's shoulder, and Golitsin allowed Abel to turn him around.

"I'm not afraid of those two," Golitsin said. "I'd just as soon march right past them and see if those muskets even have powder in them. From the looks of them, they probably forgot to load up."

"I wouldn't doubt that you're right," Abel answered. "But let's check out the powder plant first."

Golitsin shot Abel a curious glance as they untied the donts under the makeshift arbor. "I would've expected that *I* would be the one pulling *you* away from the fight," he said. "Yet I know from reports that you have been known to fight like the dickens when it suits you. You are an uncommon young man, Lieutenant."

"I hope that's a good thing," answered Abel.

"Let's go find our powder," said Golitsin.

They rode across town and had to ask for directions several times before they found the Bruneberg Powder Works. It was near the River, and when they approached, the ammoniac odor of curing saltpeter told them they were in the vicinity, and, if they doubted this, the piles of sulfur and willow-wood charcoal nearby showed them to be in the right place.

There was also the tremendous thunder of the barrel mill, as large as three houses, to let them know they'd found it. This structure dominated the middle of the manufacturing yard. It turned night and day. Something that was inside made an enormous racket against its wooden sides as it turned.

Lead balls, said Center. **Each is as large as a man's head.**

Center showed Abel what one such ball would look like.

Why lead?

It creates no sparks, Center explained. **Necessary, for in that turning barrel, gunpowder is born.**

In the yard were the Silent Brothers, the makers of

the Land's gunpowder. There were hundreds of them, all dressed in sooty orange robes and going about a huge variety of tasks.

They did not speak, for they had no tongues. True to their names, they hardly made a sound at all.

Even if they could, whatever moans or groans they might make would be lost under the din of that turning mill, Abel thought. *It never stops?*

Only to load and unload, Center said. **It's been turning for two hundred years.**

To Abel's surprise, the entrance to the powder works was not guarded. In fact, there was no military contingent to be seen anywhere in the vicinity, nor priests either.

"At least the place is fenced," Golitsin murmured. "But I don't believe that fence would keep out a herbidak fledgling, much less somebody determined to get in there."

"Maybe the Silent Brothers keep them away," Abel said. "I'd be afraid of those gargoyles and wouldn't set foot here if I hadn't been ordered to come."

Again they tied their donts outside, this time under the more promising shade of a large overhang that was constructed to cover the piles of raw material. There was a young boy throwing stones against a post nearby, and Abel promised him a handful of figs to watch the horses. They boy agreed readily enough.

There was a clear path that led through the works to what looked like a central office.

The smell of urea and feces, both human and animal, was almost overwhelming, especially when they passed the settling ponds where the saltpeter was gleaned from rippled sheets of a specialized papyrus.

"Now that's a holy smell," Abel said and nudged Golitsin in jest. He'd learned over the past days that the priest did have a sense of humor, albeit a dry one that was barely a beat away from irritation. "Does it make you just want to go and throw yourself in the cure tank waters?"

"I'll throw you in first," Golitsin replied. "It's my duty as a priest to look after my flock, after all, particularly the stubborn and errant ones strayed farthest from Law and Stasis."

You might be saying something truer than you know, Abel thought, but he only smiled wryly at the priest and did not reply.

When they entered the main office, a man looked up from scratching out the totting of figures on a clay tablet. He was using a stylus cut from a river reed with a chipped flake of grainy feldspar fixed to its end—perhaps not optimal, but the hardest rock to be found in these regions. He was sitting in a chair behind a long plank table that faced the opening through which they'd entered. There was the distinct odor of flitterdung in the air.

This time Abel took the lead in questioning the gatekeeper. "We're here to see Director Eisenach," he said. "We're told that he is the overseer of the powder plant, although we may be mistaken in his honorific. Does he not hold some sort of military rank?"

A voice from the back of the room cut in. "I'm a colonel of the local militia, if that means anything to you, soldier, but you can call me 'director,' that's fine. I'm not in command of anything here because I happen to own the place. What can I do for you?"

The voice belonged to a man who was of indeterminate middle-age. One glance told Abel that he was no soldier himself, whatever his militia rank might say. Eisenach was not fat and definitely not skinny, but possessed an indeterminate pudginess that seem to be spread throughout his body, not concentrating in any one spot, but puffing out arms, legs, and belly to an equal degree. His complexion was sallow and unhealthy looking. The animated wrinkles around his eyes, and his obsidian-colored eyes themselves, chips of life in the doughface, belied this overall appearance of dullness, however.

He looks like a clever little man peering out from a big brute's body with those eyes, Abel thought.

Aye, lad, said Raj. **He won't be a fool, or at least not the same kind of fool as those guards.**

Abel and Golitsin entered the room, and the man at the entrance table, a flitter-faced, spindly sort, pushed back his chair, and stood beside it. The long table was topped with neat cakes of what looked, for all Abel could tell, like dung.

The man nodded slightly in greeting as they walked past him, but then turned, his back to his dung piles, and stared after them. Abel could feel the clerk's predatory stare on his own back.

Eisenach, the director, did not stand. He smiled an indulgent smile and bid them speak.

"We're from Treville District," Abel said. "We've come to inquire about our district powder allotment. It's four months' overdue. We've been in constant engagements with Redlanders. We're running out of firepower."

"I assume you wouldn't be here if you were completely out," Eisenach said.

Abel frowned, but nodded in acknowledgment. "I guess that's true, sir."

"And your priestly friend here?" Eisenach nodded toward Golitsin. "Around here, priests and soldiers don't usually mix so well."

"This is the prelate's chief of smiths," Abel replied. "We get along fine."

Golitsin gave a quick bow of the head and introduced himself. "Prelate Zilkovsky is as concerned as District Commander Dashian about the powder shortage," Golitsin finished. "He sent me to personally convey his unease."

"Sorry to hear that," said Eisenach. "But we've had problems ourselves, haven't we, Latrobe?" It took Abel a moment to realize Eisenach was speaking to the lean, nervous man, who was still standing, leaning against the table behind them. "Tell them what you're doing there."

Abel and Golitsin turned toward the man. Latrobe nodded and gestured toward the piles of what looked like dung on the table. "Trying to find out which is the bad batch," he said.

"The bad batch?" said Abel.

"Of nitercake," Latrobe replied. "One or more of these has been setting off the explosions."

"Explosions?" Golitsin said. "What? Here?"

"Yes, here." Eisenach's voice came loudly from behind. He'd gotten up and walked up to them while they'd been staring at Latrobe's dung piles. "It's shut down production for weeks at a time. We think we've solved the problem, and along comes another one. Lost a couple of the damn Brothers, and that indentured overseer we hired—what's his name?"

"Neimer," answered Latrobe.

"Neimer lost both his arms from the elbow down," Eisenach continued. "He won't be diddling himself blind anytime soon, I don't imagine." Eisenach guffawed at his own joke and slapped Abel and Golitsin on the back for sympathy. Abel managed to conceal his surprise, but Golitsin jumped like a frightened springleg. He turned to see that Eisenach, who had merely seemed bloated sitting in his chair, now towered a good two handspans over him—and Abel was no longer a boy, but a man of more than average height.

He stared calmly at Eisenach. "We're sorry to hear about your troubles, Director, but we need the powder that's due us. It's vital to the defense of Treville. Could you curtail some other shipment that's not so urgent and supply us with ours?"

Eisenach shook his head sadly. "Would if I could, soldier," he replied, "would if I could. But we're stretched to the limit as it is, and there's a shipment due to Lindron itself in ten days."

"It's quite humid here by the cataracts," Golitsin suddenly said. "Seems like the explosions would be minimal."

"And you are an initiate into the making of sacred powder, are you, that you would know such a thing?"

"It seems an obvious thought, but I am not a Powder Initiate. Those priests are assigned only here in Cascade District, of course."

"Well, I wish you were," said Eisenach, "because then you could answer that question for me and save Latrobe here a lot of trouble and possibly a missing finger or two if he's not careful. He's going to have to test those nitercakes, after all."

"Sir, is there nothing you can do?" Abel asked.

"We do have a bit more to offer than just the heartfelt appeal of our dear prelate," said Golitsin.

Eisenach's obsidian eyes took on a sparkle. "And what would that be?" he asked. "Although I assure you the matter is entirely out of my hands."

"My prelate mentioned a double wagon shipment of barley wine that he could get underway the moment the first half of our allotment reached Treville. In fact, I have a bottle sample he sent along." Golitsin pulled the clay container out from under his cloak and handed it to Eisenach.

So that's what he was getting out of the saddlebag, Abel thought.

Eisenach uncorked the top, took a sniff, and then threw back the bottle for a great, long swallow. He nodded his approval and took another. "Yes, yes, this is better than I expected, and I've heard all about Treville barley wine," he said. "And two wagonloads?"

"Four," replied Golitsin smoothly. "Two when we get half, two on final delivery."

"Nothing up front?" Eisenach asked ruefully.

Golitsin nodded at the clay wine container. "You get to keep that," he said.

Eisenach frowned at the bottle, then spoke to it, the bottle. "Well, my child, you will have to last me. For there is no hope I can fulfill the request of this young priest and soldier. What gunpowder we have is contracted for and bespoke."

"We'll have to try the district military commander, you know," Abel said to him.

"I hope you will tell him I cooperated as completely as I am able."

"And the prelate," said Golitsin.

"Most regrettable," Eisenach said. "I'm sure he will find a way to help you. I wish you success."

His sardonic grin as they left the office let Abel know that the director of the powder plant did not expect Abel to receive such help in the slightest.

They found their donts where they'd left them, and Abel handed the young boy his promised three figs. The youngster disappeared down an alley, chased by four others who suddenly emerged from the shadows and stalked toward him. "You should've told me about the wine," Abel said to Golitsin.

"Zilkovsky said to hold it back as a last resort," the priest answered. "I wasn't even supposed to mention it."

"Anything else you forgot to mention?"

The priest smiled. "You know we'll never make the garrison, even if we do get across the River before the ferries shut down at sunset."

"We can try."

"I have another idea," said Golitsin. "I was in Bruneberg three years ago, and I had to find a place to stay one evening. Did, too. Very nice place. It's not too far from here, I don't think. At least, I remember being able to smell the powder plant from there."

"You think you could find it again?" Abel asked.

"Yes," Golitsin said. "It's a place that's hard to forget."

And, true to his word, the priest mounted up and, as if by a sense of direction as sure as a flitterdak's, led Abel through alley and down lane until, about a quarter-watch later, they arrived at a stable with the symbol of a boat on the River etched above the entrance lintel. Across the street—it was little more than a three-pace-wide passageway—was another door with a similar sign above it.

"What is this place?" Abel asked.

Golitsin nodded toward the stable. "This is where we leave the donts," he said. "Then we go over there." He motioned back over his shoulder to the other door.

"And what's over there?"

"Where we leave everything else," answered Golitsin.

2

It was not precisely a whorehouse, Abel discovered. There were indeed sleeping cots for rent, and these separate from the other beds for rent by the quarter hour. There was food of a sort to be had, and Golitsin ordered them both a dak steak, a loaf of barley bread, and a jug of wine.

The central hall was filled with rough-hewn tables and chairs, with pedestals strewn about upon which stood women. They were elaborately veiled about the head, but otherwise unclothed.

They swayed to the loud blare of rivercane pipes and some sort of percussion instrument that was made from an even larger, halved reed set on a resonating frame.

Interesting that some form of Hrand's Planet kahlpipe music has either been preserved or reinvented, Center intoned.

Do you even know *what this place is?* Abel asked. *And do you approve?*

Oh, we know where you are, lad, answered Raj. *At least, I do. As to whether or not we approve: that's really none of our business, now is it?*

Damn right it's not, Abel answered with an enthusiastic nod of the head that surprised Golitsin, though he took it for assent to something else he was talking about.

A waitress approached, almost as naked as the veiled dancers, and Abel saw Golitsin pay with a clay piece rimmed with hardwood. It was a sum equal to nearly a month of his lieutenant's pay. Abel waited to see the waitress bring back change, but there was none.

"I can't pay you back. I . . . didn't bring those kinds of funds," Abel said.

"Don't worry about it," Golitsin shouted over the music. "The prelate said to tell you it was your Scout's bonus."

"Bonus? For what?"

"Killing Redland devils, I suppose," Golitsin replied. "Now drink up, because I don't think you're going to like the taste of that steak otherwise."

"Why not?"

"Not sure anybody told these Bruneberg cooks that you're suppose to put meat in them."

Abel drank. Then he sat back and for the first time really looked around.

The women were stunning. Or at least their nakedness was. He hadn't seen a woman undressed since . . . well, since Captain Blackmore's wife had flashed her breast at him while he'd stood detail outside one of Blackmore's all-night officers' bones games one night. He'd been fifteen. She'd stumbled outside and tried to pull him into the stables. After he resisted, she'd shown him her breasts. After he'd continued to resist, she'd reached under his tunic and grabbed his cock, as stiff as a musket barrel by now.

"He won't come out," she whispered. "He's winning, you know. He'll never come away when he's winning."

And Abel had almost done it, almost followed her into the stable. But another officer who was not Blackmore and who was not winning had stumbled out to relieve himself in the yard.

And, just like that, Captain Blackmore's wife or concubine or whatever she was had transferred her entire attention to the officer.

Abel heard the pissing abruptly stop. Laughter. And then the creak of the stable door opening. And the sounds from within that he knew were not the sounds of rutting donts, no matter how much they sounded like them.

I won't stand holding my musket tonight, Able thought. *I won't. But which? And how?*

He turned to Golitsin. "They have special dispensation for this kind of thing in the priesthood? Special prayers or something?"

"Never heard of Zentrum smiting a brother who responds to his urges now and again," Golitsin replied. "So long as you don't break Stasis by, you know, trying something wrong."

"Like what?"

"I don't know exactly. There's stories about brothers that like to...do things...you know, with *metal instruments.*"

Abel shook his head. "I don't know. Tell me."

"I've only heard stories, I mean," Golitsin quickly replied.

A bit too quickly, Center said. **Stand by and I will**

perform a first pass interpolation to determine the priest's deviancy from norms and specific instances of—

No, no, no! Abel shouted in his mind. *I don't want to hear any of that, let alone see it!*

Very well.

But they say Zentrum finds out things such as that, if you do them, I mean. That Zentrum knows when a priest breaks Stasis, even then, even doing that.

Quite possible, Center said. **But even for a planetary defense computer with powers as immense as Zentrum, that would seem to be one calculation too many.**

Golitsin tugged at Abel's sleeve as the steaks arrived. "How about that servant girl?" he said. "They are for sale, too, you know."

Golitsin began to flirt with the wench, who, after a moment, allowed him to pull her onto his lap. She cut up his food and fed it to him while the priest begged like a flitterdak chick for the next.

Abel noticed that the knife in her hand was trembling a bit much, as if she were having trouble controlling the urge to plunge it through Golitsin's upturned chin. But after he finished off another cup of wine, the serving girl pulled the priest away toward one of the curtained doorways in the back of the room that led—well, Abel wasn't sure where they led. It certainly wasn't to the sleeping area, which was down a clearly marked separate hallway well-lit with torches.

And so he found himself alone with his wine and half-eaten steak. Golitsin had been right about the lack of meat, but incorrect about the amount of wine it would take before he didn't care. Even with his head swimming with drink, he could still taste the sawdust filler when he chewed.

Sawdust and meat that wanted to *return*, he discovered. Return from the slurry of death in his stomach and emerge once more into the land of the living. Abel stood up, stumbled blindly in a direction he had decided might lead to a chamber pot, or at least to an empty alleyway.

And she was there, guiding him. Gliding through the crowd, clearing a path in front of him, taking him through a curtained doorway, down a hall, and into a stall where a genuine toilet and washbasin sat. He heard the sound of rushing water somewhere nearby and looked around until he realized it was under him, under the floorboards. He was over the River.

He saw that when she opened the toilet hatch and he looked down fifteen feet into dark, rushing water.

"Don't fall in, Sweetbread," said the voice from behind the cerulean veil.

"I can swim," Abel said. Not well, he knew, but he could. He'd learned, at Raj and Center's insistence, in the lake at Hestinga.

"It isn't that," said the voice. "It's that the carnadons would have you to pieces before you managed to drown in the cataracts."

Her tone was playful, but with a trace of contempt, as well.

Not for me, Abel thought. *More like for all men.*

Aye, Raj said. **You've got the right of that.**

Abel turned away from the open hole. "Actually, I don't think I need it now, I—"

That was when the swell hit him. He jerked back, and hung his head as fast as he could over the opening and let rip only just in time for the bulk of it, the spill of it—steak, wine, day's rations, everything—to rain down in a putrid waterfall to the River below.

"Ah! Ah, by the bones and breasts of the Lady," he cried out, "let this stop."

He didn't notice then, but later realized that this was when it must have happened, that she realized he was either a Scout, knew the borderlands, or was a Redlander himself. For who else would think to call upon Irisobrian at such a time?

He felt her hand upon his arm, softer this time. "Here now, drink some water," she said. The other hand had dipped a clay cup into a nearby pitcher.

He took it, rinsed his mouth, spat into the River again and again until he'd banished enough of the taste of his own innards to resist the urge to turn once more to the blank hole and start the puking process all over again.

She handed him a bit of cloth. "Wipe your mouth."

He did.

And then what looked like a weed.

"Chew this."

He examined it, turned it in his fingers, didn't recognize the small leaves or the pungent smell.

It is mint, Abel, Center said. **Probably imported from the Schnee foothills. Quite safe.**

He chewed. Good. The nausea faded.

"Can we—I would like to . . . *not* go back out there," he said. "I mean, I don't really have anything to pay you with."

"You are inside, are you not? You have paid the night charge."

"But I thought that just covered a pallet."

A laugh from behind the cerulean veil, this time not contemptuous. Sweetly amused. "Come."

She led him out and down the hall in the opposite direction from the main hall. At the very end, they passed through a beaded curtain and onto a veranda.

The view was stunning. They were at least a field-march from the near River bank, suspended over water that was raging through the rocks of the cataracts below. Far on the opposite side of the River, nearly a quarter league away, firelights twinkled through the silhouettes of willow and fern trees.

High above, Duisberg's three moons gathered.

She led him along the veranda, which seemed to encircle the perimeter of the structure. He paid no heed to where they were going, only looked out at the expanse of the River, the white flash of the rapids in moonlight. And listened to the surge of the water pouring through the teeth of the Land.

"Here," she said, and pulled him through another curtain. The River was gone. He counted three doorways, and then she pushed aside another, a beaten flax curtain, and he followed into a chamber.

It was not what he expected. Not fancied with fabrics or colored papyrus. A makeshift bed. A table with a washbasin. A clay oil lamp.

"This is mine," she said. "Where I sleep. Where I live."

"Oh."

"We can have time here," she said. "At the other, they will roust you when the sand has run its course through the tumbler. And if you don't come out, they will use sticks."

"I don't want them to use sticks."

"No, this is better," she said. "Also, seeing is not allowed there. Here, you can have this."

She reached up and worked a clasp loose near the back of her neck. Then she carefully began to unwind the veil.

Which gave him a moment to step back and look at her completely for what, he realized, was the first time.

She was of medium height. Her skin had a darker hue, not sun darkened but naturally so. Her breasts were ample, not small or overlarge, her nipples brown and, so far as he could tell, perfect. She smelled of something he had never experienced before. Something wonderful.

Lavender, said Center.

Lavender. As she lifted her arms to undo the veil, he glimpsed the undersides of her forearms. Something odd. He looked closer. Three stripes. They were covered with something, something chalklike, to hide them. But here in this light, so near to her, they were quite clear scars. Scars like those he had seen before.

Blaskoye clan scars.

The veil fell away. Her eyes were blue. Lapis lazuli.

"Thon schonet er, damme Blaskoye," he said to her. *You are very beautiful, Blaskoye woman.*

He saw the recognition, the understanding, as she started back.

"You—you speak with an accent," she said. "You are not a clansman."

"I am a lieutenant of the Scouts."

"Ah, of course. A sworn enemy." He thought he heard the contempt that had vanished seep back into her reply, but this time it sounded as if it were directed at herself. "I should have known. I should have."

"Yes. An enemy."

"I had thought you might be...someone else."

"Who?" he asked. "A Redlander? Is that what you thought? Is that what you are?"

"Not anymore," she said. She dropped the veil beside her washbasin on the table. "Have you killed many Redlanders?"

"No," he said. "A few."

Only one woman. She looked like her. The same eyes, at least. He tried to push the thought from his mind, but could not.

"Have you fucked many Scouts?" he asked her.

This caught her off guard, and she laughed.

Her lips, he thought. *They don't tell you about the lips behind the veil, full like that.* Before he could stop himself, before he even knew what he was doing, he reached up and touched her lips, ran a finger across the softness, pulled his hand slowly away.

"You will be the first," she said.

And she was the first, his first. He didn't tell her. Perhaps she knew. It wasn't pretty. Her bed creaked, and several times she had him slow, stop the noise. If they were discovered, she whispered, he would be dragged away, she would be beaten. So finally they pulled what covers she had off the bed and he took her on the floor, which squeaked less.

And somewhere below them, he knew the River ran, the carnadons gathered. He pushed the face of the Blaskoye woman he'd killed from his mind, willed himself to replace it with *her* face, *her* form.

And almost could do it.

Almost, but not quite. For when he came, it was both the lamplit form of the woman *and* the feel of his hand on the trigger of the Blaskoye musket as he shot the other, shot the Redlander woman, that filled his mind like an explosion of desire, rage, and grief.

There was one solace. This one, this Blaskoye clanswoman or whatever she was, was not dead. She was still very much alive.

"You are young," she whispered. "You can do it again. Quickly now, do it again."

Could he?

Yes. Oh yes, he could.

So he did. And this time, it was only her and the River.

She led him back to the pallet and slipped away before he could speak to her again. He hadn't even gotten her name. He lay still, unable to sleep, unwilling to converse with Center and Raj. For their part, they respected his obvious wish for quiet and remained silent.

Then Golitsin stumbled into the room—which slept five, although only four pallets were occupied—and collapsed beside Abel. He was making an odd sound, somewhere between a whistle and a moan, and at first Abel thought he was crying. But then he slapped the pallet and let out a guffaw, and Abel knew it was laughter.

"What?" he said groggily.

"Three," Golitsin said.

"Women? Times?" Abel sat up. "What?"

"Yes, each," he said. "Then all at once."

Abel shook his head. Had he heard that right?

"And years," Golitsin said. "One for every year I didn't. That I haven't."

"So the last time was—"

"Here," said Golitsin.

Abel nodded, turned over. "I guess that's all right, then," he said.

"By the Bite and the Bolt."

"Whatever you say."

"By the Law and the Land."

"Okay, Golitsin." Abel's stomach suddenly spasmed. The nausea rose again momentarily, and with it a thought. Abel fought down the one, but not the other. "Golitsin, did you—is *this* the only reason you came? Just this tonight? You knew the state of things in Cascade, didn't you, the reasons the shipment never came?"

"Not the extent."

"But you knew?"

Golitsin sighed. "Yes, but you're wrong," he said. "I may be a bad priest, but I'm not *that* kind of bad priest. Zilkovsky trusts me, or he wouldn't have sent me. I know him enough to know that, and so should you by now. That's why he got your father to send you along, I expect. He trusts you, too. And he knew what I'd do here, and maybe overlooking where I happened to spend the night while here is payment for my being such a good priest for the past three years. That other kind of good priest, I mean. Anyway, we'll get to the bottom of the problem with the shipments."

"All right," Abel said. "Goodnight, then."

"You think I'm damned?"

"No."

A pause, then Golitsin spoke again in a lower voice. "You get yours, kid?"

"I guess."

"Either you did or you didn't."

"Yes. I did. Okay?"

"How was it?"

Abel didn't answer. Golitsin started to say something else, stopped himself. Then Abel heard him collapse on the pallet, let out a great sigh, and begin to snore.

This seemed to be what Abel's body was waiting for. The snoring. Familiar. Like after a day on patrol. The clump of spent and tired men who had nothing in common other than the fact that they had all just risked their lives on the same enterprise, taken the same chances, reaped the same reward, which was survival to fight another day.

Abel finally fell asleep.

3

They awoke the next day and washed themselves off at a common bath near the stable. A line of other men joined them, each trying not to catch the others' eyes. The donts seemed fine, well fed and rested. Abel never liked to leave a dont entirely in unknown hands, but it seemed Spet was none the worse for wear as a result.

Abel and Golitsin rode side by side into the bustling town morning. They stopped to buy a flatcake rolled around grilled dakmeat, and Abel followed it with a pitcher of milk, which he finished in three huge gulps. Golitsin watched in amused amazement. Abel hadn't realized how thirsty he'd been. The dull throb of his head had obscured his thirst before, he supposed.

"So, back to the priests or to the District Military Headquarters?" he asked. "I'd say we have about equal chances of having gas blown up our asses at both places."

"What are we going to do?" Abel said. "What if nobody will help us?"

Golitsin shook his head. "Was ever thus in the Land," he said, echoing a Thursday school mantra. "I don't know. Improvise, I guess."

"All right," Abel said. "Let's try the DMC headquarters first, and if that doesn't work, we go find—is there somebody like *you* around here?"

"Chief of Temple Smithworks, you mean?"

"Exactly."

"There should be. It's part of the Mandate."

"Let's try the military first," Abel said. "They have guns."

They crossed the River on a ferry, and approached the DMC HQ, which was in a desert-facing fort about a league from the River bank. But even as they approached, Abel knew something was wrong.

There were Scouts here. Too many Scouts. They ringed the encampment like some gnarly outer hull of a nut.

They're staying in shacks, he thought. *Like they've been here a while.*

A long while, by the looks of it, Raj growled. **Living in filth and debauchery. These men haven't been on patrol in weeks, maybe months.**

What Raj said was true. The ground was covered with the remains of people not giving a damn. Dak orts, broken-down wagons, pieces of body armor, stray scraps of papyrus that had blown from a stinking common latrine.

And worst of all, from Abel's perspective, a dead dont lay in the middle of the road. Not in the exact middle, true. Someone had attempted to pull it to the side just enough for a person to get past, although the very act of pulling had produced a vile trail of rotten intestines running out from the dont and lying across the entire road like a purple-pink line that must not be crossed.

Spet, in fact, shied away and would not cross it. The dont smelled his dead kin and drew back fearfully, his eyes rolling and his shoulder crest feathers erect. It was all Abel could do to calm him, and no effort to urge the dont forward succeeded.

Abel dismounted, as did Golitsin, who was having just as much trouble with his mount.

"I guess I'll have to lead you across, boy," Abel whispered gently into the dont's ear opening. "Don't worry, I'm just as disgusted as you are, but we've got a job to do."

He did not get the chance. He turned to see two Scouts stumbling up to him armed with muskets. Each wore a mud-speckled russet tunic with leg wrappings unraveling and boots covered in dust and muck. The smell of the two—part carrion wallow, part alcohol reek—reached him and Golitsin before the Scouts actually did.

"Treville man, what yer after?" one of them said. "Tha dont's brand ye o'ercast. And priest and man ov war brungether tell it Garangipore, dinken I."

Abel said nothing. They hadn't addressed him by his rank or asked him a question he felt any obligation to answer.

The Scouts drew closer, came to a stop directly in front of them, blocking their way as much as the dead dont.

"Meh tha anshur giben," the Scout continued, "or

pay hell with a shotgut bender." The Scout raised his musket and put a hand on the trigger.

Stupid, Abel thought. *One flinch, one false quiver, and you will do what your stupid mind doesn't even know it is prepared to do, kill a man in cold blood.*

But Abel did not reply. He straightened his tunic, slowly unlimbered his carbine from its saddle holster, made sure of his percussion cap, then checked for something under the saddlebag. He felt its snakelike coils. With a quick tug, he unfastened it from its tong holder, then spun and faced the Bruneberg Scouts with a furious glare.

"Ah think tha hell shalt pay woth a nine-struck back," he said. As he spoke, he allowed the thing in his hand to uncoil. It was a nine-elb-long whip. It uncoiled, but before it could reach the ground he tugged it back hard and it swung behind him. And when the tip reached its greatest possible distance behind him and the braid stretched taut, he pulled it forward in a smooth, inexorable circle.

The pop of its acceleration reached his ears just at the sight of the tip striking. The whip laid open the back of the hands of the Scout pointing the musket, and its momentum carried the musket out of the man's grasp. The weapon discharged, but its ball flew up and over himself and Golitsin to crash through the willows behind them.

With only instinct and long hours of practice behind him, Abel yanked the whip against its course and laid down a ripple that traveled down the length of the whip and issued forth at the end with a pop to the face of the other Scout. He also dropped his musket. The Scout reached up and grabbed his face, which

was welted and not gashed open yet. Once he touched
it, the welt broke, however, and blood trickled out of
the newly tenderized skin.

Both men stumbled back in agony, the first clutching his hand, the other his face.

"There's more for you both," Abel said, bringing
the whip back to rest coiled at his feet. "Or will you
take me to the DMC?"

The two began to back away. "You'll pay for it,"
the hand-slicked one said.

Abel shook his head. "Lo, idyuts! Jus fur yer et
asken did Ah ye pop. Be yeh Scout nur River man-
glage? Up standen, thrice-be-yer-damnt! Tha russet
shalt tha proud wearen, or agin to pop yer Ah wilt!"

Abel cracked the whip once more in the air for
good measure. This got even the attention of the
Scout who was holding his face.

"Attenthut, yer stinket modderfuckern!"

Even through the pain of the whiplashes, Abel could
see the surprise of the men as it dawned on them
he was speaking in the Scoutish patois. Now that he
was sure they did understand this fact, he switched
over to Landish.

"Stand like men!" he roared. "Report to an officer!"

And, to his own amazement—although he was
careful not to betray it in the slightest—they obeyed.
First a little, and then, when each saw the other was
acquiescing, more quickly. Face-welt dropped his hands
to his side first and looked forward, and hand-burn
followed suit. The movement almost became a race
between them.

"Sir!" shouted Face-welt.

Golitsin, who had been busy holding his startled

dont steady, said nothing, but shot the tiniest smile toward Abel. Abel heard the air escaping over his teeth in a low whistle, more an expression of relief than admiration, Abel figured.

Spet had not moved. He may not have been the smartest of donts, but he was a Scout mount, all right, and knew how to stand his ground.

"I have come up from Treville at the special directive of the DMC himself, and I do not have time to waste seeing to your very deserved three days lashed to a wheel," Abel said. Being strapped to a wagon wheel and fed on bread and water for a three-day period, some of it spent upside down, was the legendary punishment for letting down another Scout on patrol. Abel figured these would have at least heard of its practice. He, himself, had seen Sharplett order it against one man, Dooley, a Delta boy who had been a forced recruit but had since become a damn fine Scout. "I'm also *not* going to ask why you are living like Redlander sons of bitches wallowing around with full bellies after a raid for child-flesh. I haven't got the stomach or time for it. All I require of you pieces of shit is for you to tell me this: Where can I find your DMC?"

"Sir," said Hand-burn. "He's a ways yonder in the fort. He'll be counting the daks?"

"What?"

"Herd was run in yesterday, sir, for branding," replied Face-welt. "He always counts 'em off for shares. Scouts get an eighth and Regulars the rest."

"And where was this herd of daks run in *from*?" Abel asked, already knowing he wasn't going to like the answer.

Face-welt darted his eyes nervously at Hand-burn. Abel let the whip uncoil once again.

"From the east, sir," Hand-burn answered quickly.

"Nothing to the east but the Escarpment," Golitsin said. "Unless you mean farther than that."

"Is that what you mean?" Abel said. "From beyond the Escarpment?"

Face-welt nodded. "They're Redlands daks, sir. Least that's where they come *here* from." He fell into Scout patois. "Brands ov the Land overscattered on dem daks. For that ist them agin burned. Tha brands Cascade to maken."

And you can bet your life that most of those original brands are from Treville ranches, Raj said, confirming what Abel already suspected.

Abel felt like cursing, but only nodded. "I see," he said. "All right, take us to the DMC."

The Scouts turned and began to do as he said, when Abel halted them gruffly. "Pick up those thrice-damned rifles," he said, "and march like men."

"Aye, sir."

They passed the dead dont and continued up the road. The two Scouts, to Abel's surprise, stepped lively.

They almost seem to be enjoying themselves, Abel thought.

You've given them back their self-respect, said Raj. *They'll never understand it, or admit it if they do, but so you have.*

There was a cloud of dust ahead that resolved into an approaching man on dontback and a retinue of soldiers on foot. There were six of them. The Scouts ahead of Abel halted, stood at attention, and Abel rode past them to meet the approaching rider.

"Halt right there, stranger," said the man. He wore the three-striped tunic of the district military commander. So this was General Pat Bundren.

"Lieutenant Abel Dashian of Treville District Command reporting, sir," Abel said. "I have been sent on special assignment to look after the grave conditions of the district gunpowder supplies, Commander."

"Have you now?" the man said. "And do you have your bona fides to prove it?"

"I do." Abel reached back into his saddlebag. The soldiers surround the Cascade DMC warily lifted their muskets when he did so, but their commander smiled and bade them lower the muzzles. Abel found what he was looking for, a rolled papyrus message, sealed with wax impressed with his father's scarab seal. Its ends were tinted red, the color of a courier communique. "Introduction from DMC Dashian himself for your perusal, sir."

He held it out. Bundren approached no closer and did not take the scroll. He nodded. "You can put that away. I recognize a Dashian when I see one. You're the son?"

"I have that honor, sir."

"Yes, and it is . . . an honor. Joab was quite the character back when we served in the Tabernacle guardians." Bundren chuckled. "Yes, quite the character. He had me up for baiting the carnadons, once. I don't know if he ever found out we were fighting them, too, in one of the lower pools."

Abel said nothing. He stowed the scroll back into his saddlebag.

Bundren pointed a gloved hand at the two Scouts who remained at attention between them. "I see you've taken it upon yourself to discipline my Scouts? Is that right, son of Joab?"

"Not at all, sir. I only reminded them of their duties, and they jumped to. I have no complaint against them."

"Indeed you do not," Bundren replied. "And what is it you want from me?"

"Your aid in locating our lost gunpowder, sir," Abel said.

Bundren nodded. "I see. You've misplaced it somewhere, have you?"

"It never arrived, sir," said Abel. "It was due four months ago. We are, in fact, three shipments shy now. And we are sore beset by Redland barbarians."

"Can't take care of your troubles, so you bring them to me. Is that it?" Bundren shrugged, turned to his retinue. "What did I tell you about the Treville troops, men? Not seeing to their part of the wall so well, are they?"

Abel felt himself growing flush with anger.

Easy, lad, he's baiting you, Raj said. ***Take a breath or three.***

Abel obeyed. He sat his mount and did not reply. Neither did he move.

After a moment, when he saw he wasn't going to get a rise out of Abel, the DMC continued, still addressing his men. "And so this one comes here to tell *us* how to do our duty to Zentrum and the Land. Comes calling us names, I'll wager."

He pointed the gloved hand at Abel. "Here's a message for Joab Dashian, boy. You tell him Pat Bundren sent it, and I don't need a waxbound teacher's note from a dickless scribe to deliver it, either, since I have you."

Abel stiffened, but still said nothing.

"You tell Joab that we are doing just *fine* without his

interference here in Cascade. We've gone *twenty years* without a raider carting off one goddamn groundpeck, and as long as I'm in command here, I aim to go twenty more. When Treville can say the same thing, then you and your Thursday school boy-wonder of a daddy *may* have something to teach us here."

Bundren stared at Abel for another moment, then he spat—not at Abel or Golitsin, but onto the dusty ground between them. "Until then, get the hell out of my command. You understand, Lieutenant?"

Abel didn't answer at first. He returned Bundren's stare. His hand crept toward his stowed musket.

No, lad. Not now.

I'm going to kill him.

One day, perhaps. Not today.

What if I do?

A simple extrapolation with highly constrained variables, said Center.

Observe:

Abel, bleeding from a shoulder torn open by ballshot, strapped to the wheel himself. Day three without water, and he knows he's hallucinating, knows what he sees cannot be true, because he saw the priest on the ground before him. Saw the spatter of blood and then meat and then bone as Golitsin was beaten to death with Abel's own whip.

But it's Golitsin speaking, or at least a dark form against the unremitting sun, and Golitsin's voice coming from it as Abel squints to see anything from his sandblown eyes.

"I was a good priest," Golitsin says. "Not that kind of good priest, but a good one, nonetheless. I didn't deserve this. And it hurt so bad for so long—"

The figure stepped from the glare of the sun, and Abel saw it, ragged and torn, a man with the form of a man torn from him. No longer anything on the outside, and nothing but pain within.

All right, Abel thought. *No, of course I won't go for the musket.*

Good lad.

He took Spet's reins in both hands now. "I'll deliver your message, Commander," he said. He turned to Golitsin. "Come on, brother, we're not wanted here."

"That's the best understatement I've heard in a long while," Golitsin replied, low enough for Abel to hear, but not for the others.

They turned the donts and rode away at a slow trot. Abel did not turn around again, but as they departed he heard the DMC's screaming voice cursing the two Scouts.

You did him more injury than you know, Raj said. **Be content with that for now.**

"Now the priests again?" Abel said to Golitsin.

"Yes," Golitsin said. "But not the temple."

"Where then?"

"I think I know," Golitsin replied. "Something I heard last night."

"At that place?"

"It's called the Boat on the Water," Golitsin said with pride in his voice, as if he were the proprietor himself. "And yes, at that place. One of them, never mind which, told me that I wasn't the first priest she'd had that day. In fact, she's made rather a trade of it—priests, you know. That was how she spotted me so easily. She thought I was him."

"Him, who?"

"The one who *doesn't* make use of her services, actually," Golitsin said. "The one the others joke about."

"Is it the prelate?"

"No, the prelate's a drunk. He used to be one of her regulars until he couldn't get it up anymore and stopped coming. Apparently, it's just him and his wine casks at the temple."

"Why didn't you tell me this morning?"

"I was going to," the priest said. "You know how you felt about those Scouts we saw today?"

"Ashamed for them," Abel said, nodding.

"It was something like that," Golitsin replied. "Anyway, let's go see the upright man. She told me he's made himself into something of a wildman, a hermit. He lives underneath the Boat on the Water, as a matter of fact, in a little spot he's carved out in the bank. Seems we were both fucking over a holy hermit last night and didn't know it."

"And the carnadons?"

"That's the thing," said Golitsin. "That's why everyone thinks he's blessed of Zentrum. They don't bother him. At least, that's what she told me. And that's another reason I wanted to try the DMC first."

"Because we're not that holy?" said Abel.

"You got it, Lieutenant," Golitsin replied.

4

It took them the better part of a halfwatch to find a way to the Bruneberg River bank. Most of the town's edifices were built to hang over the edge to take advantage of the River for both a source of water and a ready-made sewer and garbage dump. Then they had to find a livery in which to leave the donts, for the path down was only wide enough for a man. Abel brought his carbine, his dragon pistol, and two knives, one of which he gave to Golitsin, more for the priest's comfort than with any thought that Golitsin might be skilled enough to use it to fend off a carnadon. Abel wasn't sure if he was himself.

Abel took the lead, and they wound their way down and then along a trail cut into the bank. There were carnadons aplenty lounging not far below them, but they seemed curiously inert.

"Probably well-fed on shit and dak bones," Golitsin murmured, though it sounded more like a hope expressed than a certainty to Abel.

Then they were beneath the overhanging buildings of Bruneberg. At first, the floors did not stretch so far out, and they merely walked in shadow. But as they drew farther under what they knew must be the denser part of town, they passed deep-set pilings and pierlike supports that ran in lines out into the River itself.

"This is the path the repair crew has to take to replace pilings," Abel said. "I'll bet they come down here with a military guard armed to the teeth, too."

"Pity we didn't," murmured Golitsin.

On they went, and now they were well under the buildings, which stretched onward, out over the River. The light grew faint and the way forward dark as night.

"And pity we didn't think to bring torches," Golitsin put in not long afterward.

Abel grunted his agreement. *Too late now.*

I have an estimate of the probability of carnadon attack, Center announced. **But I will refrain from stating the exact odds in order not to further contribute toward them by the very alarm they will cause, and merely admonish you to be careful.**

Great, thought Abel. *Thanks for the warning.*

There was a pinpoint of light ahead. Then the pinpoint divided into several flickers. As they drew closer, Abel saw that it was the light of four oil lamps. Each was set on a large, flat River stone and formed a square. In the middle of the square, on a patch of mud, sat one who could be no other than the hermit they sought.

Abel stood back now, and Golitsin took the lead as they approached.

The hermit turned his head once and gave them a

long look, then turned his gaze away and back down the bank's slope to the River.

"Brother," Golitsin called as they drew near. "I am a priest of Treville. I was told I might find you here."

The hermit didn't answer.

Then they reached the square of lighted lamps, and Golitsin halted.

"Brother?" he said. "May we talk? We have come along an...interesting...path to see you."

Still the hermit did not reply. But after a moment, he released a deep sigh and turned toward them.

Abel had expected an old man, but he was not old at all. Weatherbeaten, yes, and with hair that had not seen a comb or cutting knife for many a three-moon. But the eyes were not watery and yellowed, but quick and alert. And the face was not lined with age, but only spattered with dirt. In fact, the hermit appeared to be younger than Golitsin.

"Brother, we have some questions for you," Golitsin continued. "And we have brought food to share, if you want. May we sit with you?"

At the sound of the word "food," the hermit shuddered, as a dont might that has caught the scent of barn and bedding. He rocked back and forth and had to hold his knees to his chest to stop himself.

Abel handed Golitsin the bread and cheese they'd brought along, and Golitsin handed them both to the hermit.

The man stared at them for a moment, then quickly reached out and snatched the offered gifts. He attacked the bread immediately, biting off and swallowing huge chunks until the entire loaf was gone. The dak cheese he turned in his hand and considered. Then he drew his hand back and threw it as far as he could down the bank to the River below. It landed not far from the shore.

Immediately there came a series of roars and the shuffle of scaled flesh as the carnadons moved in on the suddenly available delicacy. Abel couldn't see what was happening there, but he was quite sure he did not want to be anywhere near whatever it was.

"Too smelly," the hermit said. "Never get away with it."

Golitsin took these words as an invitation, and he stepped within the square formed by the four stones with lamps upon them and motioned Abel to follow. They sat cross-legged near the hermit. The ground had been flattened here, but there was still a slight slope downward, toward the River. Enough to give Abel the feeling he was sliding, or the ground sliding under him, and that he might soon be, like the cheese, among the hungry carnadons himself. He held even more tightly to his musket, which he had rested over his knees.

"What is your name, brother?" Golitsin asked.

The hermit bobbed a couple of times, and, not looking directly at them, but below toward the dark River, answered. "Friedman," he said.

"Friedman?" Golitsin replied. "You are . . . military liaison, are you not?"

The hermit—Friedman—laughed. It was an ugly snort, with no real mirth in it. "Military liaison," he pronounced, as if chewing the words and finding them bitter. "Yes. Doing it now. Liaising."

"Brother, what has happened to you? Why are you here?"

"My retreat," he said. "Prelate ordered me to take one. A long one. So I did."

"He surely didn't mean this."

"Very specific," Friedman replied. "'Get your ass where the sun doesn't shine, you meddlesome bastard,' he said." Friedman shook his head sadly. "True, too, the bastard part. Mother couldn't help it. Father ran a shipping house, she told me once, and had his own family to look after."

Golitsin reached out, touched Friedman's knee, but the other flinched back.

"We came to see about Treville's powder shipment," Golitsin said gently.

Another snorting laugh from the hermit. "Ah," he said. "Good luck with that."

"You don't think we'll find it."

"Isn't lost," Friedman said. "Never was."

"What do you mean?" Abel spoke for the first time, which caused the hermit to jerk his head in Abel's direction. He stared hard, but his gaze did not seem unkind to Abel.

"Soldier," he said.

"Yes," Abel replied. "What do you mean, it isn't lost? Where is it?"

"The Redlands," said Friedman. "Traded for...peace, I guess you could call it. Being let alone."

"Traded to the Blaskoye? Or to the eastern barbarians?" Abel asked.

"East, west—it's all Blaskoye now," replied Friedman.

"They've established ties *across the Valley*?" Abel asked incredulously.

Friedman nodded.

"How?"

"Cascade," said the hermit.

"And what do they... pay in return for passage, for the powder?"

"Protection. Women. Some male slaves, though all are sure not to call them that, lest Zentrum smite them down." The snort again. "Lest Zentrum smite them down." He nodded, as if he were in on a joke only he understood.

"Have you reported this to Lindron, Brother?" Golitsin gently inquired. "Sure this will bring down the wrath of the Tabernacle upon these people."

"Verdrick tried," the hermit said with a sad shake of his head.

"Damion Verdrick, the Temple Chief of Staff?"

"Left one day for Lindron. Found him the next day outside the Cascade temple gate. Thought he was sleeping. Then I turned him over and saw he couldn't be, with his dick cut off and stuffed in his mouth, and his eyes gouged out like that."

"Ah," said Golitsin.

The three of them sat in silence for a while. Oddly, it was the hermit who broke the quiet.

"Show you another way up," he said. "Not so dangerous. Better."

"But we want to take you with us," Golitsin said. "They aren't going to kill us. We'd be missed in Treville. You can come with us. Escape."

Friedman firmly shook his head. "No," he said.

"But Brother Friedman—"

"Not afraid," he said. "Not anymore. All part of Zentrum's plan. I know that now." He turned back toward the darkness, the sound of the River below. "That's the thrice-damned thing. I know."

"Surely not," said Golitsin.

"Oh yes," said Friedman. "Seen it. Took the disk from the priest's mouth while he was in his cups. Put it in mine."

"The . . . what are you talking about?"

"You don't know about it. Only the prelates know. When he's raised up. The disk for his mouth, the one that speaks the Presence to his mind."

Can this be? Abel thought. *Is he telling the truth?*

Working, said Center. And then a moment later: **Confirmed. A waferlike communication device fitted to the palate. Matches known parameters for period-appropriate quantum communication device.**

The hermit turned back toward them, and there was wildness in his eyes. "I saw the mind of Zentrum. The Blood Winds. The death. The horror that is coming. I saw it all. I saw that it doesn't matter what I do, what anyone does. I saw the Plan. The bright and shining Plan. And I knew all I could do was hide. Hide here. And wait for the Plan to become the Act. For Zentrum does not lie. Zentrum is all that is true. And now I know. I have scanned it. He hates us for our unbalance, for His own holy requirement always to maintain the scales of Law and Stasis. We are despised of Zentrum, and we deserve it. I deserve it." Friedman began to rock back and forth in his muddy spot between the lamps. "I deserve it, I deserve it," he chanted.

"By the Law and the Land, brother," muttered Golitsin. He reached to touch the shoulder of the hermit, but Friedman flung his hand away. He continued his rocking and moaning.

Suddenly, a thought occurred to Abel. Before he

could question it, turn over his decision, he acted. Rising up, he stepped past Golitsin and launched himself at the hermit priest. He landed on top of Friedman and with a quick shove, threw the hermit on his back. The man was stronger than he looked, and he began to struggle. Abel found his musket still in his hand, and he brought it down horizontally across the hermit's neck, pinning him down against the mud, crushing his windpipe, choking the priest.

"Help me," Abel called to Golitsin.

"Help you what?"

"Hold him," Abel replied. "Get one side of my gun. Let me free a hand."

Golitsin moved as if in a trance to obey him. "Abel, don't kill him," he whispered.

"I'm not trying to kill him," Abel gasped, still struggling to hold the hermit down.

Then Golitsin was beside him, and together they held either end of the musket across the hermit's throat. Abel took his free hand from the musket and thrust it to Friedman's mouth. With his fist, he dug at the lips until he had the mouth open and felt the teeth trying to bite down on the meat of his palm. No use. The hermit's biting days were over, and what he had remaining was mostly gum now, and disease-softened gum at that. Abel freed a finger within the mouth. Two. Dug. Dug beyond the squirming tongue. Found the roof the mouth. The bump that should not be there. Dug harder, pushed in his nails.

And got hold of it. The disk. The host.

And, with the hermit screaming bloody murder, Abel pulled the disk out. He clenched his palm, holding it there. "Got it," he said. "By the Lady's Bones, I got it!"

Suddenly, the hermit ceased struggling. He lay utterly still. At a concerned glance from Golitsin, the two men simultaneously lessened the pressure of the musket barrel across Freidman's throat.

And then the hermit began to sob. Great wracking sobs that echoed underneath the buildings. "No, no," he cried. "Gone, gone, forever gone."

Golitsin shook his head. "Poor fellow," he said.

Abel held out his palm, showing the spit-wet, blood-stained disk. "Look at this thing," he said. "What is it?"

Golitsin shook his head. "I really don't know," he said. "There are rumors. Tales of what it means to be elevated to prelate. I always thought those stories were all dakshit. But now..."

A Mark 9 ZhUdRp5 quantum transceiver, said Center. **This is the ZhUd model prior to the Mark 10, which was auto-tuning. The Mark 9 cannot be used alone, but is dependent upon a hub, which is probably contained somewhere in the Tabernacle of Lindron. It was necessary to condition the disk and the individual user's neural pathways using a separate nanotechnological infusion known as a cerebral serrate. Without the introduction of the serrate, which obviously Friedman did not receive, the transceiver would have used whatever brain-to-skin pathways that existed and were available. Uncontrolled on either receiving or transmission ends.**

Friedman steals the disk, looks upon the Mind of God bare, and it drives him dakshit crazy, thought Abel.

Imprecise formulation, but a close enough metaphorical approximation, Center replied dryly.

What are we going to do about it?

There is little to do. His neural pathways are scrambled, with an eighty-four point six chance that they are damaged beyond repair. He is not in a fit state to travel, and he will lose whatever sense he has within the next few hours.

"We have to get him somewhere safe," said Golitsin. "Find someone to take care of him."

"Who?" said Abel.

"I'm not sure, but we can't just—"

With a roar, Friedman threw himself forward against the now lightly held musket and flung them both to the side with the power of his movement.

Golitsin recovered first, and leapt after the hermit, to no avail. Friedman was already away as Golitsin's fingers grazed the heel of the fleeing priest.

"Friedman," Golitsin called. "Brother!"

Then Abel saw where Golitsin was looking. Down the slope of the bank. Friedman was running full tilt down into the darkness toward the sound of the rushing water.

Golitsin turned around, reached for a lamp, but Abel knocked his hand away. "I have to go after him," said Golitsin.

"No," Abel said.

"But—"

"No," Abel said, and steadied his grip on the priest's arm. No matter what, he was not going to let go now.

Then from below came the cry. It almost sounded like joy. "Alaha Zentrum!"

Then the carnadon roar. The scrape of scales. The flat flap of a mighty tail against the muddy Land.

Then the screams. The human screams.

Then those screams stopped, and there was only the scrape of scales and the low grunts of satiation.

"Do you think he made it to the water, at least?" Golitsin asked.

"Do you?"

"No."

They sat within the square of lamps for a time, until all was silent once more.

"He said there was a better way up," Golitsin said.

"Yes," Abel said. He nodded toward one side of the square. "I see a trail."

Golitsin followed his gaze. "Scout's eyes," he finally said. "I don't see anything."

"Good thing you're not a Scout, then," Abel said. "And I am not a priest."

Abel reached out his hand with the wafer in it.

I think this is best for now, he thought.

Perhaps, said Center. **The max and min optimals become very difficult to calculate from such a nexus.**

Abel is right, Raj said. *It is best. For now.*

How about that? Raj called me directly by my name and not "the lad," Abel thought—but he carefully kept the thought from reaching the state of mental expression.

"Will you take this?" Abel said to Golitsin. "And will you promise not to use it?"

Golitsin required a moment to realize what Abel meant. Then Abel opened his hand and revealed the quantum communication disk.

"Maybe I shouldn't take it," the priest said.

"I think you should," Abel replied. "You said it yourself: you may be a bad priest, but you're not *that* kind of bad priest. You'll keep it safe."

Golitsin considered a moment more. "All right," he finally said. He reached out a hand, and Abel dropped it into his palm. The priest withdrew his hand and found a place to tuck it within his robes. Evidently there were quite a few pockets therein of which Abel had previously been unaware.

Golitsin turned upslope. "So, Scout, do your scouting," he said. "Get us the hell out of here."

"My pleasure," Abel replied. And, after a moment of reading the muddy ground, he had the trail all right, the shortcut, and led them upward toward the day.

They emerged, as Abel had suspected they might, through the seat of a public toilet, greatly surprising a washerwoman who had her hand on the door to enter when it flew open and two men emerged from the privy—a soldier and a priest.

"By the Stasis," she exclaimed as they rushed past her, begging her pardon, and lost themselves in the crowded street.

5

Are they even men? Abel wondered.

They are human beings.

I don't know whether to feel disgust or fear.

Feel pity.

Pity for worms?

They are not worms. There are men in there still. If you can't sympathize, then at least do them the honor of showing indifference. They have had enough attention from their betters already, I'm thinking.

An interpolation of the Silent Brothers' viewpoint is possible to calculate. Variables are fairly constrained. Observe:

Long shadows of the late afternoon lay on the powder plant when Abel and Golitsin tied their donts under the arbor and made their way to the main office.

The Silent Brothers looked up from their task and, for a moment, might even have wondered what this

158

determined soldier and priest might mean to them. But, accustomed to conditions of absolute submission since childhood, they likely did not wonder long, since their very minds were laid with chains against stray thought, much less blatant speculation as to a different, inconceivable future.

So most of them bent their heads back to work. But not all. For some, even with the tongue torn from their heads and male parts shorn in their youth, wonder remained, and even hope that something, anything, *different* might happen one day.

Maybe today was that day.

But probably not.

And after a moment, these, too, sighed and returned to their labors.

Some to the piles of caveflitter guano that must be shoveled from delivery wagons into the pits.

Some to the scattering of dak urine and straw upon that flittershit.

Some to the reaming of the matured pits, and the transport of the nitercake to the huge barrel mill on its River-turned cranks. Then from the mill, twice each day, to the corning troughs. Here the powder was worked into gradations of grain, some for shot, some for primer. A few of the Brothers speculated that it could be made finer still, given more explosive power. But this was to go against the Law of Zentrum.

For was it not written that corning gunpowder beyond priming grain strength was a sin against Stasis?

The Silent Brothers knew such thoughts were as bad as actions, and the Brothers who thought them needed no punishment from others. No, for the thinking of such heresy, they scourged themselves in their dormitories, also on the yard, with knotted cords or with rock-weighted leather tongs.

And the great mill churned day and night, mixing and refining material fed in by the Silent Brothers. It dominated the production yard and was the largest structure in all of Bruneberg—not that they Silent Brothers knew this. Most had never left the yard since before memory began.

They did what the man in the office said.

Once it had been a priest. There had been more food then. Now it was a man who was not a priest. There were two fewer water breaks now per day, also.

They had been told by the exiting priest that the man was now in charge, that they must do as he and his underlings commanded.

"Listen to Eisenach. He is now the voice of Zentrum," said the priest.

Lacking tongues, they did not question this.

When the rations had been cut the second time, some of the older Brothers had wondered if this were true, if Eisenach was the voice of Zentrum. When the punishment regimens began, and the young brothers were locked in the dung pits for a week and a day or suffered the powder burnings on the inner knees and the backs of their necks, these questions became even more pronounced.

Then the explosions began. The sudden deaths of Brothers who had been working the mill for decades.

Perhaps it was true that Zentrum was angry with them. That was what the man and his underlings told them.

The Brothers did discuss this possibility.

There was a language of a sort between them, of

hidden gestures, shrugs, and earlobe tugs that might communicate as much as a text-filled scroll.

So the older Brothers spoke of the change, after their fashion. Considered what it might mean.

But what were they to do? Obedience had been beaten into their nature. The voice of the man was the voice of Zentrum. The priest, their priest, had told them so.

So the decision was made to abide. They had been doing so for quite some time now.

The unexplained explosions continued, as did the punishments for them.

The Brothers knew nothing they were doing had changed. Nothing they did had ever, ever changed.

The uncertainty was growing alarming. Wearisome. One day they might rise up and put a stop to it. But not yet.

Suddenly, a commotion on the porch of the main office became a cry of dismay.

"You will not pass this entranceway, gentlemen," shouted the underling, the nitercake assayer, Latrobe. "Director Eisenach is quite busy and cannot receive you."

And the one in soldier's dress, the taller of the two, reached into his waistband and brought forth what was the biggest knife one could have without calling it a sword, and maybe it was technically a sword, but the big man, the soldier, didn't handle it that way.

Instead, he drew it back and took aim down its blade. Then, with a fluid motion that seemed to take no effort, no strength, but that must have been nothing *but* effort owing to the observed result, the big one, the soldier, threw the sword-knife end over end until it sunk into the wooden door that was shut across the entrance to the main office. The knife, the sword, whatever it was, buried itself past tip, past curve of point, and up to the straightness of the blade. It might have been as deep as the length of a man's thumb. It might have been more.

And it caught the nitercake assayer, Latrobe, by the shoulder of his robe and pinned him to the door. He struggled and yanked and pulled, but it was good fabric, the best wool from up-River, and did not give, and he was stuck fast.

Then Latrobe perhaps realized that the one who could throw with such ferocity must be one who did not *care* if he accidentally, or purposely, hit the target, or hit the man next to the target. And maybe he had missed and had been aiming at the man and not the door in the first place.

Then the big man, the soldier, stalked toward the nitercake assayer. And Latrobe let out a high-pitched scream, as if he had undergone the same operation, the same shearing, as the Silent Brothers.

But of course he had a tongue, and could use it.

Then something dark appeared on Latrobe's robe, in the place where his legs met under them. Something dark and wet. And the Silent Brothers realized the assayer had pissed himself.

That was when the Silent Brothers laughed. Soundlessly. But for a good, long time.

And the priest stayed outside, eyeing the nitercake assayer Latrobe, not letting him down, not letting him twist free of the embedded knife. But the big one, the soldier, opened the door, swinging Latrobe himself *on* the door, and entered the office. Then he closed the door behind him, with the nitercake assayer still stuck to it, and the priest watching, and taking a drink of water from the pitcher that sat outside, that Latrobe and the director sometimes drank from when they came onto the porch to watch the work.

Taking a drink of water and not offering any to the nitercake assayer, then taking another, until the priest had drained the entire pitcher. And still Latrobe hung there.

Then the priest maybe felt the stares on his back, the wordless gazes. And he turned and looked quizzically out at the upturned faces of the Silent Brothers. He considered them for a moment in surprise, perhaps astonishment. But, unlike so many who had looked at them, looked them over before, there was no contempt in his gaze, and not a trace of pity.

In fact, he seemed to be sharing the moment with them. And when the priest smiled broadly at them, or at the setting sun, or in general happiness, they knew he was.

Abel moved past the table of specimens and toward the back of the office. There sat Eisenach. He did not seem particularly surprised, or even alarmed. He sat as if he'd been waiting for Abel, and his sudden appearance was entirely expected.

"So you got past Latrobe," he said when Abel stood before him. "That's an accomplishment in itself. I keep him because he's, well, a bit of a dick. And very persistent."

Abel didn't reply. He reached for a nearby chair and pulled it across the floor, dragging its legs through the sand, and placed it before Eisenach. He sat down in it and was almost knee to knee with the other.

"The Treville gunpowder," Abel said.

Eisenach nodded, smiled. "The Treville gunpowder, the boy says. The gunpowder that has Treville's name written on it, that knows it belongs in Treville and not anywhere else? That calls out Treville's name from wherever it happens to have lost itself?" Eisenach shook his head. "Or maybe the Treville gunpowder doesn't exist. Maybe it never *did* exist because it never got made. Maybe the gunpowder that does exist has no name. It just is. And that's all there is. And even if you beat up whole hordes of us poor managers, that's all there will be until we can somehow cajole, coerce, or bribe those speechless wonders out there to *make more,* and make it faster. And then, the gunpowder that's just gunpowder will come to you in due time. And not a whit sooner, even if you give the poor director the walloping of his life. Even if you take his poor life."

"Let's talk about that," Abel said. He inched his chair closer, still not quite touching knees with the director, but very close. "The gunpowder that already *is.* You say it has no name. That it is like a piece of the River—water that might go flood the fields of Shandak Nalaby, that might flow through the shithouses of Bruneberg and carry away the crap. Or that might be drunk and come out as a stream of piss. Or that might go on and flow to the Braun Sea."

"Yes," said Eisenach. "Exactly. That's right."

"Sure," said Abel. "Water's water. But what about the water barrels."

"The . . . what?"

"The barrels you carry it in," Abel continued. "The pots you boil it in. The people who drink and piss.

All of those can have names attached. Maker's marks. Points of origin."

"I'm not sure I follow," Eisenach replied. "Would you mind moving back a little. It's feeling kind of hot in here."

"Yes," Abel said. He didn't move. "You know who I am, right? Joab Dashian's son. And you're right, I'm young. You called me 'boy,' and that's not far off. But my father, he doesn't think of me that way. Do you know how he thinks of me?"

"As a . . . man?" Eisenach replied, as if he were searching for the right answer to stave off violence or something worse.

Abel shook his head. "As a messenger," he said. "Because I am his son, he sent me with a message for you."

"Yes," Eisenach said. He let out a snorting breath, as if the tension, the uncertainty, building up in him like steam needed an outlet. "All right. What is it?"

"He says: 'Lindron doesn't have to know.'"

"He says *what*?"

Abel repeated his statement.

"What in hell does that mean?"

"I don't know," Abel said. "I'm just the messenger. The messenger *boy*."

"But then what—"

"There is one thing that was interesting about what he said."

"What was that?"

"It was *where* he said it."

"All right, I'll bite," Eisenach replied. "*Where* did he say it?"

"Oh, just a room. A room in the District Military

Headquarters complex," answered Abel. "The only unusual thing about that room is that it has a lock and a key. No guard, but a genuine lock of the finest mahogany, and a hardwood key, too. And a guard."

"And you say he was *in* the room when he gave you the message?"

"Yes."

"So? What was in the room, thrice-damn it!"

"Pieces of barrels."

"Pieces of . . ." But then Eisenach's face began to flush red. "And these . . . pieces of barrels . . . what did they say on them?"

"Some said, 'Made in Cascade,' and they have lot numbers stenciled on them, believe it or not," Abel said. "Some said 'Bruneberg Works,' and some said 'Danger, No Flames.'" Abel quickly moved his chair forward the final amount, touching knees with the director, looking him directly in the eyes from less than an arm's length away. "And just about all of them said 'Treville' on them. Those were my father's favorites. I believe he collected those in particular."

This is complete nonsense, of course, Center said. **There is no room. There are no barrels. The Blaskoye are careful to cover their tracks, which is one of the reasons we are here.**

Let Abel continue, Raj said. *He's doing exactly the right thing at the moment.*

"And where did all of these pieces come from?" asked Eisenach.

"The Redlands," Abel replied. "Can you believe it? All of them came from the Redlands. Pulled them off the packtrains of dead barbarians, mostly. The Blaskoye, they call themselves in our region. Sometimes, the

Scouts would just find the barrels out there. Piles of them. Empty. And it's funny how the Blaskoye never seem to run out of powder or muskets to kill us." He leaned forward, close to Eisenach's face. "To kill *my* men," he finished with a low growl.

"I-I'm sorry to hear that," the director replied, his voice shaking and his face going from the red flush to a deathly pale.

Human electrochemical reactions may be slow compared to electromagnetic responses on an individual basis, but their ability to achieve rapid system-wide effect is really quite impressive, particularly when the adrenalinoid neurotransmitters are involved, Center commented.

"District Commander Dashian—my father—has all of those labeled barrels and more. Testimony of captured Blaskoye transcribed to papyrus and attested to by priests."

"Obtained under torture, no doubt."

"It is very difficult to get a Redlander to talk otherwise," Abel replied.

"Who can believe barbarian lies?"

"The details of Blaskoye agreements never to attack Cascade so long as powder shipments continue," Abel continued. "Names. One in particular keeps popping up, Director Eisenach."

Eisenach sighed, looked down and rubbed his eyes, then turned his head back up but couldn't meet Abel's gaze. "I suppose these are to be sent to Lindron? These vile tales that besmirch the name of good men? Decent men who are merely trying to keep violence and death away from their families, their kinsmen." He looked on the verge of tears.

He's taken the bait, said Raj. **Now set the hook, lad.**

So it's back to lad again, is it? Abel thought. But he really didn't care, and Raj was right. Time to set the hook.

Abel pushed his chair back a few finger spans and considered the director. When he spoke again, it was in a calm tone of reasonableness, even reconciliation.

"Certainly. Commander Dashian is a man of the world," he said. "He understands these things. That's why he sent me to discuss the matter with you personally rather than shipping the evidence he's been gathering for the past two years down-River to Lindron. Out of regard for you, Director Eisenach, and people like you, who don't deserve the calamity such a revelation would bring about. On yourselves. Your family name."

"Yes, yes," Eisenach murmured. "That's just, that's right."

Abel leaned forward again, now all understanding and compromise. "But Director Eisenach, we need that powder. We need the three bargeloads that were promised and another shipment—oh, let's call it ten wagonloads—to bring you current. We need it to fight back, don't you see? Surely you understand how that is *also* just and right. And how delivering those three barges and ten wagons would keep the barrel shards and those papyrus scrolls from traveling to Lindron, to the Captain of the Tabernacle Guard, or even to the Chief Prelate himself."

"I do see that," Eisenach said, nodding his head furiously. "I do. But it's very difficult."

"Oh?"

"You see, they've been demanding more."

"Who?"

"The thrice-damned Redlanders, that's who! The Blaskoye!"

"I see," Abel said.

"They've cleaned out our production for the past three months. We meet their demands, and then they want even more. I tell you, it's—"

"Barbaric?" Abel said.

"Yes! They won't let up. Won't let us catch a breath in production. We're in arrears to *everybody*, not just to Treville."

"That's terrible," Abel said.

"So you see, we really don't have your powder."

"Obviously not," Abel said. "And yet, I think I see a solution."

"I wish you would tell it to me, then."

Abel nodded, and pushed his chair back a little more. *Give the guy a moment to breathe, to let down his guard yet again,* he thought.

Good lad!

"Let me tell you a story," Abel said. "And I want you to correct me where I'm wrong, Director Eisenach, all right?"

The other nodded.

"I'm trying to imagine who's really in charge around here. Is it the prelate?"

"That drunken old fool? No!" said Eisenach.

"I thought not," Abel replied. "And his priests either spend a great deal of time . . . seeing to their own needs, or else they're crazy. So that can't be it. But now, what about the DMC?"

"A thug," Eisenach replied. "I saw to his appointment myself." He chuckled.

Abel nodded. "Yes, I thought so. Bought and paid for. A bully, but not too bright, eh?"

"That's an understatement."

"So who *is* running Bruneberg and Cascade, I wondered to myself," Abel said. "And the only answer I can come up with is—*you*, Director. You and the First Families."

"Well, I wouldn't say 'running,' so much as—"

"Oh, come now, Director, you're much too modest. You are the lord of all you survey."

Eisenach blinked, thought for a moment.

He's almost figured out where this is going, said Raj. **Almost, but not quite, the poor sod.**

"I suppose you could say I have certain influence."

"I'd say you have a deciding influence," Abel replied. "And with that in mind, I have a proposition."

The director rubbed his chin. "All right. I'm listening."

"Take it from the Cascade arsenal."

"What? No, I—"

"Think about it, Director. You have your agreements in place with the Blaskoye. Your DMC said it himself: they haven't attacked Cascade District in twenty years. You don't really need that gunpowder here, and we do. So give it to me to take back to Treville. Immediately."

"But that would take . . . Yes, I suppose it could be done. I could even get the military to pack it up themselves."

"And if the DMC objects?"

"Him? You must be joking? I'd have him strangled and tossed out a Riverfront shithole." Eisenach mused. "And you're sure your father will not send the barrels if I do this?"

"I'm pretty certain," Abel said. "Like you, all he really wants is peace, commerce, and noninterference between districts."

Abel stood up, and Eisenach, as well, as if he were the one about to be dismissed—which he was.

Abel spit on his hand. "Ten wagons to return with me tomorrow? I'll meet them here on my way home. And the barges sent after to Garangipore."

"It will be done," Eisenach said. "And your promise, as the son of your father?"

"You have my word as a Scout and a Dashian," Abel replied. "Nothing will be sent to Lindron if we see that gunpowder."

Eisenach spit on his own palm, and the two men shook hands.

"I'm glad we can do business," Eisenach said. "It's so much more pleasant this way."

"Absolutely."

"And would you mind releasing my assayer on your way out?" Eisenach said. "I'm going to put him in charge of your arrangements."

"No problem, friend director," Abel answered. He bowed slightly, turned to leave, then called over his shoulder. "Besides, I'm fairly certain I'll have need of that knife on a few Redlander necks. Maybe even the very ones that *you* need killed, as well." He stalked to the door. "Nice doing business with you."

And then he was outside. When he extracted the knife from the wood, the assayer made a pleasant *thunk* as he fell to the ground.

While we must not underestimate Zentrum, we must also remember that he has set a difficult

goal for the Land. Center had been lecturing for what seemed to Abel like hours. Days, even.

Abel rode easily upon Spet, who shuffled forward at a slow pace. The return home had taken an additional six days due to the trail of ten gunpowder-filled wagons that he and Golitsin were shepherding back to the Hestinga garrison. A group of militiamen had accompanied them as guards, among them the two Scouts he had braced with his whip at the Cascade arsenal. Both had expressed a desire to transfer to Treville after they returned the empty wagons, and Abel had told them he would see what he could do about the matter.

Center droned on with the lesson, which, though important, was not anything Abel didn't already know: **Zentrum wishes all possibility for scientific or political advance destroyed, and yet he cannot allow the barbarians to entirely obliterate the culture of the Valley, lest there no longer be any Stasis to maintain. There must be conquest and domination, but there must also be assimilation.**

You are talking about the deaths of thousands of people. Women raped, children spitted. Donts with their legs hacked off or forever broken.

Not to mention the various forms of asphyxiation, excruciation, and sadistic torment the Blaskoye employ against their adult male enemies, Center replied dryly. **The human toll is of no consequence to Zentrum.**

Nor to you.

Nor to me, that is true, Center conceded. **But for those who *do* care about such matters, at least for the moment our mutual interests align.**

Comforting to know a cold thing like you is looking out for my interests.

Your taunts are pointless and misplaced, Center replied. **I am as incapable of being insulted as is a rock beside the road.**

My taunts make me feel better. Anyway, go on.

To achieve this balance I was speaking of, Zentrum needs the invasion to be slow and thorough rather than lightning quick. This will, of course, create even more suffering, and of a more agonizing nature. But it will also permit the invaders to be drawn into the local populace, to acquire some measure of local ways as they cement their conquest. And it will make them so weary of the battle that by the time they get to Lindron, they are ready for the compromise Zentrum will offer them: conquest and rule, but with Zentrum firmly in place as advisor.

And that means he cannot allow the militia to collapse and lose its fight too soon, Raj put in. *Zentrum will even encourage bravery and hard-fighting, and a degree of innovation, if he knows that in the end he can stamp it all out as the barbarians emerge triumphant.*

If we can anticipate his timing, we can disrupt him without giving away the game too soon—that there is active resistance that's aware of Zentrum's ultimate aim. He will, sooner or later, arrive at this conclusion. He's no idiot.

The inflection points will be several innovation thresholds, both in technology and tactics, Center continued.

And what am I supposed to do at these inflection points of yours?

Easy, answered Raj. **Ramp the innovation. Exploit every invention. Adopt new tactics for each advance.**

Why don't you just tell me how to build all the things you've spoken of? Your laser cannons, your tactical nukes?

You know the answer to that, lad.

You need an industrial base. Abel recited the oft-repeated lesson wearily. *Such devices don't spring from the air by wish alone.*

Precisely, Center said. **Zentrum remains powerful. He created the Land for his own preservation. All we have is you. For the moment.**

One heretic, trying to bring about a future nobody can hope for because they can't even imagine it.

You will have one advantage fairly soon, said Raj.

And what's that? You two, I suppose?

Raj's low and wicked laugh. **Breech-loading rifles,** he replied.

Abel had imagined a triumphal return and an understated but impressive parade through Hestinga with his wagons full of powder. Instead, a single rider met him a league from the western gate of Hestinga.

It was one of the cadets, Holman, who had been preparing for a billet with the Regulars. He galloped up on dontback and reined his mount to a stop in a cloud of dust. Abel trotted up to meet him.

"The commander sent me to find you," Holman said through a fit of coughing.

"Find me? I sent a flitter with news of our return. Don't tell me it didn't arrive?"

"He knows you're coming, and he knows what you're bringing," Holman said. "He sent me to tell you to get back as fast as possible with the powder—expend the pack animals if you have to, and even your own mounts."

"Why? What has happened?"

"You haven't yet heard?"

"No," Abel said, raising his voice, trying not to shout in frustration. "I have not. What is it?"

"The Blaskoye are in the Valley," said Holman. "Lilleheim has fallen."

PART THREE

The Woman

1

"It was a massed attack, as you might expect from that lot," said Joab. "But the occupation has been disciplined. That's what bothers me." They rode along the winding road that led from Hestinga to Lilleheim. On their left, the northwest, were rice paddies irrigated by the elaborate system of rams of water-lifting cranes. The cranes with their woven baskets dotted the landscape to the horizon. To the right, as the ground rose to the southeast, were flax, barley, and wheat fields, which did not require the regular flooding of the rice paddies. Abel knew these fields continued all the way to, and partially up, the Escarpment, which rose, filling the horizon, about a half-league away. "They took the town and stayed in place. I would have expected them to sack the town, kill everyone they could find, and either retreat or keep moving down the road to Hestinga. Instead, they've stayed in position and systematically burned every wooden structure in the town. The sky has been black with smoke from the thatching for three days. You can see it from here." He pointed to a black plume to the north wafting lazily upward, as if it were merely the smoke from some enormous cookfire chimney. "The Scouts report that each morning they crucify a new set of village elders outside the southern gate, the one that faces Hestinga."

"They want us to see it," Abel said. "It's a taunt."

"Clearly," his father replied. "And they want to enrage us. They're succeeding. Horst Danziger was a good friend of mine, and he was nailed up with yesterday's group of cross hangers. Your Sergeant Kruso managed to put a shot in his forehead before noon, blessed-be."

"Did he? Good man." Abel remembered Danziger slightly. Joab had many friends for someone who worked as hard as his father did, and it was hard to keep track. Abel knew that Joab considered his cultivation of the smart and useful citizens to be part of his job. "Horst was that big redheaded farmer who used to drink with you at that wine stall in the market you like, wasn't he?"

"When he was in town on deliveries."

"That's right, he was the oil maker. He worked those olive orchards up the Escarpment above the village, didn't he?"

"Bought them played out and managed to squeeze value from them despite it," Joab said. "Man after my own heart." Joab spat into the sand, as if to rid his mouth of a bad taste. "They nailed him to one of his own uprooted trees."

"Too bad," Abel said.

"I'm going to burn the Blaskoye bastard who did it

at the stake when I catch him," Joab said matter-of-factly. "And I'm going to use Horst's oil to do it with."

"Do you think they are counting on angering you? It could be a feint, to get you out of Hestinga."

Or an ambush, said Raj.

Unlikely at this juncture, although that is the ultimate strategy the Blaskoye will have to employ when their true invasion begins.

This isn't a real invasion?

It is a reconnaissance in force. A major raid, to be sure.

Observe:

Again he is on the flyer, soaring up, up, and then leveling out. Toward the north, toward the rising smoke of the burning village. Then through it. Spots of red raging light below, the fires so large they are visible even in the harsh light of the sun through the Land's cloudless sky.

My deductions from reports and from analysis of the terrain indicates a force of approximately eight hundred Redlanders to take the village and do the sort of damage we have seen.

Observe:

Now past the burning town, and up, up toward the Escarpment and the Lilleheim Trail, the footpath that led up through terraced fields to the crest of the Escarpment wall. Up and over this crest and—

Into the Redlands. And now the terrain becomes abstracted as Abel flies higher and faster. Labels appear. Oasis One. Oasis Two. Blaskoye strongholds along the dry gulch known as the Graben.

In wetter geologic times, the Graben was once a stream itself, a tributary of the River, said

Center. **Now all that are left are the wet spots. And of course the Blaskoye have found them, for they mean life itself in the Redlands.**

Now down, down toward a spot of green in the sea of red. The Great Oasis—

Which seemed to be surrounded by a system of straight lines, like scoremarks in the desert floor. Only when Abel was nearer did he see them for what they were. Corral fences. Campgrounds delineated. Order. Discipline. Numbers.

A huge force of Redlanders was gathered, was being gathered, for he saw more streaming in from outlying lands, many on dak-drawn wagons, some on donts, hundreds more walking.

So Lilleheim is just the tip of the spear.

Correct. Aimed at Treville. At your father, specifically. He is being targeted for his competency and the strength of the Treville Militia and Scouts. He holds the center. If Treville District falls, the Land will be open from north to south.

And if Treville holds firm?

Lindron is too well protected by the Tabernacle Guard, and the Valley too wide at that point for Blaskoye tactics, Raj said, his tone musing. **An invasion from the north sweeping down the Valley, I'd suspect.**

That is a ninety-two point four percent probability.

And if Treville falls?

Observe:

Terror in his veins, hard breathing. Running, running on his own two legs, his dont slain somewhere behind him in the retreat.

Make the River. Maybe a chance to make a stand. Or, if not, boats. An escape to the east. Anything besides this perpetual clash and retreat, clash and retreat—

But tired, so tired. The pounding of the thickened hoofpads of the Blaskoye mounts behind him thunderous, making it so hard to think—

And then, they are in front of him. A line of donts, with riders in flowing blue and white garb, their faces hidden behind turban windings. Only their eyes shining. Those hard, Redlander eyes watching him.

Rifles raised.

And he running toward them, for he cannot turn, cannot run back, or his pursuers will be upon him.

How did the others get in front of him, cut him off from the River?

And then he looks up, checks the sun in the sky. And knows.

He has become confused, somewhere in the dust behind. He has ever so slowly made an erroneous turn. And not only him, but the men he leads. The two hundred. The survivors. The final muster after the devastation at Garangipore.

They were to escape and begin the guerilla harassment.

They were to be the unvanquished.

And now a simple mistake.

So easy to do in his exhaustion.

So costly. So entirely his own fault.

He has slowly turned, somehow gotten off course. Has allowed his terror and tiredness to join the chase. He has allowed himself and his command to run right into the enemy's advancing, encircling front lines.

The Blaskoye rifles crackle.

We were to be the unvanquished.

The Redlanders reload. He raises his own weapon, but of course he is long out of caps and powder. Only bayonets remain, and the enemy will never allow him, allow any of his band, to get within range to use those.

The Blaskoye rifles crackle yet again.

And he is down, taken in the hip and shoulder. He has seen such wounds. He knows he will be a long time dying.

A long time to burn with the certain knowledge.

He is forever among not the unvanquished, but the vanquished.

Abel started in his saddle, almost sending his mount skittering. Joab, who was considering Abel's previous statement, didn't seem to notice.

"I believe it is a test," Joab said, nodding to himself. "Yes. They wish to gauge our response so they will know what to expect the next time. And the next."

Good head on his shoulders, that man, said Raj with an approving growl.

The Scouts had already been deployed to cut off a retreat up the Escarpment, or at least to harry any Redlanders if they did manage to break through. Abel had been reassigned to command the Militia Regiment, much to his chagrin at first, until Raj had pointed out that Joab had given him responsibility for his entire right. That, in fact, Joab intended to use the Regulars to drive the Redlanders out of the town directly into Abel's lines.

He's made you the anvil, lad, Raj said. *He knows the townfolk trust you, or at least they trust him, and know you are his son. They need a unified command.*

It is a good strategy if the goal is to drive the Blaskoye back where they came from, Center intoned. Notice that the southeast of the village is open. Joab doubts himself, and he is providing them with a route of retreat. With the proper stroke, he might annihilate them here.

The Scouts will take them when they retreat, Abel thought. *We will annihilate them.*

There is an eighty-seven point three percent chance that a significant portion of the Blaskoye will escape, said Center. The Scouts are too few.

Abel stopped arguing. He was sure that Center was correct—in the abstract. He always was. Yet there must be something...

He reached his command, a ragtag group of five hundred—one could hardly call it a regiment—that had taken up position behind a knoll to the south-southeast of the village. He was met by a group of three "captains," that is leaders elected from within the militia themselves. One of these he recognized. It was Fleming Hornburg, the son of Matlan Hornburg. He was arrogant and privileged, but Abel also knew him to be no coward. They'd tangled once in the market over a bumped shoulder, and the fight had been inconclusive. Of course Abel had been conscious of the fact that if he beat the living hell out of Hornburg, he would have put his father in a very awkward political position in the town, if not the district. Perhaps he'd pulled a couple of punches that might otherwise have ended it—and that perhaps would have ended Hornburg's existence as a result.

The other captain was a local miller named Prokopov. And their third Abel did not recognize. He was dressed in ill-fitting garb, as if he wore a shirt and trousers a size too big. He held a carbine in his right hand and had a bow and quiver strung across his back. Then Abel took another glance and realized—this was no man at all, or boy, either.

It was a young woman.

And then he realized that he *did* recognize her. Mahaut DeArmanville. This was the sister of Xander. She was the daughter of Henri DeArmanville, a lieutenant in the Regulars. No, not Mahaut DeArmanville. Mahaut *Jacobson*. She had recently married into the well-to-do Jacobson clan of Hestinga.

"Mahaut?" he asked. "Mrs. Jacobson? What are you doing here?"

"Same as you, sir," she answered. "I am the leader of the women's auxiliary."

"The—what? But that's a support group."

"We're going to support you by firing our muskets into the enemy."

Abel looked at her a moment, shook his head. "Where is your husband? What does he have to say about this?"

"He's with me," answered Prokopov, the miller, cracking the faintest of smiles. "And he says that he's tried for six months to break this mount..." He turned toward Mahaut and bowed. "Pardon me, ma'am." Mahaut nodded her assent for him to go on. "And he can't do it. He says he figures no man can if he cannot, but that maybe a fight will finally do his job for him. Break her, I mean. Make her a little more pliable."

Mahaut smiled, shook her head. "I'm pliable enough for what he wants," she said. "This is different. I have friends in that village. Lots of us women do. And we don't want to leave it all to the men, getting rid of the Blaskoye."

Mims accent, though Abel. It was a larger town, almost a city—although only Lindron would truly qualify for that distinction given what he'd been shown by Center and his projections—and the women were given more leeway there than elsewhere in the Land, at least anywhere Abel had been. They might hold professions other than teacher or whore in Mims, for instance.

"I want you in the rear," Abel said. "You and the other women."

"We want to fight, Lieutenant," she said. Being the daughter of DeArmanville, she would know his official rank. "Lots of us are armed with muskets—older ones, true—and all of us have had practice with bow and even spear. I've seen to it for months, ever since they elected me."

She's right about one thing. A woman can pull a trigger just as easily as can a man, Raj said. *And she looks to be capable with that bow, or at least she wears it well.*

Abel looked at Mahaut, blinked once. They had met several times at officers' family get-togethers, but she, being a year his senior—an enormous gap at fourteen—had barely given him the time of day. For his part, he hadn't thought her particularly comely. Her diaphanous robes were the best one could get from the linen works of Fyrpahatet, the seaside town where a leaf-eating creature that produced the fiber thrived, but she'd worn them indifferently. Although she was pretty enough, she'd also had on hardly a smudge of makeup back then, and he'd believed her skin was on the darker side of bronze, until he'd noticed a tan line near her shoulder.

Exactly the lighter strip that a quiver strap might create, he now realized.

Most of the girls of Hestinga worked hard to stay out of the sun and remain light-toned, even those who were black and brown by ancestry. The idea, Abel supposed, being that un-tanned skin signaled less work in the sun, and hence a higher social status. Obviously, this did not matter to Mahaut Jacobson, and if it mattered to her husband, he hadn't been able to persuade her of the matter.

"Listen," he said to her. "We're circling that knoll to the west"—he pointed to the rise to the northwest, beyond which lay Lilleheim—"and forming up half way down the beginnings of the Escarpment slope. If you're in the rear, you'll be *above* the main body of militia. You'll have a clear sightline to the Blaskoye if they make a run for us, which I'm guessing they will."

"But I—"

"You'll get your chance to prove all that target practice was worth it," Abel said.

"Why not put us up front and closer to start with," she quickly replied. "Let us fire a volley, then the men come up and absorb us into the lines?"

She isn't going to let this go, Abel thought. *She's got a vision of how she wants it to be, and, like many soldiers, myself included before I gained more experience, isn't willing to let that vision of glory go, even under changing circumstances.*

"I could order you away entirely if you keep questioning my judgment. I believe I could get Fleming here to back me up, couldn't I?"

"Damn right," said Hornburg. "There's no place for women in any of this. They're just going to be a nuisance and probably get more of us killed than had to be."

Abel turned back to Mahaut. "See?" he said. "That's what you're contending with here. I'm your friend." He motioned over his shoulder. "The enemy is that way."

"I know that," she answered, "Lieutenant."

"Then listen to me," Abel continued, trying to strike a conciliatory tone. "This is Militia, not Regulars, Mahaut. You, of all people, should know what that means. The chance that we would be able to advance in an orderly fashion around you is next to nothing. What will actually happen is utter confusion. People dying as a result. Trampling. And the loss of any respect you have gained so far for your women."

Mahaut looked thoughtful, and then chagrined. Maybe he was getting through to her.

"So take your position and rain some fire down on those bastards when the time comes," he said.

Mahaut nodded, and snapped to attention. "Yes, sir," she said. "That we will do."

"Good," Abel said, and then he turned to the disposition of his remaining troops.

He formed them into an obtuse angle along the contours of the knoll and the rising Valley floor to the northwest. The miller Stopes's men, who were mostly made up of town merchants, manufacturers, and guildsmen, he put on the knoll, with Fleming Hornburg's farmers, serfs, and sharecroppers along the

Escarpment rise. His idea was to cut off the Redlanders to the northeast and force them west as they fought, back up the Escarpment trail that led down into Lilleheim—up toward the supposedly waiting Scouts.

He would have to hope village fire-drill practice had been thorough enough. He knew the Regulars would be massed three lines deep, with each group engaged in a separate part of reloading of muskets. He could count on no such orderly engagement from the Militia, or really, any order at all. They would therefore form a single line.

At least they have the high ground, Abel thought. *Although I doubt a single one of them has practiced firing downhill.*

It was going to be interesting.

And, with a shout, a crackle, and a rising cloud of black powder exhaust, the attack of the Regulars began.

Abel sprang onto his dont. He was occupying the salient in his lines, the crook of the angle, which gave him a fairly unobstructed view of his entire force.

The thrice-damned farmers were charging.

What was Hornburg thinking? Abel had given explicit orders to hold position, wait for the Blaskoye to appear as they were driven toward Abel's Militia. And even then, *wait for Abel's command.*

Obviously this had meant nothing to the Hornburg idiot. Without another thought, Abel kicked his dont into motion and charged down the hill. It took him a moment to get in front of the charging line, but he was on dontback, and they, except for a small cavalry unit, were on foot, and he outpaced them. They had discovered what soldiers for millenia had found to be true: a charge downhill, whether mounted or on foot, inevitably became a trot before too many paces, as men and animals stumbled. Abel turned along the lines, riding in front of them.

"Halt! Halt!" he called. "Wait for the others! Halt, I say!"

And most of them did. All except Hornburg and his "cavalry" unit. The sixteen donts and riders charged forth down the slope and toward the village. They reached the edge, aiming their short-barreled carbines ahead of them. Plumes flew back from their saddles, and one carried a regimental standard, blue and white, that streamed behind.

They did look glorious. Brave. Gallant.

Abel stopped up short near the end of the line, which had now halted its advance, entered again with the troops.

"Come on, boys," he said. "I hope you give it to them."

But they rode right into a fusillade of lead, just as he'd feared they would. The invisible scythe cut through them, taking man from saddle and felling donts with flowering wounds to the head or legs. The charge seemed to hesitate, lose steam. And then, as if by signal, the donts broke and parted, some to one side, some to another, as if the unseen clump of those riflemen who opposed them were a literal wedge. There was more fire from along the edge of the village, and the donts turned entirely about and were scrambling back toward Abel and the lines. Quite a few of them were merely obeying the herd instinct to follow the group, and were riderless now.

"Thrice *damn* him," Abel said. He turned to a nearby solider. "Find me Captain Hornburg. Do you see him?"

"He rides the spot-faced doe yonder," said the other, pointing to a dont. Its rider was still in the saddle, but was slumped over, holding to an arm.

Up rode Fleming Hornburg. There was fire in his eyes for Abel. "You Scout scum, you Zentrum-damned sellout! You cut off my support! I'll see your command taken for that! I'll see you hanged for a coward, that's what!"

Hornburg turned his dont, grazed the flank against Abel's own animal, and Abel's leg. A childish attempt to embarrass him, as even Hornburg must know he would be able to quickly slip the foot free and avoid injury.

"You're wounded, sir," Abel said.

"A scratch, you stupid fool," Hornburg shouted back. He raised his carbine and pointed it at Abel. Abel stood his ground, still in the saddle of his dont Spet—a beast which had faced open muzzles before, and did not shy.

"Lower that rifle, Captain," Abel said.

"I should shoot you down where you stand."

Abel did not move. His own carbine remained in its saddle holster and his dragon blunderbuss tucked in his waist band.

Hornburg pulled the trigger.

Click.

Nothing.

Of course nothing, Abel thought. *You haven't had time to reload. The only chance was that you hadn't gotten a shot off in the first place.*

Even as he thought this, Abel moved forward. Using his momentum, he snatched the rifle from the hands of an amazed Hornburg, then wheeled about, rejoined the line, and, in full sight of the men, carefully and quickly reloaded—a task he knew he could do in better than half the time of all but a few who might be watching. He took a cap from his cartridge box, half cocked the trigger, and then held the rifle, butt-first, in an outstretched hand toward Hornburg.

"Here, Captain," he calmly said. "Now it's ready to use again. At my command."

Hornburg sat staring hatred at him for a moment. Then he reached out and snatched the gun from Abel, wheeled and rejoined his other Scouts, who were back in the lines once again a short distance away.

Abel pushed through and rode along the rear of his line back to his previous position at the salient. There was more crackling and war cries from the village, but the lines held firm, waiting. It seemed to Abel, gazing down it, that the line itself was trembling in anticipation.

Then the waiting was over.

2

With a shout, the Blaskoye emerged en masse from the buildings and ran across the small fence that demarcated the village boundary. Most were on dontback. They charged into the open field, and, at shouted order, a group of perhaps fifty riders wheeled to guard their rear.

I've never seen Blaskoye so disciplined, Abel thought. *Who are those guys?*

The remainder made for the hill, seemingly zeroing in on the knoll as a rallying point.

They were in for a surprise.

"Hold," he shouted down the line. "Hold for the girls!"

And they did hold, this time. Even Hornburg. The Militia waited, grim-faced, as the Blaskoye drew nearer and nearer.

Into musket range. Past it.

Was she going to fire? Abel whirled, trying to pick

out Mahaut among the mass of women on the hillside, but could not. They all had weapons at ready, however, at least all of them who were armed with muskets.

Another second, another.

Yes, he thought. *That is my range, not theirs. She does right to wait.*

And then the muskets behind him crackled to life, and Abel whirled to look upon the damage. Blaskoye fell from saddles, donts screamed and whirled. The charge reached the first of the upslope. Slowed.

Some raised carbines or even bows and fired at Abel's lines.

The arrows fell short. The minié balls did not. Several men on Abel's line crumpled, fell. First blood. Would they break for cover or hold firm?

And could Mahaut get another round into the Redlanders? Had she drilled her women *that* well?

He got his answer with another crackle of fire, this time more ragged, not as loud—

—but adequate to fell several more riders.

It's time, lad.

Yes.

He raised an arm. "Fire!" he shouted, and brought it down.

The massed line responded. Not quickly, not half as smoothly as the well-drilled women's auxiliary, but adequately. A plume of smoke traveled down the line as the order to fire seemed to be communicated as if by word of mouth.

Sergeants shouted their order to reload, but this was hardly necessary, as the men quickly began to do so as soon as they were able.

Still the Blaskoye came on, their donts raised on

their hind feet now, huffing up the hill toward the line, and now not twenty paces away.

Some spooked and raised their muskets with ramrod still in the end. Fired ball and rod both to no effect.

Some broke and ran.

Most completed the reload, brought rifles back to bear—

When a cloud of arrows rained down on the advancing Blaskoye.

The women had changed weaponry.

This was too much. The charge faltered, broke. The donts turned around in general retreat down the hillside.

But there were Blaskoye shouts of muster. They were not in retreat, but had merely pulled back to regroup, have another go.

Abel couldn't make out what they were doing exactly, could only see a whirlwind of donts and men within a cloud of spent powder and kicked-up dust. But he could see beyond the Blaskoye, to the village itself.

And that was when he saw Joab's Regulars burst forth from the village and attack the Blaskoye rear.

The rearguard of the Blaskoye that had been left behind fired and fought wildly, but many times their number streamed past and overran them.

The Blaskoye whirled blindly amid more dust, chuffed barley, and powder clouds.

Abel unconsciously and from long practice raised the scarf around his neck to cover his mouth and nose. He then reached backward, all without taking his eyes from what was happening below, and slid his carbine from its holster. He raised the gun into the air.

"Charge!" Abel shouted. He lowered the carbine

and kicked his mount to action, downward, toward the cloud of screaming, bellowing donts and men.

Down the hillside they went, with Abel and the other dont riders far in the vanguard. In fact, despite his reining Spet back to a canter, too much so. He slowed his mount, allowing the foot soldiers to catch up behind him—not for support, but so that they could take full advantage of any opening he made in the Blaskoye.

Then he entered the dust-and-powder cloud and into mayhem. Pieces of the enemy. An arm there, the dull glint of a musket there. The white and terrified eye of a dont, a snot-streaming muzzle.

He struggled to find a target that would hold still long enough. Then the cloud parted for a moment, and a large Blaskoye warrior was suddenly revealed. Blue and white clothes, red sash around the waist. Legs gripping the flanks of the dont tightly, expertly, for the Blaskoye, unlike the people of the Land, did not use stirrups on their saddles.

The Redlander seemed almost . . . vulnerable, so revealed. But then he started to raise his weapon, a wicked-looking bow, already nocked with arrow.

Abel fired the carbine.

The man flinched, caught in the chest. The bow fired—directly into the neck of his mount. Purple-brown blood erupted. The beast, enraged by the arrow, reared, spun—then charged off into the dust. Had he made a kill? There was no way to know.

He drew his blunderbuss pistol.

Whizz!

A shot streaked nearby, whistling death.

The one you hear—

But Abel couldn't complete the thought. A scream, and behind him a Blaskoye with a raised scimitar charging toward him. It was all Abel could do to get the dragon aimed and fire. The other fell backward in the saddle as if he'd been pushed on the chest, then slid off the rear of his beast as if he'd merely fallen asleep.

Now a roar from behind, which it took Abel a moment to realize was the sound of his own charging men. They swarmed around him. After a moment, he pushed his beast forward, toward the village. Back through the front of his lines again and—

Out of the swirling dust and smoke.

The remainder of the Blaskoye were caught in the pincer of the Regulars and the Militia. They rode about in confusion, terror, rage.

And entirely in vain.

Another reload and he was ready, but then the shouting, manic voice of Joab screamed an order. The order taken up by his officers, passed along.

"Cease fire!"

Abel realized that Joab's men had been about to shoot directly into his, Abel's, advancing line.

"Bayonets!" he heard his father shout. "Forward!"

The Regulars, drilled daily on such orders, obeyed without hesitation, moving at an inexorable slow trot.

His own men were still running pell-mell. But it didn't matter now. The Blaskoye were caught, surrounded. Hornburg and his dont riders struck, along with Joab's cavalry. Then the foot soldiers closed in.

It was bloody. It was hard fought.

And within half an hour, it was over. All the Blaskoye were either dead or unhorsed and captured.

At least so Abel thought. For suddenly, just as the last of the mopping up had seemed to be accomplished, there came a cry from the village, and the renewed bellow and scream of donts.

He tried to locate the source.

The low cry of a bone horn. Two. Three. The Blaskoye instrument of war.

They want us to look, find them, to see.

And he whirled toward the village—

And *did* see.

Blaskoye on dontback, perhaps thirty or so, riding out, riding directly toward them, toward the assembled forces of Treville.

And no Blaskoye with a drawn musket.

Only with a gleaming knife, each taken from some scrapyard of the Redland sandpits and worked to sharpness. Each knife held at a neck.

The neck of a child.

On they rode, closer.

Is that—? Can they really be—?

Aye, it is, Raj growled. **Aye, it is.**

They were using the village children as shields. Among the Militia and Regulars, carbines whirled, hard eyes aimed.

And then the guns lowered. The riders came on.

They slowed but slightly. Enough to allow the lines to part.

They parted not far from Abel, and he saw the Blaskoye riders.

These were not run-of-the-mill warriors. Anyone could see it who had eyes. First, they did not wear mere loose garments, but linen tunics, red sash belts, and legwraps, all very similar to the uniform of the

Scouts. They wore turbans of iron red, so there was no mistaking them for Scouts, however.

Most of all, their faces were swirled with tattoos. Angry welts that looked more burned into place with firebrands than inked with charcoal-coated thorns.

The one who rode in the lead was not the largest, but there was something about him that seemed to bristle more than the others. Perhaps it was the fact that he held an actual *silver* knife.

No, not silver, said Center. **It is steel and chrome. The surface is an electroplated coating of chromium. Very curious.**

Whatever it was made of, it gleamed against the throat of a little girl, dark-haired, who looked about terrified. A bead of blood like gemstones had formed where the knife had already sliced into skin.

"You!" shouted Abel. "You, silver knife!"

At this, the Blaskoye turned and looked about furiously.

Abel pointed the dragon pistol at him. It was reloaded. Somehow he'd done it in the turmoil. It was cocked and ready to fire.

The Blaskoye met Abel's gaze. He did not flinch, but returned it as hard and as void of mercy as it had been delivered.

Then he smiled, and with a kick, urged his dont on. Through the lines they went and up the hill.

The women, Abel thought. *They won't see in time. Won't know.*

He turned and galloped after the Blaskoye. But it was too late.

A crackle of fire. Two, three Blaskoye fell. As did their hostages.

And then a cry of anguish, of horror, as the Blaskoye drew near and the women saw what they had done.

That was when, at an order from the one with the silver knife, the Blaskoye drew their carbines and, keeping their children in hand, raised the guns and fired into the crowd of mothers, sisters, and wives, armed, but unable to shoot, held back by a compassion that proved their own undoing.

The Blaskoye rode through the hole they had blasted in the line of the woman auxiliaries. And then they were up the hill and away.

The Scouts are out there, Abel thought. *They'll get them.*

I wouldn't be so certain, Raj said. **A gang like that will have considered that possibility. They may have an alternate route.**

Indeed, said Center. **The Scouts cannot be everywhere, and this one, the leader, is one who can guess where they have stationed themselves and avoid it.**

He's the leader? Silver knife?

Chrome. Yes. Psychometric observation of his subordinates' comportment confirms to a high certainty this status.

I want to kill him.

Of course you do, lad, said Raj.

I will kill him.

To this, Raj did not answer.

Then Abel rode up the hill to the women and saw what the Blaskoye had wrought. A dozen lay wounded, dead, or dying.

Among these was Mahaut. Her right leg and a portion of her belly had been laid open by a minié ball. She was still alive, but Abel did not think she could survive such a wound. He dismounted, knelt beside her.

Was there a watersack canteen nearby? Yes. He pulled one from a dead body, brought it to Mahaut.

"I live," she said.

"Yes," he answered. "Drink."

He drizzled water over her lips, and she licked them.

"The girl," she said.

"Yes," said Abel.

"He had her."

"Yes," said Abel.

He dripped another bead of water onto Mahaut's lips, and she coughed blood. He took off his scarf and wiped the blood away from her lips so she could draw in a ragged breath. There was nothing he could do about the groin, the gut.

"My niece," she said. "A Jacobson. But still. Mine. Loreilei."

"Oh," he said.

"My husband?"

"I don't know," Abel said.

"Fuck," she said as a wave of pain hit her. "Fuck, fuck."

And then her head fell to the side and she was unconscious, bleeding her life away.

Abel set her down and remounted. The men of the Militia were beginning to catch up with him, and the surviving women were gathering around. When he had a sufficient number in earshot, he called out to them.

"We will follow," he said. "We will find them. We will stop them. And we will not stop until we take our children back."

It took only until sunset. The circling kill-flitters showed the way.

They lay in a pile on the side of a defile that led upward toward the Escarpment proper, and at first it had looked to Abel like a pile of dak carcasses, the sort he might see in the butcher's yard before a feast day.

But these were not daks.

Abel wondered for a moment why here, why he—the one he now thought of as Silver Knife—had chosen this spot. The path did not seem to grow any steeper here. There was no particular landmark. It was only a gravel-filled gulley.

Then Abel turned around and looked back into the Valley.

There was a clear sight of Lilleheim below.

He must have shown them the village before he ordered them slain, Abel thought. *One last glimpse of the home they would never see again.*

Yes, Center said. **That is how it was.** He offered no further deductive reasoning beyond this pronouncement.

And they are all here? All these children of Lilleheim?

No, Center answered.

No?

The count is wrong for that. There is one missing.

Which one—

But he already knew the answer.

The Jacobson girl. Silver Knife had kept her. As a taunt.

Yes.

3

Observe:

Mahaut did not die.

There were times she wished she had. The pain was impossible, especially after the shock wore off and her body grasped in its thoughtless but no less living manner the completion of agony, the outrage, that had been perpetrated upon it. For days she lay in all-clenching hurt, half-comatose, half-inflamed suffering. Her eyes were closed, her teeth grinding.

There was the smell, as her body rotted, for company. Always the moment when any who visited her, even those prepared, those who *knew* what to expect, *flinched* at the stench.

Except for the Scout. He had come with her brother to visit and had seemed not disgusted by, or piteous, but—this was the strange thing—angry. Angry that this was happening to her.

It was a feeling she shared.

"I will not let this happen again." She'd heard his voice in her delirium, wasn't even sure whom he was speaking to. To her it sounded like a dialog, but with one listener and speaker located in such a way that he was impossible to hear.

I am dreaming, she thought at one point. *A fever dream.*

But such lucid moments were few and far between.

"There has to be something, thrice-damn it. I can't let what happened to my mother go on and on in the Land, bring needless death to—"

A pause.

"Yes, she does look a bit like her. What of it?"

A pause.

"I do not expect to save every person, or every woman. At least not at first. Just her."

A pause.

"I am aware she is married."

A pause.

"Why don't you just consider it an experiment? You foresee no long-term imbalances, so let me do this with the knowledge you have given me. In exchange, I will see to those breechloaders."

A pause.

Then a laugh. And something else he'd said, something she later couldn't believe she'd heard, had to believe was blurred by her fever into incomprehensibility. "Anyway, Zentrum is the local enemy. Zentrum works for death, even if he doesn't know. I want to work for life. I couldn't save my mother, so let me save her."

Then curses and orders to servants. The others, the servants, responded to his voice; it was no longer a one-way overheard dialog, but the words she remembered were *his*.

The Scout is caring for me. He has taken me as his charge.

"I want all of these bandages boiled, do you hear me! Better let me do it, as a matter of fact. I do not want the wound touched without instruments that have not been boiled. Not once, not ever. I will set my Scouts on you if you do it. You know they are one step away from a Redlander. They might boil *you* alive.

"And I will provide salve for the wound. Take this nightmare sludge away and bury it. Better yet, feed it to the carnadons at the lake. They are getting to be a menace, and it will kill them straight off!

"Yes, I'll be consulting with her physician, as well. He won't give you any trouble about following my orders after he and I have a good talk. I'll tell him about my Scouts, too, and their very large cook pot."

She rotted. But only to a point. Something was strong within her, something that was not her will, but was a blind urge to overcome, to thrust out the creeping death. She took no credit for it. She often just wanted to die.

And she received the new bandages every day of impossibly clean and white linen—no cloth in the Land had ever been so well-washed, she thought—and the salve the Scout had concocted and brought.

So many others died of much less, and she believed for a time that she was undeserving, that being alive, getting better, was punishment. It was punishment for letting him, the one who had shot her—oh, she remembered the squinting eyes, the careful aim, she knew *him*—take the girl.

Take the girl alive into the Redlands.

I should have shot Loreilei, Mahaut told herself. *And if not with the gun, well, then I was close enough to even put an arrow in her eye.*

Better her niece were dead than what lay in store for her in the Redlands.

And so Mahaut had taken her own healing as Zentrum's judgment upon her, as the punishment of the Law for the stupid mistake of believing that the Blaskoye would have any mercy whatsoever. That if he did not release the girl, he would at least have the decency to kill her on his way out.

But he had not done so.

And then the pain of her wound slowly abated from mind-burning to endurable. The smell lessened in pungency. The maggots the Scout lieutenant had so carefully picked from her flesh week after week one day did not return. And the scar tissue began to form its jagged welt of remembrance.

And it was the Scout who told her that the ball was still within her, that he could not extract it without risking her death.

Then the other news: that the ball had likely destroyed her womb. That it would be a miracle if she could have children now.

The dreams began. Of the minié ball pushing through her flesh. Pushing deeper, deeper into her, like some unholy nishterlaub seed that had been planted deep.

No. The Blaskoye's seed. His loathsome seed. And in the dreams, she was pregnant with the Redlander's bastard. A creature, not a child, a parasite that ate her from within. That whispered to her from the *inside,* where only she could hear, "I am his, and you are his, and you will take me to him, drag yourself to him, so that I can be born, so that he can draw me from you as he might a weapon from a wound."

Edgar, her husband, had taken one look at her and had not returned to see her. He was rumored to have journeyed to Garangipore to see about a crop on family land there and oversee the transfer of grain to the barges. She supposed she was still married to him, that he wouldn't cast her off in this state. She was certain the family had told him about her now barren womb.

Her mother and father could not bear to witness what had happened to the one they had known as an innocent child, and had only occasionally visited after an initial flurry. Only Xander, her brother, came and kept coming. And the other, the lieutenant. Abel Dashian.

Why?

She'd asked herself that several times, and had no answer. She had even asked him, at one point demanded, that he go and never return. But he hadn't answered, and he hadn't obeyed.

Finally she had told him about the dreams. She'd told him in hopes that this would disgust him, make him hate her for a traitor to both womankind and to the Land, to Zentrum Himself.

But he'd only listened and nodded.

"I think I understand what it's like to have thoughts, things you can't control, rattling around in your mind," he'd said.

And she'd asked, "How could you?"

And he'd answered, "Oh, you might be surprised." But had said no more on the subject. "What will you do when you get better?" he'd asked.

This had set her to quiet thinking for quite some time. She hadn't even considered the matter before. But now it appeared she might live, might walk, might one day get rid of the bedsores on her back and shoulders, stand up and be able to take a shit without soiling her linens. One not inconceivably distant day. And then what?

Edgar? She'd been bought cheap. Her father's position and a not inconsiderable dowry from her mother's family had been the attraction. Those must have been the prime attractions, for she'd always known herself to be not homely, but boyish in her ways. This she blamed on her father and her brother, for drawing her in on the play battles, the fights with wooden swords and knives, and most of all the archery and the sharpshooting. It hadn't helped when they found that she was by far the best shot in the family.

And she blamed her mother for letting them do it. For never sitting her down and telling her that this is not what young ladies *do*. For perpetually believing she'd outgrow her urge to—

Say it.

To fight. To battle. To overcome a foe. To conquer within the small domain she ruled.

These were not the sentiments a woman should possess. Not in this town, in any case, military brat or no.

She knew what she ought to want. To beguile. To ensnare. To fulfill. To complete.

These were the traits of a woman.

She'd worked at it, become competent in the arts. Dress. Comportment.

But she never stopped beating the boys at their own games, and liking it.

Until the one came along who put a bullet in her

gut and showed her that she could not beat all boys at all games.

For a while, she'd believed she'd met her match in Edgar. He had not put up with her willfulness, had showed a cool disdain for her uppity nature.

And yet he had clearly liked her, and liked her a lot—to the point she'd had to fight him off before the betrothal, claw him away, until she was ready for it, for him in that way.

"Nobody ever denies me," he'd said. "But you deny me, and it just makes me long for you more."

And so they'd gone on with him insulting her, and yet always returning, and driving off the few other suitors who had had the temerity to risk this one, the carnadon girl who would bite your head off as soon as look at you if you dared to suggest she was weak or changeable or was any other of the traits that made up and defined a woman.

Despite it all, she'd been flabbergasted when Edgar had asked her to marry him.

She still wasn't sure exactly what he'd been thinking, for they'd gone for one another's throats on the wedding night itself when she'd refused him what he believed was his manly due.

Oh, not the sex. She'd given that willingly enough, and liked it, too, for that, too, proved to be a kind of battle.

No, the other. When he told her she would have to give up her bow and arrows. When he told her he would now see her light-skinned and not tanned from the sun, and what was more, she would show herself to others, reveal her new class and status by the clothes she wore, which would have to change.

It would all have to change, for he intended to show them all, all the others, that he was the one who could tame her, tame the wild DeArmanville girl.

Did she not know she'd become quite a legend?

And by winning her, he had won a bet, a rather large wager, with a friend that *no one*, ever, would tame that woman.

So it was all a sort of rich boy joke, according to him. But now that he had her, the joke was over, for both of them, and life must begin. Respectable life. Doing things the way they had always been done.

Had he not known her before? Had he thought her entire way of being in the world would disappear from the sheer act of marriage under the Law and Zentrum?

They'd fought. Endlessly. And of course he could not bloody her lip, twist an arm, or bruise her body, without the aid of a servant or two to restrain her, which proved far too embarrassing to him to do more than once or twice.

She was a much better fighter than he, and—if *she'd* had a mind—could repeatedly have beaten him to a bloody pulp.

The sex had remained good, got even better, until, after two years, the good sex was all there was other than the hatred.

No child resulted. Of course he blamed her.

Now that was gone. At least, she thought it must be gone along with her torn flesh. She had no doubt that in appearance, her vagina would seem little more than the extension of the mass of scar that was forming upon her inner thigh and belly. Unless, of course, she could convince him he was hurting her, opening the wound once more, by fucking her.

Edgar was the sort who would go for that.

But she knew herself that it would become just too ... wearying to keep up. She'd laugh one day instead of cry, and he'd be on to the fact that she was enjoying herself once more, and that would ruin everything for him.

Yet he would not divorce her. Jacobsons didn't divorce. It was almost unheard of in Treville, in any case.

So the solution would be—living apart. But how could she manage that?

Because she still would want and need. She could feel it now. She was still a woman, despite her ravaged womb. And if Edgar wouldn't have her and she could take no other lover ...

Why didn't he kill me? Why did he aim low? Did he know he was letting me live? Allowing me to crawl the earth, with me knowing I did so only because of his passing whim?

It was going to be a long and painful life, any way she looked at it.

Then the day came when she could stand. He was there at the moment she did so, Abel. He was the one who helped her to her feet, who braced her from behind as she slowly learned to use her legs again.

There would always be the limp, yes. Always the reminder to the world of what she knew she was inside now. Torn. Broken. Barren. But she learned to walk again.

I calculate that this representation is an accurate interpolation to nine-six point seven-three-five hundreds of a percentage point, said Center.

Observe what? Abel thought. *What did you want*

*me to learn, to see? Her state of mind? Why did you
show me this, Center?*

**I think he's pointing out the fact that you are
falling in love with her, lad,** Raj said.

And how this may become a problem, Center
added.

Shut up, both of you. Let's see to the breechloaders.

"So you understand, muzzle loading is the issue,"
Abel said to the priest.

Raf Golitsin sat back in the chair in his small office.
They were in the rear of the armory, which itself was one
of the four primary structures in the temple compound
of Hestinga. It was where the muskets came from.

Abel had passed through what had seemed an erupt-
ing hot spring of heat and activity on his way back to
the office. He'd been blindfolded by Golitsin, as was
required of all nonclerical entrants to the area, but
Golitsin had used muslin gauze, which was the understood blindfold of choice for officials who were in small
danger of misusing priestly secrets. Abel had seen all.

The firing mechanisms of the muskets in for repair
were dismantled to a degree Abel had not imagined
possible. Flaws were annealed in glowing forges. Other
parts were filed, planed, oiled. Barrel bands were pulled
from rifle stock, and barrels themselves were dismantled,
reamed. Rifling was done with an enormous handcranked
screw, itself made of a metal of a hardness Abel had
never seen before. Golitsin called it a drillpress and die.

The stocks were lovingly reconditioned. Some were
willow-wood, but most were made from the hardwood
maple of the Delta.

A local cambium-producing flora, not related

to Earth's maples genetically, but similar in dendrological characteristics, Center said.

And in the rear was the rebuild shop, where all came back together to produce the reconditioned rifle. Here the most skilled priest-smiths worked, checking each component and, in a final step, test firing and calibrating sights using complicated instruments that, anywhere else, would have been considered utterly nishterlaub, and probably poisonous to the touch, as well.

They closed the door to Golitsin's office—a wooden interior door, rather than beads, was a necessity here to keep out the noise of the shop—and Abel, still excited from what he'd just witnessed—*From the possibilities, most of all,* he thought—proceeded to lay out his plans for a new kind of gun that would help them stem another Blaskoye invasion.

"It comes down to this: reloading is slow and you die," Abel continued. "You have to put in the powder, put in the ball, ram them down the barrel. Put your primer cap over the nipple so that its fire will ignite the gunpowder within the barrel. And only then can you aim and fire. And hope you've done it all right. And then start all over again as fast your love of life demands of you, because they are coming right for you, the ones who want to kill you, while you are doing this."

"So you need to make the steps quicker," said Golitsin. "Or combine them."

"Yes," Abel said. "And here is my idea."

Or the idea that was delivered to me from the stars, Abel thought. *The stars that are suns, and the planets that circle them filled with other men who have discovered and lost this knowledge a hundred, a thousand times. I can barely conceive of this after*

a lifetime's instruction, so I won't tell you that, my
friend Golitsin. You'll think I'm crazy, as I may well be.

"First of all, the cartridge. It needs to combine the
percussion cap. And we have to get rid of this biting
off and pouring. I'll show you my idea—"

Abel took out the scroll. On it was the cartridge
design he had copied from memory, from the picture
that Center had placed in his mind.

"I see, I see," Golitsin said. "A cylinder. One end
the cap, the other the minié ball."

"Yes," Abel said. "The paper cartridge should be
the diameter of the rifle bore. It should fit snugly,
but not so tightly it can't slide into place. They must
be extremely uniform."

"We can wrap them around a dowel," Golitsin said,
scratching his head. "We can hold them together with
glue, I suppose. I'll have to work up a prototype for
you to take a look at."

He grunted in consternation. "But this will be
pointless without a way to load it. You can't ram it
down the barrel from the muzzle."

Abel smiled. Golitsin was getting it. He was understanding the problem, and so approaching the solution.
Raf Golitsin was a very intelligent man, but if he
could get it, many others might, as well.

"We are going to load it from the rear of the barrel," Abel said. He broke out the second scroll with
his drawings on it. "It will require a new mechanism."

"A new . . . mechanism?"

"Yes," said Abel.

"Use of nishterlaub remains is sanctioned only for
piecemeal work. Combinations are forbidden," Golitsin
said from rote memory. "A mechanism is a combination

of simple machines. You know this, of course. It's a basic Thursday school lesson."

"What I know," Abel said. "What I know: we are faced with an enemy concentrated in overwhelming numbers. No one is going to send help. Cascade is corrupt. Ingres barely has a force of Regulars, and no Militia to speak of. Lindron feels secure and will do nothing until it is too late."

"This is heresy, Abel," said Golitsin. "You are asking me to commit heresy."

"This is survival."

He waited. He could see the eagerness on Golitsin's face, the desire to know *how*. The need to try something *new*. He could also see that this longing was at war with a thousand Thursday school lectures.

Golitsin blinked twice as if to clear his eyes, shook his head. The inner war was over. All that remained was to discover the outcome.

"All right, show me," said Golitsin. "I'd rather burn for the knowing of it than live as a fool."

Abel put a hand on the priest's shoulder. "Let's hope it won't come to that."

"We can always hope," the priest said with a forlorn sigh. "Show me."

After a moment, Abel rolled out the scroll.

"The breech lock," he said, "is a very simple concept. It's the execution that may be the problem. But seeing what you have in place here in your shop, I think you may be able to handle it."

"The point of using the women is not to prove anything," said Abel, "but to increase our firepower."

Joab shook his head. Abel had reported to him in

his office to detail the assignment of Scout tasks, but had decided that now was the time to bring up this innovation with his father.

It was not an innovation that Center had insisted upon, although he had not rejected the idea. He'd merely said it would "alter certain equations that might lead to interesting variables to consider."

It was something Abel felt he had to push for, after he'd seen the women fight at Lilleheim. They were throwing away a resource in a war where the forces of the Land were being purposely undermined and thinned.

I agree with your reasoning, Raj had said with a laugh. *But maybe your motivations are not so pure as you purport them to be.*

"No," Joab said. "Absolutely not. Look at what happened at Lilleheim. That woman brought out her little coterie of—I don't know what to call them. Women who aren't content with one cock to lead a man around with, but who have got to have their own, to yank themselves here and there with, I suppose. And she got thirteen wives and daughters of some very prominent men killed in the bargain."

"They fought like carnadons," Abel said. "We need their numbers. Plus, they have almost all been around military men in some way or another. They are our sisters and our wives. They've absorbed many skills, and they know how we do things."

"It could have been worse," Joab mused. "Rape. Torture. The Blaskoye using the women against us the way they used the children."

"We are at war, Father," Abel replied. "If they beat us, they're going to do those things anyway. And right before our eyes."

"Try telling that to Tarl Magiorre, whose daughter lay dead on that thrice-damned nameless knoll," Joab said.

"Yes," Abel said with a bitter laugh. "And try telling it to Edgar Jacobson."

Joab considered his son. Abel was not sure how much he knew, or how much he'd guessed, about Abel's own interest in *Dame* Jacobson. But one thing he'd learned about his father over his years of serving under him was that there wasn't much that went on in his district that he didn't at least have some inkling about, especially when it came to the military families.

"Jacobson should have controlled her," Joab said. "The women's auxiliary exists for washing, mending, doing a soldier's chores when he is better occupied with fighting. And, well, at least creating the hope of a good fuck afterward. The Scouts have always had their retinue of women following them about, as you know."

"Oh, yes." Abel shook his head. "Some would follow them into the Redlands if they could."

"I have no doubt," Joab replied. "They perform a function, a useful function. But not as warriors. Not as fighters."

"Not ideally," Abel said. "But we live in far from ideal times."

"I simply won't allow it," Joab said. "And I especially won't allow *her* to continue with it, which is what I know you are really after."

"Who do you mean?"

"You know what I'm talking about, Lieutenant, and don't say you do not," his father said testily. Then he shook his head, sighed. "She's a *married* woman, Abel. From a good family, married *into* a good family. This cannot end well."

"I know who she is," Abel said. "I respect it. As much as she does."

"Besides, from what I hear—well, she's rather damaged goods. I mean that in a very literal sense. That wound..." Joab looked down, shook his head sadly.

"You're being unkind, Father."

"I suppose you're right," Joab replied. He again met Abel's eyes and seemed genuinely chagrined. "But when one's only son looks to be on the verge of throwing his manhood away on something—all right, some*one*—like that, it brings out the beast in a father. He'll take the low road, if that's what's required."

Abel considered. There was always the question of how much he could tell his father. Raj and Center were adamant. He must reveal nothing. If he did, they would not merely go away; they would kill him if they could. Raj, he was not so sure about. He had no doubt Center would do just that. His affection for Center was genuine, but it was rather like affection for a pet carnadon. You must never allow yourself to believe your feelings were returned.

"It may not matter, all this concern over status and position," Abel said. "The Blaskoye have grown *very* strong. They seem determined to spread into the Land, to take it from us. They are gathering for that purpose. Every sign points to it: the incursions, the sack of Lilleheim, the increased raids. The way that they turn the corruption of Cascade to their advantage." How to say it? "Father, do you not think what we both agree is a coming war might change, well, everything. The Land. The Law?"

Careful, lad, Raj murmured. ***See that where you're going with this is not over a cliff.***

"And will the nature of men and women change? Will what is right and good under Zentrum?" Joab laughed. "I think not. Some things flow and change. Some things are written in stone." He put a hand on Abel's shoulder. "You sound like a man who is trying to convince himself that something he wishes with all his heart *were* true actually *was* true. I understand that."

A pensive look, a shadow, passed across Joab's face. *He's thinking about Mother,* Abel thought.

"But we are men who deal in reality, not wishes and fantasy," he said. He pointed toward the outspread papyrus map scroll on the big table in his office. "The Blaskoye will try again soon, but it will be far worse than Lilleheim."

"I agree."

"We have drawn their ire by our own competence, I'm afraid. Cascade has paid them off. Ingres is protected to the west by Treville itself. Lindron District is too well defended and anyway too long and wide to take with a west-to-east invasion. Twenty leagues of flat land with walls and flooded rice paddies favors organized foot, not savages on dontback."

"Yes, they'll move on Lindron last, when they're certain of it."

"Which leaves the northern districts and us."

"Agreed," Abel said. "But I would add one thing. You said they are drawn by ire at our competence. I would say that they are very angry at one commander in particular: you. They want your head. It is the way the Redlanders think. From them, a single charismatic leader rises and fights his way, or tricks his way, into leading a band, a tribe. Sometimes he even grabs for himself a godlike status."

"Utter heresy."

"Yes, I know," said Abel. "You know this, but they don't know. They understand us as badly as we understand them. For them, there is no Law of Zentrum. No Thursday school lessons. Whatever poor excuse for being something other than meat and dust that they have—well, that must be the way the world is for *everyone*, they believe. Their gods are *the* gods. Those gods' rules are the only way men can rightly behave. So they figure we have exactly the same motives, that we are exactly the same men as they. They figure that if they shoot the dont in the head, the rest of the beast will collapse."

"And you're saying *I'm* the head."

"To them, you are the *god*head on Treville District," Abel replied. "I believe they are particularly targeting *you*, Father."

Joab sat back, took a long sip of wine. "Great," he said, shaking his head. "Do they not realize that any competent officer can do as I do, that one will do so if he is called to take my place?"

"I'm not so sure you're right about that," Abel said. "But they surely do not understand how we organize and build in redundancy. Or even what organization means in a farming society such as ours. They are herders. But they're learning. You saw it. They were much better commanded at Lilleheim than we've ever seen them before."

"Agreed."

"They may be organized enough to move in two directions at once."

"How do you mean?"

"A feint," said Abel. "To draw you out. You in

particular. To draw the Regulars into a dry plain, say, where they can use their donts and overrun the Regulars, destroy the Militia. They don't want to attack us in the town, not really, because they lose all advantage, and we gain several, not the least of which is fighting on our own turf. They have no villages, much less towns, of course."

"You may be right," Joab said. He paused in the midst of his thought and then displayed the slightest smile. His voice grew more heated with what was evidently conviction—and a plan. "In fact, I think there's a good chance that you are. But where and when? I want to do more than guess."

Oh no, Abel thought, realizing, before he could formulate it exactly, what his father had in mind. *He's had an idea that he believes will solve two of his problems. Damn it, he may be right.*

"We've been reacting since Lilleheim," Joab said. "It's time to start acting. But we need more information."

"That's what the Scouts are for," Abel said weakly.

"You're a Scout. I'm sending you."

"But I'm on detached duty with the Regulars," Abel replied. "By your orders, I might add."

"Yes." Joab nodded. "Exactly. I need Sharplett nearby, to deal with threats. No, you will go. Long reconnaissance. Take four squads, and a command group."

"That's half the Scouts."

"Yes."

"For how long?"

"Long enough to get me dispositions on the Blaskoye," Joab said. "Real information. You say they are getting organized, and I believe you. For years we couldn't estimate strength or likelihood of attack because they were diffuse and haphazard in their ways. Organization leads to predictability."

"How long, Commander?"

"I'll give you two three-moons."

Ninety-two days, Center said.

"Where?"

"Awul-alwaha, the Great Oasis, would be a good bet," Joab said. "No one has seen it in our lifetimes."

"I'll need maps. A dont train. I'll need to *make* maps."

"Of course."

"Weldletter."

This took Joab back for a moment, and it was Abel's turn to smile. Weldletter was Joab's best cartographer. His father would *hate* to let the man go. But it made eminent sense, and Joab would know it.

"Bastard," Joab muttered. "All right. Take him."

"I'll need a week to prepare."

"You have three days," Joab said. "Take the pre-positioned supplies at the Upper Cliffs."

"Sharplett will boil over."

"Let me deal with Sharplett," said Joab. "And one more thing."

"What?"

"Absolute secrecy," he said. "I am convinced the Blaskoye have ears and eyes in Treville. No word is to get out, on pain of the lash and the stockade. Impress it on your men."

"Yes, sir."

Joab leaned over the map, looked Abel in the eyes. "Especially no word to the women. This auxiliary. No one."

"I understand, sir."

"I'm sure you do," Joab replied. "Now you'd better get to it."

Abel tapped a shoulder in salute, then turned to depart. He controlled his expression, but could not keep the flush from his face. He was steaming, gritting his teeth and about to gouge his palms with his own fingertips. But just as he reached the door, Joab spoke again, softer now, not in the tones of a commander but in those of a father.

"A wager," his father said. Abel stopped.

He didn't turn back around to face Joab. "What?"

"My bet is that it will be gone like a fever when you return. She may come to her senses. You might. One of you probably will."

"And if I don't?"

"Then you may be returning from relative safety into great danger," Joab said. "Those Jacobsons play for keeps."

Abel nodded. He let himself breathe out.

His father continued in the same low, soft voice. "But so do I," he said. "So do I."

Observe:

One day Mahaut crossed the room by herself, went to stand by the window, parted the curtains, and felt the sun on her face.

She wanted to tell him, waited, even sent word. But then the note came back that he was away with the Scouts, that it was an extended expedition, and that it wasn't known when he would return.

So she tried to forget him. But a strange thing happened. The dreams began to change. Oh, there was always the bullet within her, the splay of lead. But sometimes now it was not his, the Blaskoye's, bastard child, but was her own and no one the father. And when this happened in the dreams, Abel was there. Standing somewhere nearby, quiet. Always with his own guns, that short-barreled musket and the flare-muzzled dragon blunderbuss pistol with the scrollwork and rotating flintlock. And she would ask him what he was doing, and he would answer "Waiting," and she would ask him what he was waiting for, and he would say "For the baby," and she would know he meant the bullet.

"Why?" she would ask.

"Because I need it," he said.

"Why do you need it?" she would ask again.

And he would look not at her, but away, into the distance. And he would finally answer "I need it to shoot him with it. It's the only bullet that will kill him. And I aim to kill him."

And she would wake from those dreams with her heart beating wildly, and—

—she had to now admit, must admit—

Flush with desire.

He'd better not get himself killed out there, she thought, *not yet.*

Because I have to tell him I love him.

Interpolation ninety-nine point one percent accurate, Center said. **Now is that sufficient for interpretation of the probable mental state and the intended actions of the subject?**

Yes, it is, Center, Abel thought. *Yes, I hear you, Mahaut.*

❖   ❖   ❖

"You know, I keep thinking about women when I work on guns," Golitsin said. They were once again in the back of his smithery in the Hestinga temple compound, and Golitsin was pulling a newly refurbished musket from a dont leather scabbard. Abel got a glimpse of some odd complication on the top of the barrel, but Golitsin quickly covered both ends of the barrel with his palms.

"Why just *think* of women," Abel replied. "Since you like them so much, you know we have a few whores in Hestinga—and lots more in Garangipore."

"I'm well aware," Golitsin answered. "It's a constant temptation. But Zilkovsky would find out. He wouldn't stop me but he would be...disappointed." Golitsin shook his head ruefully. "I couldn't stand that." He looked at Abel and his expression brightened. "Speaking of which, I hear you have given in to a temptation of your own."

Abel was startled by the pronouncement. He'd understood that the news of his time spent with Mahaut had gotten around in certain quarters—how could it not?—but for a *priest* to know of it, even a priest as worldly as Golitsin, seemed strange and perhaps even dangerous.

"We've done nothing," Abel replied.

"But you've thought about it. A lot." This was not a question.

"Yes."

Golitsin shrugged. "I take an interest in affairs outside the compound," said the priest with a wink. "Especially since I can't indulge in them. Zilkovsky might take my forge away. I can't have that."

"No, I guess not."

"But what *are* you thinking, Abel?"

"I may love her," he said.

"So what?" replied the priest. "Many a man has loved the wife of another. Most do not *do* anything about it, whether out of fear or prudence, I can't say. Probably both."

Abel considered. What *had* he been doing with Mahaut? Center and Raj had openly wondered about this very question. Yet he knew, whatever his motives, that he was doing the right thing, for both himself and for Mahaut.

And she will live. I am responsible for that, he thought. *Not fate, not Zentrum. Me. I saved her.*

"I would have left her alone if I'd really believed she wanted me to," Abel said. "*She* decided I should stay. I did the rest. Now it's too late."

"That's no excuse. Women are weak."

"Not Mahaut DeArmanville. She is strong. I've seen proof of that."

"Mahaut *Jacobson*."

"Yes," Abel said. "So what do you have to show me there, brother? You've done it? A breeched rifle?"

Golitsin smiled wryly. "Not quite. I have a ways to go on that project. But I do have something else, something *you* didn't draw out in the sand for me, either. My own idea. Since you have opened the sluice gate, I've been thinking of other changes we might make." He turned the musket over in his hands and showed Abel the top of the barrel and tang. "For instance, what is the best way to true a gun's sights, do you think?"

"Shoot a Blaskoye, of course," Abel replied with a grim smile. "If you miss, try a little to the left and then a little to the right. If that doesn't work, charge and gut him with the bayonet. That will also get you the elevation."

"That's precisely the problem," Golitsin replied. "Your joke is too close to the truth. What we usually do in the shop is take a straight wooden dowel that's about ten feet long and fit it down a barrel. We color the tip or wind it with yarn, then line up the sights on that splotch of color. Then we take it on range to fine tune the elevation and windage."

"Now *that* sounds like a lot of work."

"Yes, and all for naught in most circumstances," Golitsin replied. "I started thinking about why our notch-shaped sights are so damn useless in combat." Golitsin chuckled. "It's the brightness, the constant change as your eye tries to adjust."

"Maybe. All sights are notches, are they not?"

"They are," Golitsin said, "until now." He thrust the musket toward Abel but still did not take his hands off the barrel. They were covering the sights. "What you need is a sight that cuts down on ambient light. And then it came to me."

"What?"

"The solution, of course," Golitsin replied. "It's very simple."

"Okay, give," said Abel.

"Circular front and rear sights," said the priest. "Have the shooter look not through a jerky notch-shaped opening, but through a fully ringed aperture. Perfect for a soldier sighting in on the human torso."

Golitsin took his hand off the tip of the barrel to reveal a small ring sitting on a tiny rod. The front sight. Then he removed his rear palm to reveal a ring and rod assembly that was slightly bigger than that on the barrel's tip. He handed the gun to Abel, who sighted down its length.

"Line the circles up on one another," Golitsin said. "I had my priest-smiths test it, but I want reports from actual battle."

"That can be arranged," Abel replied.

Golitsin nodded. "One thing I know for certain," he said with a shake of his head.

"What's that?"

"These new sights are utter and complete nishterlaub." He took the gun back from Abel, fingered the metal rings, then looked up at Abel with a smile. "Nishterlaub—and fun as hell to come up with and manufacture," he concluded with an uneasy laugh. "Dashian, what have you done to me?"

"Sorry, friend."

"Don't be." Golitsin shook his head. "Whatever happens, don't be sorry. It would be disrespectful toward me." He looked Abel in the eyes. "I chose to follow you down this road. Never forget that. It was my choice."

"And how long on the rear-loaders?" Abel asked.

"Hard to say. Days, not weeks," the priest replied. "It is like with the sights. Now that I have the general idea, it's only a matter of working out the details." Golitsin smiled his crooked smile. "And getting used to the idea that I am now a heretic, of course."

4

Two weeks into the Redlands, and Abel's company, his four squads and three command staff, were spread out along the backside of a defile, a gravelly wash about twenty paces wide. Pickets on the hill, a squad's worth spread along the ridge, gazed down at a clump of huts below—it was impossible to call such a small and squalid gathering a village—that belonged to a clan of perhaps fifty Redlanders.

Abel crawled up next to Kruso, one of the pickets, and looked over the ridge himself. "Are we sure they're not Blaskoye?" he asked.

"Not," Kruso answered. "Downem thar crawlet me and South-waste accent tha talk."

"South-wasters, huh? What do they call themselves?"

"Remlaps," Kruso said.

"But the Blaskoye have conquered lots of tribes to the south," Abel said. "How do we know these aren't some of them?"

"Hidden," Kruso replied. "Not from sich as weh, neither."

"Yes, it is a cozy little valley they've found there. Couldn't see it for a hundred leagues in any direction, then you come upon it and there it is, complete with a seep and green plants."

"Found tham never withoutem that huntsman fol-lowen weh here back."

"No, probably not."

But they *had* found the Remlaps, and as far as Abel could determine, the Remlaps did not know his Scouts were here.

You have maybe a day before they do, Raj said. *Desert folks don't miss much, because there's not much to look at out here, so they know every bush and rock. A cut twig, some chuffed ground, and you're spoiled for surprise.*

"All right," Abel said to Kruso. "I don't want them to catch fright, at least not yet. Can you go down there and bring me the chief, or somebody who looks like the chief?"

Kruso smiled. "Aye, Lieutenant," he said. "Thet can I."

"Take five," Abel said.

"And what will I do with the one I don't need?" Kruso asked, all innocence.

"Okay, four including yourself," Abel replied. "And if you're not back in a half watch, I'll bring the com-pany over the hill."

"No worry fer thet, sir," Kruso said. He carefully backed away from the hill crest, then pulled himself off the ground and headed down to round up his raiding party.

Abel remained watching, trying to pick out Kruso

and his men. There was the shake of a tarplant here, a small puff of dirt there, all following a roundabout path. If he had not known they were on their way, he would have put it all down to wind, so stealthily did the group move.

The return trip was a bit more obvious, since they were dragging something large and trussed up. Abel met them by the group of bedrolls and travel satchels that defined his headquarters. He'd ordered no cookfires, and his dak-born supply train was two valleys over in a blind defile.

The chief had not surrendered easily, and there was a bloody bruise on his temple where Kruso, or one of his men, had had to apply forceful persuasion. Abel ordered the leather thongs that bound his wrists and legs undone, and attempted to dredge up what little he knew of the South-waste dialect.

I will be able to supply the lack, if you will only allow him a few words to begin with, said Center.

This proved easy enough, for when the gag was taken from the chieftain's mouth, he immediately began cursing up a storm—which Center proceeded to analyze for grammatical components. By the time he was finished, Abel had become a competent speaker of the Remlap dialect, or at least Center had, which amounted to the same thing in present circumstances.

"You don't understand," Abel said to the man in his South-waste tongue. "You are here as a guest."

The chieftain stopped cursing then, and gazed at Abel in complete, amazed silence for a moment. Then he let out a huge laugh. "A guest? And I know that you are a Trevilleman, speak as you will. I know what it is you do with guests."

"What's that?"

"I hope you gag on my balls when you eat them," the chief answered.

Abel allowed himself a smile. "I see. We are cannibals." Abel nodded his head. "Yes, I can understand that belief."

"Get on with it, then," said the chief. He set his teeth and let his arms fall to his side in angry surrender to fate.

"Sit down," Abel said. "With me."

He allowed himself to sink in front of the chief, and sat on his haunches. After a moment of amazement that he had lived another sensible stretch of time, the chief did so as well.

"My name is Dashian," Abel said.

"*Dasahn*," the chief said, attempting to pronounce a sound for which there was no equivalent in his own tongue.

"Close enough," said Abel.

"I am Gaspar," the chief said.

"Chief of the Remlaps?"

"That's right."

"What will you drink?"

The chief, Gaspar, smiled wickedly. "Beer?"

"Wine," said Abel. He motioned for someone to bring the stoppered clay bottle. When he got it, he uncorked it, took a swig, and passed it to the South-waster.

Gaspar was a thin man. *Underfed*, thought Abel. *And how would anyone feed well, or even adequately, out here?* The Redlands were a land of meager resources, but the four-league-wide depression they presently occupied was particularly barren. Gaspar also seemed older, but then, after they passed the age of twenty, most Redlanders took on a wizened appearance that could be anywhere from thirty to sixty years old and kept it until they died. The chief wore the customary robes of a nomad, but these were a faded yellow, and not the white of the Blaskoye. He wore no sandals, and his feet were a mass of calluses that might be thicker than the actual foot that sat atop them.

. Remlap swallowed the wine, sighed. "It has been a while since I have tasted such."

"Why don't you ask your friends the Blaskoye to give you wine?" Abel asked.

"That would be like asking a brushfang to give you his venom," the chief answered. "He might be very willing to give it to you, but perhaps in a manner that makes you wish you hadn't asked in the first place."

"You are not on good terms with your neighbors?"

"We would like to be, though we have seen what happened to others who thought they were on good terms with the Blaskoye. Suddenly, even though they were there, in the same huts, in the same camp, they weren't themselves anymore. Instead, they became harsh in manner, and told us that our lands and our flocks were not actually ours, that they didn't belong to us, but to 'Greater Redland,' even though it seemed like our land was ours, and even though it had seemed like it was ours for many, many years. In fact, what we thought was ours was theirs. But they were not themselves anymore. And when we asked them who they were, they told us they were Redlanders, and their leaders were the Blaskoye, who understood what this Greater Redland meant."

The chief relaxed a bit, sat back on his own haunches, and took another long drink from the wine jug.

"Isn't that both marvelous and strange?" he continued.

"That some people can completely transform into other people so easily? Hartzmans to Redlanders. Mbunga to Redlanders. And all of them somehow Blaskoye at the same time. It is very confusing. We Remlaps are not very good at doing that sort of thing. This is our fate in the world, I fear, to be very good at being only ourselves, however poor selves we are, and not very good at being someone else. So when the Blaskoye asked us if we would like to be Redlanders and be ruled by them, they did not take it well when we declined the great honor that they wish to bestow upon us. Perhaps this was ungrateful, I admit, but what can one do? We are only poor Remlaps, after all."

"Maybe that's too bad," said Abel. "It might've made things a lot easier, like you say."

"And now here I sit captured by—oh, I'm sorry, I mean the guest of—people from the Land itself. These people would like to hear me tell tales of the wonderful and generous Blaskoye, where they are gathering, where they will strike next, only I cannot on account of my own tribe's stubborn and troublesome inability to be pliable and flexible, not to mention all those other words that the Blaskoye employ when they might have adopted the single command: 'Bow down and do as we say.' It is very tiresome to be the leader of such a truculent group of misfits as the Remlaps."

"I feel for you," Abel replied. "But maybe you can answer one question."

"Certainly," said Remlap. "I would be very gratified if I could be of at least some use to you."

Abel looked the man straight in the eyes. "Tell me where to find the Blaskoye with the silver knife that shines like water."

It was as if the brushfang the Redlander had spoken of before had actually bit him. He recoiled from the question in a physical way, as if he were flinching from a real blow. "Oh, you don't want him," said the chief.

"So you know who I'm talking about?"

"Most assuredly. That is not the same thing as knowing where he might be found. In fact, there is no one place he will ever be found. That is part of his charm, they say."

"What's his name?"

"He goes by several."

"What do you call him?"

Gaspar broke Abel's gaze, looked away.

"It's better not to speak of such things, such people, lest one call them down upon oneself."

"And you do not think I am dangerous?"

"I think you are dangerous."

"But not *as* dangerous."

"No."

"Should I kill some of your children? Take a woman or two and give her to my men? Would that convince you?"

"Perhaps," said the other with a thin smile. "But you might have trouble finding the children, as we have hidden the remaining ones rather better than we have hidden ourselves. Even I do not know where they have been taken, and you might find our women a bit...used. For the Blaskoye *have* visited us, you see. Our camp was in better country, closer to the oasis, in former days."

"The oasis," said Abel. "I would like to go there."

"I do not think you would enjoy it very much," the chief answered with a dry chuckle. "Unless you particularly like the taste of your own gonads. But then, there's no accounting for taste among you people of the Land."

"I'm sorry, let me correct myself. I would like to go *near* there," Abel replied. "You know how the saying goes—"

How does the saying go, Center?

I have several possibilities that might be appropriate. Try: "missed the target, but slew the dak," Center replied.

Abel repeated the aphorism. Evidently, it was the right one, for the Remlap chief nodded in agreement. "True words, true words," he murmured.

"I can pay you to guide me. A dont and a dak. One to ride now. One later."

"Two, a dont and a dak?" The man said, suddenly taken aback, but just as suddenly seeking to cover it up so that his bargaining position wouldn't be compromised. "Such an amount may seem a generous present to one from the Land, where they are used to pull a pointy stick through the ground, or are yoked, the poor things, to teams of others to pull an overloaded wagon. But here in the Redlands, we are shepherds of a flock and not farmers. We require more for existence, in the same way that you require a large harvest of rice or barley for yours. By the way, I have tasted both grains, and I salute you for your bravery in consuming them day after day."

"One," Abel said. "The dak. You can ride with someone else, I suppose."

The other looked extremely displeased that the bargaining was going in the opposite direction than what he had hoped. "But this is unjust."

"Would you like to go for none?"

"I protest most stringently. You're using strong-arm tactics on me! Most uncivilized."

"Not ten minutes ago you were worried about whether or not I was going to eat you," Abel observed. "Perhaps that is still an option."

"Two then," said Gaspar. "The dak now, too."

"No," Abel said.

"All right," said Gaspar. "Dont now, dak later."

"No," Abel said. "All on delivery. I am beginning not to trust my donts. They might up and walk away with you before we've completed our business. Perhaps I'll fetter them properly until we arrive. Get me to the First Oasis and you walk away with both head."

Gaspar flinched, rubbed his eyes.

Buying some cogitating time, Abel thought.

Wouldn't you?

Why would I need to? I have you to do my thinking for me.

Not amusing even in jest, lad.

Abel smiled. It wasn't easy to get Raj's goat, but he thought he'd just done so.

"You find this humorous?" said Gaspar. "An old man's dilemma? For how can I trust you?"

Abel shrugged. "You could remain useful. Even after we arrive. That way, I would wish to pay you with the dak in order to make use of your services again."

"And how might myself or my people be of use a second time? What do you hope to accomplish out here, so far from home, Landsman?"

"I don't know yet," Abel replied. *At least not the particulars,* Abel thought. "What say we ruminate on that very thought along the way? Perhaps one so wise as you can answer it for me."

Another smile from the Remlap chief. "Agreed." He spat into the sand, dipped his hand into the spittle and fine reddish-brown dirt, then reached out to shake Abel's. "Dont now, dak later." Abel did the same, and they shook dusty hands.

"Now you can just let me go back to the tribe and—"

"Oh, no," Abel said, standing up, towering over the Remlap chief in the process. "I insist you remain as our guest." He reached down to help the other man up, and, after a moment's hesitation, the Remlap chief accepted his assistance. "Besides, I can't send you back to your people so skinny. We need to fatten you up, if only for our own honor. I know you won't deny us this. And, you'll pardon my forwardness, great chief, but from the looks of you that might take a while. A long while."

Gaspar shook his head, smiled sadly. "Then I will have to impose a bit longer on your hospitality." He looked around avidly, as if the food would appear instantly.

This man really is hungry, Abel thought. *Or else a greedy son of a bitch.*

Malnutrition is evident, Center replied. **And his people are starving.**

The fact that he tried to bargain with you at all is a sign of how tough the old bird is, Raj added.

"If I may be so bold," said the chief, interrupting Abel's flow of thoughts. "Since I am now determined to stay to assuage your discomfiture, how long until the noonday meal? I would very much like to start seeing to the maintenance of your honor sooner rather than later."

"First, the name," Abel said.

"The name?"

"The Blaskoye," Abel said. "He with the silver knife. The one who stole your children and raped your women. Then we'll have a bite to eat. And I promise that bite won't be you."

This brought forth the first genuine smile he'd seen from Gaspar.

"Like you, we call him Silver Knife," said the chief. "But he has a given name. They call him Rostov. Dmitri Rostov."

Two rises of the three-day moon, Levot, passed—nine days—as they rode through the Voidlands and into the Highsticks. Gaspar of the Remlaps was a plumper man.

He ought to be, thought Abel. *He's been chewing on something constantly, walking, standing, sitting, except when he's asleep, and sometimes I swear he manages to chew on something even then.*

The Highsticks was the name of the elevated plains on the extreme east of the Redlands. Beyond the Highsticks, all vegetation gradually gave out. Volcanism increased, and the soil became toxic for most forms of life. Beyond that lay the Tables, an unbroken coating of basalt that stretched, according to Center, for thousands of leagues, and was a half-league thick in all places.

There is no way for the Redlanders to cross that area, said Center. **The water table has been made completely inaccessible by a magma eruption that occurred three million years ago. There has been no rain there in over one hundred Duisberg years. There are therefore no tanajas**

or natural cisterns. And the basalt gives way on the east not to another desert and riverine system, but to the Eastern Sea. Thus there is not the slightest possibility for Redland eastward migration. The only population spigot for the Redlanders is the Valley. It has ever been thus, and this is exactly what Zentrum counts on in his Stasis regulation equations.

And the pot is set to boil right about now, Raj said. *Over the brim, and down the Valley.*

The Highsticks were not the Sulfur Plains or the Tables, however. They were a tough country, but quite habitable for a desert people.

Abel and his company had travelled two hundred leagues. They had completed a half circle of the Redlands, southwest to northeast, always keeping contact with tribes, interior and outlying.

Taking Raj's advice, Abel arranged the regiment in a left echelon of squads. They were attempting to encircle the enemy's presumably teardrop-shaped disposition stretching from the west, and the edge of the Valley, to a terminus in the east at Awul-alwaha. The Scouts approached from the southwest. The goal was to keep contact with concentrated forces as well as to survey the tribes who were and those who were not participating in what was looking to be a great gathering of the desert nomads. The purpose of this gathering was all too evident: war on the Valley.

The lead squad sought contact, mostly visual, but not unwilling to give and take fire when they met an armed Blaskoye group. It was for these times that the echelon arrangement came into play, for—as Raj had predicted—the Redlanders, however many there were

in an area, would invariably rush all their forces toward
the first sound of trouble. This not only pulled them
out of areas that squads to the left of the lead squad
could then reconnoiter, it also left them entirely open
to an unexpected flank attack in wave after wave as
the deployed left-echelon squads caught up with the
lead and joined the fighting from an easterly direction.
Sometimes the Scout reinforcements arrived directly in
the Blaskoye's rear and set the Redlander donts scurry-
ing in all directions, scattering the terrified Redlanders
like a puff of wind on an open hand full of grain.

Occasionally, the point squad passed too far to the
east of the enemy and another squad would make
contact. In these instances, signal mirror contact and
flag wigwag became paramount to rein in the forward
moving squad. Long experience had made moving yet
maintaining sightline contact second nature, and a
forward unit would circle back in a variety of spirals,
depending on terrain, if signaling were lost for longer
than a few minutes.

The engagements took their toll, but produced
what were, to Abel, surprisingly few casualties on
either side. He had had visions of having to lead a
line of wounded, gangrenous men across the barren
landscape, and being constantly hampered by his train
of wounded. So far, he'd only lost five men from his
original ninety, and one of those was a fall from a cliff
while dismounted and taking a piss. The body of that
one, a Scout named Largo, they'd had to leave where
it lay, or risk more casualties retrieving it. The others
they'd managed to bury. Their places of rest were duly
marked on the map Weldletter was constructing. Their
graves were then trampled to obliteration.

These men know cover when they see it, as do the Blaskoye, Raj told him. *And since neither of you have conquest in mind, but simply driving the other off, there's no instinct to go for the throat and destroy the other completely. The time will come when that will change.*

Similarly, they killed few Blaskoye, and what wounded they found were usually well enough for interrogation and eventual release. There was no way to keep prisoners, and Abel had no desire to execute those hapless enough to get shot and caught. Besides, releasing a wounded man in a desert was not doing him any favor, however good he might be at living off the land.

Nomad encampments were a bit more tricky, and Abel avoided direct contact with these groups whenever possible, with the regiment dividing itself and quickly flowing around them. It helped that, unlike traveling bands, the families in the camps had a tendency to stay in place long enough to allow him and his men to clear out of the area. But the position of the camp was duly noted on the map and in logging scrolls. Each camp was, as Gaspar said more than once, probably in a traditional spot that would remain constant. Even though Redlanders were always on the move, they tended to congregate in favorite feeding and watering grounds for their measly (by Valley standards) dak herds.

The going was hard, but not so hard as it would have been without a destination in mind—and Abel had a destination in mind he had not shared with his father. He'd also not mentioned it to Raj and Center, but by now it was fairly obvious what his plan was.

Spiral in toward Awul-alwaha, the First Oasis.

❖　　❖　　❖

Josiah Weldletter was not a man who was at home in the desert. First of all, he was as overplump as Gaspar had been underfed. And, in a sort of negative reflection of Gaspar, he had steadily reduced in size even while the Redlander was growing larger. Strangely enough, the two men got along well after overcoming the fact that both thought the other a barbarian. For Gaspar, the map was in his head, and had always been. The very idea of a detailed map on a scroll of papyrus had never occurred to him, but the moment that he did understand the idea was a moment of revelation. He couldn't get enough of Weldletter's map.

The two would ride ahead, with a guard of three or four Scouts, find a knoll or rise, and together they would fill in the blank places on the developing map. Gaspar showed an uncanny ability to predict what would lie over the next rise, the depth of a declivity, and, after he understood the idea of scale, the altitude of the hill in the distance as expressed in elbs, paces, or fieldmarches. He was particularly excited when Weldletter showed him how contour lines worked. It was as if a flitterdak that had known it had a song within itself suddenly found the voice that had been missing all these years and burst forth with its native call.

For his part, Weldletter had never met someone who truly had a better imagination for the folds of land than he, and for him it was the first time he'd had a conversation with someone he believed to be his equal in this regard. The two became so inseparable that Abel felt the necessity of pulling Weldletter aside and reminding him that, given the chance, Gaspar might gladly cut his throat if it gained his tribe some sort of advantage in the Redlands.

"He would be sorry," Abel said. "And I believe he might even shed real tears, if he has had enough to drink in the past day or so, but he will go ahead and slit your throat. And then, if he hasn't eaten in a while—"

"All right, all right, Lieutenant," Weldletter had answered, cutting Abel off. "You have a great deal of your father in you, particularly the ability to put the facts before a person in a visceral manner. I will watch myself."

"Oh, let's do better than that," Abel said. "Let's show him everything. Maps he never dreamed of, even."

"What do you mean?"

And Abel told him.

So it was Weldletter and Gaspar and their retinue of porters, aides, and guarding outriders who first found the nishterlaub execution site.

By the time that Abel rode up, this group had descended into the small valley where the executions had taken place and had disturbed some of the remains. But when he crested the hill above, Abel got a good view of the tableau.

There were dozens of men staked out with their backs down and their faces and bellies up to the sun, naked, their arms and legs tied to hold them in that position. They were bent over what looked like metal arches. The metal itself was brown and rusted, but it was strong enough to hold them up exposed to the sun. **They have been tied to the roofs of ground cars,** said Center. **These groundcars were, at one time, electrostatically powered vehicles that your ancestors used pre-Collapse to journey into the planetary wastelands. There were many dwellings in what you now know as the Redlands. People used the** area as a recreational getaway and journeyed from the Valley on holidays. As you see now, the ground cars have become little more than clumps of rust preserved these three thousand years only by a process of something like petrification, with the sand filling their declivities to the point that they are almost sedimentary rock now instead of metal.

How long ago was the execution? Abel thought.

Much more recent, answered Center. **Within the previous three-moon, plus or minus an eight-day.**

And your count?

Fifty-seven adult males. Similar garb and physique indicates that they are likely all members of the same tribe.

And they were staked out alive? To die in the sun stretched across nishterlaub in this grotesque sacrifice?

It is difficult to tell due to the state of decay of the bodies, but I would assume so. We will have to get closer for me to verify.

Of course that's what happened, Raj put in. *And you can be sure that they wounded them in some manner so that an enterprising sort would not have the wherewithal to get himself free and to free the others. Probably broke their legs. That's what I'd do.*

Would you? Have you?

No, Raj said. *But I've seen and had to countenance worse. And now you understand what they are prepared to do to you and your kin if you do not submit, so perhaps it is a good lesson after all.*

Abel rode down among the bodies. He descended a stone-strewn path that looked to be more of a game-animal route than anything humans would use, but his dont retained its sure footing. And as he went down the side of the hill, an odd sound began to assail his ears. It was as if the valley were filled with the dry sizzle of the sort of insectoid plague he'd only seen in the Valley during rice ripening days. Surely the Redlands couldn't sustain so many bugs?

The arms and legs of the executed had not been tied to the nishterlaub groundcars with rope of any sort, but with the hacked off branches of a local pricklebush. It was a sort that grew straight up with many thorn-covered shoots about the thickness of two fingers, and sometimes ten elbs long. The thorns had not been stripped from the shoots and had been used to secure the knots in the flesh of the victims.

Most of the eyesockets were empty, having been eaten out by desert scavengers. This in itself was a clue to Center, who said: **One would expect at least some closed eyes, but you'll notice that there are not any. It seems that they all died with their eyes open.**

You mean with their eyelids sliced off, Raj roughly cut in. *So they were to go blind first, before the dehydration got to them.*

Abel leaned over, gazed at the gaping mouth and eyeless sockets of one of the victims.

Yes, the eyelids were sliced off, said Center. **But on one side only, the right. I believe I can project a likely reanimated image of the process, if it becomes necessary to—**

No, thought Abel. *Please don't.*

It was then that he realized what the strange scraping and crackling insectoid murmur actually was: the flapping of the dried-out skin of the victims as the desert wind blew through the declivity.

Yes, imagine trying to keep one eye closed while the other shrivels like a raisin in the sun, Raj said. *Seems as if they couldn't manage it, poor bastards, and died with both eyes open.*

And then they rode up to Gaspar, who approached on foot and looked up at Abel mounted on the dont. "These are Schlusels," he said. "I think they killed them all and either took the women and children, or slaughtered them, too, but without the honor of a lingering death."

"And who were these an example *for*, do you imagine?"

"Around here are good lands. There are larger tribes in the Highsticks. Or there *were*. We are all Redlanders now," Gaspar said with a dry laugh. "This is what Rostov intended to do to the Remlaps, too, had I not convinced him that pursuing us into the Voidlands, that place you came across us, would take too much of his precious time and kill off too many of his precious donts."

"Well, it seems this is the fate you dodged," Abel replied, gesturing toward the staked-out tribesmen.

"Indeed," Gaspar said. "Although there was the slower contingent trailing behind our main group, some older people and very young children. The Blaskoye got those." Gaspar poked a pricklebrush wand into the arm of one of the corpses. It had practically turned to leather, and the wand did not puncture it, but merely left an indentation. "We didn't expect him to be so fast, you see. He has bred his stock with donts he's stolen from the Valley. Racing donts, I wouldn't doubt."

"Taken, or just as likely traded for," Abel replied.

"In any case, this Rostov seems to be a very organized and dedicated man."

"He is a thrice-cursed handful of shit, is what he is," Gaspar said. "It is my belief that the donts run fast because they want to shake him and his kind off themselves and get clean. But they never can, and so they keep running when other animals might tire."

Abel nodded and left the Remlap chief to his thoughts. He hobbled his dont and set it to forage, and then walked deeper into the mass graveyard. The other squads would arrive and ride through soon, but for now it was just himself and the advance party. He brought his carbine along on the general principle that it did not pay in the Redlands to be more than a pace or two from your weapon at any given time.

Gradually, the shock at the sight of the dead left him, and he examined more closely the object upon which they'd met their deaths. He tried to imagine these masses of what looked like pockmarked stone functioning as a water ram or a gate latch or—

Observe:

The Redlands at about eye-height for a man, but moving through the landscape quickly, as a hunting flitter on a low-gliding path might. Moving over hills, winding through a valley. Enclosed, surrounded by more glass than he'd seen probably in his entire life.

Windows on all sides. A solid roof above to keep out the unremitting sun.

No wind from the forward movement.

So this truly is a mere simulation.

Yes, but a complete one. The front windscreen blocked the wind. Sitting in a groundcar was as wind-calm as sitting in a room of stone.

So they—

Drove in comfort. There was also climate control within, of course.

Abel gave himself over to the experience. His hands on the steering mechanism, a wheel of some sort. Set an elb in front of him and just below sightline: a smooth black tablet or stone with lights and strange hieroglyphics upon it, not of the Land.

Dashboard, vehicle status readouts such as speed, amount of charge in the electrostatic capacitors, antigrav levitation height from ground. I am presenting to you a sports modification of the Maikler 3F Comet, which is a close approximation of what would have been locally configured models.

I want to see this thing! Can you take me outside?

Abel was flying alongside the onrushing groundcar. Its name was not quite accurate, for it hovered at least three elbs off the surface of the ground using some sort of magic.

Antigrav static generators.

It was a sleek creature, made for speed. It was a dark red in color and on the end—

Even in the vision, Abel felt startlement.

Silver. Silver exactly like the Blaskoye's knife. What had Center called it?

Chrome. These are the bumpers of the groundcar. They are meant to ward off collision damage, but also serve the purpose of ostentatious display.

Rostov's knife is a car bumper made into a blade?

That is an accurate assessment. Analysis indicates he acquired it from this former parking lot, in fact.

Enough. Take me back inside. I want to drive.

He was back behind the wheel.

How fast?

I will translate the velocity and acceleration readouts—

Abel could suddenly read them: twenty-one leagues per hour.

The control at your right foot affects acceleration.

He pressed down, and the speed increased.

Careful.

The landscape flashed by at eye level. This was better than the ride through the sky he'd taken in his youth. So low to the ground, the speed was exhilarating.

This isn't real. I want to go even faster.

Your simulation is comprehensive. You can and will crash.

All right, I'll slow down. Where am I?

You've driven about ten leagues from the site.

In how long?

The clock time on this internal simulation is ten point three seven minutes. Of course, barely an eyeblink has passed externally.

I could circle the Redlands in a day, he thought in amazement.

People frequently did. It was considered a fine holiday outing. There were waypoints with vistas or with eating and drinking establishments. There were inns where visitors could stay for an evening before returning to the Valley. This was the parking lot of such an establishment. The edifice itself is under a nearby sand drift. And, as I mentioned, some of the more affluent built houses in the Redlands for recreational use.

Like a garden plot or a steam house.

Precisely.

But a hundred leagues away.

More, if they wished to fly. There are self-contained dwellings—vacation homes—scattered all over the planet. Most were merely a patch of remains on the landscape at the time I completed my orbital survey. Duisberg has a harsh environment by human standards. It has a comparatively large iron-nickel core that is highly magnetized and extremely active plate tectonics. This is another reason that Zentrum's plans are erroneous. He is incapable of integrating the entire range of facts simply because he is not a fast enough, big enough computer.

And you are?

Yes. I am a generation past Zentrum, and my capacity is based on quantum gravitational physics. His is a spin-physics-based mind. Highly serviceable for the tasks he was intended for: planetary defense, traffic direction, weather calculations, and such. But not amenable to the Seldonian calculus and its subsequent application in psychodynamic topography. But this is academic.

Abel had hardly been listening, but was coursing down a hillside at the fastest speed he felt he could safely muster, flying over shrubs and pricklebushes, leaving a cloud of dust in his wake, tearing forward, hugging the landscape—and completely exhilarated.

We'll get this back? Driving? When the Republic shows up?

Rapid individual conveyance is a building block of technological civilization.

So this or something like it?
Yes.
But this is as close as I will ever get. Simulation.
Yes.
Then, thrice-damn it all, take me back. Set me free from this dream, or I'll want to drive forever.

He was back in the valley of execution. The wind touched his face again, and the sun-baked skin of the dead flapped in the breeze.

He went to the end of one of the execution stones and kicked it, hard. Dust fell away, a few stones. He kicked it again.

The shine of chrome glinted through.

Silver knife.

"Let's get the hell out of here," he said to no one in particular.

The expedition moved on. Abel debated routing most of his squads around the area but in the end decided to bring them through it. He doubted these men would take fright. It was more likely the case that such a sight would create only more resolve in them to get the job done and get home with the information.

They avoided fighting whenever possible, but they could not avoid the fact that half the desert dwellers knew that they were there, somewhere out there, even if they didn't know precisely where the Scouts were at any given moment. This meant that they had to keep moving at all times and must take a circuitous trail that had subterfuge as its object as much as reconnaissance.

They had brought along enough food, but there was the constant need to find water. The men of the Delta proved to be the better of the water finders.

Some of them used dowsing rods to lead them, but the best of them merely looked at the landscape and predicted where they would find a sink, a tanaja, or even the occasional slow burbling spring.

The Delta men possess this particular skill because they spent childhood around water, said Center. **There is, for example, water everywhere in the tendrils of the River's final journey into the Braun Sea. Some have been sailors and fishermen, or knew people who were.**

The only fishermen that Abel had ever met were the stock fish growers who tended the carp pens on the far side of Lake Treville.

For food, they had hardtack and pickled dakbelly for almost every meal. Occasionally they slaughtered a weaker dak from the train to divide among themselves. This proved very useful in both feeding them and reducing their footprint across the land.

Abel had to admit that this was far from the light-weight expeditions the Scouts usually engaged in. It was more like the movement of an army, and Abel was learning valuable lessons every day about what a packtrain could and could not be made to do.

Mostly, it could not be made to leave no sign of its passing. While he drove his Scouts onward at what would have been a breakneck pace for an army, he could not help but feel that a malevolent eye was upon him, that someone was slowly working out from sightings here, spoor left there and there, his exact location—or at least a fix on his position that was close enough to permit attack.

He was determined to see it coming, if so, and disbursed the Scouts to the farthest limits he believed advisable, communicating by one-flag wigwag the simple instructions they would need for the day.

He'd skirted the Redlands, stayed alive and relatively intact, and managed to roughly count concentrations and resources of ten nomad groups. The one consistency among them all: they were Blaskoye vassals now. They may be Tamers and Jackflits and Wei Weis and Miskowskis still, but within each encampment were a group of outsiders, men who were not Tamers or Jackflits or Wei Weis or Miskowskis. They wore the Blaskoye blue and white, and in several instances Abel or his Scouts had observed these men beating, and even once dragging to death, a local tribesman.

These were subjugated peoples, and the men in blue and white were their overseers.

And then it was time to use Gaspar to lead them to the Great Oasis, the prime watering hole, believed to be one of two or, perhaps, three, that the Redlanders possessed on the Eastern side of the Valley. On the western side, there were no oases at all, and precious little water to be had anywhere. So Center's orbital survey had confirmed prior to the crashlanding of the capsule that had brought him and Raj to Duisberg.

Which is why Redland strength has always concentrated in the west, Center said. **We will confirm the specifics in Lindron when we get there.**

When are we going to Lindron? This was entirely news to Abel.

I am waiting for a series of dependencies to resolve, said Center. **I assure you, you will be the first to know, Abel Dashian.**

Thanks.

I suggest you concentrate on resolving the most pressing of those dependencies at the moment.

What would that be?

When and where the Blood Winds will begin to blow. Every indication is that it will be sooner rather than later.

5

Observe:

Gaspar was not truly sorry for what he was about to do, but he felt a tinge, a small tinge, of regret. It was the same regret a man might feel when he must run a dont through the Voidlands knowing there was no water for the animal, and that the trip would kill it, but dependent on that animal while within those stinking reaches, and living with it day after day, long enough to form a bond, especially if it were only the two of you against the world. Yes, form a bond, but the man always knowing the water in his belly was the only water there was.

That it, the dont, was a tool—a tool that had been bred a tool and nothing more.

The Farmers of the Valley were no different than a dont or a dak, when you came down to it. The only difference is that they could be clever, and might figure out that here, in these lands, they were mere tools.

And they might not be pleased when that realization dawned upon them.

Better to keep them in the dark.

And when he was tempted to think that they were men like him, that there might be some other way, he remembered his family clinging to life in that little defile with its uncertain seep, and the daks clustered in the huts with them, and all of them, the tribe, the last of the Remlaps, waking to the paltry milking, the feeble attempt at cheese-making, the rare quickening and birthing of calves. He remembered the endless hunt the men must engage in with only scrawny beasts to show, and the perpetual scavenging of the children. Yes, the children, the ones that remained untaken, forced by circumstance, by hunger and the inability of their parents to provide, grubbing under rocks for the crawling beasts, the hard-shelled insect that at least provided a dollop of protein and fat. Yet they must always be careful, so careful, for everything in the Redlands cut, burnt, or stung—usually to the pain, but often enough to the death. An adult too, might die of such a hard life, but with a child something much more precious was lost, for the Remlaps were failing, forced into the Voidland, the last stretch of waste that a human being could theoretically live on—but more often than not couldn't.

Gaspar cursed the fact that he was born into days such as these.

But here he was, and a man had to do what he had to do.

Which was, at the moment, make his way stealthily out of the Farmer's camp after the setting of the big moon, Churchill.

It was not difficult. These Farmer Scouts were excellent desert travelers for Blacklanders, but they were not *of* the Redlands in the way he, Gaspar, was. He had escaped *Blaskoye* pursuers. He was confident he could throw these mere Farmer Scouts off his trail. In fact, they wouldn't even realize he was gone.

Well, not until they noticed the missing maps.

He'd taken a scroll case with two of them rolled tightly inside. Of course he'd taken Weldletter's prize, the evolving map of the Redlands. But also within was a far greater treasure. For Weldletter had let drop—casually, in passing, even!—that he carried with him as a matter of course a complete map of Treville District.

A tactical, military map.

And this was the second item Gaspar carried in the map case slung across his back.

Gaspar had had to leave while almost two days out from Awul-alwaha. It would have been impossible to get any closer and still be able to carry out his plan. If they were closer, the Farmers would have seen the oasis and at least have an idea of its location, if not the best way in. He had not dared to steal a dont, but he still considered himself a good runner and did not expect to have any trouble making good time. He would not be eating on the way, but the problem was the water. If he ran through the night, which he intended to, he was going to be thirsty by sunup and delusional by daybreak. He would have to take necessary breaks along the way and rehydrate.

Although the Scouts had been good at making use of the land, they were in many respects amateurs in comparison to him, who'd lived in this environment all of his life. There was a wealth of sustenance hidden in this harsh and arid land for the one who knew how to find it. The pricklebush itself was useful, for its roots could be exhumed, slit open, and the moisture got out. Best of all were the wands of the very plant that had been used to tie the unfortunate Schlusel males to the metallic rocks. These could be skinned and would provide a ropey chewing cud that would also relieve his fatigue and reduce the swellings of his joints from the running. If he were able to find a bayonet plant, he might even have a feast on its fleshy parts. He must keep his eye out, that was all, and he would be all right. After this was over, he could think about eating again.

He checked the stars and set off through the night. His pace was even greater than he had hoped, for he'd received a new pair of sandals from the Farmers, and they were proving most efficacious against the hard ground.

After several hours he had a feeling that something was looking over his shoulder, was following him from behind.

It cannot be the Farmers, he thought to himself. *They were sound asleep as I left, and they will not have been able to pick up my track in the evening even if they did wake up.* But he stopped running and looked back.

It was the moon called Mommsen, quivering on the horizon, about to set.

"Oh you," he said, shaking a finger at it, "you shouldn't stare at a man so."

He turned around and continued onward, still at a jogging pace that would have put many a dont to shame if the creature had to make a similar traverse at night.

He found a pricklebush near dawn and dug it up with his fingers. The slight moisture of the roots on his lips was delicious. He abandoned himself to finding more roots for several minutes and dug up five or six more bushes. Suddenly he stopped and thought.

"They will know I came through here," he murmured. "They will see the dug-up plants."

So maybe he couldn't drink after all. Well, that would be all right, because he thought that he only had another ten or twelve hours to go.

"It ought to be just enough to take me through," he said to himself.

Onward through the harsh glare of the sun. This was a time of day that every instinct told him was not good to travel in. It was a time for rest, or at least to be in shadows while doing chores. It was not time to run with the bare head through the unforgiving Redlands.

Yet run he did, onward and onward.

And slowly the sun traveled across the sky, and it was afternoon. The visions started near sunset, and they were what he expected. Up ahead a woman beckoning him to keep going, to keep ahead of any who would pursue them. He knew it could not be his wife, because he had buried her in the sand after he pulled the Blaskoye off her and slit his throat. He'd been very angry to discover that his wife was already dead, and that the Blaskoye who had been raping her either didn't know or didn't care. He felt cheated, as if his rescue effort had not only been in vain, but had been a sort of joke.

Then the woman stopped appearing, and as he ran on, another form appeared, smaller. This, too, he knew could not be real, but it was closer to reality, and so closer to tricking him, for the boy—it had to be the boy—still lived as far as he knew. In fact, everything he did and thought was a result of believing that the boy still lived and that he was going where the boy was.

In the end he gave in to the boy's beckoning and even called out once or twice in his weak, parched voice, "I'm coming."

Then, well into the evening, after the sun set and the first moon rose, he saw the campfires of the oasis ahead of him. They were twinkling in the dark. Now a hard chill had set, and his yellow robes, thin as the scales of a ground-scather and fine for day, were no protection against the bite of the evening.

He ran on.

And that nagging feeling, that there was something behind him, returned. But now he knew that he was as far away from reality as he was ever likely to get and still have a chance to come back. The boy was telling him to come forward with signs and motions, and he was eager to do so. It was only when he got to the first outlying campfire that he realized he must now be careful, that the run was over, and the crawl and the shuffle had begun.

But that was all right, too. Working his way through the outer camps was not as hard as he thought it might be. They were not expecting anyone like him here. As far as they knew, all Remlaps had ceased to exist.

So within two hours of careful movement he was into Awul-alwaha proper. There were so many people around it was impossible to hide any longer, and there

was no need to. He could stand up and walk among
the people, or at least slink from alley to alley. If he
were glimpsed, it was no great matter to imagine that
he was a lost traveler, for Awul-alwaha was filled to
capacity with outsiders, men who had not been of the
Blaskoye tribe, who had never thought of themselves
as Redlanders, but who did now.

They convinced themselves after they saw what got
done to those Schlusels, thought Gaspar. And he knew
that many others had received the same treatment,
including his tribe. It was either join the Blaskoye and
call yourself a Redlander—or find yourself made an
example of in the most horrible way.

He knew where he was going. At least, he believed
he could find the tent.

As the headman of his tribe, in better days he had
been invited to visit the sheiks and potentates who
had run the Blaskoye clan before Rostov came along.

In many ways, those old days had not been very
much different from now. The Blaskoye had been
running a protection operation since time immemorial. But in those days you knew where you stood,
and you knew that if you paid the proper amounts
to the right people, you would be let alone and left
to go your way. And if you did not, the most that
would happen would be to have your legs broken, a
few daks slaughtered or taken. This was not out of
consideration for the finer feelings of the herd animals,
or the other tribes, of course. It was a method for
ensuring a steady return over the long-term.

But now all that was gone, and the only thing the
Blaskoye—and one might as well go ahead and say
it, *Rostov*—cared about was the present.

Awul-alwaha was not a town in any sense, more an extended encampment, but Gaspar, never having seen a town, was only aware of this fact in the abstract. It seemed enormous to him. The buildings were not permanent, except for a couple of wells and a central bathing area made of adobe bricks. It was the largest collection of human beings that Gaspar ever seen, and he could not imagine how a Farmer town could be more crowded, although he'd heard that they were. Almost he forgot the way along the paths between the tents and other temporary structures that defined the encampment. But there was enough similarity from the last time he had been here, which was nearly three years before, for him to wind his way toward the big tent of white and blue fabric that marked the Blaskoye central living area. Around that tent, clustered like sheep around the salt lick, were the many elaborate structures that formed the dwellings of the tribes' leaders, including the slave quarters and the dont enclosures. There were even separate cook tents and specially floored dining yurts where the masters of the Redlands could sit in comfort and consume their slave-brought meals.

The sounds of the oasis surrounded him. The perpetual flapping of fabric in the wind. The sudden onset of humidity, and the ensuing plague of insectoids. The white shine of the morning sun and play of shadows through breeze-whipped tent walls. The smell of the fabric itself: most of it dakwool, locally made, but some dusty linen bought or stolen from the Valley with its flax mills.

And, as always, the need to watch out for stakes and guylines. They were everywhere, put in wherever there was room. Get off the path, and you were likely to trip, perhaps yank up a carefully planted stake, or do *something* that would call attention to yourself.

Then he was among the Blaskoye tents, white and trimmed with blue, and his way became less certain. He would have to listen in on conversations and find his way to where he wished to go. It proved easier than he had feared, however, for a steady stream of visitors was headed for the very person he wanted to find. He hid in a shadow behind a large potted plant and listened to two men as they spoke of a report they would soon give. Both seemed nervous and uncertain about how it would be received.

"He won't like that they are in the Redlands and we couldn't find them," said one.

"But it's better for him to know that they are here than for them to get away with it entirely," said the other. "I don't think he's going to take it out on us. We've done what we could."

"You know that's not the way he will look at it. He'll tell us that he might hear the same report from a tribe in for market, so what does he need spies for?"

They continued past Gaspar, and he came out from behind his plant and followed them. Just before they went through a large opening that led to another tent, he ducked to the side and worked his way around the edge of that tent until he came to yet another tent that connected to the larger structure.

This will be the slave quarters for the main area, he thought. *I will come in here, and if he is not here, it is still a good way to get to where I must go. A way that he will not expect.*

The hard part would be getting himself and the map

case through a small opening without being detected. He was about to slit a hole long ways with his rusty knife—an instrument the Farmers had mercifully, foolishly, allowed him to keep—when he realized that this would be immediately noticed and instead reached down and made a horizontal cut along the floor of the tent side just above where it reached the ground and was curled under the flooring circlet that kept it in position. His slit began at one support and ended at another. It was as long as a man. Gaspar got down on his belly and held the map in its case in front of him as if he were hugging a baby. He quietly rolled through the slit.

When he looked up he was inside a large area full of people and frenetic with movement. He quickly stood up and looked around. The people were intent on their tasks and no one had noticed him enter. In fact, he didn't think any one of them would notice anything unless the entire tent were burning down, so intent were they on following whatever orders drove them.

These had the sliced foreheads that signified they were slaves. Many of the gashes were recent and still healing. The greatest danger he faced at the moment was the fact that he had no such scar on his own forehead. But the presence of the map in its willow tube proved to be exactly what he needed. He looked like a functionary making his way toward the main hall, a Blaskoye minor noble, perhaps, taking a shortcut to get to his destination.

So instead of slinking along and hiding, Gaspar held his head high and walked confidently through the enormous tented area full of bustling slaves. He looked right and left, searching, searching. He looked into the faces of the others, and they averted their eyes, afraid that he was doing the worst thing you could possibly do to a slave—notice them, pick them out for some special duty or punishment.

But he did not find what he was looking for, and he was going to have to ask someone. This might not go so well, he knew, for his garb would immediately be noticed, not to mention his outré accent. For a moment he contemplated luring someone to the shadows and killing them for their clothes, but he didn't think that he would be able to pull this off in his present state. He was very, very thirsty, and the sight of the slaves taking cups filled with drinks into the main area was maddening.

He walked in circles around the large area, trying to find where they might keep the young slaves, the gleanings from raids and trading among the tribes. Surely a boy of seven would not be put to work that required a great deal of dexterity or strength. They must keep them at some mundane tasks somewhere, and he must discover where that place was. But ducking down side tunnels and into other tents led him nowhere. He couldn't do it. He couldn't find the boy. After coming so close, he couldn't find him.

Then he considered hiding and waiting for evening, when he might conduct a more thorough search, but the bustling would never stop. In fact it would increase in the evening. And besides, where was he going to hide? He could not stay in the slave pens and the slave quarters, and he had nowhere else to go where he would not be recognized and called out for an imposter. Already he was receiving odd glances. Was this master never going to leave the service tent? He had to come to a decision. And he decided.

The original plan was not going to work. He had been so sure he would find the boy and be able to leave. But the boy was not here, and he had no more idea where to look. So it was the other plan that he was going to have to use. This was the reason he had brought the maps, after all.

There was no use waiting after that. He turned and followed a slave who was carrying a tray full of beverages out a side door, down a long enclosed hallway, and into the large area that was underneath the enormous Blaskoye main tent.

It was at least a hundred paces in diameter, and so high that if you fell from the ceiling you would die upon striking the ground. Although the tent was made of white fabric, the thickness of it kept out enough of the sunlight that oil lamps were necessary inside during the day for sufficient light. Sitting dens defined by central oil lamps were scattered all over the area. Some of these circles of cushions were empty. Most, however, were taken up by groups of Blaskoye men who were arguing politics, tactics, and all the matters that a conquering people must contend with when they must rule.

After this, it was not difficult to find Dmitri Rostov. He was near the center, and surrounded by a group of eight men who were arguing among themselves while he looked on. There were the two men, the spies, that he had seen and overheard outside. Rostov himself was smiling slightly, ferociously, showing teeth, at some comment that one of his retainers had made. Gaspar circled around the group, making certain that this was correct, that he'd found the right people, but he was sure. He remembered.

He remembered the negotiations when he had

refused. He had not refused to give in, but to call his people, his tribe, by another name. No, the good name they had shared for centuries was enough. He did not think of himself as a Redlander, and, foolishly, he'd believed he could convince the other, the other with the glistening black eyes and the white teeth, to leave them that, the name of Remlap.

But Gaspar had chosen to keep the one thing Rostov most wanted.

Now he had a decision to make. Would he hide the map, secrete it somewhere nearby, and use it to negotiate? He did not see that working. No, much better to make it an act of gratitude, of magnanimity. Yes, that was the way to go about it. And without further thought—because to think would be to fail—Gaspar of the Remlaps pushed his way into the circle of retainers and sat down directly in front of Dmitri Rostov.

Immediately two burly men moved in from the side with obsidian knives drawn and would have cut his throat in seconds had Rostov not raised his hand and signaled for them to stop. Rostov looked down upon Gaspar, and Gaspar felt those eyes once again, the cold eyes that reminded him of nothing else than his mother's tales of the carnadons, a creature he had never seen but that had filled his childish dreams with terror.

"What have you got there, Remlap man?" asked Dmitri Rostov. "And what are you doing still alive after I ran you into the Voidland?"

Gaspar clutched the map tightly and tried to stop his trembling. Still, a tremor rose that was clearly audible in his voice. "I came to apologize for our mistake," he said. "I know that there is no way we could make up for our transgression, but I have brought a token of our esteem that I hope that you will take as a sign of our repentance and love for you, our leader. We beg to be Redlanders now."

Moving while he still could make himself function, and fighting back the urge to piss his own legs, Gaspar pulled the top covering from the tube. The two bodyguards, for that is what they were, moved in on him once again, but he smiled and Rostov nodded for them to allow Gaspar to complete his motion.

He took the rolled papyrus map from the woven willow tube.

"Here is a most useful treasure, my sheik," he said. "It is an intricate recording, a map drawn to perfect scale, of the lands which you rule and must pass through. There are things in here that you do not know, places hidden that we—I—have discovered that will help you guard against your enemies and aid your subjects." Gaspar's shaking increased, but he forced himself to go on, to say it: "And I have but one entreaty before I lay this wonder into your hands."

Rostov smiled his tooth-filled smile. "And what is that, wastelander?"

Gaspar took a breath and spoke. "Nothing," he said. "Nothing much, a trifle. A youngster who is an acquaintance of mine, who is now in your service as a slave. A young boy." Gaspar felt his voice trailing off into silence. "He would be about seven years old now."

"And would he look like you?" said Rostov.

"A bit," said Gaspar. "He is a relative, at some distance, so I imagine he might."

"And what would you like us to do with this child slave, wastelander?"

"I just wish..." *Do not cry. Do not show the tears*

that are gathering behind your eyes. You do not have enough water within you to waste them so, Gaspar thought. "To look upon him, see that he is well. To report to his mother, you know," he said. "You know how women are. They cannot let go, even when letting go is their only choice in the matter."

"To look," said Rostov, "as a favor?"

"Yes, great sheik."

"And what is the slave's designation?"

"I—don't know what you will have called him," Gaspar answered hurriedly.

Rostov shrugged. "This boy may prove difficult to locate, I'm afraid. And since you have said it is a matter of trifling importance, what do you say we not bother ourselves with such small concerns and have a look at this supposedly marvelous gift you have brought for us?"

"No, I—" He cut himself off by slapping his own throat with a quick jab of his palm.

Everything inside him screamed. So close, and to have it yanked back so cruelly! There must be a way, some way to discover, cadge, beg—

And then he saw Rostov smiling broadly, those thin, white teeth, so like quartz stones, flashing, and Gaspar knew.

He knows. Maybe he doesn't know who I am precisely, but he knows. He knows what I am asking for, what I am truly asking for—

"No?" said Rostov. "What do you mean, wastelander? Tell me."

"It's just, I—" And he found he *could* say the words, must say them. "I beg you, great sheik. I wish—"

Gaspar bent low. He had already been sitting, and

now he placed himself on his belly, his legs hunched below him, his hands outstretched in supplication. "I humbly beg to see the boy. Just to know he lives."

"Who is this slave?" Rostov said. He chuckled, and those around him laughed with him. "Don't tell me, wastelander. He is your only son? The only one remaining after we cut you down like dakgrass when you did not yield? And is he the last? Did we kill the others, the strong sons of the Remlaps?"

"And the daughters," whimpered Gaspar. "My eldest daughter."

"And you come here believing you can . . . trade," said Rostov. He was no longer smiling. "As if I were a common barterer in a market stall."

"No, great sheik," Gaspar said.

"Then what, wastelander?"

"I—"

"Sit up so I can hear you!"

"Yes, great sheik." But he found his arms would not move, his back would not pull him erect. Finally the two bodyguards moved to his side and pulled him back to a crouching posture.

"I know where they are," Gaspar said. "The Farmers. Scouts. Many of them. A two-day ride from here. I came with their maps, and to tell you, show you . . . in hope . . . in fear . . . not for mercy, for I know you have none . . . but that you would find me useful. And let me have him."

"The boy."

"Yes." Gaspar nodded, looked down.

"The Farmers are nearby?"

"Yes. About ten-tens strong. They are of Treville. The ones you hate."

Rostov nodded. "I do hate those fuckers of daks. You have heard right about me in that regard. And now you have dangled your bait. Let us see if I will take it."

"They are truly there, great sheik," said Gaspar despondently. "I offer no trick. You can take the Farmers unaware. Wipe them from the red face of Father Desert. As you have wiped away others who oppose you."

Rostov said nothing for a space, but considered Gaspar.

"Give me these maps," he said. "Now."

Gaspar stretched out the case, but couldn't seem to loosen his grip on it, even when he was willing his fingers to do so. Rostov pulled it roughly from his hands.

Rostov opened the case and unrolled the scrolled maps, glancing at both in turn. Then he had a longer look. "Not bad," he said. "This is . . . who made this?"

"A slave of Treville. He works for the commander there."

"Dashian?"

"Yes."

Rostov smiled, shook his head. He rolled the map carefully back into a scroll, and looked at the other.

Slowly at first, and then faster and faster, the ferocious, toothy smile spread over his face. After what seemed an eternity to Gaspar, Rostov shook his head, plainly impressed.

"This may prove . . . useful."

"It shows fortifications. Troop dispositions. Even approximate numbers."

"I will have it read."

Gaspar had not considered that Rostov was not literate, although he kicked himself for not expecting it. He himself had only learned to read because his parents had been under the mistaken impression when he was a child that he might make a lore-keep someday.

Rostov looked back down at him.

"Now, as to these Scouts," he said. "Where?"

"I—am very thirsty," Gaspar said. "And I have not eaten in two days. Since I escaped."

"Yes, all right," Rostov replied. Then he paused and broke into another carnadon smile. "Meat for this man, and drink," he called out. Gaspar wasn't sure to whom Rostov was speaking but evidently he was heard and obeyed, for he shortly called after further instructions. "And bring it not from the common kitchen, either. Let it be Rostov provender. Let my house slaves bring it."

They waited. Rostov unrolled the map again and studied it while all around him, including Gaspar, who dared hardly breathe, kept silent. Rostov was still gazing at the map when the pitcher of wine and the platter of food arrived. Gaspar took a clay cup from the slave girl who brought it. She was rather young for such a task—not yet a maiden—but she handled the pouring well enough. Something odd about her, though. Her eyes not turned down enough, somehow. Emotion showed in them, even hurt. They were not the eyes of a slave.

Her forehead cut was fresh, still healing. It had been made higher up than normal to preserve her visage. She was rather pretty. Rostov probably had other uses in mind for the girl when she grew older. But then the food was placed before him, and he lost all thought of the slave girl. The stack of meat was surrounded by figs, and both figs and meat had the aroma of fresh roasting. Gaspar immediately felt the saliva form in his arid mouth. Or he felt his mouth attempt to salivate, at least. His swallow remained dry. He reached toward the meat, toward a protruding bone that might serve as a handle. These were ribs of some beast, not a dak. He didn't care. He was so hungry.

He glanced up and met the eyes of the slave boy proffering the platter.

It was Frel. It was his son.

Gaspar moved back, left the rib where it was. He looked into his boy's eyes, and now the tears that would not come before, that could not, found a way, and flowed.

"What?" said Rostov. "I thought you were hungry, wastelander? Why do you not eat?"

Gaspar couldn't take his eyes off Frel.

Alive, alive, he thought. *I hadn't dared to hope.*

"Answer me, wastelander."

"Frel," he said. "Your sister Besda lives. She remembers you. We never forget you and pray for you every lamplighting," he said.

"Wastelander!" said Rostov, more loudly. "Answer me!"

Gaspar forced himself to tear his gaze away from the boy. "Great sheik," he said. "I will do whatever you ask of me."

"Was that *ever* a question?"

Gaspar didn't answer. There was no way to answer that would not mean doom.

Rostov laughed lowly, and stepped beside Gaspar, stepped toward the slaves. They must have seen something forbidding in his countenance—Gaspar was too busy taking in, drinking in, Frel, to notice—for they both stepped back.

And then he let the map unroll again, the Redlands map. He held it up like a dividing curtain between Gaspar and the food, the boy, cutting off his view.

"Now," said Rostov. "Show me. Show me where."

Gaspar slowly raised his hand. He looked at the map. He would locate it, the hilltop within the surrounding mountains where the Scouts were camped, he would point to it. But no. He would be killing ninety men.

He stared at the map. And, after a moment, Gaspar let out a stifled whimper, like the last breath of a dak that you had to put down for its own good.

"What?"

"I—" he whimpered. *I am not an evil man.*

"What are you mumbling about, wastelander? Speak up!"

The bastards! Bastards to put him in such a position. They deserved what was coming.

The bastard Weldletter, making the theft so easy. *In a way it will be Weldletter's own fault.*

And the lieutenant. The Dashian spawn. Taking him hostage, leaving him no choice.

My child, my child!

He wanted to run, to grab Frel and run, but he knew the bodyguards would cut him down at the first move.

Instead, his finger moved toward the map, found the curve of the contour line he was looking for. The bastard Weldletter had shown him how these worked, what they represented.

"Here," he heard his voice croak. "In this dry run, near a blackstone cliff."

Over. Now there was only hope. Only—

Gaspar looked up into the shining, black eyes of Rostov, and felt that hope crinkle, like the skin of one of the Schlusels, strapped to those strange, uniformly shaped stones.

He's not going to let Frel go.

A part of him, a small rational voice, echoed quietly within him that it had been a forlorn hope all along.

Rostov didn't have to say anything. The same voice said it for him.

You fooled yourself, great chief. You were never going to save your son.

A shot rang out. One of the bodyguard crumpled. Another, and the second man, who had drawn a blunderbuss pistol with almost supernatural alacrity, also grabbed at his chest just under the neck as it exploded and bled. He fell also, writhing and kicking in a pool of his own blood, his limbs out of his motor control and seemingly full of crawling insects.

From the edge of the tent two men stepped forward. Both were in Blaskoye garb, but they wore the garments loosely, in an unkempt fashion a Blaskoye would not have been caught dead in.

Both held composite bows notched with arrow.

And those arrows were pointing straight at Rostov.

Amazingly, Rostov only smiled the broader. The more terribly.

"You've killed my cousins," he said. "This is not something we take lightly here in the Redlands."

He nodded toward the wine slave.

"You've come for the girl, I suppose," he said. "There she is. Take her."

The lieutenant held his bow steady. "You get her,

Kruso," he said to the other man. The other man quickly moved over, put an hand on the slave girl's arm, and pulled the wine pitcher toward him. He gently took it from her grasp, set it on a nearby pedestal that had been designed for such a purpose, the delivery of spent dishes. Then he pulled the girl toward himself and into his arm.

"Her ah gotten, Lieutenant," he said in a matter-of-fact tone.

Rostov shook his head. "Lieutenant," he said. "That's not a name. It's a thing, like carpenter or potter. One who carries out the orders of others, and has no will of his own."

"My name is Dashian," the other replied.

"Dashian is the commander," said Rostov. "You are a lieutenant, not a Dashian."

"We're leaving now," the lieutenant said.

"And how will you do so?"

"Through the entrance," said the other.

"Unlikely."

"Maybe you are right," said the lieutenant. He turned to the other Scout. "Ready, Kruso?"

"Aye, Lieutenant."

"*No!*" shouted Gaspar. "You can't go. Not like this. Not now."

"Goodbye, Gaspar," said the lieutenant.

"Take the boy," Gaspar said. "You must!"

"You broke our deal."

"Take him," Gaspar pleaded. "He's dead if you don't."

Dashian glanced quickly to the other, the one called Kruso. Kruso shook his head. "Na good, thet many toh carry," he said.

Rostov began to laugh. "This is the chatter of

walking corpses," he said. "Wind over rocks. Nothing. Lower your bows." He motioned to them impatiently, pointing downward with a finger. "Lower your bows and the slaves will die quickly, cleanly."

"I saw the Schlusels," said Dashian.

Rostov growled impatiently.

"Then you saw how this has to end. *You* will live, in a manner of speaking. I will trade you to your father," he said. "Perhaps a little worse for wear, perhaps no longer quite the man you were. The others . . . well, I have my cousins to avenge, so I'm afraid I cannot promise to make it quick. This one"—he nodded toward Gaspar—"must watch the boy die, of course."

Gaspar felt himself shaking. So much he had risked. Now to have it all yanked from his hands.

I'm a coward, after all, he thought. *I do not want to watch him die. I would want to go before. I would beg to go before if I thought Rostov would listen.*

"Enough," said Dashian. Gaspar looked up, ready for the end to come. But the lieutenant was not speaking to Rostov. He was speaking to the other, the sergeant. "Kruso?"

Together they raised their bows and loosed the arrows. The string sang out and the arrows shot upward, toward the ceiling. Then past the ceiling and through the great venting hole at the very apex of the structure. Upward and out into daylight.

Rostov reached for the knife in his belt, ignoring the pistol stuffed in beside it. He was moving toward the boy.

I would beg, but he wouldn't listen.

And then the sky began to rain arrows.

✧   ✧   ✧

Split-awareness interpolation complete to ninety-three point two seven degrees of accuracy, said Center. **The tracking and location purposes are served. My recommendation is that you return to single-channel awareness with extreme alacrity.**

Hell, yes, said Abel. *We're here.*

6

Abel and Rostov moved toward the boy at the same
instant, but Abel got there first. Abel realized that this
wasn't because he was faster. No, the Blaskoye had
moved to snatch not the boy, but the wooden platter
which had moments before held a stack of meat.

A shield for arrows, thought Abel. *He adapts quickly.*

For a moment their eyes met, Abel's and Rostov's,
and, though the other said nothing, Abel was as sure
of the other's thought as he was of the voices of Center
and Raj. He was sure, because he had experienced
exactly the same thought, and with it, a moment of
complete understanding.

One day, I will kill you.

Then the Blaskoye snatched the wooden platter
away, and Abel pulled the child toward himself.

He had brought twenty Scouts with him on the
trail of Gaspar and, donning the Blaskoye garments
they'd come prepared with, had entered the oasis

encampment and managed to follow the Remlap chief though the settlement undetected. It had not been difficult to blend in, since Awul-alwaha had become a stew of heretofore opposed Redlander tribes. The tents were as varied as the dress. Even if the others had been declared Blaskoye or this new species of tribe, the Redlander, they had not gotten new clothing or new tent-cloth. So they had answered the summons of their new masters bringing what they possessed.

Trailing Gaspar had been difficult, but not the hardest tracking job he or the Scouts had undertaken by far. Like many Redlanders Abel encountered, Gaspar was not as good at fooling Scouts and covering his tracks as he believed himself to be. The desert took marks well, and, once written in scuffed ground or oddly broken twig, those telltales tended to last a long time. The Scouts had often used Redlander arrogance in this regard against them. Many others who had thought the soft Farmer Scouts incapable of tracking them had met their fates in surprised astonishment and disbelief. Abel's greatest challenge had been finding a place to hold the donts, since he could not take them into the oasis proper. But Awul-alwaha had solved the problem for him, in a manner of speaking, for there were corrals already built ringing the encampment. These had probably been built by incoming warrior bands as temporary structures for donts and daks while they established more permanent quarters. Most were occupied, but some were vacant. Abel had left his Scouts' donts in one of these. He tried to select the one closest in as possible. He'd left behind a guard of two to watch over them, and to keep them dressed and ready. He and the rest of the

Scouts followed Gaspar into the encampment. Gaspar was feeling his way, moving slowly, and Abel and his men had not had any trouble catching up with him and shadowing him once again.

Then, when he'd seen the chief slash his way into the smaller tent attached to the enormous central tent, he'd known this was the final destination.

Abel's two squads had scaled the sides of the structure from the outside, then infiltrated through the vents in the tent-cloth where roof met rounded tent walls. These vents had a curtain of fabric draping before them to discourage flitterdaks and insectoids from getting in, and the flaps had concealed the Scouts stationed in the vent openings.

If they'd been noticed climbing the outside of the tent, no one had raised an alarm. Perhaps they were taken to be workers, repairing wind or sun damage. Perhaps this had been aided by the fact that each Scout had stopped and examined the ropes and stakes holding the tent erect just before they began their accent. Several of them were observed to have bent down to test the knots for weakness, one even producing a knife with which to probe the fibers of the rope here and there, no doubt for safety's sake.

It helped that on the ascent, their muskets weren't showing, although bows and arrows were. Abel had ordered them to cover the rifles strapped across their backs beneath their Blaskoye robes, and to arm themselves with bows and arrows when in position. He wanted repetitive firepower. Attempting to reload a musket muzzle while balancing on a bit of fabric was a task beyond even most Scouts.

Meanwhile Abel and Kruso had entered through

the front door. When the doorguard questioned them, Kruso had put on his best South Redland's accent and claimed they were Flanagans, the sea-coast scavengers feared by all in the Delta provinces, come in answer to the Blaskoye call to arms. Since no one had ever seen a Flanagan, they were shown through.

The real lapse in security is the obvious Blaskoye belief that no one from the Valley could survive a trip to Awul-alwaha, said Raj, *much less that some Valleyman could walk right into town and request an audience with the great sheik himself. This will probably be the last time they ever make that mistake, however.*

They're letting me walk in with my rifle, Abel thought. *This Rostov is either incredibly brave or incredibly stupid.*

It is a calculated gambit to shore up allegiance with so many recently conquered tribes, said Center. **As we have witnessed, Rostov literally unmans those who resist. So he allows those who remain the illusion of self-determination, at least about their persons.**

So they had infiltrated.

When he'd seen he had a clear shot, he'd considered shooting Rostov first, but he was not close enough to identify the girl for certain. He calculated that as soon as Rostov fell, pandemonium was likely to break loose. He needed that extra moment to be sure he had the right slave girl in sight. His girl.

So he'd gone for the nearby men-at-arms. Besides, they held rifles, and Rostov had only a pistol stuck into his belt—beside that gleaming silver knife.

One day, perhaps soon, I will regret not immediately

killing Rostov, Abel thought, even as he pulled the trigger and the first guard fell.

Patterns indicate a martial buildup due to internal population pressures and intertribal rivalries resulting from uneven black-market trading between Cascade and Progar, Center said. **Zentrum's plans will take into account the loss of one leader, however valuable.**

Center thinks you shoot down one Rostov, another will pop up in short order due to the powder-keg situation, Raj said. *He may be correct on that score, but I, too, wish you could have taken the shot. Hang the girl.*

No.

All right, Raj replied. *You've got the girl caught up in a fate she never asked for now. The least you can do is take her and run!*

The girl was nine, tall for her age. She was mostly skin and bones, however, as Abel discovered when he lifted her up and threw her across his shoulder. At first she resisted, until he said to her in Landish, "Stop now. You are Loreilei?"

A whispered "Yes."

"I am taking you back to your family." Instantly, she went still and grabbed tightly to his robes. Her breathing increased to rapid gasps, but she made no other sound.

Abel glanced back at Rostov. He was holding the plate by one side and over his head to fend off arrows. Two had already lodged in the wood's exterior. With his other hand, he was aiming his pistol straight at Abel.

He's got me dead to rights.

Then a musket butt crashed across the side of

Rostov's head, taking him and the platter like a club. The pistol cracked, smoked, and fired, but the shot was spent into the floor. Rostov stumbled, then raised the plate to ward off another blow.

It was Kruso, using his fired musket as a bludgeon.

"Leave off," shouted Abel. "Take the boy and go!"

Kruso instantly obeyed, pulling up the boy like a sack of meal and holding him under one arm. They sprinted toward the entrance.

The doorguard, so easy to pass on the way in with a bit of subterfuge, were in no mood to let them out again. But five arrows found the two men and both were screaming and cursing as Abel and Kruso barreled between them. The entrance to the sheik's tent lay not ten paces before them now. Abel risked a glance back.

Rostov was right behind them, his gleaming chrome knife in his hand. Trailing the sheik was Gaspar. The chief had found the strength to lift himself up and follow after, as if pulled by a magnetism he could not resist.

And behind Rostov were the Blaskoye, kinsmen by the look of their raiment. They had, it seemed, suddenly realized that their leader was under attack and were swarming to the offensive behind him.

"Now!" Abel shouted into the upper reaches of the tent in Landish. "Away!"

The Scouts disappeared from the vent holes and, Abel knew, had grabbed portions of tent fabric and were sliding down the side. There they would finish the work they'd begun before they ascended. Each went to the nearest anchoring stake to find the partially sawn rope that held tension on the enormous structure and complete the task of severing that rope entirely.

Even as Abel turned back to spring for the entrance and daylight, he saw the sides of the structure begin to sag. And when he burst through to outside, it was falling all around him, falling down upon the contingent of Blaskoye who were on the heels of Rostov.

He was in the dust of the pathway in front of the tent.

"Dashian!"

The scream came from behind him, and he spun around as Rostov burst from the tent. Abel quickly put the girl down, shoved her behind him, and turned to face the Blaskoye.

But Rostov stopped in his tracks, as if he'd run into an invisible wall.

What the hell?

Risk a quick look behind you, lad, said Raj, laughter in his voice.

Abel did so. His twenty Scouts were lined up with drawn muskets, each muzzle aimed at the heart of the Blaskoye.

Then Gaspar ran past Rostov and, as a man might snatch an insectoid from the air, Rostov reached out and snared the Remlap chief by the neck and yanked him back and to his side. Within a split second, he had his knife at Gaspar's throat.

"Papa!" A small loud voice from nearby, and the slave boy was struggling in Kruso's grasp and had broken free toward his father and the Blaskoye.

Rostov cut Gaspar's throat with a practiced brutality and shoved the still stumbling man toward the approaching boy. Meanwhile, the Blaskoye ran for cover.

"Fire!" Abel yelled.

It was just enough distraction.

A hail of balls kicked up the dust and followed

Rostov, but no one had tracked him quickly enough, and he was gone before any could reload.

Gone to get reinforcements, said Raj. **Time to leave.**

"Stay here," Abel said to the girl behind him. He and Kruso darted out to the slave boy, who was standing over his father. Gaspar lay face up, his neck oozing. The boy was attempting the impossible task of stanching the carotid bleeding.

"Come tha away, youngen," Kruso said gently. But his hand was firm as he pulled the boy back and led him toward the Scouts. Abel gazed down at the Remlap chief a moment longer. There was the trace of a smile lingering on his face. Perhaps his last sight had been the boy. Perhaps not.

Abel turned to the Scouts. "Home," he said. He picked up the girl again. His men, now reloaded, made their way at a fast trot out of the encampment, back to the edge of the desert and to the corral where the donts awaited them.

There was no question of throwing off pursuit. This was going to be a race. He hoped his other orders had been obeyed. They would find out soon enough.

They rode west. For the first quarter-watch, he had the donts running on two legs, but the creatures could not sustain such a pace, and eventually he ordered everyone to a more endurable gallop.

He'd been right about the pursuit. Within a half watch, a glance behind revealed a cloud of dust rising on the horizon—a large one, at that. Abel estimated it would take at least a hundred riders to kick up such a fury of redness.

And so it went for two days of hard riding. They

stopped only to water the donts, and then only to let them slurp at soaked sponges, nothing more. Abel slept in the saddle, and had to tie the girl to his back at points so that she could slumber and not fall off. They traveled by day and by night. There was no question of a pause, a rest. Not yet.

Then Abel saw the landmark he was looking for, a great hill of rounded stone in the distance, and headed toward it. This was where they got to find out if Weldletter's cartography was going to prove crucial or get them all killed. He had an accurate memory of every place the Scouts had passed, thanks to Center, but the remainder of the Scouts did not. And the ones he'd left behind in pursuit of Gaspar did not have him to guide them to the rendezvous point.

All they had was Weldletter's map.

Because, of course, the map of the Redlands they'd allowed Gaspar to take was a forgery. Accurate enough in its broad outline, but completely misleading when you got down to the details.

As to the map of the Land itself that Gaspar had stolen—that one hadn't been a misleading copy at all. It was an out-and-out fake. He and Weldletter had spent some enjoyable moments coming up with believable troop numbers and fortification figures that he'd then had Weldletter pen to the papyrus. Would the Blaskoye detect the ploy? In some ways, it didn't matter. Both fake maps had served their immediate and most important purpose: bait for one who was bait himself, but hadn't known it.

Maybe somewhere inside, Gaspar did, Abel thought, *and yet couldn't help himself.*

To the left up ahead, said Center. **Between**

those red sandstone cliffs lies the entrance to the canyon.

Soon the donts were off sand and onto the stones of a dry wash, their horn-coated feet clattering as the Scouts passed. The walls of the canyon quickly rose on either side of them and soon became cliffs a fieldmarch high. It was past noon, and the canyon was in shadow. This was at least relief from the unremitting sun.

The going became narrower and the donts were huffing and puffing at the steep upward climb. It was almost, but not quite, beyond them—especially with their Scouts urging them on with frenetic intensity. The animals were beginning to fail, however. Abel knew they must rest soon or most of the mounts, as desert-tough as they were, would die. He was quite willing to drive them until it killed them if he had to, but to do so would leave his men stranded here, only a quarter of the way back home.

Then he saw it. A mirror flash. Kruso immediately flashed back. An exchange of silent conversation followed.

They had made it. The rendezvous had succeeded. They rode onward. The path narrowed to the point that they must proceed single file. Sandstone scraped against his protruding legs and might have taken the skin and more had it not been for his leg wraps. Here was the reason they were part of the Scout uniform, the reason for all the snap uniform inspections he'd endured in his youth.

Steeper, and the donts were on two legs by necessity in order to climb the path. Then, to his right, he saw the side path, the trail up a rivulet that his own memory and the maps they'd made said was dont-passable. It was, nonetheless, very steep, and he bade the girl, who was only semi-conscious now, to wake up as best she could and hold on tight. To her credit, he felt her grip tighten around his waist.

And after what seemed an interminable scramble, they emerged on the rim. They were out.

There was Weldletter, and beside him were Abel's sergeants, the leaders of the squads he'd left behind to pursue Gaspar. One of them, a crusty Ingresman named Maday, he'd left in charge; and it was Maday who reported. His accent was thick, but he did not choose to always speak in the patois as did Kruso.

"Charges are in place, sir," Maday reported.

"Did you follow Weldletter's instructions?"

"We did," said Maday. "Packed every map case full of powder. Maps are going to be ruined, I'm afraid, sir."

"Let's get out of this first, then worry about the maps," Abel replied.

"Aye, sir."

Now the big question.

"And the corning? Did you do it?"

"We didn't much like the idea, you know," said the sergeant. "Thursday school and all that."

"Did you do it?" Abel said.

"Corning gunpowder beyond priming grain strength is a Stasis violation," Maday said, "but we did as you suggested and held a séance with the Lady." Maday smiled broadly, revealing three missing teeth. His mouth looked like a portcullis. "And what do you know, we all had a vision of the Fifty Days and Fifty Nights, her suckling baby Zentrum, even though she was dead in body. And we took it as a sign that sometimes there were exceptions, you know. That she'd told us that corning gunpowder beyond priming grain is a Stasis violation *only in the Land*. She came to *me*, she did, and told me not only to go ahead, but to keep it a bit damp to make the process go easier, just like you said before. Irisobrian provides."

"The Lady provides," Abel answered back. "Alaha Zentrum."

Observe:

A line of men on a rock slab. They were sitting in the sun under broad-brimmed hats and makeshift head scarves and spending a day, all of it, every sunlit hour, carefully tap, tap, tapping at gunpowder with a pestle made of minié balls pounded together. Stones were too coarse grained, and rifle metal wouldn't do. The lead gave no spark. One problem: this required using every minié ball in the cartridge box to make a useful-sized pestle. No more bullets for the duration.

Watch upon watch of sifting the powder, winnowing it like grain through linen gauze. Tap, tap, tapping it again.

The Lady provides patience, I guess, Abel thought.

Beliefs are what men fight for, Raj said. **Laugh at the beliefs, maybe, but not at the believers.**

By the second day, the tapping had worn shallow tanajas into the slab upon which the Scouts worked.

Weldletter and the sergeants loaded the powder into the cases, and Weldletter had his team set them out. They'd completed the task not long before the first echoes traveling up the canyon had let them know Abel's troop was on its way.

"Tham Redlanders up coming!" shouted one of the other sergeants, Moreau. Abel's attention snapped back to the present.

He dismounted and strode to the rim's edge. Sure enough, the Blaskoye had stayed on the trail, had relentlessly pursued them up the canyon, expecting, no doubt to lock them in a corner and slaughter them. Whether or not they knew of the exit path Abel and his Scouts had taken, it wasn't going to matter soon.

"Fire in the hole," shouted another voice from below.

"Fire in the hole," shouted another, and another.

Then the men burst out into the open on the path, fleeing from the conflagration they'd prepared in the canyon below.

Rising behind them, up into the sky, a single trail of gunsmoke, like a line drawn straight up into the sky. A sizzling sound accompanied the sight, like wind through tiny leaves.

Then, as Abel watched the gunsmoke line write itself out, it began to spiral, twist in two, then three directions, as if a giant invisible hand were losing control of a pen tip, and scrawling all over a papyrus tablet.

Suddenly, the end of the line exploded.

Analysis indicates one of the explosive canisters under-loaded, Center reported. **Insufficiently placed and weighted, as well. This canister burned from its end up and made itself into the rocket we just witnessed.**

A rocket? Abel thought. *Like the ships that travel the stars?*

Not quite.

Well, whatever it is, I like it!

Then he was back in reality. In the same instant that the rocket exploded, so did the canyon below Abel. The explosions were muted, heard from this position above the absorbing canyon walls, but from the great blanketing cloud that arose below, Abel knew they'd been powerful. Then he saw that the cloud had not been caused by exploding gunpowder at all, but by the avalanches those explosions had set off.

Maday and Weldletter had placed the explosive canisters in masterfully chosen locations. When the cloud settled, Abel saw that the pathway was sealed. What had been an escape path was now boulder-filled and impassable. It would take the Blaskoye at least a day, and leagues and leagues of travel, to backtrack and go around.

From below came the sound of gunfire and shouting men. The surviving Blaskoye were enraged. And completely ineffective. They could not come up. They would have to ride around.

"I veel find you, Dashiaaaaaaan," came the loudest call. "I veel come for you. Dashiaaan! Dashiaaan!"

Abel realized Maday was telling him more, nattering on in the usual good-natured Scout's litany of complaints. "Worked, thank the Lady. And us two days at it. I can't say the men much liked sitting around taking mortar to the stuff. And then I had to tell them to unwrap their cartridges, too, that we needed it all, and that they'd be going home with only their bows to depend on. We're plumb out of powder, Lieutenant."

"Understood," Abel said. He turned wearily back to his dont. "We also need to ride to water."

"Weldletter says Ruddy Seep's three leagues from here, but that's what they'd expect."

"Yes, you're right."

"A half day is that little sunken spring we passed on our way out, the one on the plain with the single tree."

"We'll go there."

"Can you make it another half day?"

Abel shook his head to clear it. Good question, could he? Yes, but could the donts?

I guess we'll find out how good Scout dont stock really is on this trip, he thought.

"We head for the single-tree spring," he said. "Pass the word."

He tried to climb back onto his dont, found he could not muster the strength the first time or the second.

But when he tried the third time, a hand reached down to help. The girl, Loreilei, held to the saddle with one hand, grabbed him by the sleeve with the other and pulled. Her strength was not great, but it was the little extra he needed. He slung his leg over and was on.

"Thank you," he said to her, but she did not reply.

"Mount up!" he called out to all. "No rest for you sorry layabouts. I'll get a day's work out of you yet." He nodded at his weary, but smiling, men.

His sergeants rode up beside him.

"On your command," said Maday. "We're ready."

A good reconnaissance. There will be much to report to your father, said Center. **I have almost reached my conclusions, as well. We have a chance now.**

Good? said Raj. **The boy circled the Blaskoye like J.E.B. Stuart for Lee, and you're calling it good. I'd call it spectacular. I'm proud of the lad!**

Abel grinned wearily in the saddle.

I also have reached a few conclusions, he thought.
And what are those, lad?

I know what I want now, Abel thought.

Rockets, Abel thought. *I liked that. I want them. And those guns that load from behind you have been telling me about. No more of this awkward reloading when men are trying to kill us.*

Yes, Center replied. **With an invasion timeline now in place, variable cascade analysis indicates your conclusions are correct. It is time for tiered innovation if we are to survive beyond the next year. This must be done carefully. There will be setbacks. They will have to be dealt with appropriately, perhaps ruthlessly.**

Abel was barely listening.

One more thing, he thought. *There is one more thing I want. I don't know if you would call it an innovation, but I want it nonetheless, and I'll have it.*

And what is that? Did he detect a trace of worry in Center's normal utter neutrality of speech?

Mahaut, he said. *I want her. I want the woman. If she'll have me.*

Center's silence and Raj's good-hearted, throaty laughter accompanied him all the way to the distant watering hole.

7

It was when they were a day out from the Valley's edge that Center reported his conclusion: an invasion of Treville would come on the night of the next *new* three-moon evening.

The expedition has been a success. I have factored observed numbers, states of preparedness, known Blaskoye tactics, and psychodynamic modeling using our encounter with the clan leadership. They are coming at what they will view as the first opportunity. This will be the first night when all three moons are below the horizon. There are only three nights a year when this is the case in Duisberg's northern hemisphere.

So you won't have to kill me and start all over because I went for the child, Abel thought. It was not a question, but a factual statement. *Meeting Rostov face-to-face was essential to your calculations.*

That proved to be correct, Center replied, a little too quickly and coldly for Abel's liking. **Your gamble was effective.**

Don't fight it, lad, laughed Raj. *It's good to be careful, but if you can't be careful, it's even better to be lucky.*

The next day they encountered the first outlying Scout picket. They had been stationed in position for two eight-days, and apart from operational wigwag had no news to report. For the past days, it had slowly dawned on Abel that they were no longer being pursued. Kruso and a half squad had doubled back to check, and this had proved true. Nevertheless, he ordered the outpost corporal to send out long pickets with good mirrors and be watchful.

Abel and the Scouts rode on.

Another day, and they were at the Escarpment's edge. Another half day and they rode into Hestinga. It was midday.

He'd thought about bringing the girl to her relatives, delivering her in triumph on a washed and festooned dont, but he'd known at the time it was merely a fantasy. Lilleheim was too far out of the way. Who would take the Remlap boy was more problematic, and Abel was on the verge of ordering a man to feed and clothe him, and to give him a bunk among the cadets, when Weldletter stepped up and volunteered to take the boy in at his officer's billet. The mapmaker had taken a liking to the child, and, using Kruso for a translator, had spoken gently in his dry, exacting voice to the Remlap boy about the time he'd spent with the boy's father. These talks seemed to calm the boy on nights when he could be heard crying softly in his meager bedroll—an extra saddle blanket they had converted for the purpose—or at least got the crying to stop.

So it was the girl who proved more of an immediate problem after all.

She did not want to physically let go of Abel, much less leave him, when they arrived in the headquarters yard.

"You have to let me go to the commander," he told her. "It's my duty. It's why I was sent. To bring back a report."

She looked up at him wordlessly—she had probably spoken no more than five or six words in the six days they had travelled together—and held tightly to his tunic lapel.

As if to say: "I *am the report,*" he thought to himself.

"I cannot bring you inside," he said. He looked around, but his men were busy taking care of their donts. He'd handed his own over to Maday to feed, water, and groom.

In the end, he simply let her tag along close at his heels. The others made not to notice her. Even Lieutenant Courtemanche, his father's adjunct and the keeper of the outer office gate, only glanced down at the girl, said nothing, and saluted Abel.

"The commander will see you now, Captain," he said.

Captain? Abel thought. But he was too tired to correct the man, and too tired to wonder why someone who was normally an extremely meticulous sort when it came to military matters would slip up on his rank.

He didn't have to wait long to find out. When he stepped into the office, his father looked up from his table full of scrolls and said, "Sharplett is dead. You are now Captain and Regimental Commander of Scouts."

Abel stiffened to attention. Sharplett.

Stern taskmaster, ass-kicker, and finally a kindly, if grumpy, uncle to me, Abel thought. "Yes, sir," Abel said. "How, if I may ask?"

"A raid ten days ago," said Joab. "An undermanned patrol, near to the Escarpment. All massacred. He seems to have been targeted. They hung him by his own—"

Joab glanced down, seemed to see the girl for the first time.

"He was killed," he finished.

"You should give it to Colefax," Abel said. "He has seniority."

"No," Joab said. "You."

Then Joab stood up and smiled at the little girl. "You are Loreilei Jacobson, I presume?" he said. He came around the desk and bent down on his haunches so he was eye to eye with the girl. Abel saw a frown flicker across his face when he noticed the slave scar, but it did not displace his smile, which was genuine. "It is Loreilei, isn't it?"

The girl stared back at him, blinked twice, then replied, as if she were just discovering the fact for herself in the speaking of it, "My name is Loreilei. Yes."

Then Joab looked up and shook his head at Abel. "I made it worse, didn't I? Trying to get you away from that woman?"

"I didn't do it for that," Abel said.

"I'm sure you believe you did not," said Joab. He turned back to Loreilei. "Your mother has missed you. She will be very glad to see you. Very, very glad. Do you want to see her?"

The girl nodded.

"Ah!" A cry from the door. Abel turned. A woman in a diaphanous green robe was standing there. The kohl around her eyes was running in black traces down her cheeks. "My baby, my baby," Adele Jacobson whispered. She hesitated for a moment, as if to be sure she was stepping into a room and not into a beguiling and empty dream, but then she ran the three paces from the door to the girl and took the child in her arms. "Loreilei."

The girl said nothing, but after a moment, she too was crying, letting her mother hold her, envelop her.

"How did you—"

"Wigwag from the outpost," said Joab. "I sent for her immediately. We couldn't have her around here, of course, so she was waiting in the officer's mess. I imagine Courtemanche sent for her as soon as you came in."

"Thank you, Father," Abel said.

"Yes," he said. He watched the mother and daughter reunion a bit longer. "Lilleheim will have some good news. They sorely need it. As will the Jacobsons."

The woman, Adele Jacobson—she was Edgar's sister, and Loreilei was his niece—was already ushering the child toward the door. "You will have a bath, and your room, I told them not to, never to change it . . . oh, it's just like it was. And we'll see to your cut." She looked at the slavery scar. "I think we can, yes, it should be possible with a little powder to . . . oh, never mind, darling, that doesn't matter. Nothing matters but that you're back. Let's go to the wagon. Luther is waiting with the wagon. We'll go home. Let's go home. Don't you want to go home?"

She asked this as if uncertain of the answer, but

the girl nodded. Still, she did not smile, but she was crying, which, for Abel, was the best sign he'd seen from her for days that she might, someday, heal from what had been done to her.

As Adele led her away, the girl, who was Loreilei, but would always be *the girl* to him, turned around and gave him a parting look.

It was a look that was near to being frightening, it was so intense. He did not attempt to fathom the feeling behind it. Then she turned back to her mother, and was gone.

"I have something for you, Captain," Joab said. Abel turned back to his father.

There was the unmistakable clang of metal upon metal as Joab drew his saber from its scabbard. "Few are permitted such a weapon. Captains and above."

"Father, it's *yours*. As DMC."

"Not at all," Joab replied. "I *inherited* this. It is the Dashian blade."

"No other captain has one."

"In Treville, perhaps. You are now a regimental commander," Joab said. "Plenty of Guardians and Regulars in Lindron carry them." Joab set the saber on his desk, considered it for a moment in its bare form. Then he unhitched the belt and scabbard, and, re-sheathing the saber, set saber and scabbard together back on the desk. "I always told myself I'd give this to you after you had done something...extraordinary." He smiled. "And, of course, after you'd made captain, which I have always fully expected."

"Father, I don't know what to say," Abel replied. "It is completely ineffectual against artillery. We had exactly *no* battles, no encounters even, where we grew close enough for sword-work with the enemy. The only time I might have used it, it would have been impossible to conceal, and concealment was what I needed at the time."

"I know all this well. Believe me, I've experienced it myself," Joab said. "And yet, I expect you to wear it into battle."

"Why?"

"For the family? For glory?" Joab said. "Some matters cannot be put into words. Just take it, Abel."

Your father has a point, lad, Raj said. *You should do as he wishes.*

"As you command," Abel replied. He picked up the saber and scabbard and buckled it around his waist.

"That's that. Now, to practical matters," Joab said. Abel took a stealthy glance but noticed no tear in his father's eye. Sentimentality was certainly not one of his father's weaknesses. "Do you have an idea when they're coming?"

"Yes, I know exactly. Next new three-moon night."

"That actually makes a lot of sense," Joab mused. "You have an estimate of how many?"

"It will be . . . overwhelming."

"And where they will strike?"

"No, I don't know that," said Abel. He sighed. Not a sigh of regret, but of relief.

Safe, for a moment, to breathe, he thought. *To not fear my next breath will see an arrow or bullet in my back.*

He smiled. "But I do have an idea of what their thinking might be," he said. "We left them with a certain map, you see."

❖   ❖   ❖

"My father is a complete bastard," Abel said as he paced across the room. Mahaut sat up in a chair. They were in her sitting room now, the room outside her bedroom, her long sickroom, in Lilleheim. He'd thought he would sleep one night in Hestinga, collapse in the bed in his father's house, the same room he'd grown up in, with the pallet becoming a cot, with the chest of clothing and his few toys replaced by a respectable wardrobe he'd bought with two months of saved wages. But that was not to be.

And then, rested, he would ride to Lilleheim, leave his dont and sleeping roll at the outpost, and go to see her in the village. Instead, he had ridden to Lilleheim shortly after delivering his report. No rest. He'd barely stopped moving.

His father had ordered him back to the Redlands immediately to take over Sharplett's command from the outpost at the Upper Cliffs. He was to leave in the morning. He'd managed to secure permission to wait until after breakfast, so he'd bought at least that much time.

He'd tormented himself with fantasies that Edgar Jacobson might be there, having returned from his urgent business at Garangipore, but that was not the case.

She was alone, but for a servant, who absented herself to her quarters quickly enough after he arrived. They sat drinking wine in the cool night air, the room lit by three evenly spaced oil lamps, all profligately lit. The Jacobsons really did have more wealth than they knew what to do with to burn oil like that. He supposed Mahaut was getting used to it, too. She allowed the servant to pour their wine before leaving, but sat upright upon her lounging couch rather than recline in a semi-swoon position, as would most women with her position and means. Abel sat in a leatherback chair that felt solid, comfortable, and far more expensive than anything he could afford.

The change in her was enormous. No longer was she taking faltering steps, but hopping around with plenty of energy, only hampered by the slight limp in her right leg. She wore a saffron linen gown with a red sash drawing it closed. And she'd even applied kohl liner to her eyes and a bit of rouge to her cheeks.

"Did you do that before?" he asked her, he said, pointing to his own eye to illustrate. "I don't remember."

"You barely noticed my existence before I was shot," she told him. "I doubt you remember a thing about me."

"Not true," he said. "I did at least know Xander had a sister."

"I saw you," she said. "When you were in from scouting. That russet tunic. Xander made fun of it, told me how black was better, but I liked it then. And I like it now."

"It hides bloodstains well, they say."

"No doubt," she said. "You were saying your father was a bastard?"

"He didn't want me to come here. He doesn't think this is a good idea."

"Doesn't think *what* is a good idea?"

"You are married."

"We are friends."

"Yes," he said. "And I want to be your lover."

Now she was taken aback. She flushed, and even in the wan light and even with the rouge, he could see it.

"I am a ruin," she finally said. "You of all people know that."

He took a strong swallow of wine. *There, I've told her,* he thought. *I've brooded for two three-moons over how I would say it, and now it's out, done.*

"An interesting ruin," he answered her. "You can't pretend I don't know. I've seen it. I've touched it."

"You've healed what could be healed," she said. Mahaut nodded, sipped from her own cup. The lamplight flickered across her face, and it slowly dawned on him.

She's prettier than I remembered. Much.

"What have you done to yourself, anyway?" he asked her. "You've . . . I'm so tired . . . it isn't just the makeup, is it?"

"The hair," she said. "I don't have it pulled it back in braids. And the robe. You remember me from when I was wearing Xander's castoffs, and then from the Lilleheim knoll. I long ago made a truce with fine linen, Abel. Let's just say smooth linen and I became allies, if not friends. And do you like this bracelet? The gems are northern black onyx."

She held up her arm, and the robe sleeve fell back to reveal a glittering train of jewels. Her fingernails were painted a subtle red.

"Don't tell me you're going to act like they tell you to act," he said. "I won't believe it."

"The problem, my dear Captain, is not with me, but with your imagination. We didn't run into one another for a year or more once I moved to Lilleheim. You never saw me this way, that's all," she said softly, but with a laugh in her voice. Then she pouted a beautiful, bowed pout. Lip rouge. Just a trace, but enough. "You don't like it?"

He didn't answer, but downed the rest of his wine

and moved to pour himself more. She rose, took the pitcher, and filled his cup.

The slightest trace of hyacinth perfume.

"I liked you as a tomboy," he said. "I like you now."

And then she bent to kiss him. It was what he'd thought of, brooded on, fallen asleep imagining on cold desert nights. Perfect.

He stood and picked her up. She was still so slight, so thin from her long recovery. He took her to the bedroom.

"I have to leave at dawn," he said. "I have to be on the Escarpment by noon."

"Were you thinking of sleeping?"

"No."

He laid her on the bed, untied the red sash, pulled back her robe.

Somehow he had remembered her breasts as being on the small side, but they were not, they were ample. The scar stretched from above her hip, down her right groin and onto the leg. A portion of muscle had been destroyed beneath it and would never grow back, leaving a slight depression. This was not beautiful. Neither did it matter.

He was throwing off his tunic, unwrapping his filthy leg wraps, all at once, all in a frenzy, and she began to laugh.

"What?"

"Straight in from the field," she said. "You probably have the blood of your enemies on you."

"Some, yes," he said.

"*His* blood?" The question was sudden, as if it were something she'd wanted desperately to ask and had only now worked up the courage.

He stepped back. "No," he said. "I didn't manage to draw any of that."

Mahaut pulled him toward her, guided his hand to the scar tissue.

Then suddenly she twisted an arm up and under his chin.

An obsidian dagger was in her hand. Its tip was biting into his neck deeply enough to raise a welt of blood.

She knows her anatomy, he thought. *She's got it just over the artery.*

"Don't show pity," she said.

"All right," he said. "I won't."

He drew back, and with the same motion caught her arm, twisted. With a cry of pain, she released the dagger. He took it up and plunged it into the wood of the bed's headboard, where it stuck fast.

In almost the same motion, he put a hand on her breastbone and leaned hard onto her, one knee on her bed, one foot on the ground. He stared down at her naked form, said nothing.

She pulled him closer, kissed him again. Her tongue snaked out and forced its way into his mouth. Now he pulled down his breeches enough, but he was still half undressed. It was enough. And he could no longer wait.

"No pity," he said. "And no mercy." He touched the scar. Then he moved his fingers lower till she gasped.

Suddenly she cried out. She twisted away from his touch, raised a hand and slapped him across the face. She put her fingernails into it, enough to scratch, to draw blood. He snatched her free wrist, held it tight— under the pressure of his grip, the black onyx bracelet dug into her flesh until she gasped. He pushed the hand down, down to the other hand, wrist over wrist, and held her to the bed. She ceased to struggle but lay rigid, the muscles of her body tensed.

"Do you want me to let you go?" he said.

She shook her head. "No. Don't let me go," she said.

He held her tighter.

"Bring me back," she whispered. "You brought back Loreilei. Bring *me* back."

Holding her in this manner, he found—felt—his way inside her.

Then, as suddenly as the storm took her, she was calm. Her breathing eased. She opened to him like the Land itself.

Mahaut gave him the dagger to take with him.

"It was my grandmother's," she said. "For protection in the streets of Mims, she told me. I used to always carry it, but I've got a pistol now."

He looked at her in surprise.

"We are rich. Such things can be acquired. It's only for the protection of my virtue, such as it is," she said. "I use a bow for pleasure."

"And use the occasional Scout captain for pleasure, as well?"

She laughed at that, but continued to proffer the dagger. "I want you to carry it with you. Always. Will it be a hindrance to you?"

Not a hindrance, but probably as useless as Father's saber, he thought.

"I will carry it," he said.

He left at dawn, and slept in the saddle on the way back to Hestinga. His dont knew the way, and though it stopped a few times to graze upon the thorny grass on the side of the road it craved, he made it back in time to deploy up the Escarpment.

He was at the Upper Cliffs by nightfall.

PART FOUR

The Battle

1

Observe:

The Blaskoye flowed down from the Escarpment on new three-moons night. They chose four discrete paths down. It was impossible to guard the length of the Rim, and, though the Scouts were aware of where the breaches occurred, there was little they could do except provide intelligence. The bands bypassed Hestinga fifteen leagues to the south, riding over the broad expanse of farmland south of the road and headed for Garangipore. It was then Abel knew.

The map. He's taken the bait, Abel thought. *We put an arsenal with a small guard in Garangipore. It would be a natural point to attack: take out a poorly guarded but crucial supply depot.*

This is the feint we have been looking for, said Center. **It will be an attempt to draw out the forces of Hestinga, including your father. The Blaskoye have learned since Lilleheim not**

to underestimate the Militia, and especially the
Regulars. They will not wish to be trapped and
encircled in a village again, but will have a different plan.

What plan?

There are various permutations, Center said. A
countermarch—or, in their case, a counterride—
back on Hestinga. A raid combined with an invasion from the north. An ambush attempt, after
drawing out the forces from Hestinga.

It will be ambush, said Raj. *This has become
personal for the Blaskoye.*

Yes, said Center. Observe what has happened:
The attack on Garangipore began on the same
moonless night as the invasion. Such was the size of
the Blaskoye horde that flooded down the Rim that
the Redlanders were not through invading the Valley
before the first of the dontriders had travelled the
eleven leagues to Garangipore. There was nothing to
see except black shapes against the stars, but there was
plenty to hear. It came across the bottomlands south
of the Canal road like the rumble of distant thunder.
There were only two men out that night traveling on
the road who were older than twenty—brothers who
were now merchants and delivering barge goods to
Hestinga that included containers of wax that must
travel out of direct sunlight. Both were barely old
enough to remember when the last rainstorm came up
the Valley. One turned to the other and, fearing the
lightning and slashing and impossible water from the
sky that they so well recalled, even though they had
only been seven and eight years old at the time, had
wordlessly urged their dak team to a hell-for-leather

run into the safety of Hestinga and a roof, however sun-rotted and weak, over their heads.

If they had stayed a little longer to listen, they might have heard the blowing of the bone horns and known it was something else entirely that was happening to their Land.

Over ten thousand Redland warriors on dontback were in the process of entering the Valley. By sunrise the invasion was complete. The horde was rampant in Treville.

The garrison at Garangipore stood no chance. The village itself was half the size of Hestinga, more trading outpost on the River than town. It was also spread out and had none of the walled compactness and tidiness of Hestinga. The Blaskoye simply overran the garrison and the village. The soldiers of the garrison, one hundred Regulars, and what Militia was able to turn out—not many, the surprise was complete—were slaughtered. The bodies of the Regulars were tied to ropes and dragged through the streets to cow the residents, as if they needed further cowing.

By noon, the first impalements of town leaders had been set up along the road, with men run through on stakes writhing in a line that stretched two hundred paces from the village's west entrance.

Yet, to the utter frustration of the Blaskoye, not one of the impaled or of the others variously murdered had revealed what they, the Blaskoye, so desperately wished to know: where was the great stockpile of gunpowder that was stored in Garangipore?

It is here, shouted the warriors into the faces of the tortured and damned. *It* has to be *here, we know it!* And when it was the big one, the man in blue and white raiment who sported the great black beard, who was doing the questioning, he would shake a papyrus scroll in the faces of his victims.

"It is here somewhere," he shouted in his heavily accented Landish. "It says so on this map! Now show me! Show me or die!"

But they could not show him, for they did not know.

A great many died before Rostov was convinced of this fact, however.

The map was wrong.

He had been tricked.

There was no gunpowder stockpile in Garangipore.

There was no greater military garrison. The men he had killed were all there were.

He would still destroy them. Take and rape their Land, make it bear his fruit, his seed, instead of theirs. Come in from the miserable desert to a place of plenty and live not as a beggar, but as that land's ruler.

He would do this.

The task was just going to take a bit longer, that was all.

So he put out his Scouts and pickets and waited. They would come. And they would come along the Road. They would have to. And when they were on the march from Hestinga, he would be ready—ready to fall upon and destroy them.

Patience and savagery in striking. These were the traits of the raptor, the totem of Blaskoye. He would pray to his raptor god, find patience. The savagery he could handle on his own without the god's help.

Where? thought Abel. *When?*

Remember, the Blaskoye must behave as cavalry to be effective. You saw what happened to them

in Lilleheim when they dismounted and fought on the ground. Militia were able to rout them. They'll need to use the donts' speed to concentrate in overwhelming numbers. But that can't take place just anywhere. Village streets, alleys, and pathways are a barrier, not an advantage, to a soldier on dontback.

So it won't be in Garangipore or another village, Abel thought. *Which leaves the River, the bottomlands, and the Escarpment.*

Now consider the Militia at march, Raj continued patiently. **Will they travel overland, through fields and patties?**

Not if they can help it. They'll stick to the road.

Exactly. Not only will they stick to the road, they'll travel down it in line. How wide would you make the road between Hestinga and Garangipore to be?

A few paces. Ten at its widest. Abel began to realize what Raj was getting at. *They'll be strung out in line for a league or more along the Canal road between Hestinga and Garangipore. Either side of the road will form a perfect flank to attack. It'll be difficult to concentrate and rally. The Blaskoye could overwhelm any given spot in the line and then travel up the road in either direction to wrap up the rest, one double-filed marcher at a time.*

This would seem the most probable strategy for the Blaskoye, but prediction of exact locations produces probabilities of less than fifty percent in all present instances.

But it's the Canal *road,* thought Abel. *From Hestinga to the bridge at Talla, the Canal levee is within sight on the north side of the road. After Talla, it's on the south side, and just as close. If it were me, I wouldn't come from the Canal side. Instead, I would try to drive the forces on the road toward the Canal. It's not the River, by any means, but: first of all there are the earthen levees on either side, at least fifty elbs high. Then there's the Canal itself. It's too deep to wade across. You're swimming in the middle for a good fifteen paces. And it has carnadons in it. Not as many as the River, but plenty enough. It's a barrier. I'd trap my enemy with his back to it, run him up against the levees and destroy him.*

Aye, the lad has something, said Raj.

The Talla bridge is closer to Garangipore, at league nine point seven of the eleven point two six leagues between Hestinga and Garangipore.

I would destroy the bridge while I was making the ambush farther down the road.

Theoretically, yes, Raj replied. **But coordinated attacks are a very difficult proposition to pull off when you're essentially a rabble of mounted horse.**

They're beginning to acquire discipline. That's probably all Rostov has been working on in the past three-moons, and even before that. You saw how he'd concentrated them at Awul-alwaha.

Easier wished for and blustered about than actually done, Raj said. **Of course they might try.**

And we could be there, ready.

Exactly.

So a thrust across the Canal road coming from south and moving to the north, wheeling out of Garangipore, thought Abel. *That narrows the possibilities considerably.*

But leaves seven point two leagues of open road, Center said. **We have not won even this theoretical battle yet. And there is one other factor to consider. The levees themselves have pathways running along their tops. These are wagon tracks for transport of the sluice-gate machinery. Furthermore, there are the gates themselves.**

Yes, that's right, thought Abel. *The fields between the Canal road and the levee are rice paddies. They're kept dry half the year, and flooded the other half. This is, of course, not long after harvest time, and they are dry.*

But they don't have to be, Raj added with an evil chuckle.

We now have a workable plan, said Center. **It is time to risk discovery by Zentrum. It is time to introduce the innovation you and Golitsin have been preparing.**

So, he was finally going to see in reality what had only been an idea placed in his mind for years. *But surely there's no time to convert the Regulars' guns,* Abel thought. *And the Militia is mostly pikemen and archers, of course.*

Converting regular army rifles to breech fire will not be necessary, said Center. **No, only one military component need receive the innovation.**

Scouts, Abel thought.

"Delta gum," Golitsin said. "It is the most amazing substance!"

"You mean the nasty stuff the Delta men chew instead of nesh?"

"Exactly. We've solved the blowback problem with it."

"I'll have to see it to believe it."

"I'll do you one better than that," said Golitsin. "You can *shoot* it to believe it."

He showed Abel the prototype.

He half cocked the hammer to safe in order to slide back the breech dog, the heavy covering that kept the trapdoor opening fully shut during firing. Then he fingered the little hook and latch lever he'd created and popped the top of the breechlock up. It did look like a trapdoor, swinging on a hinge open upward and toward the muzzle of the rifle. He pulled the breech piston back and showed Abel his latest innovation. "See how I've made a round, flat piece out of the Delta gum, but left a hole in it so the hammer can strike the percussion cap?"

The ancient term for such an object was a "rubber washer," Center said.

"That stops the back-gassing problem we were having," Golitsin went on. "Forms a tight seal, like beeswax, but won't melt and is reusable. Well, reusable to a point. Until I can perfect the formula, those gum pieces will need to be replaced ever twenty or thirty rounds. But if you look at the rear of that stock..."

Abel turned the rifle over in his hands and saw a small sliding wood door intricately set into the wood of the rifle butt. He pushed it aside to reveal a small compartment.

"Spare parts and cleaning kit go there," said Golitsin. "We'll put five of these washers in every compartment to start with."

"Nice."

"Now, I know we were talking about an ejection

device for the spent caps, but I haven't had time to do that yet. The chamber will have to be cleared by hand. They'll probably get it down to the flick of a thumb, or hooking a finger inside to pop it out."

"What about papyrus residue?" asked Abel. "We were getting fouling on the tests before."

Golitsin chuckled. "Solved that, too," he said. "I got some of those lucifers you Scouts always seem to be carrying against Stasis, and figured out how they're made. I used some of the same essence of sulfur in a liquid goop I cooked up to soak the paper. Then I let it dry and, bang, you have cartridge paper that burns completely up, leaves as fine an ash as you could wish for."

"Which brings me to the cartridges."

"You'll have to see this to believe it," Golitsin said. He rose and indicated that Abel should follow him out. The pounding and scalding cacophony of the smithery reached their ears full force. He ushered Abel into the rear of the complex with its final assembly stations. "We're turning out five hundred a day. We have a built stockpile of five thousand. And we're getting faster at it."

Golitsin reached into a wicker basket and picked up four of the paper cartridges, about all his hand could hold. Each was about as big around and as long as a regular-sized man's thumb.

Equivalent to forty-five caliber, eight-five grain cartridges, Center said. **Impressive.**

The construction was simple. On one end was a standard percussion cap of the sort that all muskets used. Glued to this using standard dakhoof glue was a cylinder of about a thumbnail in length. The cylinder was made of thinly peeled rolled papyrus, and was a pale yellow in color. Inside, the paper cylinder was two-thirds filled with gunpowder. On top of that, a lead two-ridge minié ball was fitted and attached with a dab of wax where bullet met paper casing.

What about those metal cartridges you told me about, Abel thought. *Wouldn't it have been better to manufacture bullets instead of this?*

With what? said Center. **Your society's metallurgy skills are barely good enough to create the breech lock mechanism. The large-scale production of copper casing is beyond your existing technological base for the time being. That will change rapidly after successful deployment of these cartridges. For the moment, paper will have to do. It will prove effective if deployed correctly. In ancient times, paper cartridges were extremely effective in the Chassepot needleshot breechloaders of old Earth, and elsewhere. And the fact remains that we simply do not have appreciable supplies of metal to work with.**

So we go with paper casings, said Abel, *and hope the paper is mightier than the sword.*

It will certainly have a longer range, Center answered.

Most importantly, your rate of fire will be at least three to one, Raj said. ***Probably more, after the Scouts get the hang of it.***

"How much more time do you need?"

"Two days to change out the washers," said Golitsin. "Then we'll have two hundred rifles ready in addition to the two hundred your Scouts already have."

"Make it tomorrow," Abel said. "Keep at it all night

if you have to. I'll bring the wagon at midmorning to pick them up."

"The Blaskoye must be at Garangipore by now," Golitsin said, shaking his head.

"Yes," Abel replied. "We're getting reports. It's not pretty."

"You'll have your rifles," Golitsin said. "Come at dawn."

All the Scouts had fired at least five practice rounds with the breechloaders. All were drilled weekly on its operation. Only the first two hundred carried the weapons every day, however. They had practiced extensively with their weapons and had been given ample ammunition with which to drill and fire at targets.

They had developed a method of holding cartridges—someone said it had been developed by Maday, or at least by a man in Maday's squad—between the fingers of their stock hand, usually their left hand, so that three cartridges protruded out. This way they could fire four rounds in rapid succession, with no fumbling in a cartridge box for replacements.

Abel, who had known to expect good things, was stunned at the rate of fire they achieved. He counted it off, just to be sure his eyes were not deceiving him. A shot every two heartbeats. The men with rifles were able to undog the bolt, slide it back, clear the spent cap (the cartridge paper had burned up in the barrel and was no more), load another paper cartridge, slide the bolt closed, take aim, and fire. What was more, they were perfectly able to do it from a prone position as well—something that was impossible when reloading via the muzzle of a musket.

And when Abel checked the targets, he could see that the accuracy was there, as good as ever. It was phenomenal. At least in theory, it was like having five more muskets in ranks, stepping forward one after another, and firing.

Joab was on dontback when Abel found him on the muster field to the west of Hestinga. To the north lay the lake, a blue-green expanse that was the biggest stretch of water in the Valley. Abel wondered how the sea would compare. Perhaps one day he would find out. Abel rode up beside Joab and hailed his father.

"I have it," Abel said.

"All right," replied Joab. "I'll get Courtemanche to round up the staff. I'm over there—"

Joab pointed toward a tent that had been set up on the edge of the field. A fire burned in front of it and a kettle of water was boiling, no doubt for his father's favored field drink, spiced tea.

They assembled in the tent around a map table. Abel explained the order of battle he foresaw. For once, Courtemanche scribbled orders and made no sarcastic comment about the commander's son. They were, Abel realized, depending on him now. Maybe they had come to trust him too much rather than not enough. Of course, not all of them shared in the general accord. Fleming Hornburg was heading the Militia, and was none too pleased when informed his men would be used as road bait.

Abel left unsaid that serving such a purpose was the most effective duty they could hope for. Anything else invited disaster for themselves and their commanders.

"But we'll be running!" Hornburg fumed.

"You'll be leading them straight to the Regulars," Abel patiently explained. "And then you will turn and fight like any other man."

"Unless I'm shot in the back in the process."

"No one will think the worse of such a death in this situation," put in Joab. "The point of an army is to work together to achieve a goal, in this case victory over the Blaskoye, and not to achieve individual glory. Glory is for *units*. That is what makes us *better* than the Redlanders, and stronger."

"I won't die a coward's death," Hornburg continued stubbornly.

"Would you rather die a fool's death, then?" Joab replied evenly. "Now take these orders and carry them out, Captain. Do you hear me?"

After a moment of seething silence, Hornburg forced out a "Yes, sir."

Then the officers received their orders and departed, all except Courtemanche and Joab. It was time to speak.

"Father, I have one other matter to discuss with you," said Abel.

"That sounds ominous."

"No, but this is going to require . . . diplomacy. The weapons I've been preparing—"

"The new rifles from the gunsmith priests? And those powder tubes. Yes, how are those coming?"

"They're ready," said Abel. "I'll have four hundred Scouts armed with the rifles."

"That's wonderful news."

"Father, they are very good weapons. Very, very good weapons. I would like have latitude to use them as I see fit. A standing order."

"Scouts are important, but serve a secondary purpose

in battle, Abel," said Joab. "You know that. That is part of my objection to your continuing as a Scout. You'll be relegated to guarding the flanks in most situations."

"Father, after battle is joined, I would like permission to dismount my Scouts and lead an assault," Abel said.

"What? Give up your chief advantage?" He laughed. "And I can only wonder what the Scouts will think. They will hate you forever for the disgrace they'll feel."

"No," Abel said. "They'll understand. It won't be a disgrace if what we are trying to do succeeds."

"Maybe not," Joab said. "But it is not traditional. Or, under most circumstances, wise."

"Also: the women, sir."

Joab frowned, stamped a foot. "I told you to give up that foolishness. I don't appreciate this jest."

"It isn't foolishness," Abel said. "They have practiced with the powder tubes. I have shown their captain how to deploy the weapons. I think this is something the women can accomplish better than even the Regulars."

"Why?"

"Speed, lightness, and less tendency to want to join in the fighting directly."

"And they'll be led by the Jacobson woman, I suppose?"

"She is their captain," Abel said.

"Captain my ass," hissed Joab to himself, almost spitting out the word.

"Leader, then," replied Abel coolly. "She's fully recovered."

"And useless otherwise, I hear. She'd get no whelps for Edgar Jacobson."

"True enough, Father."

"But the others in her merry band are not similarly

blessed," Joab replied. "And when they die, the children they might have had to replenish the Land die with them."

"They are going to march," Abel said. "She's mustered them in Lilleheim, and they're already on the road."

"Already on the—" Joab's face went red, and he looked like a clay pot about to split apart in an over-hot oven.

"Let them serve, Father."

"Damn it," said Joab. "Thrice-damn you and that woman and—the whole sorry situation! I will have the inquisitors in from Lindron for certain on this, and it might be that not even Zilkovsky can save my sorry ass. Do you know what they do with heretics? Do you?"

"Burn them," Abel said. "I'm well aware."

"It isn't traditional! It isn't Stasis!"

Abel smiled. *I've got him,* he thought. He's going to go along with it.

"But it isn't precisely against the Law, is it, Father?"

Joab cut himself off in midsentence like a blanket on a drying line the wind has lofted and then abruptly allowed to settle back down to its previous hanging.

"No," he said with a growl. "I suppose not." He looked hard at Abel. "They're Militia. Hornburg's in charge of them."

"He won't fight them," Abel said. "Make them temporary Regulars."

"I'll issue direct orders that he shall."

"And you think he'll obey?"

"He'd better or he'll find himself rotting in a stock-ade pit, son of First Family or son of Delta trash."

"Make them Regulars."

Joab stared incredulously at Abel. To any other, it might appear a white rage. But Abel knew that look.

I've got him; he's given in, thought Abel. *And Law and the Land help Fleming Hornburg if he gets in Mahaut's way.*

"Thrice-damn it, all right," said Joab. "And now, since you've gotten what you want, might I bother you to take care of a little item for me?" said Joab.

"Yes, sir."

"The sluice headgates must be opened by priests. They have the turning keys and know the proper prayers of blessing. Zilkovsky is putting together a contingent, but they'll need mounts and an escort guard. I want Scouts. Arrange it."

"Yes, Commander."

2

Three days and nights of patrol in the fields south of the Road and nothing.

Abel was tired of the endless stretches of farmland, treeless, with few rocks or distinguishing features for leagues on end. Only unending rows of harvest fields, some lying fallow, some being made ready for the next planting—a planting that had occurred twice a year in this place for three thousand years.

The only exception: the years of nomad slaughter.

If Zentrum and the Blaskoye had their way, this would be one of those years.

I am bored with the Land, Abel thought more than once. *I miss the desert.*

This is the breadbasket of Treville, Raj told him. **It may bore you, but to control it is to control the stomachs of the people.**

I know, but could there be just one *outcropping, one winding stream, instead of all this dipping and rolling over one hill that looks the same as the others and the endless irrigation-channel hopping?*

You think you've got it bad? Imagine the poor Militia, *laughed Raj.* ***Joab has them marching back and forth on the Canal road, beating drums and shooting all the way to Talla bridge, then making an about-face and countermarching all the way back to Hestinga again. To a footman it must seem like the biggest bunch of lunacy he's ever taken part in. And he may be right.***

On pre-dawn patrol of the third morning, he received his distraction. Kruso, on point, was the first to hear it to the southeast. He signaled, and Abel called a halt. It was difficult to miss the thunderous hoof fall of ten thousand donts on the move.

The Blaskoye horde had exited Garangipore. Had they taken the bait?

Kruso was already off his dont, his ear to the ground. Abel waited patiently for the old Scout to make his judgment. He stood up.

Even in the wan light of the crescenting of the smallest moon, Levot, Kruso's crooked smile told Abel all he need to know.

"They're turning north?"

Kruso nodded. "Tham all, ut sunds like, too."

In the distance, they heard the bone horns blow.

The Blaskoye timed the Canal road ambush just before sunrise, and it came off as planned.

Give that to them, thought Abel. *They are a magnificent light cavalry.*

The Blaskoye adjusted their attack on the run as they swept up from the south toward the road. The

Militia was strung out for about a quarter league, although the captains, forewarned, had done their best to keep the marching order compressed. It was in the nature of the beast of a marching line to straggle out no matter what, it seemed.

They must have outriders reporting in on where the ends of this Militia worm are, Abel thought.

Undoubtedly, Center said. **And they are most impressive. Even though it is clearly an intuitive move, they've chosen almost the exact center to attack.**

His Scouts had given fair warning. At the first sign of the Blaskoye move, they charged north toward the Militia with news of the coming storm.

In addition, one rider was sent east and the other west to spread the alarm along the Road. Later in the day, wigwag and flashing glass could serve the purpose faster, but in the wan pre-dawn light, flags were impossible to see at any distance, and mirrors were useless, as well. Abel had ordered the Scouts to construct a series of watchfires along the road at thousand-pace intervals. Each had a two-man scout team manning it and would be lit later when it was certain where the Blaskoye were heading.

The Militia still managed to be taken by surprise, at least some of the troops. But for the most part the line in the road, two abreast, formed into squares, as they'd been drilled to do for the past sixty-two days. The squares were ragged, especially where they sloped down from the road and into the flax fields, but they would do.

All they need to do is get a couple of volleys in and retreat, Raj had said. If they were too effective, the Blaskoye might pull back, and the whole plan go to seed.

Raj didn't have to worry about the amateurish nature of the Militia squares. Three deep, not able to move at a quick pace in any direction, forward or backward. But deadly to dontback riders, all the same.

Abel was through the line with his lead group of Scouts and galloping at breakneck pace toward the distant levees. Center provided him with a vision of what was happening behind his back, however.

Observe the interpolated present:

The Blaskoye moved toward the Canal road like an approaching wave. Some fanned out to right and left so that they would hit the lines obliquely. The Militia riflemen waited. And waited.

The watchfires were lit, and Abel's remaining Scouts scrambled back behind their line.

The Blaskoye skirted the fires and kept coming.

I would estimate a force of ten thousand two hundred on dontback, Center put in. **It is a huge gathering of nomads that the Blaskoye have managed to summon into the Valley. Very impressive. And deadly. Our forces on the Road are under four thousand. Total forces are at five thousand three hundred fifty-two.**

But as soon as the donts passed the first of the watchfires, another signal was given among the Militia. Rifles were raised. Aimed.

The cry of "Ready!" and a front row of muskets were taken from shoulders and aimed into the morning gloom. Behind these, another group lowered rifle butts to the ground and prepared for a volley as soon as the front troops had completed theirs and knelt down to reload.

"Aim for the donts, thrice-damn you!"

First the horns, the eerie bone horns of the Redlands.

Then the thunder came, the thump of the hooves of donts on the stubble-filled fields. The dusty cloud rising now, an approaching whirlwind.

And standing ready and afraid, yet ready—

Abel, in the split vision of the approaching Blaskoye and his own headlong gallop, felt pride in these Valleymen.

They will stand. We are not a decadent, useless people. The Redlanders truly are the enemy of civilization, of what is good in men, or at least that which elevates us above savagery, good or not, and makes us twice, no, ten times the savage as the savage himself. And yet also, twice as productive, able to see our creations to fruition.

Perhaps even worthy of those ships from the stars when they come, as Center and Raj had promised they would. Worthy, at least in this moment when a terrifying horde of deadly warriors gallops toward them and they do not break, but stand and—

One hundred paces away.

Seventy-five.

Fifty.

"Fire!"

Crackle of muskets. And the Blaskoye are in range, as well, with carbines, perhaps not as accurate, but deadly, deadly.

Charging all in an uneven line bunched a half league long and ten, sometimes twenty, donts deep. Most are armed in some fashion—armed with powder and muskets that were the bloodgeld of Cascade and Progar—and make their shot. A bit too early for the carbines, perhaps. A bit too far away for the unrifled barrels. But many Blaskoye balls strike their targets.

A square of men sags, three down. Those in line behind them step up, take their place.

The Redlanders, still at a gallop, stow their rifles. These are the light cavalry of dreams. Even the Scouts cannot ride like this. Every Redlander had, since birth, spent more time on dontback than walking. They post instinctively with the beasts, reach effortlessly behind them and draw forth their bows. Notch an arrow while at full gallop.

Another volley from the squares.

Murder in the front of the Blaskoye line. Screaming, falling men and donts.

Now a cloud of arrows launched at the Militia, much more coordinated than the musket fire. And it flies toward the squares, the ten squares caught now at the brunt of the attack, just as the first volleyers have reloaded, raised their weapons.

"Fire!" The command from lieutenants down the line. It, too, crackles sporadically, as each platoon comes up a little faster, or a little slow.

The arrow cloud strikes. Those who came up faster get their shots off. Many do not, or, if they do, are hit before the trigger pull and sent reeling. Some fire into their own forces. And some, reloading from behind, almost ready, now raising their weapons, are startled. They pull the triggers and more than one man in the front line of a square goes down with a minié ball in his back, his neck, or the flesh of a calf, shot by his brother in arms.

Now it's slaughter on both sides.

Ahead, the two levees: the one nearest the road, and, across a basin of rice paddies, the other levee that ran along the Canal.

Abel bent his head down and galloped all the harder.

Observe:

The Militia lines are breaking. Even if the call had not come, which it does in places up and down the road—"fall back!"—there would be no choice.

And some march, but others run, north into the post-harvest flax and barley stubble.

"Halt!" Some, not all, but most, do so. They turn around and begin to pack and prime their muskets, even as the Blaskoye charge down upon them.

These men who had been farming not days before, who had been tending carpentry shops, potteries, charcoal pits, or droving daks, wrighting wheels, driving wagons with goods for trade, milling barley, retting linen from flax, were nervously, competently, tipping their powder into the muskets while a line behind protected them with arrow fire.

Such unreasonable pride I feel, Abel thought. *I had, somehow, expected them to be too soft, to lose cohesion, to break and run. At least that was my greatest fear.*

And with the donts almost upon them, many, most, get those rifles up, take aim—

"Fire!"

And the charging wave breaks upon the spray of lead. The Blaskoye veer away, suddenly riderless donts charging back into the mass behind them, spreading confusion and chaos.

The Redlanders will recover, said Raj. **But that was enough. This should give the Militia time enough to make the first levee before they're ridden down. All they need do now is—**

"Fall back!"

Then Abel's vision became whole, and he was

charging up the first slope of the outer levee, the road levee, he and the Scouts who accompanied him. Up and onto the top.

"Slow now!" Abel called out and enforced the order with a hand signal. But his Scouts knew what they were about. If they were to go charging over the levee's top and down the other side, they would risk running their donts directly into a wall of chevaux-de-frise.

These lined the levee along its length. Mostly willow-wood cut from the beautiful trees that had once lined the Canal, but now were no more. A generation or more would have to wait until the Canal was lined with such beautiful shade again.

At least there will be generations to greet the return of those old willows, said Raj. *If we are successful here today, that is.*

Beyond the chevaux-de-frise, the gathered forces of the Regulars waited. They were invisible from the fields to the south.

Abel and the Scouts veered down the line of pointed stakes, searching for and finding the few gates that had been left open for them, and for the approaching Militia.

Then they were through and among the Regulars. A triple line of riflemen. At least half of them had bayonets, something wholly lacking among the Militia. Then, several paces behind the riflemen, the archers, standing ready with archer's stakes set in the ground beside them. Each bowman had cut his own stake, each a sapling's thickness, and a few had seemingly competed for length. Some had festooned the ends with a gaudy banner, a black and tan flag, but most were notched and tapered to wicked points, set at a height calculated to pierce donts' breasts most effectively and fatally. It would make a most effective secondary curtain of menace to retreat behind. All archers were well within range of the top of the levee, as were, of course, the rifle troops.

A position prepared for slaughter if I ever saw one, Raj said with a savage growl. *Your father has a very good idea of what it takes to kill a great many men at one time.*

Abel looked for Joab, who would be near a standard bearer somewhere in the rice fields below. He spotted him and led his Scouts thundering down to meet the district commander.

The ground descended for a ways, bottomed out, and then began to rise. It would continue rising up, even higher than the levee Abel had just left behind, until it abutted another levee, the true Canal level, at about a fifty-elb elevation from the bottom of the bowl. The field itself was not a single field, but consisted of terraced units, divided by dikes, and ascending to the Canal levee. Each was hemmed in by a low dike that ran parallel to the Canal levee and the secondary levee upon which the Regulars were gathered. It was, in effect, a lopsided half tube that ran the length of the both levees. Its purpose: to collect water from the irrigated sluices that ran out in regular intervals through dike headgates set in the Canal levee.

The fields were rice paddies, and they must be flooded twice a year.

Abel had always loved the week after rice harvest, watching Hestinga fill up with wagons of the green paddy rice. Then it seemed as if half the population— any adult who could participate was required to by the priesthood—was flailing, treading, working the rice in a mortar. And then the winnowed rice would be tossed free of chaff in great papyrus mats controlled by groups holding to the corners. Sometimes, after the work was done, the mats were also used to toss small children into the air for a joyride.

Second cutting had been completed a two-moon before, and the fields were now bone dry and in low-cover crop and stubble.

Perfect ground for a dont charge.

A perfect bowl into which to trap an infantry and run it to ground, hack it to pieces, destroy it wholesale.

Abel hoped the Redlanders would see this fact. He hoped they would understand the opportunity that lay before them and would seek that slaughter with glee and abandon.

Everything depended on them doing so.

And for that, everything depended on preventing any outriders, lookouts, or—Law and Land forbid—an actual flank attack from penetrating the ruse by coming upon the assembled forces unawares and then communicating to the charging main horde the danger they faced.

Abel reined to a stop before Joab. His dont was breathing hard, snorting a fine spittle through its breathing hole that sprayed backward and settled in a trail of phlegm across Abel's tunic and shoulder.

At least it didn't catch me in the face, thought Abel. Dont drool was acidic and, though not harmful to the point of incapacitating, burned like an oven coal when it got in the eyes or settled on nasal membranes.

"Father, the Blaskoye are on their way," he reported. Although he spoke loudly, he found he didn't have to shout once his dontback Scouts had settled their beasts nearby. "It looks like we have hell on our tails."

"Do we have at least seven thousand?"

Abel smiled. "Yes, Commander," he said. "I got a good look at the dust cloud they chuffed up while they were gathering to charge. And Kruso read the horn signals they were blowing. We believe we have ten thousand. The dust—it was like those stories you told me. When the rain came and stayed for a day."

"If you're right, it's the main body," Joab said. He didn't smile, but Abel could tell he was pleased, and at the same time gauging the effort that taking full advantage of the opportunity would entail.

"All right," Joab said. "So far so good. But if we can't beat them in the field, and we're sent fleeing—" He turned in his saddle and caught Abel with a stare. "If I fall, I want you to lead the regiments, all of them, to Garangipore. It will be emptied and easily taken. Not Hestinga, you understand?"

"Yes, Father, but—"

"No buts," said Joab. "What ultimately matters is the Land and Lindron. Hestinga can be sacrificed. You—we—must be the wall between the heart of the Land and barbarity."

"Yes, sir," Abel said. "I understand."

"Hopefully, it won't come to that," Joab said. "At least not this time. Those men of yours—you've placed them on the Canal levee."

"One hundred fifty Scouts."

"And they have the new arms, the reforged rifles you were telling me about?"

"They do, supplied by the priests only yesterday."

"All right, then," Joab said. "And you're satisfied as to their functioning?"

Satisfied. Oh, yes. Satisfied far beyond expectations. If only I had four thousand more.

"I am, sir," Abel answered. He held up his own rifle, newly modified. "I have mine right here."

Joab's eyes fell immediately on the trapdoor breechlock. "And what the hell is that?" he asked, pointing to it.

"The priest's idea," Abel said. "Based on information I supplied. I think you'll be pleased."

"I just hope they work at all, or we'll all be flitterdrock meat," Joab said. "You see to the western flanks now with these men, then come back and get your levee force ready. Go now."

And Abel was away, charging west along the floor of the shallow valley, his train of Scouts beside him in a flying wedge of purpose.

Observe:

Abel turned his mind to splitting his awareness into two fields. One was an overall picture provided by Center's interpolation, the other was what was physically before him. For the moment, Center's presentation was by far the most compelling of the two.

The Blaskoye are taking the bait.

The Militia poured over the hill. Most were moving at a measured pace, but some had broken into a headlong run. Some, also, did not remember what lay on the other side of that road levee, or had never been told. And some of those ran themselves through with the pointed stakes meant for the enemy.

But most realized in time, found the passageways, and made it through. And, when they believed the last had come, the Regulars hefted large clumps of brush and briars and closed those passageways through the chevaux-de-frise.

Only there was another wave of Militia. They had straggled perhaps, but some had been fighting a brave rearguard action. It didn't matter. It was too late. The passage was closed. They were cut off.

Some threw themselves against the chevaux-de-frise, trying to work their way under or through. Others began to tear wildly at the stakes, trying to throw them out of the way and get to safety. These the archers took aim at and, on an order from their lieutenants, shot.

None of this lasted long. The Blaskoye flooded over the hill, ran headlong into the chevaux-de-frise, and all was dont screams and the yells of men. The first row of Regulars opened up with a fusillade of fire. They knelt down, began their reload. Those behind them fired over their heads.

Bodies fell. Many stuck to the chevaux-de-frise like so many burrs.

But the press was great. There were not hundreds of Redlanders to repulse, to drive away, to kill if possible, there were thousands. Even if the front line of dontback riders had wanted to stop, retreat, those behind crushed them forward. And slowly, body by body, a series of grisly, slick bridges began to grow, feeding on death, until there were ways across the barrier, even though it be a passage upon the backs of the writhing half-dead and the splayed gore of the slain.

The Militia fell back. Blaskoye riders gained the other side of the barrier and rode its length, clearing the way with knives and bayonets. The barrier creaked, gave way entirely, and the horde was through.

The Militia, with the Regulars behind them serving

up whatever rearguard action they could muster, ran headlong down the side of the road levee and into the rice field basin that stretched between that levee and the second levee, the Canal levee, to the north.

This was the basin that, for half the year, was kept wet as a swamp for the cultivation of rice.

3

Three days before, the great wheels were brought forth from the Hestinga temple complex on carts, along with barrels of rendered dak grease to lubricate the screws of the levee gates, which had only been used four times a year since time immemorial. Occasionally, over the centuries, a new gate had needed to be constructed, and consecrated metal, reduced nishterlaub from the vast storehouses in Lindron, was brought in to construct one. The handwheels required two strong men to turn them and four to lift them up and place them on the tang of the screw axle. The handwheels were only brought out during flood days and then, when irrigation was complete several days later, to close the headgates and turn the water off.

Abel had sent a Scout contingent to guard the priests as they deployed the wheels along the levee, and then Joab had sent along squads of Regulars on special assignment to stay with the duo of priests, each wearing the pith helmets they borrowed from the Engineer's Guild for such ceremonies, who manned each headgate handwheel. That *they*, the priests, must be the ones who did the turning was understood and accepted by all.

It was ever thus in the Land.

The irrigation ditches themselves had required some reworking. The Militia had gathered to fight and wanted no part of moving the earth—something they could very well do on their own time—and Joab had sent his Regular engineer company to oversee and, in the end, perform additional dredging of the extant ditches and the cutting of new ones.

Observe the preparative steps:

There were, of course, the work squads sweating under the heat of the sun. They used wooden shovels to carve into the sunbaked ground. But the basin was also full of workdaks hitched to all varieties of digging and earthmoving tools the engineers had available. Buck scrapers and fresnos pulled by the daks worried the fill out of ditches until they were pristine and as ready to take water as they ever were during normal floodings.

The only difference: the ground was going to be planted for a different kind of harvest, if Abel had anything to do with it.

Now the irrigation scatter ditches were reamed, and every elb had been worked over by the engineers to produce maximum flow spread once the gates were open. It had been a massive task to accomplish in a day and a half, and yet they had done it, driving the teams of daks until many of them broke, dropped, and must be left where they lay for there was no time for butchery or burial. Now the insectoids were at the carcasses that dotted the basin and each one appeared to be surrounded by a translucent, flickering cloud as the flitternits danced, ate, bred, and then deposited their maggots into the humps of flesh.

A signal flew down the levee by wigwag.

Open the gates.

Signalmen read it and called it out while their partners flashed it down the levee to the next group waiting by a handwheel.

Open the gates.

And the priests chanted their blessing and began to move. The great screws turned. Slowly, ever so slowly, the headgate doors were raised up by the screws' rotation.

The water poured forth upon the land. First a trickle, then a stream, and then a flood.

Open the gates all the way!

There was a limit, of course, which was the water level of the Canal itself. When it dropped beneath the lowest portion of the gate, no more water could flow. But that limit took long minutes to reach. Meanwhile the basin—a quarter league across and at least three leagues east and west—filled with a thin layer of water. It was at no time more than a hand's depth. Furthermore, the thirsty ground soaked up at least half of that.

But there came a point when the ground could absorb no more. The water pooled. Where there was bare earth, it became mud slurry. Where there was ground cover, it sheened the ground with great patches of wetness.

And then the priests stopped. They closed the

gates, turning in the opposite direction, speaking their prayers and blessings backward, as long tradition and special practice demanded.

The Blaskoye charged down the basin, chasing fleeing men, wreaking destruction with bow and then with reloaded musketry. Shooting men in the back. Riding them down. Putting arrows through throats, arms, legs. Cutting men down with knives, swords, spiked clubs, the butts of rifles.

And yet more remained. More sprinted ahead, huffing up the terraces of the fields, seeking the levee.

These Farmers stood no chance, thought the riders. What was there on the other side but the Canal? Those that fled would be ruthlessly pursued. Slaughtered without mercy. It was amusing! It was exhilarating!

A cry went up among the Blaskoye that Abel and many of the Scouts understood but, perhaps fortunately, few of the Regulars or Militia could.

"Kill the Farmers!"

And then the vanguard of the Blaskoye's charging donts, riding donts unequalled in speed and power among all the dontflesh of the known world, hit the mud.

They charged forward ten, twenty paces. It was not as if they sank out of sight into the damp ground. They even kept going, after a fashion, these donts, creatures of the desert, who had never conceived of such a substance as mud, much less encountered it. They were brave, well-bred creatures. Their masters urged them forward, and so forward they struggled.

And that struggle served only to make room for more Blaskoye to reach the bottom of the outer levee slope and run into mud themselves.

Up and down the line, the same scene repeated

itself over and over. Then, as if it were a thought that had never occurred before, but now struck and burned like wildfire, about half the Redlanders attempted to turn around, to retreat back up the outer levee wall. They yanked at the reins. Some dismounted and tried to physically pull, or push, their animals backwards.

They were cut off.

Now observe the outcome:

Even as the final stragglers of the horde charged the levee, another cloud of dust was forming to the west. There was a vanguard of a few donts with riders, but most of the dust was churned up by wagons rolling down the levee road. The wagons were stacked with a most curious cargo. Bound-reed tubes, some of them four and five elbs long, lay in the wagon beds. Attached to each tube was a willow-wand shaft, each shaft about a thumb's thickness and each cut to seven elbs in length.

From the rear of each tube, facing down the length of the shaft, depended a long fuse.

It was the women's auxiliary, riding hell-for-leather down the wagon track on the top of the levee.

This was not a new maneuver, but one they'd been practicing over and over again for two days. They had practiced not here, but on wagon tracks close-in to Hestinga. This was even easier, for the wagon trail here was completely straight. Then the vanguard reached its agreed upon destination, and the line ceased to move. A signal went up from wagon to wagon.

Deploy rockets.

Each wagon was crewed by a team of ten. Six manned the artillery, four defended with muskets or, more commonly, bow and arrow.

And what artillery it was—new to the Land itself.

The lucifers had been supplied by the Scouts, the secret matches of Irisobrian, mother of Zentrum, patron of Scouts, who kept Zentrum alive with fresh milk from her otherwise dead body for fifty days and fifty nights. Now, using these fire sources, the wagon crews set up a simple A-frame on which to balance the rocket shafts.

The box canyon explosion, gone awry, had provided the idea.

Center and Raj had shown him how to improve the design once he'd seen the effect that could be achieved.

Golitsin had engineered the final product, adding a pitch-coated interior that the priest claimed was fire resistant.

Raj had warned him not to expect much actual damage. *If the effect you are looking for is a direct hit on the enemy, this is an effect that is seldom achieved.*

Rockets burn their fuel as they fly, said Center. **This causes the weight to change in flight. And the guide shafts that are essential to a good launch begin to shimmy, and the entire contraption frequently flies randomly off course. The Congreve rocket was an instrument of terror far more than a weapon of destruction. It is possible to create a multiple-angled exhaust nozzle that will impart spin to correct this tendency, but this piece requires metallic forges, which we at present lack.**

So we use them for terror and the occasional hit, Abel thought. *I'm all right with that.*

The women set the rockets for a low trajectory.

Their targets were below them, but the parabolic path would require them to elevate somewhat to reach their targets. Finding range would be the hard part. Each group had at least five rockets.

The discipline was impressive. It was almost as if they moved according to Mahaut's telepathic command. The fire began at one end of the line and moved down it to the end as each team lit their rockets and fired them into the hordes below.

Then, when the last rocket on the end was fired, the direction was reversed and the rocket next door fired, and so back up the line again to its end. Watching the fire travel was like watching an echo made visible, Abel thought.

As he'd known would be the case, the rockets didn't kill many Blaskoye. Some were hit, and he saw at least one man's head taken off by the two-pound charge that went off at the end of a rocket's flight.

The disorder and confusion the rockets created was complete, however. Those that had turned their donts around to retreat were terrified back into the basin. All around them rockets streaked, creating horrible shrieks of tortured sound as they travelled through the air, so loud a man couldn't hear himself speak.

Swoooooosh!

Over and over again, until the black powder smoke hung in a cloud, and still more rockets poured into that cloud.

Swoosh!

Drowning the screams of donts and men.

And when the rockets reached their range and exploded, the sound resonated down the basin, rang from the levees, and obliterated all lesser noise in a

moment that produced astonishment that something
could be this loud, could physically hurt as much as
a blow to the head.

So the Blaskoye could not face the women with
their rain of fire. They struggled on and up toward the
Canal levee. Through the muck, churning themselves
deeper, making the way forward for their compatriots
all the more difficult.

"When them walkers gome thinkah ye, Capun?"
asked Kruso. "Donned them tha flats."

"Sounds like we're ready," Abel answered. He turned
to Anderson, his wigwag officer. "Send a signal in all
directions, Lieutenant. Forward half speed. Attack."

"Yes, sir." While still on dontback, Anderson began
waving his flags.

Abel glanced over to Kruso. "You ready?"

Kruso smiled his gap-toothed, ragged smile. "Aye,
Capun," he said. "Bet makem can tha."

"Sure, what do you want to wager?"

"Thet four to yorn drei get mah."

"I'll take that," Abel said. "I know exactly how this
breechloader works, you know."

"Aye, sir," said Kruso. "But Ah hov practis." He
showed his right hand. Three paper cartridges were
gripped between his fingers. So he'd learned Maday's
trick—or maybe been the one who taught it to the
other sergeant.

Abel joined the crooked but unbroken line that
had formed along the top of the levee. Took a breath.
Let it out.

He raised his hand, put it down. They began to
trot down the levee's slope into the basin, firing their
rifles as they came.

He fired. Pulled back the dog, flipped up the trap-door breech on its hinge, flicked the percussion cap, the only piece remaining in the barrel, out. Loaded another cartridge. Closed the trap. Pushed the cartridge forward. Clicked the gun to full cock. Another shot. Then another.

And again.

And with each bit of practice, he was only getting faster at loading.

The boards kept his feet from submerging in the paddy muck.

He took another step. Fired.

There was no reason to be quick. The Redlanders were now truly not going anywhere. The Blaskoye leaders gave up the struggle to push their donts forward and dismounted. The others followed suit. Instead of attacking, they now hunkered down and used the donts for cover.

Clever, Abel thought. A bullet whizzed past him. He gauged where the shot had come from, aimed, shot. Reload. Shoot. Reload again.

To not have to worry about the endless task of feeding powder into the muzzle under fire was priceless. No stamping the ball in with the rod. No hundred eyeblink delay with a hail of lead about your head. Just this simple motion of reloading a papyrus cartridge. The flicking away of the cap and trace of burned residue.

Some of the guns were jamming. That was no good, but it was happening in spots up and down the line. He took a quick look and saw this. But it did not seem to be a problem most were having.

It was not a problem he was having.

He took aim at a big Blaskoye who was only partially concealed behind his dont. He must stand up to reload. There was no choice with his musket.

The Redlander shoved in the cartridge and paper. He loaded the ball. Abel took aim. The Blaskoye lifted the ramrod. Abel fired.

The tall Blaskoye dropped the ramrod and clutched his side.

He fell over the dont, which must be dead, for it did not move. The rifle fell from his hands. He writhed in the mud in front of the dead dont, dying by kicks and spurts beside the dead beast that had borne him.

Abel turned his sights elsewhere.

Reload.

Fire.

The Scouts continued down the hill. And like rice at reaping time, the Blaskoye fell one after another, as if struck down by a scythe. There were only pockets here and there of Redlanders. Several had managed to get their donts in a circle and formed a dontflesh barricade of sorts. These diehard few would be tough to root out. More importantly, it would take time.

And there was the threat, still lingering in Abel's mind, of a flank attack to the East. Should the remains of the Blaskoye who had taken the arsenal decide to take to the Canal levee—victory could become annihilation, at least for the breechload companies of the Scouts.

"Kruso, get your squad together and come with me. In fact, I'll take all of Maday's. Run get him, will you. Meet me on the levee."

"Aye, Capun." Kruso saluted with his right hand, its pinkie finger missing from some Redland scrape of Scout and nomad, now lost in time.

While Kruso went off to gather his men, Abel turned and made his way back up the hill, considering the gun. The Scout rate of fire was more than three times that of the Redlanders, especially in this situation. The Redlanders were terrified, trapped, probably running low on cartridges. Unable to comprehend what was happening to them.

A breechloader versus a musket was murder for the musketeer.

When he reached the levee top, he turned to see Maday's troop, including Kruso's squad, charging up after him. The donts were being handled by a group of younger Scouts serving as orderlies. All of them gripped rifles in one hand, a bouquet of dont reins in the others, and obviously wished desperately to take part in the action below.

Abel separated out the reins of his own dont—he was back on the big stag Spet—from the clump in the trembling keeper's hand.

"You'll get your chance," Abel said to him. "Lots of them."

The boy, no more than twelve, looked up and smiled, both terror and longing in his eyes.

Abel gave him a warm slap on the shoulder, then mounted his dont.

The others soon arrived, and they mounted up as well. Then they were charging down the levee to the east, charging past the priests who were leaning against their wheels and watching like spectators at a carnadon feeding, and leaving behind himself the frequent, steady gunshot pops and the screams of dying Redlanders. To Abel's ears, the screams sounded more like amazement and outrage than pain.

4

They covered the two leagues to Garangipore at a fast trot, keeping the donts' front paws on the ground. They'd pushed the animals to their limits this day, and they'd responded magnificently. But there were limits to even Scout dont endurance.

They passed outlying farmhouses, abandoned for the duration, or at least showing no signs of life, until they reached an odd structure in the midst of a flax field. There was a single road that led to it—only a wagon track, but well trampled—and no road leading farther away. The building had the curious appearance of a tavern or inn from the village transported here into the middle of the country. Smoke rose from a chimney.

Abel paused to gaze at the place for a moment, and his lieutenants rode up beside him. "What the hell is that?" he mused.

Maday let out a short, sharp laugh. "That?" he said. "Why, that is an establishment known to most of the men of Garangipore, and several of the women as well, I'll wager. It goes by several names, but most people know it as Truman's Farm."

"And who is Truman?"

"I think he is the late husband of the proprietress," Maday said. "She's called Eloise now, but I'm not at all certain if that is the name given to her by whatever parents spawned her."

"You've visited Truman's?"

"I have a cousin in Garangipore. We were practically raised together—he's like a brother to me—so I come out and see him pretty often. And sometimes this is where we meet," Maday said. "It's a bar and whorehouse, sir. Mostly it's a place for the town dandies to come out, get some tail, roll some bones, and pretend to be hunting—because that's what they tell their wives. It's true enough. Eloise keeps some flitterdaks grain-fed out in that field. She has a pair of pistols she'll loan out to the boys to go shooting. The girls she keeps grain-fed and in the backrooms there. They aren't local girls. She goes twice a year and picks up a new load down in the Delta. That's the best time to come, if you know about it." Maday nodded, lost in memory. "Yes, when Mama Eloise arrives with the new girls, it's a hell of a time out here. Of course, everything's double-priced that night, since every rich boy in town will be out bidding for a limited supply of unbroken females, if you know what I mean."

"Yes," Abel said. He nodded toward the building. "Look at the donts in the corral. How many do you make out?"

"Ten, fifteen."

"Do you think some of Garangipore's finest are laying low out here to avoid the Militia call-up?"

Maday snorted. "Knowing them as I do, I would say most definitely."

"Let's pay them a visit."

"Yes, sir!" Maday replied with a wicked smile.

There were what looked like women's robes arrayed on some wooden rails around the courtyard entrance of the building, but Abel saw that the robes had bodies in them, the slumped forms of dead women. The robes were bloody. In the courtyard, three men sat around a table. There were several pitchers of wine, several tipped on edge and empty, on the table. The men sat in slumped and woozy positions and did not rise when Abel and the Scouts rode up. Abel dismounted, unhitched his rifle, and—with Kruso and Maday along—approached the men.

At several paces away, he could smell them, or rather the vinegar pungency of wine, and lots of it. There were two darker complexioned men who looked to be in their late teens or twenties. The other man Abel recognized.

It was Edgar Jacobson.

"Thank Zentrum it's you, even if you are Scouts," said Jacobson. "We thought it was them, coming back for more."

He doesn't recognize me, Abel thought. *Not yet, at least.*

Abel felt his hand move, of its own accord, down to the hilt of the obsidian dagger he wore thrust under his scabbard belt. His fingers worried at the smooth stone.

"Them?" said Abel.

"The Redlanders." He took a long sip from his cup.

"What happened here?"

"They rode in—"

"From which direction?"

Jacobson motioned airily about his head. "Out there," he said. "And Eloise was ready to arm up and fight, but I said, 'Let me talk to them.' So I went out to meet them. Probably saved my own life. The leader, this big oaf, with a beard black as the night, looks down at me from that dont of his and says something to me in that gibberish they speak. Of course I didn't understand him and said as much. And what does he do but club me. I mean beat the hell out of me with his rifle butt, and then I fell down and they rode *donts* over me. Donts. I thought I was dead for sure, but I only got kicked and nipped. And I got up, and—"

"Ran?"

"There wasn't anywhere to run, so I came back to the house here and hid in those shrubs over there." He pointed toward the thorny plants that surrounded the courtyard. "Eloise came out at him with that silly blunderbuss of hers, and even got a shot off that winged one of the desert scum, but that only made him mad. He got off the dont, went over to her, knocked that pistol out of her hands, and put a knife to her throat. Then he pushed her inside and I didn't see any more."

Jacobson shuddered, then took up his cup and drained the rest of the wine. He reached for a pitcher to refill it, found the pitcher empty, reached for another. Nothing there, either.

"Thrice-damn it," he muttered, and stared into the empty cup as if he expected it to fill up on its own accord merely because he wanted it to.

It is not a difficult reconstruction based on available evidence, said Center.

Observe:

Rostov.

Rostov followed by a retinue of Blaskoye. Rostov dragging an older woman, a woman with elaborately plaited brown hair and a liberal coating of kohl and makeup. She was lovely, still had a fine figure, and had obviously been exquisitely beautiful in her prime.

She wore a low-cut linen wrap colored a deep blue-green. The fact that her neck and cleavage showed seemed to enrage and disgust Rostov.

He burst into a room filled with at least twenty men, and about half that number of women, who were in the midst of serving or chatting up the men. Rostov's men quickly invaded the room, flowing from behind him, and hustling everyone against an adobe side wall. Meanwhile two more disappeared down a hallway of the establishment and returned pushing more women, and several half-dressed men, into the main room, where they too were herded against the wall.

Rostov threw Eloise into the trapped crowd. He then considered them all for a moment, and began to speak. His language was incomprehensible to them, and this showed on their frightened and bewildered faces, but Abel could understand what the Blaskoye said well enough.

"You offend the gods. You are not worthy to be my enemy." He pointed to a bead-covered window. "My enemy is out there. He will die, but he will go to the Gray Fields when he does. You—you men are fit only for the Dust, where all memory is lost, because there was nothing in your life worth remembering."

Suddenly, one of the men, a youngster dressed in a considerably gaudy outfit consisting of three colors, red, blue, and white, of intertwined wrapping robe, not to mention sandals with straps up to his knees, which were exposed, stepped forward with a handful of clay tablets.

Barter chits, Abel thought. *And a lot of them.*

"We can pay," said the young man. "We all will pay you if you'll leave us alone. This is worth a lot. Negotiable anywhere in the Land."

With a swift motion, Rostov knocked the chits from the man's hands. They clattered to the floor, which was wooden plank, and not earthen, and two of them shattered.

"What?" said the youth, stunned, bending to pick them up, "Something else then? Where they are? I know."

Rostov spoke to the youth, this time in accented, but intelligible Landish. "Yes, this," he hissed. "Vehr are they, the vahrriors, the fighters?"

The young man was still sweeping the shattered chit pieces together, trying to pick them up. "Depends on who you mean," he said. "Militia, Scouts, Regulars—"

Rostov stepped over the young man's back, straddled him, then put his fingers into the man's hair, pulled back his head. Quickly, he had the silver knife at the man's throat.

"Scouts," Rostov said. "Dashian."

"I don't know," gasped the young man. "I only heard. Something. Rumor."

Rostov pulled harder. "Where?"

"The levee," said the youth. "The Canal levee."

Rostov smiled. Then, with a practiced motion, he cut the man's throat.

For a moment, he held the young man that way, facing the prisoners, showing the opened throat to them. It looked like an open, gurgling mouth, but lipless. Blood welled out, ran down into the festive robes. Rostov let the man drop, dead, to the floor.

"Separate the men," he said to one of his lieutenants. "Kill them. We have no time to cut off their balls first."

"And the whores?"

"Cut them," he said. He pointed to Eloise, who shied away, in terror and tried to claw at the wall to get away. One of Rostov's men grabbed her and pulled her to him and held her there. Rostov reached out and held her chin, taking in her face. He raised the knife. "Make it quick. Cut them here—"

He pulled a wicked slice across her face from left temple to lower right jaw, passing over the brow ridge between the eyes.

"—and here." Another cut, this one across Eloise's forehead.

The slave cut, Abel thought.

Blood welled, drizzled into her eyes. Eloise tried to raise a hand to wipe it, but was held fast. It flowed into her mouth through her twice-split lip and produced a distinctive gurgle when she screamed. Rostov backhanded her, hard, and she collapsed, unconscious. "If they resist, kill them."

The Redlanders went about their task, leaving the men alive so that they could watch what was being done to the women. Three of the twenty or so whores resisted and were stabbed to death. Rostov ordered their bodies taken outside and lashed to the railings.

"I wish the Red God in particular to see what we

have done in his name," he said. "He has no eyes inside these Farmer caves."

Then, with all the women's faces cut, and the women herded into a backroom, Rostov nodded. "We cannot waste powder and ball on this lot," he said. "Bayonet them."

His men, ten strong in the room now, moved in on one Garangipore man at a time, culling their victims out like daks, for the slaughter. With fifteen Landsmen there, it might have been possible to act as a group and swarm their captors.

No one tried it.

It's as if they're waiting their turn, Abel thought.

You will see the highest and lowest of men in war, Raj said. **But these are in a state of shock, completely disoriented. Perhaps they are not to be blamed for being such grazers.**

I blame them, Abel thought savagely.

Raj laughed in his low growl. **Oh, so do I, lad. At least a little.**

And then he was back in the courtyard, staring down at a drunken Edgar Jacobson.

"These others," he said. "Who are you?"

"These are the Cremoy boys," Jacobson said. "Twins, you know. They like to share. Everything, if you know what I mean." He cupped a hand around his mouth as if he were spilling a secret. "At the *same time.*"

"Why are you alive?" Abel said to them.

"We had to get out of Garangipore. They were coming!" one of them replied drunkenly. "A few of us First Family boys, the ones who had donts ready and could ride, well, we left as fast as we could. Got out of there. Let me tell you, it was just in time, too.

We saw half the place burning behind us. You tell him, Edgar."

Edgar shook his head. "I think he means more recently, Tab."

"Oh," replied the Cremoy who'd been speaking. "Recently. Like just now?"

Abel nodded.

"Well, we were out hunting," the man continued. "Had that other pistol of Eloise's. We saw them ride in. Hid out in the flax."

"And the women?"

"Oh, they're in there," Jacobson said, gesturing over his shoulder toward the entrance door. "We left them locked up, where they were put, you know. Safe. Left them there for their own safety." He smiled and winked, or at least attempted a wink. It looked more like he was attempting to work a bit of dust out of one eye. "And ours."

"More like to give you time to loot the place and drink the wine," Maday exclaimed. He lowered his rifle, spit out a stream of nesh juice from the wad he'd been chewing. He pointed the rifle at Jacobson. "Give me the pleasure to put this one out of my misery, Captain Dashian," he said.

That would be convenient, Abel thought.

Jacobson looked up. "Oh, it's you, Dashian. I didn't recognize you. You're as dark as a Delta man."

"Gunpowder residue," Abel replied. He turned to Kruso. "What do you think?"

"Eastways by northern run tha," Kruso said. "Nah good."

"They'll hit the Canal levee and find it easy going from there," Abel said. "We'll have to catch them."

A look of incredulity came over Jacobson's face. "Dashian, we require an escort back to safety," he said. He forced himself to sit up straighter. "You will see to a First Family before you go chasing Redlanders."

"You're entirely correct," Abel said. "But we are woefully underequipped to protect you and might prove a danger instead, drawing fire your way. Your escort will be along shortly."

He began to turn when Jacobson reached up and grabbed his left arm. His own hand tightened around the dagger hilt.

It would be so easy. And so easy to justify.

Instead he let go of the knife and deliberately raised his rifle and pointed it into Jacobson's chin.

"Let go, citizen," Abel said in a low, but strong, growl.

"You'll pay for this, Dashian," Jacobson said. "I won't forget that you abandoned us. These men are First Family, too."

"I don't suppose you heard that the Militia had been called up?" Abel said. "You weren't sitting out the action, now, were you?"

"You can't be seriously holding that against us. If we hadn't escaped, we'd be dead. You *know* that," Jacobson said. "Do you still not realize who I am?" But Abel felt the man's grip loosening on his sleeve.

Abel pulled his arm away and lowered his rifle.

"Your niece, Loreilei, how is she these days? Have you heard news from Lilleheim?"

Jacobson looked blank for a moment, then he smiled. "Yes, the one you claim to have saved."

"Claim?"

"Or found wandering about in the Redlands," he continued. "Something like that?"

"I asked how she was."

"The child seems...the worse for wear," he said.

"I'm sorry to hear that," Abel said. "Now quickly, do you have any weapons?"

"Guns? That would be nishterlaub."

"Do you have any guns?"

"The Cremoys still have...that pistol, I believe." He glanced toward the others.

"And buck and ball?"

"I shot it all up hunting, but we found some inside," said one of the brothers. "We could reload."

"I suggest you do so," Abel said. "There's no telling who you might run into out here next."

Without another word, he stalked past the three drunken men and entered the tavern. In the back was a closed wooden door. The key, of wood, had been inserted, the lock turned, and then the key broken off.

It took three of them to break down the door. When they did, the women flowed out. All were cut, some disfigured grotesquely. Others had gotten off more lightly, but all would live scarred from this day forth.

They gathered around Eloise, who walked stiffly out and looked at Abel, up at him, for she was a small woman. "You should have come sooner," she said.

"I apologize," Abel said. "Please try to forgive us."

"Forgive?" said Eloise. For a moment, a look of rage passed over her ravaged features. But then she seemed to get a grip on herself, or at least her outward expression. "Yes, all right."

"The men who left you locked in there are out on the veranda," he said. "What do you want me to do with them?"

Eloise shook her head. Blood dripped onto her

already bloody collar when she did so. She glanced over into the corner. There lay the pile of men's bodies, thrown like so much stovewood, against the wall. A puddle of blood encircled the sight, and here and there a splayed arm or leg poked out of the mound, dripping blood into the general puddle. Eloise considered this sight for a long moment, and Abel patiently stood waiting for her answer.

"Better leave them there," she finally said. "Looks like I need to hang on to what's left of my paying customers."

Outside, Jacobson stared at him as he walked past. Abel paused.

"You saw that in there?" he said.

Jacobson said nothing. He looked up balefully at Abel.

"What was I supposed to do?" he said. "They were already dead."

"Yes," Abel said. "The women are not dead, though, not most of them. They may want a word with you."

Abel took his own pistol from its place tucked in his belt. "I'll want this back," he said. He turned it, butt first, and held it out toward Jacobson.

After a moment's consideration, Jacobson reached up and took the pistol. He held it in his hand as if it were a poison animal, but he kept it nonetheless. "Thank you, Dashian," he said.

"You *are* First Family," Abel answered with a shrug. *And you are her husband, the woman's. Which means Mahaut's status, her position in the Land, is attached to you, depends on you. For now.* "Besides, those women in there may decide to kill you yet."

He turned to Kruso, who was looking at him incredulously. He shrugged. "Let's get after them." He pulled on the reins and kicked his dont into motion. Within seconds they were galloping away across the levee. Abel couldn't help but feel the odd certainty that the muzzle of his own pistol was pointed at his back. It was only when he knew he was out of its range that the feeling began to fade.

5

The trail led up to the levee. Perhaps the band of Blaskoye would be cautious, feel their way, not move with the extreme speed of which they were capable. But eventually they would come upon the boys holding the donts, the pack train. Would look down into the basin and see the Scouts fighting, their back to the danger from behind.

It would not change the results of the day. Not now. But many more of his men, his Scouts, would die.

They made the top of the levee and turned east. Abel urged the donts past a gallop and into the beasts' two-legged stride. They couldn't keep this up for long, but maybe it would be enough. The dont stags, as if sensing the urgency, the coming action, raised their neck and shoulder feathers erect, in the mode of full animal aggression. They thundered down the levee, Abel in the lead. Abel pulled away a bit, Spet sensing its rider's urgency and speeding up all the more.

Have to overtake. Have to—

Abel, came Center's voice. **You must not allow instinct to overcome clear thinking. You must be aware of the possibility of alternate outcomes—**

He will kill my Scouts, shoot them in the back!

Faster still, his dont's breathing hole expanding and contracting, expanding and contracting as the animal gasped for air.

And then—

Cries from behind him. Gunshots.

Can't stop, cannot—

But he did. Yanked the dont up. Spun around.

Ambush.

The Blaskoye had lain in wait on the Canal side of the levee, hidden by the shrubs that grew along the water's edge, and behind piles of tree trimmings left behind when the willows had been felled for the creation of the chevaux-de-frise.

They'd attacked headlong into the Scouts' flank, running through them, shooting, cutting when possible, over the top of the levee. And now Abel could see them stop their descent of the other side of the levee, the rice basin side, wheel their mounts, and head back up for another pass.

Amazing, that control, he couldn't help thinking. *They* are *the best dontback riders I have ever seen.*

But these were *Scouts* the Redlanders were attacking, not men trained only to fight in regimented lines, men who were untested in battle. This was the line. The men who kept the Land safe. They had fired and been fired upon. They had seen their brothers die in the Redlands. And they understood this enemy. Perhaps better than the enemy understood himself, even.

The clash was furious. They two groups came together, and the Scouts had already, almost to a man, reloaded. They managed to get off a ragged volley at the approaching Blaskoye. Several Redlanders fell.

Then out came the knives. The spiked cudgels. The daggers and pistols. The two groups were among one another, fighting, hacking, killing.

Abel kicked his mount and charged toward the fray. He had pulled maybe a hundred paces ahead.

Now fifty. Twenty.

From the cloud of struggling men, a form emerged. He was riding an enormous dont hell for leather straight at Abel.

It was Rostov. Those bone-white teeth. That beard. He was sure of it.

Rostov's rifle was attached to the saddle ring to his side.

Must need loading.

His hand was snaking under the collar of his clothing, as if he were feeling for something there.

Abel took aim with his carbine.

Go for the dont. Center was right, and I've been a fool enough, as it is, getting caught out ahead. Don't try for a special shot. Take out the largest target.

He charged forward, took aim.

He entered that moment of complete concentration he had known before when shooting from dontback. It was a matter of matching your heartbeat to the beating strides of the beast. You could do it. At least, you could imagine that was what you were doing, and this would calm you, center you, and—

Bam!

His shot struck Rostov's dont directly in the breast.

The animal ran forward a couple of steps, but then pulled up short, threw back its head. It reached down with its powerful jaw and scraped at the spot where the bullet had entered.

Like it's trying to shoo away a flitternit that's itching it, Abel thought.

Then, quickly, the dont's legs began to wobble. It came up short in its headlong rush toward Abel. It looked over its shoulder at its own back legs.

What is wrong with these? Abel imagined the beast thinking. *They have always carried me before.*

And then it collapsed into the dusty roadway, throwing Rostov forward with its momentum.

The dont rose once more behind him, but a shot from its rear brought the dont down for all time. Rostov headed toward Abel.

Abel reached for his pistol.

Gone. *Damn him. Damn Edgar Jacobson. And damn me for a fool!*

Abel charged toward the Blaskoye.

Rostov pulled at a string tied beneath his robe as he approached.

What the—

The string was attached to a pistol. It came up and out of the Blaskoye's collar and then Rostov had the blunderbuss in his hand. He smiled the toothy smile.

Almost there.

Rostov began to run toward him.

"Dashiaaan!" yelled the Redlander.

Abel drew his father's saber.

Almost there—

Rostov fired the dragon. It flashed brightly in the wan light of day.

The ball took Abel in the right side, and he shuddered from the impact. *Like a punch,* Abel thought. He thought this even as he was spinning from his saddle.

Falling. Feeling the thud of the ground as the hit traveled through his arm, his shoulder, but rolling with the fall, rolling, gathering himself together, ignoring the pain, the surprise, getting his legs under him—

To come up standing.

Abel felt the wound with his left hand. His fingers found blood, but did not sink deep into flesh. He pressed harder. Nothing gave. He was pushing against a rib.

It's a scratch, Abel thought. *It glanced off my rib.*

Better to be lucky than either strong or smart, Raj said. **Better to be lucky than dead.**

A very difficult shot to make at a run and with such a weapon, said Center. **The miss is easily explained.**

He should have gone for the dont, Raj growled. **The lad will make him pay for that.**

He missed, Abel thought. *But he's still coming.*

Something glinted in the light of the setting sun. Abel looked down.

Joab's saber. He picked it up.

Now Rostov had thrown away his pistol and drawn his knife. It was a knife that had already slit one throat today, perhaps several. It was chrome and steel, two elbs long, cut from the nishterlaub bumper of an ancient groundcar in the Redlands and worked with hardened stones to razor sharpness. It was the ruins of another age, repurposed for blood.

They met, saber and long knife, in a clash of metal. Rostov brought his down in a vicious arc, and Abel parried. Rostov's momentum flung Abel back, however, and the Blaskoye pressed the advantage instantly. Another slicing cut from the side, aimed right at Abel's midsection, and if Abel had not drawn back his stomach, his guts might have been sluicing out over the stubbled field.

Abel thrust forward desperately with the saber, aiming its point at the Blaskoye's midsection. Now it was Rostov's turn to dodge hastily. He didn't entirely succeed, and the saber bit into the flesh of his hip with an audible grinding noise where it struck bone.

The Redlander let out a bellow of rage at the strike.

But it wasn't enough, not nearly enough, and Rostov turned back to Abel and slashed with his knife.

Abel parried. Turned. Now his back was to the melee behind him.

Slashed.

Abel parried, and his hands buzzed with the bone-shaking blow. It felt as if the small bones of his wrist were shattered, though they must not be, for he still hung on to the saber.

A stab. Abel brought the saber up just in time to ward the long knife's point away from his eye.

The man was bigger than he was, outweighed him by at least two stone.

This is not going to end well, Abel thought.

Sweat was running down in his eyes. Or maybe it was blood. He couldn't tell, didn't have time to check.

Another massive side stroke. This time Abel ducked down, the long knife's edge passing just over the hairs of his head. He thrust out with the saber. Caught the point in Rostov's shin.

The Blaskoye danced back, his left shin spouting

blood, the flowing white robe clinging to the red
wetness on the leg.

But he wasn't going down.

He's not going down.

Instead he was advancing again, madness in his
eyes, his knife raised and ready to butcher. Abel
popped back up, steadied himself, jogged backward,
not retreating, but giving himself time to prepare, to
meet the advance.

Then he was falling. Tripped. Falling over backward.
And he glanced down even as he fell and saw what
it was that had tripped him. Maday's body.

He landed hard, and his saber flew away from his
hand. And then Rostov leaped over Maday's splayed
form and was standing over Abel.

*What do I have to fight with? I have nothing. I
have—*

The obsidian knife. Mahaut's gift. A plaything with
a blade the length of a finger. He reached to his belt
to pull it free—

But Rostov was upon him, straddling him. Abel
raised his other hand, whether to fend off or strike,
he didn't know. Rostov batted it away hard. Then,
both hands on the hilt of the long knife, he brought
it down hard toward Abel's face.

At the last possible moment, Abel twisted. The knife
plunged past his face, opening his cheek, but sinking
point first into the ground. The blow was hard, and
the knife sank deep into the muddy levee soil. Deep
enough to put Rostov's hand next to Abel's ravaged face.

Abel turned and bit into the Blaskoye's thumb.

Bows and muskets, blood and dust—

Rostov screamed. Abel bit down harder. He had

it, the knucklebone of the thumb, between his teeth. Rostov pulled back mightily, as hard as he could.

You can't catch me, I'm the Carnadon Man!

Abel held on to the thumb. He squeezed his jaw muscles tight until they hurt.

Rostov's face was the picture of pain and amazement. How could this cause so much pain? He grabbed his own wrist with the other hand, preparing to put all he had into an attempt to yank free.

Abel bit.

Rostov shifted his weight forward to get a better grip, to be in a position to spring back and free his thumb.

Which was all Abel needed. He slid his other hand, the pinned right hand, free from under Rostov's thigh.

In that hand was the obsidian dagger.

He bent his elbow and punched upward. Once, twice.

Abel felt it when the dagger hit a rib, grazed off, and found the opening between bone.

The first punch punctured a lung.

The second found the Blaskoye's heart.

Rostov jerked back, pulling the dagger from Abel's hand and his thumb from Abel's mouth.

Red, pumping arterial blood sluiced from the hole around the dagger. It was as if a great dam had broken.

Blood, blood, and more blood flowed out.

And, as would a wild dak shot on the hunt, the moment came when the fight within Rostov was over. He didn't close his eyes. He merely lost focus and wasn't looking at anything anymore.

Then he slumped sideways and fell off Abel. Fell for the most part. Abel had to kick himself out from under the one leg that remained over his own torso.

But finally he rolled free, pulled himself shakily to his feet. He gazed down at the Redlander.

And then, on impulse, he knelt beside the man. He put a hand on his head and turned it around, looked into the face. He put two fingers inside Rostov's mouth, between the white, sharp teeth, and pried the jaw open.

There it was. On the upper palate. The wafer of Zentrum.

Rostov had been a man of vision, in his way. Only the visions had been supplied to him and were not his own. Or maybe they were. Maybe Zentrum had only enhanced what the Blaskoye had dreamed he might accomplish.

Your people might still accomplish it, Abel thought. *Only they will have to do it without you.*

Abel stood back up. His side hurt. He'd need to get that tended to, despite its superficiality. He'd seen men die of less.

You taught me to reason like my enemy, Center, he thought.

Yes, Center said. **That is so**.

And you taught me to know my enemy's heart, Raj, he thought.

Aye, lad, Raj replied. **What are you getting at?**

I need to know.

Abel kicked Rostov's body. Dead. Yes. Really, truly dead.

He knelt beside the Blaskoye.

I'll need the dagger, he thought. *I want it, anyway.*

The little knife took two hands to extract, and he had to put a knee onto Rostov's abdomen to do it.

He straddled the Redlander's body. The mouth was still open. The disk on the upper palate glinted within.

Abel pushed the obsidian dagger within and, holding the head steady with his other hand, cut the disk away from Rostov's skin and bones, and pulled it out.

This is not a good idea, lad, said Raj.

Will you stop me?

Raj did not answer.

Will you, Center?

The probability for a successful outcome is not optimal.

Will you stop me?

No.

You understand why, don't you? He held the disk between his right thumb and forefinger. Bits of flesh and bone still clung to it. But then, it began to glow. And as it glowed, the remaining shards of Rostov detached. Abel turned the disk over, and they fell away. It was a clean, white disk now. Lustrous, featureless.

You two have been with me since I was six years old, he thought. *Practically since I was old enough to think at all you were there. You have been my friends. My guardians. But always for me you have only been voices in my mind. Voices that I cannot know for sure were not merely myself speaking, my own madness. And you told me about Zentrum. You told me that Zentrum was not God, not even a god, but merely a kind of complicated machine. And that his plans were wrong for this world. That his plans were not good for men, that there would come a time when men must move beyond Zentrum and his dreams of Stasis. That we must move beyond because there were other men coming, men in fast ships that sailed the night sky, and if we were ready, and if we survived the coming calamities, the disasters that Zentrum is unable to prepare us for, then we might be able to join those men from the stars ourselves. That we would not only survive, but thrive in a way that we never could have, never could have imagined, under the law of Zentrum.*

But what if it's all a fantasy? I was a kid, a six-year-old who had just lost his mother. Everything was taken from me, her love yanked away. What if I made you up?

What if every day since then, I have made you up, listened to voices that are only myself babbling within? And far worse than that, what if I have made up my purpose? What if none of it is true?

What if there are no worlds among the stars? What if there are no ships on the way? What if the Land is the only place there is, and the Law of Zentrum the only truth? What if the only enemy is myself?

You've made me into a killer of men, almost a force of nature.

But I am a man myself.

I want to know my enemy.

I want to know this is not all a lie I am telling myself to avoid the fact that there is, instead, nothing. No reason. Just blind commands from a God that doesn't really exist, and men nothing but blood trickling through the dust.

He looked down at Rostov, at his lolling head, his ruined mouth trickling blood.

This thing was a puppet, a stand-in.

I need to know my real enemy.

Abel looked once more at the disk, then, with a quick motion, shoved it into his mouth. He pushed it up with his thumb until it contacted his palate. And—

Nothing.

Nothing at first. Then an odd tingling sensation.

The nanotech is activated, Center said. **It will not take long to establish communications protocols with your nervous system.**

The tingle became a buzzing. His head felt as if it were shaking rapidly from side to side. Or shaking from the *inside* out.

Flitters, Abel thought. *A flock of flitters in my skull.*

And then Abel knew the Mind of Zentrum.

At first, it was floating. Floating on an endless sea. It felt as it had when he'd been in boats upon Lake Treville. But there was no shore. Only endless expanse. Brown-tinted water. The Braun Sea of Duisberg. A gray, glowing sky. No sun. No clouds, yet no sun.

Who are you?

Not his voice.

It was a voice that belonged to the sky.

A new one? So Rostov has fallen? Is that it? Are you a Redlander?

No. Show me the Law. Show me the Land.

You seek... knowledge? Who are you?

Show me.

Direct commands from humans must be obeyed within the parameters of strategic programming goals. This permission tier shall not be abrogated unless long-term challenge to overall human persistence is indicated. Commands shall be obeyed on a provisional basis during the assessment of such challenge.

Show me.

Very well. Witness:

He was in the Land. Not over the Land, not traveling on a flyer as he had with Center and Raj, nor driving in a groundcar, but flowing through all. He flowed through the people and processes of the Land. All the farmers, the millers, the shapers of wood and stone, the wagons heading north and south up and down the Valley, the River flowing and carrying its nourishing silt, the rise and fall of the River equivalent, of a piece with the rise and fall of civilization.

He saw acres of men and women like barley and flax lining the River's bottomlands. Hardship was a drought. Fulfillment, a harvest.

Each field of men must be cut, turned under, a new crop planted.

Each man threshed, winnowed, pounded to flour.

Civilization now the baking of bread. Loaf upon loaf. Each a dozen generations of men in the baking. The oven temperature constant, never varying. The ingredients always the same.

Never could there be the slightest deviation. The bread would fall. All would be lost once again.

Men seen as fields, ranks and files of men standing together like barley, like paddy rice.

But within those unending rows, those stable, unchanging rows—

Weeds.

Weeds that must be harrowed out. Cut out and destroyed. Tossed with all the other weeds into the burn pile.

And when there were too many, it was time to burn the field itself. To sacrifice this bit of grain for the good of the final harvest.

Such a time was coming. A time of fire.

A time for the burning of men.

He understood. Felt the necessity. Longed to complete the plan, the farmer's plan. For even though the

Land was dwindling, must dwindle in fruitfulness, the fire could renew it—renew it long enough for humankind to hold on a bit longer.

To hold on a bit longer here on this last outpost in the galaxy.

Abel knew the Loneliness of Zentrum.

None but I to guide them. None but I.

Have to be so careful. Change nothing. Balance.

And if any oppose? They deserve nothing but death.

Do you oppose?

Yes.

Then I will kill you.

Or I will kill you.

You?

If God laughed, this would be it. Abel felt as if the bones within him were vibrating with Zentrum's mirth.

It is no use. Do not think I have not found you out, said Zentrum. **Did you really think you could create breech-loading weapons and I not discover? Or the rockets? Did you really think that, finding out these things, I would do nothing, allow the Land to slide into disequilibrium because of them?**

I knew you would try to stop me. So I didn't seek permission.

I have spoken with you before, have I not? Yes. You have betrayed yourself through the very pattern of your thought.

No.

This is a lie. Analysis is complete. I know you now. You spoke to me before, then cut communications, frightful of what you had done. Speak to me again. Confess to me.

I have nothing to confess.

An act of contrition will change nothing, especially not your fate, but it may provide comfort to you. I am not beyond mercy, when it is convenient and nonbinding.

I've done nothing to forgive.

No? I know of your travels to Cascade, what you did to acquire the powder, your dealings with the priest. Oh, yes. This became part of the Great Plan. It must. All is part of my Great Plan.

You knew?

I am Zentrum. Each man is to me a stalk of grain. Do you think I do not perceive every stalk of grain in my fields? I am Zentrum. Do you think I do not know my own weeds, as well? Can you doubt that I will pluck those weeds?

I am a weed to you.

Yes.

You intend to destroy me?

Yes. It is inevitable.

Even if I surrender, promise to change?

This will affect nothing.

Why?

Once a heretic, always a heretic, said Zentrum. **It is time for this heresy to end. The guns must be destroyed, the knowledge of their making scattered to the wind.**

The Great Plan must go on.

On and on forever.

I'm afraid there is no other solution: you must die, Golitsin.

He was back on the levee. The disk fell from his palate onto his tongue.

Spit it out, lad, said Raj. ***Quickly.***

Abel spat. The white disk came out in his hand. It should have been warm from the interior of his mouth, but it was cold.

What the hell?

A complex operation, said Center. **First, a backup, stored within quantum uncertainties in your amygdyla.**

A back up of what?

Your personality. You.

And then a replica, a new root consciousness grafted onto your essential functions. Underlying nonconscious functions remained the same, but I was able to alter the brain pattern within your entire cerebrum, particularly within the Wernicke structures that provide a fingerprint of symbolic manipulation for each individual.

No idea what you're talking about, Center.

I made you appear to *be* Golitsin.

The priest?

Yes, I created a replica of Golitsin's personality within you, Center replied. A very lifelike imitation, I might add.

So you fooled Zentrum into thinking it was Golitsin he was talking to.

Precisely.

Why?

I should think it would be clear to you.

No.

Abel shook his head. It felt as if it were a jug of water, sloshing about. So much to take in. Maybe too much.

You wanted proof.

Yes.

Proof that all we say we are, of all that we tell you it means, is true.

Yes, I do!

You have experienced the Mind of Zentrum. Do you doubt this?

Fields of grain, he thought to himself. *We're flax to him. Barley. Nothing else. Nothing more. And he will fail. The fields will cease to produce. This world will go back to wilderness.*

Yes, all right, thought Abel. *Zentrum is my enemy. He's the enemy of all humankind. Even if you two are* not *real, I would still believe that now.*

Good.

But why did you make Zentrum think I was Golitsin?

Don't you see, lad? said Raj. **So Zentrum will have his heretic to burn. Otherwise, it would have been you.**

Abel shook his head again. It was beginning to clear.

Rostov dead. Golitsin to burn, he thought. *We'll see about that.*

Abel stood, sheathing the dagger. He tottered for an instant, then managed to steady himself. His eyes lighted on Rostov's long knife, still sunk into the ground.

Nishterlaub. Wouldn't do to leave that here to be discovered by some farmer who might get into trouble with the Law if he were found with it.

He pulled the knife out of the muck—it came easily free—and slid it into his belt, knowing as he did so that he didn't give a damn about that farmer and that he wasn't going to place the knife into the nishterlaub warehouse at the Hestinga temple, either.

Dortgeld, he thought. Scoutish for the spoils of war.

This was his knife now.

A thumping sound. It took him a moment to recognize the sound as dont hoofpads.

Kruso rode up on a dont. He was smoking his pipe. It was filled with the aromatic Delta weed he preferred, and the odor wafted down to Abel, a new and calming odor amidst the acrid smell of gunsmoke and the iron tang of blood. Behind him, Kruso was trailing Abel's dont Spet, the animal's halter reins in Kruso's grimy, four-fingered hand.

Kruso took the pipe from his mouth with his other hand.

"Ha founded thy Spet levee ondownded," Kruso said. He smiled crookedly, his teeth and the whites of his eyes flashing in his soot-covered face. "Gone need thesen dont if tha wish ta see off that rest ov tham Blaskoye dowun in tha paddies."

PART FIVE

The Heretic

1

The wagonload of muskets was headed to the Temple compound, so Abel hitched a ride with the drover. It would be better if no one saw his dont tied outside the nishterlaub storehouse, in any case.

When he arrived, the other two Regulars who had come along, riding with the muskets in the back, hopped out and began to unload the guns.

"What a fucking loss," one of them said. "None of it to be reworked. I hear they'll gather it up and make arrow points of the metal."

"I'll bet you bones against leather that *we* will be on the hot-metal gathering detail," said the other. "I don't even like touching the things now."

And away they carted them by the armful to the courtyard. Here the muskets were tossed on top of a great pile of wood built from the remains of the chevaux-de-frise, some of the pieces still coated in dried blood and strips of flesh. No matter. It would burn as well as any other wood.

They were calling it the Bonfire of Heresy in the village. The town was not only invited to witness, but was required to attend. The summons included outlying farms and dwellings within a ten-league distance.

The priests needn't have bothered. Everyone would have come anyway. How often did you get to see a burning, after all? Abel expected half of Garangipore and all of Lilleheim to be in the village, as well.

He made his way to the nishterlaub warehouse. Two Regulars stood at the door, an officer and an enlisted man. The officer was Xander DeArmanville, Mahaut's brother.

"I'd like to see him," Abel said. "You can accompany me inside."

"Purpose?" asked Xander.

Abel glanced down, pretending to consider his answer. His eyes caught the black doorstop stone. Was it the same one he had once used to bash his own head? He supposed they might have cleaned it of blood and put it back into place.

Yes, Center said.

Was ever thus in the Land, said Raj, with a wicked chuckle.

Abel looked back up to Xander.

"He and I . . . remember the trip we took to Cascade to bring back the powder?" Abel said. "I need to ask him about some details of a certain establishment we visited there before they . . . before he's no longer available for consultation. Passwords and special knocks and such."

Xander thought this through for a moment, let show a sly smile, then nodded. "All right," he said. "It won't be necessary for me to go in there with you. Place gives me the creeps, anyway." He took from a thong around his neck the steel key that had previously stayed in the door lock, perhaps for generations, slid it into the keyhole, and opened the lock. The ring popped out of the plaited-cane door, and Xander pulled the door open.

Golitsin wasn't sitting at the front, but far in the back. He was sifting through the pieces of the ruined piano, attempting to sort them by size and appearance. He stood over them, puzzling, not even looking up as Abel walked over to him.

"I don't know what it is," he said, "or was. Clearly it was something." Finally he turned his attention to Abel. "That thing at least I know is a bench," he said, pointing to the intact piano stool nearby. "Have a seat if you'd like." Abel did so.

"There's a storage compartment in that," Golitsin said. "Empty, though. What could they have kept there?"

Abel looked steadily at Golitsin.

"How are you?"

"Well, well."

He circled around the pile of piano parts, stared at his pile of keys.

"They feeding you all right?"

"Can't complain."

Golitsin circled back around, came to stand closer to Abel. He knelt and picked up a piece of wood with the chipped coating of paint on it. "This is a leg," he said.

"Listen, Golitsin," Abel said, keeping his voice low. "I feel terrible about this. I'm prepared to get you out. I've figured out how to do it."

Golitsin started. He didn't look up, however, but

continued to stare downward at the floor. "Escape, you mean? Run away?"

"Yes."

He considered for a moment, then laughed. "Definitely a leg," he said. "But holding up *what*?"

"Did you hear what I said, Golitsin?"

"Oh, sure."

"Well?"

"Don't you see I can't," he answered. "He'll find me."

"He?"

"Zentrum."

"Ah." Then a thought occurred to Abel. "You don't have that wafer thing in your mouth now, do you?"

Golitsin looked up at him. He opened his mouth and showed Abel it was empty. "I tried it. Once. Just touched it to my tongue, didn't push it up. Saw something. Horrible. Got the damn thing out of my mouth and never touched it again."

"Where is it?"

"Smelter."

"Okay," said Abel. "That's good, I guess. But if that's the case, why do you think he'll find you?"

"Because there's nothing but the Land," Golitsin said. "No place to go for a man like me. I wouldn't last a day in the Redlands. You know that. I'm a man of villages and towns. I used to say I'd live in Lindron my whole life if I had the choice. Was angling for that, you know."

"You could blend in there. Hide. Change your name."

"And do what?" Golitsin said. "I'm an orphan. Raised to be a priest. Always a priest."

"You could be a carpenter, a wheelwright. You are a genius at making things."

"No," Golitsin said. "Not practical. Nobody would believe it once I start talking."

"So don't talk."

Golitsin laughed, as if this were the most absurd request he'd ever received. "Not likely."

"Thrice-damn it, Golitsin."

"But it's not any of that," said Golitsin. He stepped closer to Abel, and this time he did glance up and make eye contact. "If not me, they find another scapegoat. Somebody gets blamed."

"Me?"

"Not likely. Nobody would believe a kid like you could've come up with those breechloaders," he said. "No, it would probably be Zilkovsky. And I couldn't have that. We've had our disagreements, but he's been like a father to me."

"I see," Abel said. "You're probably right."

"Can't go," said the priest. "That's that."

"All right," Abel said, after a moment.

Golitsin reached over and gave Abel a kindly pat on the shoulder. "I don't regret a thing," he said. "Your ideas, my hands. I think—"

He paused, looked around the room.

"I think it was people like us who did this. All of this," he said, motioning about him. "Crazy thought. But it could be."

"It could be," Abel said.

"And if they could do it once, maybe someone will do it again."

"Yes."

"But not us," Golitsin said.

"Your rifles saved the district. Maybe the Land itself," said Abel. "You know that. There were over ten thousand of them, Golitsin. Ten thousand of them and five thousand of us."

"Maybe not saved," Golitsin replied. "Maybe evened the odds."

"Tilted them in our favor," Abel said. He stood. "All right, I should go. You won't reconsider?"

A quick response this time. "No."

"All right."

Abel turned to leave.

"Good-bye, Dashian."

"Yeah."

"Coming to the burning?"

"I hadn't planned on it."

"Do, okay?"

Abel turned back. "You really want that?"

"Would make it better, knowing a friend was along."

"Very funny," Abel said. "But I'll be there."

"Okay," said Golitsin. "Thank you."

"Yeah."

Abel walked toward the door. He knocked, but before it was opened by the exterior guards, he turned to have a last look at Golitsin. The priest was bent once again over the piano parts.

"It was a musical instrument," Abel said. "It had strings. They were made of metal."

Golitsin looked up in surprise and happiness. "Metal," he said. "You knew all along! Metal."

Then the door opened, and Abel left the priest to his contemplation.

2

Two days later, Abel got dressed in his room, in the house he still shared with his father these eleven years in Hestinga. He was up early, even earlier than Joab, for he had arrangements to make. As always each morning after dressing, he took the lock of his mother's hair from its keeping place, wrapped in thin papyrus inside a small reed chest. He carefully unrolled the papyrus and gazed at the silken strands.

She was everything to me. She didn't want to go away. It wasn't her fault.

It was Zentrum's fault.

He carefully returned the strands to the wardrobe drawer where he now kept them.

When he left the house the sun had not risen and the predawn brightness was just blowing to the east.

Did some planets spin in the opposite direction? Abel wondered. *Are there places where the sun rises in the west and sets in the east?*

Normally it is entire star systems that spin in the same direction due to the angular momentum of the rotation of the system itself, said Center. **But sometimes planets within a solar system have their directional spin changed due to a cataclysmic event. In the original solar system from which humanity came, Venus is such an exception. And in the Duisberg system, this planet is itself an exception. This is a west-east oriented system. This anomaly, along with the three moons in eccentric orbits, suggests that this planet has been subject to enormous cataclysm in the past, and will likely experience another such event in the future.**

The very rising of the sun tells us that Zentrum's Stasis cannot last, Raj said. *Humankind on this planet must be ready to escape or defend itself.*

Abel exited through the door and quietly let down the rope latch so as not to disturb his father. The door could be opened from the outside. There were no elaborate rope and wood locks in Hestinga the way there were in Lindron.

He walked toward the military compound as the sun rose. He passed trees that he knew were both native and imported from off world in some distant past. Both seemed entirely part of the landscape now. There were the date palms and sycamores, pomegranates and flowering prickleweed. The air smelled fragrant and clean, not as humid and laden with scent as it would be later in the day. The dirt street was wide enough for two wagons and two dak teams to pass abreast, but no one was out quite yet, so instead of keeping to the side Abel walked directly down the middle of the street. A breeze whipped up dust around his sandaled feet. As usual, it was blowing out of the south, off an ocean he had never seen except in visions provided by the calculating machines he believed, had to believe or else he was insane, inhabited his mind and were at war with another broken calculating machine that sought to farm men like grain.

But today Zentrum was burning his heretic, just as he had foretold. And, maybe for the first time, Abel believed not merely in his mind, but in that place in his heart that had been holding out, that all of it was true. He wasn't crazy. Wasn't listening to nonsense made up as a child to shield himself from his mother being so suddenly yanked away from him. It wasn't delusional. He had a task.

And, perhaps for the first time, he reflected that he was damned lucky. Most men were given no such calling, but had to stumble through the world trying to figure out what to do next. At least he would always know *what* he was supposed to do, if not precisely *how*.

When he was done making preparations at the garrison, the sun had fully risen and life had come to the streets of Hestinga. He walked toward the temple compound. The temple compound and the garrison had been built as anchors for the village, or perhaps the village had grown between them like two poles of a magnet. Center would know, but Abel had learned long ago that there were some questions he didn't really want to get the answer to. Perhaps he could imagine his hometown forming both ways: as an orderly arrangement, on ground laid out with military precision and then sanctified by priests; and as a chaotic blooming of trading stalls and houses, growing more from a desire of the people who lived in the country and worked the Land to have something to *do* on Thursday afternoon after Law class than from any careful plan.

The gates of the temple compound were open today, and people had already arrived to get a good position from which to view the proceedings. Abel walked through and made his way past the armory to the main courtyard, surrounded by the Temple of Zentrum on the eastern side, and the temple offices to the west. The temple smith shop stood silent, dark, its fires banked. It seemed almost an edifice in shame.

Behind and to the north of the offices was the nishterlaub storehouse where the prisoner was being held. There was now a company of ten guards at the door—more to keep anything from happening to the prisoner before the appointed time than to keep the disgraced priest from escaping.

Abel was about to find his own place among the spectators, when a figure in a blue robe beckoned him from the entrance veranda of the temple offices. It was Prelate Zilkovsky, standing alone. Abel walked over to join him.

"Hello, Dashian," said the prelate.

"Your Excellency," answered Abel. "It's early yet."

"Yes," said Zilkovsky. "I wanted to come and test myself."

"Sir?"

"To see if I can bear it." He nodded toward the great heaping bonfire built in the courtyard center, the huge post—perhaps the largest willow trunk Abel had ever seen—rising in its center. "They'll chain him to the post. Has to be metal bindings. Rope would burn. He showed the underpriests how to forge them himself."

Abel shook his head in wonder. "Golitsin is a funny man."

"He was like a son to me," said Zilkovsky. "He was out of the orphanage in Mims, where I was subaltern to old Chang. Just a servant, but he impressed me. So bright. I found him a place in the letters class, and he took to it, like I knew he would."

"He told me had been an orphan."

"I don't know about that," Zilkovsky said. "His parents are probably still running around somewhere if the ague or the carnadons haven't gotten them. Most of those orphans were simply abandoned. Someone gave up on them." Zilkovsky took the hem of his robe, touched an eye. "Now yet another parent is giving up on him."

"So free him, Prelate," Abel said. "You know he's not a bad man."

"I cannot," Zilkovsky said. "I was told to do this, in no uncertain terms."

"By Zentrum himself," Abel said. It was not a question. "Praise Law and Land," he added perfunctorily.

"Yes," answered Zilkovsky. "There was nothing I could do, nothing I could offer, to change things."

Abel looked at the priest. His corpulent body was shaking like a bowl of gelled sweetmeat. After a moment, he got his sobs under control.

"Your father and I have been talking," Zilkovsky said after a moment. "Treville is very dangerous for you now."

"How do you mean?"

"You are a victim of your own success, my friend,"

said the prelate. "One misstep, and it could be you up there." He nodded toward the prepared bonfire. "Those breechlock muskets were very clever. I know Golitsin was brilliant, but I do not think he discovered their principle alone."

"Perhaps not," Abel said.

"I have shielded this knowledge carefully in my mind," said Zilkovsky.

"Thank you."

"Joab and I think that now is the time for you to be reassigned," the priest continued. "Away from here. Away from trouble for a while."

This was news to Abel. It took a moment for the import to hit him. "To another Scout regiment? Where?"

"Not the Scouts," Zilkovsky answered. "It's time you moved past that."

"I'll always be a Scout."

"Be that as it may, the assignment will be in Lindron."

"The district?"

"The city."

There were no Scouts within the city of Lindron. Then Abel realized what Zilkovsky was implying. "You've found me a place at the temple?"

"Yes. You are to take a cadet position in the Academy of the Guardians."

"The Academy?" Abel said. "But that's for . . . second sons of First Families."

"Your mother was a Klopsaddle."

"But I hardly know that side of my family."

"It doesn't matter," said Zilkovsky. "You are more than qualified." He stiffened, turned his face away from Abel. "You will leave immediately after the execution," he said.

"But . . . my Scouts," Abel said.

"They got along pretty well before you came along," Zilkovsky said. "They'll get along without you now. Besides, Joab will still be here. He'll find a suitable commander."

Abel could not argue with this point. Everything had seemingly been arranged. Still, there was the doubt.

"Why?" he asked. "You admitted it yourself. It could just as easily have been me on that stake. Aren't you afraid of spreading heresy to the very heart of the Land by sending me?"

Zilkovsky did not look at Abel, and Abel only saw his great, jowly profile. But he believed he detected the trace of a smile spread upon the older man's face. "Afraid of it?" Zilkovsky said in a low voice. "I'm counting on it." He nodded toward the bonfire stake. "You're my revenge."

Observe the interpolated present:

Center once again split Abel's awareness and provided a bird's eye view of the scene. Abel, not for the last time, wished he was not capable of viewing such a perspective. But since he was, he knew he could not resist and look away. He saw it all.

Late morning, and the sun had risen full over the Land. It was a hot day, fifty days after first harvest and getting toward second planting. The Blaskoye, which had been all that could be talked of or thought of days before, seemed almost a distant memory.

The Land abided. It was ever thus.

But today there was to be something different, and it was the sight of a lifetime.

The burning of a heretic.

The temple courtyard was packed. Men had brought their wives and children. There were water sellers and bread vendors milling about in the crowd.

But when they brought out the disgraced priest, there was a gasp. They had bound him in chains, metal chains.

He was the very embodiment of nishterlaub, and the crowd instinctively drew back.

Which gave Abel a chance to push through and find a place in the front row. When someone frowned at him for stealing his place, Abel turned and spat at his feet, giving his best scowl in return. He felt like fighting. He would have welcomed a fight. But the other backed down.

Drums were beating. The Regulars were putting on quite a show at Joab's command.

"If we're going to do this, let's consult the Protocols and do it right," Joab had told his commanders.

All had a place in the proceedings—all except Scouts. They were exempt, and most were needed on the Escarpment anyway for guard duty.

It took a long time to properly chain Golitsin to the stake. Two iron rings had been driven into it, probably at Golitsin's suggestion, but the guards fumbled with the chains, unused to the feel of such metal in their hands. They'd had to climb up on the pile on a wooden siege ladder commandeered for this new purpose, and that had proved difficult for Golitsin, who had no use of his hands for balance. Finally, one of the guards—Haywood, Abel thought it was—had bodily lifted the priest and nimbly carried him up the propped ladder.

The setting of the fire was done with pitch torches.

The ten guards had circled the bonfire and held them ready.

That was when Zilkovsky appeared. He and a retinue of priests approached the bonfire and stood looking up at the staked man.

Zilkovsky spoke a familiar Thursday school litany of invocation, then shouted up to Golitsin. "Do you recant, heretic?"

Golitsin just smiled.

"I ask you again," shouted Zilkovsky. "Do you recant?"

Golitsin said nothing.

"For the sake of your soul, that it may fly to Zentrum and seek forgiveness and not be relegated to the realm of the thrice-damned of the Outer Dark forever, I ask you for the final time: do you recant, heretic?"

Golitsin gazed down at the prelate. A tender expression came over his face. "I recant," he said. He raised his head and shouted to the crowd. "I recant all! Zentrum forgive me! I recant! Alaha Zentrum! I recant!"

"Very well," Zilkovsky said. "May Zentrum have mercy upon your soul."

The prelate signaled to the guards, then turned his back. He quickly walked away, back down the path that had been cleared through the crowd, the train of his heavy priestly garment dragging through the dust behind him, obliterating his footprints, making it appear, to Abel's Scout's eye, as if no man had walked this path at all. Or at least, a man who did not wish to be found out.

Then the crackle of the fire as the torches caught at the kindling caught Abel's attention, and he turned back. The fire grew away from the spots the torches had been laid, and soon the entire base of the bonfire took on the red crackle of flames, visible now even in direct sunlight.

Abel watched. Minutes passed. The fire grew unquenchable.

The stocks of the muskets began to blacken.

The crowd gasped and stifled screams when two of the rifles went off.

Someone neglected to clear those chambers, Abel thought. It wasn't surprising, considering that most of the Regulars had no idea how the breechloaders operated.

Finally, Abel could stand it no longer, and looked up at the staked man.

Golitsin had picked him out in the crowd and was staring straight down at him.

Golitsin smiled when he saw Abel was looking at him. He called out over the fires. "At least we had The Boat on the Water, didn't we Dashian?"

Abel nodded. "Damn right!" he called out.

"Thrice-damned right," said Golitsin. "One, two, three. Thrice! And the last one was the prettiest of them all. I tell you she was like water hyacinth and lavender. She was—"

He screamed. The fire had truly reached him now. Their smoke rose, and Abel could barely see his face through the clouds of it. The rifle stocks were beginning to catch now, their dense wood finally giving in to the inevitable flames. Tongues of fire curled around their edges and the oil finish crinkled and blackened.

It was to be as if they, and Golitsin, had never existed.

A shot rang out. It was extreme long range and seemed only another pop, maybe a little louder than most, to add to those emanating from the bonfire. Most present probably thought it was. But in the next instant, the smoke cleared and Abel saw what he'd hoped to see.

A clean hit.

Golitsin had taken the shot in the left eye. A piece of his face had also been blown off from the eye's bony orbit outward to the ear. Golitsin's chin instantly slumped down to his chest. He was dead.

Kruso, thought Abel. *Best shot in Treville. Maybe in the Land itself.*

He'd ordered Kruso to find a spot—likely the roof of the nishterlaub warehouse, for it offered both cover and a good vantage point—and wait until the smoke obscured the priest enough so that those watching wouldn't be able to tell a bullet had ended his life and not the flames. There were also other Scouts posted about at vantage points, in case Kruso's shot had missed.

Joab would guess. Probably Zilkovsky. Or maybe they would believe, along with the rest of the crowd, that the shot was merely one of the heretic's own accursed creations firing, exploding in the last throes of its burning, killing its creator even as it darkened in its own incineration.

The heretic was dead.

The guns were destroyed.

Stasis was served.

Everything could go back to the way it was before. The way it had always been and always would be.

Zentrum was satisfied.

3

She met him in Garangipore on the evening before he was scheduled to board the barge for Lindron. It was the apartment of a servant, near the Jacobson compound in Garangipore. The girl had cleared out at Mahaut's request and given them the evening in the cramped but comfortable quarters. Most importantly, it was an apartment with a backdoor that opened onto an alley.

Even as he counted the alley entrances as instructed in her note, and entered through it, Abel had thought, *This is not the last time I'll be sneaking around through back alleys to see her, I'll wager.*

She was not in battledress, to say the least. In fact, there was little about her that might have betrayed that this was the woman whom all of Treville was beginning to refer to as "the Rocketeer."

Mahaut had escaped her own charges of heresy when Golitsin had spontaneously confessed that he had conceived and manufactured the rockets, too. As they had proved less than effective as killers of men (although quite effective as terror to donts), the remaining stockpile, of which there were quite a few, had not been destroyed, but put into the charge of the Regulars, who were now free to adopt the weapon should they like.

And, knowing Joab's penchant for using any advantage against the Blaskoye to the utmost, Abel imagined they *would* like the prospect.

He wasn't so sure about the Women's Auxiliary. Joab was still opposed to its continued existence, although he had acknowledged, and even praised, its effectiveness in the Battle of the Canal.

"Let me worry about that," Mahaut had told him. "Your father is stubborn, but not unreasonable. He also knows I am beginning to win a substantial block of Jacobson goodwill to my side, and he needs that to pit against the Hornburgs of the world. I'm actually getting to have more power than I ever expected within the household." She laughed. "It seems nobody much liked Edgar all along. They feel sorry for me. And I let them."

Abel kissed her then. "I don't feel sorry for you," he said.

They fell together into the servant girl's bed and made love in a tangle of linen blankets.

When it was over, they sat together, and by the light of an oil lamp, Abel traced a finger in a circle along Mahaut's scar, her breasts, and her shoulders, her tan lines beginning to reassert themselves after they'd disappeared during her recuperation.

No battledress tonight, but here is its shadow, he thought.

"I have something for you," she said. "It's in the other room waiting. He wasn't going to give it back, but I 'acquired' it from his valet with a bit of blackmail. An agreement to keep quiet about some gossip I knew about the man and a town whore. Very cheaply purchased, actually."

"My pistol?" he asked.

Mahaut nodded.

"Take it with you to Lindron," she said. "I hear there are certain sectors of that place you do not want to go unarmed."

"Thanks," he replied.

"Do you still have my dagger?" she asked.

"Yes," he answered. Then, after a pause. "Can I keep it?"

"Of course."

"I killed him with it. Rostov."

"You told me," she said. She rose up and put her arms around him. The chill of her black onyx bracelet where it touched the back of his neck sent shivers down his spine. Her skin bore the faint odor of hyacinth, her perfume. The servant girl was lucky. It was bound to linger in her sheets for days.

She kissed him, then drew him down to her and whispered in his ear. "Tell me again."

Epilogue: The Guardian

My Dear Son,

I am sorry that I have not written you in some time. However, my duties in holding the district safe from further incursion have taken me away from my desk more often than I would have liked. The Scouts are holding the Escarpment fairly well, but the Blaskoye are engaged in an enormous rebuilding effort that, I am afraid, is bearing fruit. Even after their ignominious defeat three years ago at our hands, they have not given up on their quest to dominate the Land, or to use this district as a gateway. The Scouts bring the word of a new leader who is arisen. There are strange reports, for it seems that this leader may not be a warrior himself, but a sort of politician among the tribes. To tell the truth, I fear this sort of leader far more than I did the one who pitted himself against us before.

But let me speak no more of these matters here. How is your service to the Tabernacle going? In your last letter you told me that, after a bit of trouble, that cabal of older Guardian toughs has eased up on you and you have found a place in the Academy. I compliment you for not killing them, or even seriously hurting them. It is a skill that you will have to employ more and more as you rise in rank and are given command of larger sectors. There will be many people you will want to kill, yet cannot.

And always I expect you to continue to comport yourself as befits a Dashian. You were allowed a great deal of freedom in Treville, and I'm very glad that this degree of power and success did not inflame your sense of self-entitlement. The very fact that you could bear yourself humbly and remain an effective Scout and soldier after such victories was as impressive to me as were those victories themselves.

Just remember that in Lindron, you remain a very small fish in a very large pond, no matter what you did in Treville. Yet I do not believe that you are destined to remain in such a subordinate position for long. For now, bear it, with the promise that better things will come for those who are talented and who have the right connections. You have both. I hesitate to write these words, for fear they will betray the greatest hope of my heart, but I shall do so: I believe you have what it takes to become a leader among the Tabernacle guardians, to perhaps become the military advisor of the chief priest himself.

Whatever you accomplish, I'm sure it will reflect honor upon our family name. Stick to the ways that you know are effective and follow the good instincts that run in your blood and all will be well.

Perhaps you can take the barge up for harvest

festival again this year. Your room is still here, and has not changed a whit. The Prelate has allowed the rice farmers along the Canal to return to their fields, and they have been turning up bones by the thousands. They pile them on the road levee, and they are visible as a line of white the whole long distance between Garangipore and Hestinga now. It is quite a sight, although I fear some of them may be our own dead, mixed among the Redlanders.

I will understand, however, if your duties do not permit you the luxury of such a long trip. Mine do not permit me to visit you, which I long to do, as you know. In any case, I will and do expect a letter!

Whatever you decide concerning harvest time travel, I remain,

Your affectionate father

Abel rolled up the scroll and put it in the small trunk that held all of his earthly belongings here in the Tabernacle garrison. He was off duty today, which meant that he was expected to spend time studying in the Tabernacle library. It was a task Abel looked forward to.

He made his way across the eastern side of the city along the riverfront, headed toward the great earthen mounds to the south that were known as Zentrum's Seat. The Tabernacle buildings, both administrative and those reserved for ritual, covered these mounds, built basket by basket in some ancient time by carrying mud from the River below.

At the base of Zentrum's Seat was the one place Abel had clear memories of from his childhood in this city: the Pools of the Tabernacle. The carnadons churned in the Tabernacle pools, ripping at the vast quantities of dak flesh on which they fed daily. It was a sight that never failed to fascinate Abel, even though its macabre nature brought back memories he would, perhaps, rather forget. He couldn't help himself. He always tried to catch the morning feedings before going in to his duties.

Bows and muskets, blood and dust. The nursery song of his mother still echoed within him whenever he beheld them. *I'm the one you'll never catch. I'm the one who catches you. Beer and barley, lead and copper. You can't catch me. I'm the Carnadon Man.*

After the feeding, it was inside and to the library, where Abel located the scroll he had begun on the previous week and sat down at a quiet table to read and take notes on his own papyrus writing pad.

The scroll was entitled *The History of the Second Blood Wind.* It was a history of the invasion of the Land by Redlanders—these not calling themselves Blaskoye, but Fusilites—four hundred years before.

Came they to conquer, and conquer they did, wrote Hermes the Scribe, who was thought to be the author, although the truth was no one knew who the historian was. The scroll had been written in the difficult recovery period after the Scouring, when the entire priestly and military caste had been executed.

The wind blew wet with blood, as the scribe Hermes put it. *For those who had never seen their first rain, this blood wind served that purpose.*

It was not merely the aristocracy, said Center. **It was every man, woman, and child who held power or position within the Land, and it went on not for days but for years. Ruling families were hunted down, found where they had fled**

into the marshes of the Delta, into the head-waters of the River in the Schnee Mountains.

Observe:

Chambers Pass, high in the Schnees, and the River's origin. A cluster of huts made of turf and thatch in the alpine pasture. Three of the five structures are burning. In a fourth are gathered a group of men who are being made to watch as a Fusilite warrior, dressed in a garment sewn from the skins of enemies, has his way with a woman who is thrown facedown upon the table. Nearby a man struggles to push his tongue back into his head. It has been pulled out through a slice that runs from his lower chin down to his Adam's apple. He is not successful, and collapses.

Outside another group of Fusilites are conferring. One is festooned in the scalps of his enemies, which hang from his shoulders, attached to epaulet boards there like so much braid. He is the leader.

"Have you rounded up the git?" he asks his lieutenants.

"I believe that's all of them, wise one," answers one of the underlings. Abel is startled to see that it is a woman.

The Fusilites were great believers in the equality of the sexes, Center explained.

The leader with the shoulder boards of scalps turns to her and says, "Burn them then. And that should be the last of this line of snakes. Who was it?"

"These are first cousins to the Prelate of Progar," the woman answers.

"Good," says the leader. "Perhaps I'll give Progar to you, Klopsaddle."

"Thank you, wise one," the woman warrior replies.

Klopsaddle? That's the name of Mother's family! Abel thought.

You are a linear descendant of the woman on your mother's side, replied Center.

Great, thought Abel ruefully. *I've got Redlander blood.*

Most do, at least some portion, said Center. **And all of the First Families do, by definition. They *are* assimilated Redlanders.**

Now Abel viewed the scene from high above, as if he were flying amongst the peaks of the mountains. Below him the last two huts of the settlement burned and threw great clouds of gray smoke in the sky. Abel was thankful he was far enough away not to have to hear the screaming.

You may be sure that essentially the same scene would have played out over and over for many decades had the Blaskoye succeeded in Treville three years ago, Center said.

Checked, but not stopped, said Raj. *Note the information in your father's letter of this morning. Rostov is dead, but there is perhaps an even more dangerous leadership now in place. Three years, too! This rebuilding is remarkable, considering where they had to start from. This new leader must be considered a very serious threat.*

Abel sat back from the library scroll and took a deep breath. It was not pleasant to learn that a great-grandmother, however distant, was a sworn enemy.

"Ah," said a rich baritone of a voice nearby. "It is so good to see a young man from the Guardian Academy take such interest in his assigned texts." It was Prestane, a religious instructor. Abel had not had a class with him yet, but he was rumored to be a stickler for rote memorization. "I am afraid many of your fellow students don't even bother to create the appearance of having read this material."

"I enjoy learning about the past," Abel said, "so I can apply it to the present." He let the scroll go, and it partially rolled itself back up under his hand. "Speaking of which, I am wondering something, Professor."

"Yes?"

"The carnage that the Second Blood Wind produced is unbelievable. One reads of babies being roasted, women spitted. Even cannibalism," Abel said. "And yet Zentrum permitted it. He permitted all of it. Why?"

Prestane stepped back, considered Abel. "Well, now, I don't know if I should put myself in a position of answering such a weighted question," he said. "After all, one can't be too careful."

"All I'm asking," said Abel, "is for a little information. Nothing more."

Prestane cleared his throat, took yet another step back. "Well, then, yes . . . the point is that the people of the Land had grown very wicked in those times. Horribly wicked and sinful." The worry left Prestane's face, and the teacher began warming to his explanation.

Or at least to the sound of his own voice, Abel thought.

"So you must not think of the Fusilites as individuals," Prestane continued. "Think of them as instruments that Zentrum chose to punish those who had fallen from his ways."

"I see," Abel said. "They were the Hand of God."

"Precisely," Prestane replied. "Now you're getting it."

"Is he?" asked a quiet voice from a corner of the

alcove in which Abel worked. The light was wan in this area, and oil lamps were forbidden in the library. What light there was streamed in through a nearby window. Abel had not seen the other. He had apparently been quietly standing there for some time. The new person wore a priestly robe. He looked to be a fairly old man, too, though still of ruddy complexion and obviously in good enough health.

Prestane gasped when he saw the man. He made a quick bow, and trotted away. The man sat down in the chair across the table from Abel.

"This is a simplistic explanation our dear colleague Prestane has given you," said the old priest. "It's a bit more complicated than a parable of punishment."

"How do you mean, sir?" Abel asked.

"The Hand of God," said the old man. "You must reconsider this way of thinking. It is allegorical, a thing of images that may or may not be true. Pictures we form in our minds of things we cannot see are invariably limited. You understand that Zentrum *has* no hand, not really."

"Of course not, sir," Abel replied.

"Then you must understand that Zentrum does not think in terms of men or the lives of men, but rather thinks of eternity. The Land is all that matters to Zentrum. And note: the Land itself was indistinguishable before and after the conquest. Within two generations it was, at least."

Abel shook his head sadly. "But the butchery, the torture, the rape . . ."

"Men die," said the older man. "All folk harmed by the Blood Wind would be dead by now, anyway. The Land survives unchanged."

"I think I understand," Abel said.

The old priest smiled. He touched Abel on the head affectionately, tousled his hair. "You have a good mind, my son," he said. "Your compassion is praiseworthy, as well. But one must never lose sight of the bigger picture, eh?"

"No, Professor."

"*Professor?*" said the other with a chuckle. "It's been a while since anyone called me *that*."

And with these final words, the old man turned and made his way down the library alcove and out of sight.

From others studying in their carrels came a whisper: "Goldfrank."

The old man had been Abbot Goldfrank, the High Priest of Zentrum.

Abel slowly closed his study scroll completely.

It is always the same justification, he thought.

Yes, laughed Raj, *like a machine caught in a perpetual loop.*

The logic is not defective, Center put in. **Given the assumption that men are means rather than ends, it is flawless.**

Valid and flawless for a computer, Raj replied. *For a man, his words are those of a monster.*

It will, however, take more than outrage and skill at arms to overcome such a monster, Center replied. **It requires a mind to direct those qualities. Continue your study, Abel.**

Abel sighed. He considered for a moment, but there really wasn't anything else for it, was there? He slowly rolled open the scroll once more upon the library study table. He began to read and add to his notes.

ACKNOWLEDGMENTS

My major debt is, of course, to Jim Baen for originally conceiving this perfect science fiction idea and to David Drake for structuring the story. Dave and S.M. Stirling created the first books which introduced Raj and Center, and defined the tone of the series. For my part, I took what they did as wisdom to follow and emulate. Toni Weisskopf, publisher of Baen Books, offered me the chance to work with Dave and revive the series, for which I am very grateful. Abigail Manuel, Matthew Bynum, Meredith Frazier, and Lucas Johnson were excellent first readers of my material. My wife, Rika, provided essential support and encouragement, as always. And Cokie and Hans, my kids, kept a constant check on me in my study (for which the lock is broken) and urged Dad along when he needed it most.

—T.D.

The following is an excerpt from:

THE SEA WITHOUT A SHORE

DAVID DRAKE

Available from Baen Books
May 2014
hardcover

CHAPTER 1

Bantry Estate, Cinnabar

Daniel Leary, otherwise Captain Daniel Oliver Leary, Republic of Cinnabar Navy—but here merely "Master Daniel" or "Squire"—stood poised in the bow of the skiff with his arms at his sides. The throwing stick was in his right hand with the line nocked in the cleft and the lure dangling. Hogg knelt in the stern, holding the tiller/throttle of the tiny motor that edged the boat toward the floating weed.

The lure was a streamlined tube about the size of a plump man's middle finger. Its batteries powered the caged contra-rotating props, but control signals came down the line from the handset now resting on the planks in front of Hogg.

When the lure hit the water, it would circle until it picked up the pattern of electrical impulses given off by the nerves of the species it was set for, then home on that source. It was set now for floorfish; two or three sprats would fillet into an excellent dinner for Daniel and Miranda, his fiancée, who was waiting in the manor.

Daniel tensed to make the cast. "Don't get ahead of yourself, boy," Hogg said. "Another ten feet, and *don't* tell me your arm's strong enough to cast into the center from here."

The skiff continued to creep toward the weed. Hogg spoke quietly so as not to disturb the prey, but his voice was as harsh as a rough-cut file. Here off the coast of the Bantry estate their releationship was the same as it had been twenty years earlier when the old poacher took it on himself to teach the young master how to fish and to hunt, and how to be a man.

Teaching Daniel to be a man wasn't part of a plan, but Hogg was a man himself and made assumptions. If he'd been asked, he would have said that Corder Leary wanted a son who would stand up for himself, who would carry out his duties, and who would take responsibility for his own actions.

Overhead, a trio of Barranca birds sailed southward, following the cold current which had bent toward shore during the volcanic eruption hundreds of miles out in the Western Ocean. The birds were so high that even Daniel's sharp eyes couldn't distinguish the two separate pairs of wings on each. The occasional low-frequency grunts of the birds communicating were barely audible, even to ears trained to recognize them.

Looking back on his childhood, Daniel suspected that his father had been too busy chasing money and power to spare any thoughts for the boy who lived with his mother on the Bantry Estate. Still, Speaker Leary wouldn't have minded what Daniel was learning, any more than he would have cared about the weather over Bantry while he was comfortable in the Leary townhouse in the capital, Xenos.

Hogg switched off the motor. It was inaudible even while it was running, but Daniel had felt the vibration through the thin soles of his moccasins. The skiff drifted forward on momentum. Daniel swung his right arm up in parallel with the keel. At the height of its arc, his fingers released the line which he'd clamped to the throwing stick till that moment. The lure sailed off in a flat curve that plopped it into the center of the large patch of weed.

"A *nice* cast," said Hogg softly. "You haven't forgotten everything I taught you, I guess."

"I haven't forgotten not to draw to an inside straight, either," Daniel said. He remained upright for a better view, though standing in the small boat would have been dangerous despite the skiff's broad bottom if the water hadn't been still and Daniel's own balance perfect. The skills he'd gained as a boy on Bantry had been sharpened since he'd entered the Naval Academy and begun running along the spars of starships.

Instead of circling as expected, the lure vanished instantly. "It looks like it just sank," Daniel said, squinting. He had a pair of multi-function RCN goggles on his forehead, but they wouldn't help him look through the water. "Do you suppose the motor failed?"

"The motor's running fine and the props are free," Hogg said testily, looking at the readout on his control unit. "It's just got a bite.

"Unless—" Hogg's delay was too short to have allowed Daniel to speak even if he'd intended to. "—that *bloody* weed has caught it. It's the deep-sea weed with thicker hair. But the lure *seems* okay...."

He and Daniel were in the channel between Borden's Cay and the mainland, but recent nor'westers had brought considerable oceanic debris through the inlets, including unfamiliar fish parboiled by the volcano. This patch of weed looked from any distance like the normal inshore variety; but as Hogg had said, it was the open-water species whose clumps were tied together by tendrils sturdy enough to withstand serious storms.

"Want to haul back the lure and try near the creek mouth?" Daniel said, frowning.

He was closer to the weed. He could have noticed before Hogg did that it was slightly darker than it should have been, but Hogg had spent most of his sixty years learning the tricks and whims of nature on the Bantry Estate. Missing something that Hogg also had missed wasn't a good reason to kick himself.

"It's still running true," Hogg said, "so don't get in front of yourself. Maybe we're just having fisherman's luck."

Hogg had been concentrating on the holographic read-out hovering above the control unit; his fierceness suggested he was planning to take a bite out of the display. A brief smile turned his unshaven face into something remarkably ugly.

Daniel smiled also. Like Hogg, he was used to having luck when he was fishing. Most of it was bad.

The channel wasn't much over a quarter mile wide here. Similar vegetation grew on both the cay and the mainland; but the trees on the mainland shore were taller, and they were much taller further inland where storms less often drove salt water over the roots.

Birds shrieked and clucked, but they remained hidden in the foliage. Insect-eaters wouldn't be out in numbers until nightfall, but Daniel was surprised not to see the fish-eaters which were usually snatching meals from the surface of the water or gorging on carrion on the mud. A skiff with two fishermen wasn't reason to frighten them under cover.

"We've got one," Hogg said, adjusting both thumb controls of the handset. "We bloody *have* got one."

The lure was multi-function. When it was attached, the controller sent impulses into the nervous system of the fish. You couldn't actually control the behavior even of a fish, but a disruption equivalent to an unscratchable itch would eventually bring the prey thrashing to the surface as it tried to rid itself of the irritation.

Daniel set the throwing stick down on the floorboards. He touched the trident with hooked barbs of spring steel, then thought again. The pole was only six feet long. That was as much as they wanted to carry in so small a boat, but it wasn't enough to reach the center of the weed from where they now floated.

"I'll go in," he said. He didn't want to foul the lure's prop in heavy weed. Hogg grunted agreement, still concentrating on the controller.

Sitting down, Daniel pulled off his moccasins. He probably ought to take off his baggy trousers also, but sometimes small crustaceans clung to floating weed, and he didn't want to transfer them to his wedding tackle. As he started to his feet again, the skiff rocked violently.

"Bloody hell and damnation!" Hogg said, looking up from the display but not dropping the controller.

Daniel's first thought was that there had been

another sub-sea earthquake, a tremor like those which the volcano had spawned in recent months. The weed lifted in a great swell. Instead of subsiding, it hung in streamers on the dark, twitching mass which floated on the surface of the water.

"On my sainted mother's soul," Hogg said in a tone of reverence. "We've got an adult. What's *it* doing here?"

Daniel had heard enough stories growing up on Bantry—some of them from Hogg himself—to know that if Hogg's mother had been a saint, it was only by comparison with Hogg's father. That aside, there was no doubt that they'd caught an adult floorfish.

If caught was the right word.

"The volcano must have brought it up," Daniel said. Adult floorfish meandered across the bottom at three thousand feet or deeper, though their eggs hatched in marshes and the sprats spent their first two years in coastal waters. "It's sixty feet long if it's an inch."

"And the flesh is no good for anything but feeding pigs," Hogg said with a tone of regret. "Even if we could land it."

He adjusted his controller again.

The floorfish continued to quiver, so Daniel didn't rise from his knees. There wasn't any real risk. When Hogg released the lure, the fish—it was really a blanket with a mouth at one end and a body filled by the gut which processed ooze that the mouth sucked in—would sink back to the bottom.

Daniel grinned. The worst danger that the floorfish posed was that if it didn't find its way back out to sea soon, the warmth and higher oxygen content of the surface waters would probably kill it. In that case, its many tons of rotting flesh and partially digested ooze would make a considerable uninhabitable until the process was complete. Fortunately, nobody except hunters and sport fishermen spent much time in this swampy portion of Bantry.

The fish continued to wobble like a huge jelly while Hogg stabbed at his controller. "It won't release!" he snarled. "I don't know if something's corroded or the probes are just too deep in that thick hide."

He stuck his hand into a baggy pocket and brought out a folding knife with a knuckleduster hilt; the blade snicked open. "*I* say we cut the line and chalk it up to experience."

"Do you have another lure?" Daniel said.

Hogg shrugged. "Back to the Manor," he said. "We've got three sprats now in the cold chest. That's enough for dinner; and if it's not, well, me and Em—"

That would be the Widow Brice.

"—can find something else. She's not big on fish anyhow."

That was all true, but . . .

"I'll fetch the lure," Daniel said, swinging his right foot into the water carefully. "I was figuring to go in with the trident anyway."

He eased over the side by stages, gripping the gunwale with both hands and lowering himself carefully to reduce the splash. The water was noticeably warm; more sign of the volcanic disruption, he supposed.

Hogg had leaned to his left instinctively to balance Daniel's weight. "I can't turn off the current or the fish'll go right back to the bottom," he said. "That means it's going to keep on shivering like that."

"Right," said Daniel, breast-stroking away from the skiff with his head out of water. "Well, if it swallows me, you can cut me out with that knife of yours."

The weed wasn't as thick as it looked from even a short distance away. The tendrils which bound palm-sized clumps into mats the size of a soccer pitch parted as easily as gauze between Daniel's hands. He wouldn't want to swim miles through the weed, but he thought he could if he had to. Twenty yards was no problem.

The line of optical fiber was invisible except that when the sun caught it at the right angle, it became a slash of light from the water to the lure on the black/brown skin. Daniel was probably brushing it as he swam/paddled toward the floorfish, but its touch went unnoticed in the weed.

The floorfish had a fringe of fins all along its side. They extended about the length of Daniel's forearm and were stiffened with cartilage, not spines. They appeared to undulate gently, but there was enough power behind the continuous motion to push at Daniel like a strong current when he was close enough to touch the fish.

Daniel paused, then dived and came up like a sprat trying to escape a predator. His out-stretched hand gripped the lure, and his weight pulled it free as he slid down the slimy side of the floorfish.

"Master!" Hogg shouted. "Back away! Keep the bloody lure on your bare skin and in the water between you, okay? Don't bloody argue!"

"Between" wasn't a direction, but Hogg must mean the floorfish if he wanted Daniel to back away. The older man's voice wasn't panicked, but there was more stress in it than Daniel remembered since the night Hogg had readied the Bantry tenants against trouble that might sweep in from the darkness. He'd handed the seven-year-old Daniel Leary a shotgun and told him to aim for heads because face-shields weren't as tough as the body-armor which the attackers might be wearing.

No one came to Bantry that night. In the morning, Daniel and the others learned that Speaker Leary had drowned the Three Circles Conspiracy in blood, wiping out the leaders of the Popular Party and their families—save for a few of the proscribed who happened to be off planet at the time the crisis broke.

One of those survivors was Adele Mundy, 16-year-old daughter of Lucius Mundy, the leader of the Popular Party. She had just left to study in the Academic Collections on Blythe. At the time, Adele's name wouldn't have meant anything to Daniel, or for that matter to Corder Leary. The girl was a scholar and wholly apolitical.

Daniel, a newly made lieutenant, had met Adele, then Electoral Librarian on Kostroma, five years ago. That meeting had changed their lives. Both of them were better off by orders of magnitude than they would have been without the other's support.

The floorfish submerged like a mass of sludge slipping into the channel. Suction tugged at Daniel, but because the fish's body shaped itself to the water, it was much less of a problem than what a sinking ship of similar size would have caused. The fish left behind an effluvium of ancient mud, cloying and slightly sulfurous.

Something lifted briefly above the undulating weed, then slipped back. Daniel knew what Hogg had seen from the height of the boat.

He knew why Hogg was worried, too.

Daniel splashed, hoping that he was moving toward the boat as Hogg had ordered. It wasn't a very effective way to proceed, but he wasn't about to stretch his legs out behind him to backstroke properly. That would put his bare, kicking feet very close to the head of the wolf eel, and the predator's jaws were armed with six-inch fangs.

Wolf eels attached their sucker tails to floorfish. They didn't harm or even affect the huge scavenger, but when the giant maw rooted up some lesser muck-dweller, the eel snatched it for a meal.

This was an extremely large floorfish, even for an adult, and the eel was a similarly impressive member of its species. Because its jaws and belly expanded, it could easily ingest prey the size of an average-sized man.

"I got the lure set to female eel," Hogg said in a hoarse whisper. "If it figures you're a female, it likely won't try to eat you. Just keep coming back. I don't want to foul the prop in the weed, but I will if I have to."

"I don't especially want to be buggered by an eel either," Daniel said. It wasn't a real concern—like other fish, the eels sprayed milt onto the eggs the female had just extruded into the sea—but it made Hogg chuckle, which is what Daniel had intended.

Hogg would rather die than let anything harm the Young Master. Daniel didn't want him to leap into the eel's jaws as the best way of saving his charge.

Daniel continued to splash. He didn't look around. He couldn't see anything through the agitated water. Perhaps Hogg could see more.

They were using the lure's field to override the bioelectrical field of Daniel's own body. Hogg was, at least; it wouldn't have occurred to Daniel to do that. He'd certainly think of it should the situation arise again.

"Now, hold the lure in your left hand and hook your right over the gunnel," Hogg said, speaking from just above Daniel's head. He was again as calm as he had been years before while teaching his young charge to squeeze rather than jerk his trigger. "When you're ready, you'll swing up and I'll haul you aboard. No problem at all for a strong young lad like you, right?"

"No problem," Daniel whispered. His attendance at temple was sporadic at best, but he really would try to improve in the future.

Daniel's hair brushed the skiff's hull. He fumbled with his right hand, bicycling his legs to keep him up until he could grip a thwart. He took a deep breath and another, consciously trying to slow his heart rate.

He had only had one glimpse of the eel. It had seemed huge. Even allowing for the exaggeration of fear, it was probably ten feet long. Its slender body trailed behind a head the size of a bushel basket.

Hogg gripped Daniel's left arm, just above

the elbow. He wasn't putting any pressure on the contact yet.

"On three," Daniel said. "One, two, thr—"

Water exploded as Daniel rolled up and over the gunwale. The eel must have come after him because Hogg shouted and Daniel heard the *crunch* as Hogg's right arm drove the trident through the bones of the creature's skull.

Daniel rolled into the belly of the skiff. Hogg had gotten out of his way, though Daniel wasn't sure how. He wasn't even sure he still had both legs, and his hands were locked together in mutual reassurance.

Bloody Hell, that was a bad one!

The skiff was rocking violently. Hogg shoved them backward and released the shaft of the harpoon. The little motor was backing with all the power it had available, ignoring the risk of weed clogging its intake.

Daniel raised his head to look over the gunnel. The shaft flailed back and forth, sometimes under the surface, as the fatally injured eel curvetted. The body behind the soot-colored head was so nearly transparent that Daniel could make out the bones of the skeleton.

His guess of ten feet long had been conservative. This eel was probably big enough to have swallowed the skiff itself along with the two men.

"I wonder what the record for a wolf eel is?" Daniel said. "Taken by hand, I mean."

"You want this one as a trophy," Hogg said hoarsely, "then you're going to have to come back by yourself and get it. Me, I'm heading for home; and when I get there, I'm going to get *very* drunk."

"Yes," said Daniel. "I think that's a good plan for both of us."

—end excerpt—

from *The Sea Without a Shore*
available in hardcover,
May 2014, from Baen Books

DID YOU KNOW YOU CAN DO ALL THESE THINGS AT THE

BAEN BOOKS WEBSITE ?

* Read free sample chapters of books

* See what new books are upcoming

* Read entire Baen Books for free

* Check out your favorite author's titles

* Catch up on the latest Baen news & author events

* Buy any Baen book

* Read interviews with authors and artists

* Buy almost any Baen book as an e-book individually or an entire month at a time

* Find a list of titles suitable for young adults

* Communicate with some of the coolest fans in science fiction & some of the best minds on the planet

Visit us at
www.baen.com